AS ... ...IE LEGACY
OF THE PAST, AS A NATION STRUGGLED
TO BE BORN, THE FUTURE WOULD BE
FORGED BY...

Torch-of-the-Sun—called Firebrand by his white enemies. He banished Gyva from his people and sentenced her to a future tinged with the blood of the past.

Jason Randolph—Gyva saved his life. Together they would build a new life on the savage frontier, until tragedy overtook them and threatened to sweep away all they had.

Andrew Jackson—Determined to avenge the cruel murder of her parents, Gyva swore to have his life. They came from different worlds, but their bold destinies were fatally intertwined.

Gyva—Forced to abandon her proud heritage, she would become Delia, wife of a white aristocrat; Mrs. Randolph, hostess to her sworn enemy. But in her heart, in her soul, she would forever be...

FIREBRAND'S WOMAN

FIREBRAND'S WOMAN

Vanessa Royall

A DELL BOOK

Published by
Dell Publishing Co., Inc.
1 Dag Hammarskjold Plaza
New York, New York 10017

Dell ® TM 681510, Dell Publishing Co., Inc.

ISBN: 0-440-12597-9

Printed in the United States of America

First printing—December 1980

For Barbara McFadden Laskowski

The many moons and sunny days we have lived here will be long remembered by us. The Great Spirit has smiled upon us and made us glad. But we have agreed to go.

We go to a country we know little of. Our home will be beyond a great river on the way to the setting sun. We will build our wigwams there in another land. In peace we bid you good-bye. If you come to see us, we will welcome you.

A Chieftain's Farewell to the Ancestral Lands of his Tribe

AUTHOR'S NOTE

In 1803 President Thomas Jefferson purchased from Napoleon a vast tract of land called Louisiana, which stretched from the Gulf of Mexico to what is now the state of Montana. The westward movement of settlers and frontiersmen, already under way, was accelerated by Jefferson's acquisition; and bloody conflicts over territorial rights to ancient Indian tribal lands began to scar the face of American history. During these years the government devised a policy called "Indian removals." A euphemism for eviction. For exodus. Such was the fate awaiting Dey-Lor-Gyva, whose name means "Beloved-of-Earth," and who was in her savage but love-filled lifetime to become the brave and beautiful *Firebrand's Woman*.

V.R.

CONTENTS

The Book of Prophecy   35

The Book of Exile   177

The Book of Exodus   363

Four Bears, motionless now for hours, lay flat against the sweet, pine-needled earth. High overhead, wind stirred in the Georgia conifers. The mountainside dropped steeply from the place where he lay waiting, and rose again, even more severely, across the gorge. There was a fast-running, rapids-filled river below, a white ribbon of light, luminous beneath the stars. Four Bears heard the thunder of the distant falls, which he could not see. He was relying on that booming tide of sound to cover his attack when the right time came, just before dawn. Just before dawn when the deep sleep comes, when even sentries sigh with relief that the night is over, and let down their guard.

Four Bears sighed, too, but with gratitude and anticipation, and listened to the roar. It was fitting that the sun and the earth and the river and the falls should be in alliance with him. The white men called this place Roaring Gorge; they could call it what they wished until they died, which would be very soon. Four Bears knew this place was holy ground—Cradle-of-the-Speaking-River, to which for a thousand thousand moons had come the Seminole and Cherokee, the Creek and Chickasaw (of which Four Bears himself was chieftain) , the Choctaw, the Sac, and the Fox, all to thank the Great Spirit for the riches and wonders he had bestowed upon his Indian children: fecund, corn-growing earth in the red valleys; pungent, healing herbs in the soft and shielding forests; animals heavy with meat and milk and young. And the vast smoky mountains that had been home since time beyond the memory of the tribal seeress, who had the divine hand-print of blood upon her face. Truly this was Indian ground.

Why did the white men not know such an obvious thing?

Clearly the white men were a challenge sent by the Great Spirit, a test to prove the wisdom and strength of Indian braves, to confirm them as warriors, and thus to reaffirm their age-old claim to this holy place, this lovely land. Four Bears clutched tightly the Red Stick that gave him immunity from bullets and blades and death, watching the blueness lighten its shade over the mountains to the east, waiting for the pale pink predawn haze. So soft was this earth, so wonderful the warm and faithful sun. In his old and battle-hardened heart, Four Bears felt great tenderness, and prayed for the safety of his one-year-old granddaughter, asleep now down there in the white man's encampment in the gorge. Dey-Lor-Gyva, Beloved-of-Earth. Yes, beloved of earth, and beloved of Four Bears, too, but now a prisoner of Jacksa Chula Harjo, as the Chickasaw called him—Jackson, old and fierce.

Andrew Jackson, who had not yet seen the circling of forty suns! How was it possible that a man so young became so relentless and bold? Had the Chickasaw nation somehow offended the Great Spirit, that such a terrible man be loosed upon them? *Ababinili,* Four Bears prayed, calling upon the force that was the sun, the clouds, the clear sky, and Spirit-Who-Dwells-in-the-Clear-Sky, *grant us victory in the coming battle. Grant that we safely recapture the infant, though she is but a female.*

Fleetingly, because there was no time now to think further upon the matter, Four Bears wondered why Chula Harjo had not killed the child. Chula Harjo did not shrink from the giving of death. He had killed the child's parents readily enough, three days ago, and destroyed by torch the village near Talking Rock where Four Bears' son, Dark Wing, had lived peacefully among the white settlers with the white woman he had taken to wife.

When the whites had first come into the territory, there had been concern on the part of the elders that intermarriages would occur. Four Bears, knowing in his heart that love was a thing difficult to confound by prohibitions, had at first hoped that the mixed marriages that did take place would bring Indian and white man closer together. But he was older now, and wiser. He saw that the whites gave on their own terms and took on their own terms. They were jackals, only jackals, Four Bears realized now, fully and forever. He had been a fool even to think that intermingling love and blood would result in a greater good. Look what had happened! The jackals had killed not only Dark Wing, Four Bears' beloved son, but his white wife as well. So now it was irrefutable. Ababinili could not have willed that the blood of red warriors be mixed with that of white jackals, who respected neither life nor land, neither peace nor living wind.

Yet the blood is mixed, he thought then. The child is undeniably the issue of a Chickasaw chieftain's son. Chula Harjo will upon this dawn pay dearly for what he has done.

Behind him, spread out in concealed positions in the bushes and trees along the gorge, Four Bears felt the taut readiness of the fifteen braves he had selected for this mission. It was a tension not of fear but of eagerness. These young braves were strong and true, and perhaps one of them would become chieftain when the time came for Four Bears to join the Spirit-Who-Dwells-in-the-Clear-Sky. These bold and fearless braves, Red Sticks in their hands, had already bloodied white soldiers along the Chattahoochee, and then along the Etowah River. They had fought, too, in the battle of the fort on the banks of the holy Oostanaula. They had fought, and fought well, and always it seemed

that the victory was theirs. The white men would
flee, taking with them their women and children, departing in fear. But always—in a fortnight, or a moon,
or two moons—the white men would return; many
more of them this time, and with soldiers.

It was beyond understanding. With every Indian
victory, Four Bears and his people were driven farther
and farther from these lands, and soon they would be
forced to retreat all the way back to the ancient villages in the mountains of Tennessee, the heartland
upon which Ababinili had breathed life into the
Chickasaw nation.

Four Bears felt the red flash of pure anger, raw
passion, arise behind his eyes, and felt the hot blood
race through his veins as if he were young again. He
was ready. Slowly, soundlessly, he rose from the pine-
needled carpet of the forest, Red Stick in one hand,
long killing-knife in the other. It was a white man's
knife, designed for death; and until the pale jackals
had come into Indian lands, such a vicious weapon
was unknown. Now every brave had one; it was a
mark of honor.

Seeing their chieftain rise, the braves rose, too, as
soundlessly as he had. Since earliest childhood, they
had learned how to be fleet and silent in the forest,
how to race like the wind beneath sheltering trees,
how to *become* the earth and the grass and the leaves
through which they moved. This was as it should be,
for heaven had willed them to be more than mere
tenants of these mysterious, brooding lands. No, heaven
had created the Chickasaw to be at one with earth,
inseparable from it through all the days.

Slowly the warriors began the tortuous descent upon
the steep wall of the gorge, clinging to outcroppings
of rock or to gnarled bushes and saplings sprung from
cracks among the rocks. The pounding thunder of the
falls obscured the sound of an inevitable pebble shaken
loose or the groan of a branch too tender for the
weight it must bear. Over the rim of the pine-encircled

gorge, the sky was now bright blue; but down inside, the air was still dark, purplish, cold enough to urge a man, even a soldier, more deeply into the warmth of his bedroll. Good. Four Bears had planned on that, and planned correctly.

Still, he had a certain respect for the canny Jacksa. The accumulated wisdom of a thousand moons dictated that a campsite must be on high ground when threatened in war at night. Thus one's enemies were forced to climb to the attack, losing the advantages of both elevation and gravity. But here, in the Cradle-of-the-Speaking-River, all things were different. A campsite on the rim of the gorge meant disaster for the white men because, if trapped, they could be driven over the side, hurled to plummeting deaths. By choosing shelter down in the gorge, however, they forced any attacker to advance most slowly, pinned all the while against steep, rocky walls, easy as targets in a children's game—unless the attacker calculated everything, and waited for the right moment, as Four Bears had.

Still in the lead, he released his grip on the stump of a tree, slid cautiously down across a mossy embankment, caught hold of a branch—and felt the Red Stick fall away from him, perhaps twenty feet to the floor of the gorge. He held his knife between his powerful teeth, which could still crack walnuts with a single crunch. But he would rather have dropped the knife than the stick, his symbol of immunity against death; and he looked around to see his braves studying him. They had seen the Red Stick fall away; and in tense, wary silence, absolutely without motion, they pressed against the rocks.

Moment by moment the sky grew brighter. There was no time to pause, and less to consider the portent of a fallen stick. Four Bears readied himself, kicked off from the rock, and dropped quietly to the floor of the gorge. There in the gloom was his Red Stick, and he retrieved it from the dew-wet grass and held it high above his head for the others to see. Then he grinned, with the killing-knife still between his teeth. It is only dangerous to drop the stick in battle, he was telling them. Otherwise there is no meaning.

The braves had faith in him. Together they advanced rapidly in the shadows along the wall of the gorge; and against the white cascade of the falls, beside the silver river, the Indians could already see the huddled bundles of sleeping enemies. But which of those dark shapes belonged to little Gyva, Beloved-of-Earth?

Four Bears halted his men, looking for sentries. He saw none. A trap? Chula Harjo thought of everything. Four Bears scanned the side of the gorge and studied the trees, squinting along the river bank. His braves, beside him, behind him, grew impatient. If a battle has been planned, there is a moment beyond which it cannot be delayed. This was one such moment. Every luck was with them, even the wind. The horses tethered by the river did not sense their presence.

The chief was just about to lift his Red Stick and give the high, hooting, blood-chilling cry of battle and assault. He was already raising the stick into the blue air, and his heart was pounding as it always did before a confrontation. His braves, anticipating blood, appeared already to be leaping forward toward the encampment, although they had not moved.

Then the thin, bleating cry of a child, piercing as a lance, rose in the cold morning air. It became a wail, bereft and need-filled, born of hunger and cold. The cry was easily audible above the rumble of the falls, and audible through the layers of human sleep, too, just as a baby's cry is meant to be.

For one long, agonized instant—perhaps for the first time in his life—Four Bears hesitated at the moment of attack. His own granddaughter would rouse the sleeping white men; they would awaken and all would be lost. Or he would attack anyway and the child would be killed. Torn between his feelings as a progenitor and his duties as a chieftain, Four Bears froze.

The crying continued, louder now and more demanding. A figure stirred and half rose from one of the bundled bedrolls.

Four Bears decided. He raised his Red Stick and shrieked to heaven and all the spirits—to the soul of his son, Dark Wing, which must be hovering about them in the very air, awaiting vengeance.

Howling and hooting, the Chickasaw rushed forward toward their enemies, who were even now leaping to their feet, clutching rifles and pistols and swords. Dey-Lor-Gyva's cry rose, frantic now, near the waning fire.

The battle itself was short and fierce, and just as joyfully brutal as Four Bears had hoped it would be. Perhaps even a white man who died in battle received some reward from whatever god he had. So let the white men die. The chieftain felt no age in his bones, none at all, as he flew down upon a blanket roll and plunged his knife down, up, down, up, down, up, and felt the heavy body jump and twitch, felt the blood hot and lovely on his hands. He rolled away, sprang to his feet, and thrust the hot blade of his knife into a young soldier crouching before him, jerking furiously at the hammer of a pistol. The man—no more than a boy—went down clutching his spilling entrails, when Four Bears jerked the knife out of him. As young as Dark Wing, Four Bears thought, whirling to meet another man, older, taller, charging at him with one of the killing-knives.

All around there was battle, and shrieking, and the smell of death, which is like the juice of sugar cane cooked too long in a kettle over the campfire, and which is like the smell of apples rotting in a pit, and which is like the ordure of a sick dog, and which is like all these things combined. Four Bears breathed deeply of the smell and gave thanks that he had lived long enough to partake of it again, and slashed with his great knife at the man who attacked.

He had reason to give thanks again.

Even here, in the dark dawn within the gorge, he saw the lank wild yellow hair, the eyes so hard and shrewd, the body that was lean and hard as a young hickory tree.

Jacksa Chula!

"Yayaeeeeeeeeee!" howled Four Bears in the ecstasy of battle. He held his Red Stick high and lunged with the knife.

Along the river the horses of the white men jerked and reared against their tethers and added the frightened sounds of beasts to the human melée. Around the campsite blood ran red on rumpled blankets, clung like dew to blades of tender, trampled grass. Braves grappled with more than a full score of white men, but the element of surprise forgives a deficiency in number. At least half of the ivory-faced hyenas lay dead already, and Four Bears sought to include their leader in that doomed contingent. He thrust at the hard belly of Chula Harjo. The high wail of his granddaughter, in her bundle by the campfire, went on unceasingly.

Jacksa saw the blade coming, tucked in his gut, and spun away, feinted, and drove in at Four Bears, knife flashing in the dawn, fire in his eyes.

Four Bears, as young and strong this morning as he had been on the long-ago day of his manhood ritual, evaded the thrust, distracted Jacksa with a quick movement of the Red Stick, and jerked his knife upward toward the white man's heart. The top of his weapon slashed through buckskin as if it were parchment, and Jacksa dropped back, blood welling from a long cut on his ribs.

Four Bears grinned and came forward in a crouch, holding the Red Stick wide in one hand, moving it, moving it slowly, trying to distract the white man with the stick, as a snake would move to charm a rodent.

But Jackson did not make the same mistake again. He kept his eyes on the knife.

The chieftain feinted again, awaiting the perfect moment for a killing thrust. He was sure of himself now, just as he always was when he first drew blood from an enemy. He did not even see the blade that came whistling through the air, cutting him high on the cheekbone, jolting him backward. But he felt the hot blood pouring down his face and tasted the sweet copper taste on his tongue.

Now Jacksa Chula was grinning at *him*.

Dey-Lor-Gyva became suddenly silent.

Around the campfire now the battle had ended. Those white soldiers who were not already dead or dying had surrendered, their arms high in the air or crossed upon their heads. Several braves lay dying, too, their Red Sticks lost in the dust. It was as the legends proclaimed: A warrior who drops his sacred shield must soon be overcome. Soldiers and Indians alike turned to regard the two men who were yet in attitudes of combat, Four Bears and Jackson.

"You are lost," the chief muttered to his antagonist. "Drop your evil steel."

Jacksa laughed. "Drop yours." Having spoken, he leaped forward once more and drove his blade at Four Bears' beaded throat, coming close enough to slash the rawhide string that bound the beads, which sparkled like tiny hailstones, catching the light as they fell to earth.

It had been a magnificent, reckless thrust. Jackson must have known that he would die anyway at the hands of the other braves, even if he succeeded in killing the chief. But he wanted the satisfaction and attacked while he was still able. Not for nothing had he earned his Indian name. But however young or however old and fierce, he was off-balance after the blow. Four Bears struck upward with his blade, and a deep, ugly gash appeared above Jackson's left eye, a diagonal slash from the edge of the eyebrow to the temple, where the big vein throbbed. Clutching the wound, Jacksa fell backward to the earth, blood running through his fingers.

Everyone waited. The thunder of the falls echoed in the gorge. A horse nickered anxiously.

"We bring you this blood," Four Bears said, standing over his victim, "to avenge the slaughter of Talking Rock."

Jackson did not move, nor did his eyes leave the chief.

"I had my orders," he said. "I was to move the Indians from that village before the buckskinners came." He took his hand away from his wound for a moment and stared at the blood. There was much of it, but Jackson had seen much more. Four Bears saw in the jackal's eyes a knowledge of possible death; but he saw, too, that there was no fear of death in Jacksa.

Against his will Four Bears was impressed. He had never given the white men much credit for courage. He considered what Chula Harjo had said. The buckskinners were wild backwoodsmen, coarser and crueler even than other white men, who killed Indians for the mere sport of it, killed them with long and lingering delight.

"It is true," Jacksa was saying. "If they had come to Talking Rock and carried away your people, every nation from the Blue Ridge to the Tennessee River would have gone to war."

"What does it matter?" grunted Four Bears, uncertain now. "The village is destroyed anyway, and my son and his wife along with it."

Curiosity flickered in Jackson's hard, gelid eyes.

The child whimpered from her blankets.

"Kill him now," muttered one of the braves. "We have many streams to ford before the sun descends."

"It was my men who were first attacked at Talking Rock," Jackson said, glancing from the bloodthirsty brave back to Four Bears. "In a village of mixed-bloods, always there are some who are hostile. To buckskinners or—to soldiers. Truthfully, I do not know who flung the first torch."

Four Bears gave a bitter laugh. "And I suppose you would deny the death of my son, Dark Wing, at your very hands? The word has reached me, and I believe it to be true. And also you pierced with your blade the heart of my son's wife."

Jackson looked startled.

Four Bears nodded gravely. "It was seen. I have heard. And I believe." He stepped forward, flicking his knife, and bent toward the bloody white man.

Jackson asked no mercy, no quarter. "She attacked me," he said to the chief. "She would have killed me."

Four Bears hesitated. His son's wife? Fighting white soldiers? The idea pleased him, even though she had been white herself, or perhaps because of it. But he remained untrusting.

"It is true," Chula Harjo said, seizing the moment. "You, who have known so many battles, must also know how wild they become. After the first torch was flung, and the village began to burn, there was no stopping the fight. In the heat of it, I was set upon by the man who must have been your son. He fought bravely and well, but . . ." Jackson supplied a gesture to indicate an acceptance of fate. "But I triumphed, and immediately a white woman set upon me with a pitchfork. I did not realize at first that she was white, for her cry was that of an Indian brave. Nor was I proud of what I had to do to save myself. It was an instinct. It was over in a moment."

"You lie," accused the chief, and gripped hard the handle of his knife.

Once again Jacksa did not flinch. If he is a liar, Four Bears thought, he is a colder one than I have ever known.

Jackson moved slightly on the ground, and Four Bears readied himself for the killing thrust.

"Remove my boot," the white man said.

Four Bears was suspicious.

"I offer you proof of my words," Jackson said, "if you wish to see it. You will do with me what you will, for you have felled me here today, and felled me fairly. But we are both, in our own manner, warriors, and, I trust, just and honorable men. Or do you deny it?"

Ah, but the jackal was clever! So now the battle-ground was one of honor. But what was this business of "proof"?

"Which boot?"

"The left."

Four Bears gestured, and one of the braves approached. Jackson wore very high black boots, the tops of them floppy and loose about his knees, which were bony and prominent beneath tight leather breeches. Four Bears gestured again, and the brave bent down, cutting the boot from top to toe in one swift motion, yet not touching Jackson's leg with the blade. He flung the ruined boot aside. A dirty bandage encircled Jackson's leg, high on the calf.

"That, too," Jackson said.

Again the brave flicked the knife deftly, and the cloth bandage fell away. The marks of four punctures, evenly spaced, were visible on his flesh, the wounds barely beginning to heal, and the skin around them blue and unhealthy.

Four Bears was pleased. His son's wife had done this? But he concealed his pleasure. "I wish that her aim had been truer," he said.

Jackson grinned icily, but did not speak.

Dey-Lor-Gyva began to cry again, in sporadic, breathless bursts.

"She is hungry," Jackson said.

"She is also my granddaughter," responded Four Bears. "It is she for whom we have come."

Jackson nodded. He had already made this calculation. "I took her from the burning house. The house of the woman who attacked me with the pitchfork."

This was the thing that puzzled the chieftain. He

had heard many, many things about this violent Chula Harjo; and the tales of all the tribes west of the Carolinas attested to his rapacity in every respect but one— Jacksa was supposedly gentle toward women. Were female children also included in this aspect of odd tenderness? Or did the white soldier have other plans? Dey-Lor-Gyva would not have been the first Indian maiden sold into slavery, or into bondage for, in due course, the sensual pleasure of the jackals.

"Why?" he asked. "Where did you intend to take her?"

Jackson's reply came readily enough. "To Pensacola. There are Seminole villages near the town, and—"

"You are lying. You meant to sell her into slavery."

For the first time, and in spite of his condition, Jackson showed real anger. "We both know," he said coldly, "that the offspring of warriors make poor slaves. I do not question your word, and I ask that you not question mine. Your grandchild is safe, only hungry. Now complete your work here, and take her with you."

It was, in its way, a challenge. Still losing blood steadily, and badly fatigued from talking, Jackson lay back down on the bloody grass, hand over his wound, and closed his eyes. Instinctively Four Bears moved toward him, knife poised. But the white man did not open his eyes. Dey-Lor-Gyva was crying. The braves were watching, and the white soldiers, too. No longer did Four Bears feel as young as he had felt during the descent from the rim of the gorge, during the battle. No, he felt again as he had at the moment he had heard the child's cry: tender and confused. It was what old age could do to a man, altering all the pure imperatives necessary to the warrior's calling. The blood ran from Chula Harjo like the thick, sweet wine of red berries prepared by Chickasaw women in autumn while the sun watched, old and cool and gentle above the high smoky mountains of home.

He stood up and stepped away from Jackson. "I

leave it to Ababinili whether you die or not," he spoke. "It is the thanks of one man to another."

Jackson wet his lips. "These are your lands. For the time being. I will accept whatever your Great Spirit decides." He appeared too weak to open his eyes, or was indisposed to do so. Four Bears, who had seen much death, was certain that he would see another if he remained in Roaring Gorge. And this morning he had lost his taste for blood.

"Bind the living," he ordered his braves, and with rope and thongs his warriors tied the white soldiers hand and foot, leaving them along the river. The Indians were confused and slightly disappointed; they had expected the taking of scalps and the delights of tormenting, with fire and hungry knife, those whom they had vanquished. But Four Bears was chieftain; and only a crazy man, or a man bent on death, would disobey him.

Four Bears strode to the tiny huddle of blankets in which the child lay crying, beating her arms against the swaddling cloth in hunger and frustration and, probably, fear. Four Bears himself was unnerved. Among his people all young children, both male and female, were almost exclusively the responsibility of the women in the tribe. Even menchildren had to be old enough to learn the ways of the nation, the skills of the forest and the hunt, before any measure of attention was paid them by the braves. So it was with trepidation and a totally unfamiliar sense of his own clumsiness, as well as with love, that Four Bears bent down and gathered up the screaming bundle that was his son's child. He had come many forests and fords to rescue her. He had killed men and was himself wounded, the blood drying now on his cheekbones but the pain still there. Yet in spite of his efforts the sheer physical fact of this baby in his arms—the braves were staring; they had seldom seen a chief cradling a child—was as disconcerting as it was joyous. And the little girl was still crying!

"Get the horses ready!" he ordered curtly, in a voice of great authority. "We must go west toward home."

And as he said it, the baby stopped crying and turned to look at him, to study the great, strange face above her, with its colored stripes of war paint, the glittering beads upon the headband, and the blood. Four Bears looked at her as well, and he was stunned to wonderment. Until this moment she had been an abstraction; but now, in his very arms, he saw a thing of incomparable beauty. Her hair was shining like the black waters of a mountain lake beneath moonlight. Her eyes were large, black as onyx, both curious and knowing. Yet how could that be? Her tiny features were perfect. Her complexion was like alabaster, like ivory.

Four Bears was astounded. This child, a product of mixed blood, seemed more beautiful than either white or red, and better than both. He did not know what to think. She was still studying him, as if trying to measure him, to judge him for what he was, for what he meant to her. Those gem-black eyes unsettled him even as he came into their spell, and he had the uncanny feeling that he was her servant even though he was her grandfather and chieftain. It was a sensation he received sometimes when he counseled with the old woman Teva, Mark-of-the-Cave, the Chickasaw seeress. Gently Four Bears turned the child's head slightly, but there was no hand-shaped birthmark on that pure skin. No, the child's power, and hence her destiny, were of quite another kind.

But he did not know what it was.

The horses were ready now, and the braves restless to be off. They would ride out of the gorge along the Speaking River until the pass was reached, then thread through the pass, far back into the hills of Tennessee. Four Bears was just about to swing upon a horse he had chosen for himself, a silver-gray beast, proud and dancing, bearing a saddle with strange gold figures: *A.J.* Then he remembered that the child must be hungry, even though she had not cried out since first they had looked at one another. But he did not know what to feed a baby.

"She must eat," he muttered to the braves, rather gruffly. He hoped that one of them would know what to do. None did.

It has been three days since Jacksa took her from Talking Rock, he thought. Jacksa must have fed her something.

The white leader lay quiet and motionless. But his blood was still flowing, more slowly now, and he was still alive.

"Chula Harjo!" demanded Four Bears. "Chula!"

No response.

"Jacksa!" Four Bears cried.

Jackson stirred, and seemed to come back from a far place. His eyes opened slightly.

"The child must eat. What do you give her?"

Jackson's dry lips parted. "Honey," he said. "Honey and water. And bread. It was all I . . ."

Then he drifted off.

"You have done your last favor on this earth," Four Bears told him, "and devil though you be, it is a good one." He had no doubt whatsoever that this act of kindness toward Dey-Lor-Gyva was random and inexplicable on Chula Harjo's part. And yet, after he had given the baby drink and a crust from a white man's leftover loaf, and even honey dolloped on the tip of his strong finger, even after he and his braves were riding down along the river, bound for home, Four Bears could not help but remember that the white jackal had wrapped the little girl well against the chill of night, and had placed her near enough to the campfire for warmth, yet far enough away for safety. He was puzzled for a time, riding with the child in his arms. He did not know why Jacksa would have done such things. He reached the only conclusion that made any sense to him: It had been some sort of trick after all. Perhaps Jacksa had planned to use the Indian princess for ransom. Or, as Four Bears had first surmised, he had intended to sell her into slavery. Certainly he had not meant to find her a home with the Seminole. Whatever the reasons, they no longer mattered. Andrew Jackson was a dead man, and that was very good.

Two days later, toward evening, the Chickasaw band, led by its chief and including its youngest princess—if with her mixed blood she could be so called— turned their captured horses from the forest trail and entered the final pass. Beyond it lay the villages of home; and as they rode along, Four Bears could hear the throb of the drums heralding their approach. Smoke by day; drums by night. Smoke and drums served not only to alert the Indians, but also to terrify the outlanders.

Four Bears rode, still holding the exhausted child in his cradled right arm—the reins were in his left hand—and deciphered the signals. First, as always, the travelers were numbered. Eleven. That meant five had been lost—five who had been, according to tradition, buried with weapons, moccasins, and a proximity to blue mountains, with the sound of water moving near their graves. Second, was the chief among the survivors? Yes, he was. Third, there were horses, which must have been captured from the white devils. Four Bears smiled. He knew what benefit the taking of horses would bring to his people. Unlike certain tribes and nations far to the west, where the level land rolled on forever beyond the Father of Waters, the mountain Indians had few horses. But they had learned well the benefit of mounts: to attack the white man, or to escape him.

And finally, when the travelers came in closer sight of the hidden brave and his signal drum, the drum beat out a last message: the child is with them.

There would be joy in the home village. That was true. But Four Bears knew another thing, too. Many

there were, and Mark-of-the-Cave among them, who
would ask whether one child, even the halfbreed
daughter of a chief, was worth so many braves. But
at that moment the little girl stirred and came awake
and looked up at him again. The heart of Four Bears
overflowed with love.

In the village night had fallen, and torches flashed
upon the wet flanks of horses and the tired, drawn
faces of the riders. Fire glinted, too, in the jewel-black
eyes of Dey-Lor-Gyva, who was wide-awake and en-
tranced by the flames, the movement, the many people. Braves and squaws alike gathered around, coming
out of the wigwams in which they had been eating the
evening meal of roasted hare and turnips, and young
boys fought over the honor of caring for the captured
horses. The braves dismounted with an attitude of
prideful self-possession that was as much a part of a
warrior's armor as his bow. Yet in spite of their fierce
calm most of them quickly sought—and just as quickly
found—the eyes of their wives or favorite women in
the crowd. For their part the women gave sign of
neither affection nor relief; an open display of passionate attachment between the sexes was not ap-
proved. Such a thing was meant for the night.

Four Bears was still on the gray horse, holding the
child. Several of the women stepped forward, and the
chief leaned down, intending to place Dey-Lor-Gyva
in the arms of one of them. But just as he was about
to do so, the child let out a wail.

"Uh!" he grunted, mostly for the benefit of the
onlookers, some of whom were struggling not to display a certain amusement at this unfamiliar aspect of
their gruff and powerful leader. The squaw reached
again to accept the baby, but an abrasive, peremptory
voice intervened.

"Do not touch her yet!"

The Indians turned toward the sound, then parted
and made way for the woman who spoke. One did not
do otherwise for Lo-Teva-Wishi, Mark-of-the-Cave.

She was the village seeress, the witch; and this small, gnarled, tough old lady, with wispy, braided hair and dark, deep-socketed eyes, might do strange and terrible things to those who were foolhardy enough to hinder her passage. The woman pushed through, squinting toward the chief and the baby he held, her old lips twisted in suspicion. Torchlight glowed on her ancient skin, which had the color of a russet fox. And from a place low on her scrawny neck, where she wore a string of black beads, spreading across her throat and upward onto the side of her face, was the pale, dim outline of what might have been the print of a human hand.

The Indians knew otherwise. There was nothing human about that mark, save that it lived upon the skin of a human being. If Mark-of-the-Cave was indeed human.

"Teva," said the chief. "It is my son's daughter."

"I know," she said, "and you ride the horse of Jacksa Chula."

The crowd hushed, and the old woman traced with bony fingertip the *A. J.* figures embossed upon the leather of the saddle.

"He is dead," pronounced Four Bears, with no little pride. "I have slain him."

The gathered tribesmen let out a sound of awe and satisfaction.

"He is not dead," muttered Mark-of-the-Cave.

Had he been a younger man, Four Bears would have been crestfallen. He would perhaps have protested the veracity of his claim, proclaimed his prowess. But Four Bears was too wise for that, and he knew too well the powers of the seeress, who now stood on tiptoe to have a look at the little girl. Dey-Lor-Gyva, who had begun to cry when Four Bears sought to hand her over to the squaw, now looked into the old woman's eyes, but made no sound. To those who stood close by, it seemed a bond had been struck between the tiny girl and the ancient crone, or as if some knowledge had been

shared, some bargain concluded. But it was Four
Bears alone who saw the expression of startled astonishment on the seeress's old face. Mark-of-the-Cave,
who must have thought she had seen everything, now
saw one thing more. She was amazed, and surprised
at her capacity still to be amazed, after all the things
she had seen that were in the past, and all those that
were still to be. Four Bears watched, too, as the old
woman gently turned the child's head aside.

"There is no mark," he said quietly. "I myself did
look for it."

"Ah," replied Teva in a tone of uncharacteristic
gentleness, her eyes still locked upon those of the
child. "Such beauty is another kind of mark. And there
is . . . something else. But I do not know it yet. Here,
give her to me."

The gathered Indians gasped in surprise. The witch-
woman of the Chickasaw nation did not perform common tasks; her touch was reserved for sacred things,
such as healing, or the casting of spells, or the reading
of minds. Perhaps she hated the beauty of little Gyva
and wished, by ancient embrace, to kill the child, or
to afflict her with lingering disease—or, merely by
touch, to turn her ugly as a snake at shedding time!

But the woman took the child from Four Bears, and
nothing transpired—at least not immediately. Teva
carried the little girl into the chief's own wigwam,
meanwhile giving orders to certain women in the
tribe to bring her what was required: water, that the
girl might be bathed, fresh blankets made fragrant by
the sun and the pine-scented mountain air, goat's milk
sweetened with honey. The women worked, and Four
Bears stood by, watching from the shadows along the
wall of his wigwam, which was the largest in the village save for the council place. The walls were covered
with the pelts of bear and mountain lion, and the
many scalps that he had taken in his life. I should
have taken another, he reflected, and he would have

been bitter save that he possessed Chula Harjo's great mount, and that he had saved the child.

"What do you see?" he asked old Teva, Mark-of-the-Cave, who, like himself, watched the woman bathe and feed the girl.

"There is a destiny for her," begrudged the seeress.

"There is a destiny for everyone. Is that not true?"

"For some it is destiny. For some it is only life."

"Ah. Her father was my son, who had the courage to follow the path of his love. Her mother died in battle, howling the war cry of our people, in combat with their best, the One-Who-Is-Old-and-Fierce."

"Such things are on my mind," murmured Mark-of-the-Cave. "But how will the blood mix? And what strengths and passions—and what weaknesses, for we all possess weaknesses—will be her heritage?"

Four Bears was surprised. "But you are the seeress."

Teva cackled, not rudely and not in derision. The sound was an expression of humility, of her own weakness. "If one knows the nature of the material with which one works," she answered slowly, "then being a seeress is not difficult. But if one does not know the nature . . ."

Four Bears nodded. Mark-of-the-Cave said no more.

The girl was bathed and fed and made ready for sleep. One of the women had brought several soft doeskins, upon which female Chickasaw babies were placed to sleep, that they might acquire softness and beauty, that they might grow to love and be loved and win a strong brave. But as the doeskins were being spread out upon the earthen floor of the wigwam, Teva stiffened. Blood surged beneath her old skin and came into the place where the mark was. Four Bears and the women saw the bloody hand take shape upon her face until it was red as fire and the veins throbbed beneath it. A dull light glowed within Teva's eyes, and she took the little girl from one of the women, who shrank back, half in awe and half in alarm.

"No!" Teva said, gesturing toward the soft skins. "Take these away. Beloved-of-Earth was born with softness and beauty. They are her birthright and already her possessions. The days are gone in which our people lived joyously in peace beneath the sun and circling moon. There is blood ahead, and dark trails, and a river of tears. No, bring panther skins, as for a manchild, and lay the child down upon them that she might win courage and grace. She will require in her lifetime the spirit of the panther, and its patience, and its stealth. And so will we all, but it will come to far too few of us."

The women did as they were commanded, and old Teva herself bent down and wrapped the child within the panther skins, and knelt beside her until Gyva slept. Gradually the blood withdrew from Teva's mark. The child slept, and Teva arose.

"It is up to destiny now," she said.

Four Bears nodded, and made a silent prayer to Ababinili. *Thou hast heard the seeress, Great Spirit. Grant the child courage as thou hast already granted her beauty. And may she be truly beloved of earth. And may she be beloved on earth.*

Long that night did Four Bears stay awake, smoking his clay pipe and sipping venison broth beside the fire, watching as the child slept.

Finally the night took him, too, and he went gently into it.

THE BOOK OF

PROPHECY

CHAPTER I

The mountains had not changed in the seventeen years since the small girl had been brought into the village, and the village itself had changed but little. There were a few more wigwams, perhaps, and a new council hall had been built. Those who had been babies or children on that long-ago evening were beginning to assume the full responsibilities of tribal adulthood. Indeed, many of the young men had already forayed against the encroaching white settlers, and those who had been blooded, who had taken the scalps that hung now from the pole in front of the wigwam of Four Bears, the dying chief, were sometimes asked to speak in council. And sometimes they were listened to. After all, the new chief must come from the young braves who excelled in the manhood ritual by which the chief was selected. The young men had set their hearts on glory.

The young women thought of the young men, and of marriage. Beloved-of-Earth—whom the tribe called Gyva—was no exception.

"It will be difficult for her," sighed the women who squatted in the center of the village, near the well, shaping grain meal into cakes that would be baked for the evening meal. Their sighs were not completely bereft of sympathy, because Gyva worked hard and well at the tasks to which she was assigned. But the women were not without envy, either, because the maiden of eighteen suns was startlingly beautiful. She was also uncommonly bold, and the women worried about that, too.

"Did you hear her speak up at the meeting of nations?" inquired an old squaw, shaking her head in wonderment.

"It was but a courtesy," spoke another. "Gyva but asked him how long it would be until the white men enter our home mountains."

The women frowned anyway. Such things were simply inappropriate, as any maiden should know.

"She is one of us," declared an old woman who, overworked through the years and approaching death, was allowed to sit by the others, to bask in the sun.

"And yet she is not," demurred Little Swallow.

The women were careful to hide their smiles. Little Swallow was a good worker, too, and fully as beautiful as Gyva, if not as exotic. After the manhood ritual, which would occur when old Four Bears passed on into the clear sky, the new chieftain was certain to choose one or the other of them. But knowledge is knowledge and wisdom is wisdom. Little Swallow was full-blooded. Could the tribe expect less of a young chieftain's wife?

The women nodded and returned to the business of slapping grain meal into cakes. Little Swallow truly had but to wait. The chief would be Torch-of-the-Sun or Hawk-of-the-Sky. There was not a woman present at the well who would have thought to spurn either one of these handsome, powerful young men. Little Swallow—with her fine bronze skin, her lush black hair, breasts full and ripe beneath a gingham shirt seized by braves at a white trading post, legs long and smooth beneath a quilted skirt—was sure the new chief would choose her.

In darker moments Gyva silently agreed. But then she thought of Torch. Never, she vowed. Swallow shall not have him.

How oddly one's feelings changed while the years

passed by. Not too long ago Gyva avoided him whenever she could.

"Little Gyva," Torch had teased her through childhood—he who was only a few years older than her.
"Little Gyva, who was nursed by Jacksa Chula, and
who cost five braves!"

He had taunted her constantly; she had hated him
then. Yet there had come a time, and not so long ago,
when she watched him leave boyhood behind, watched
his body shoot up straight and tall, watched his chest
deepen, his shoulders broaden, his face grow hard and
wise. And then one day he had spoken to her in a new
voice, one of authority and maturity, with his eyes
upon her.

"*Ixchay*, Gyva, you are well?" And, thus formally,
he passed and went about his business.

"*Ixchay*," she had said, returning the greeting. But
her body had been changing, too, and with it her
mind. The thoughts that came to her were no longer
those of games, of sweets, or worries about curbing
her tongue in the presence of the older women. No,
that day, having exchanged greetings with him in the
manner of adults, having felt his gaze, she turned to
look at him as he strode away, saw the bronze, powerful shoulders ripple as he moved, the bear claws on
his necklace brushing his skin, saw the iron muscles
of his legs hardened by bareback riding, and sensed
rather than saw the sinuous movement of his body
beneath the breechcloth. Gyva knew fully the nature
of the hunger in her—she had heard the women speaking about it in the darkness of the wigwam when they
thought she was asleep. But it had come so suddenly,
and so hard.

Days later she lay wrapped in pelts at midday,
thinking that the fever had caught her. One moment
the day was bright, and the wedge of sun was golden
where it entered the wigwam. Next moment all seemed
hazy, dark, and her whole body was wet and hot. She
felt a yielding sweetness all over, impossible to describe

and previously unknown to her. She began to give way to it, to drift with it . . . .

She started in surprise. The witch-woman was standing in the shadows.

"Who is it?" Mark-of-the-Cave, called Teva, had demanded, her face dark in the shadows.

"I . . . what?"

"Who is it? Who is the one?"

"The one? I am . . . I think I am ill with the fever."

"That is so. But not the fever you believe it to be. Who is the one?"

The seeress knew! How *could* she know? Gyva felt the blood rush beneath her fair skin, the blush that made her almost as red-skinned as her sisters in the tribe.

"I must know," Teva demanded. "It is of importance to the tribe—if not now, then later."

"Torch," Gyva answered, because she was afraid to defy the witch-woman, who had never spoken to her before, but whose sly gaze she seemed never to escape.

"Look at me!" ordered Teva; and Gyva, who had averted her eyes in embarrassment, forced herself to turn toward the old woman in the gloom. "You are sure it is he?"

Gyva nodded.

The old witch-woman was silent for a long time, deep in thought. Finally she spoke: "Child, I must give you what wisdom I can, to serve you at this time in your life. There is attraction and there is love. Remember that. Both are natural, but the one can be as much bane as the other can be gift. It is very difficult to distinguish between them, until it may be too late, and the person afflicted with one or the other might never know. It is my wish and my prayer that you should know the difference, and that whether it be love or attraction, the one you seek shares it with you."

The words were faintly ominous. "How . . . how will I know the difference?" Gyva wondered.

"You will know it, precisely," the witch-woman said. "You will *feel* it. If you are lucky."

That did not sound especially bad, Gyva reflected.

"If he called you now, in secret," Teva asked harshly, "would you go to him?"

The image of Torch came to Gyva's mind—the way he looked, the manner in which he spoke, the way he moved.

"Yes," she nodded.

"This fever of yours," said the old woman, again after a long silence, "it is not for you alone. It is for the tribe, for all of us. So be careful with it. But I tell you this. When he calls, go to him."

Then she was gone, as if she had not been there at all.

For a long time afterward Gyva lay wrapped in the sleek panther skins that had been hers as long as she could remember, thinking of the seeress's words. Suddenly she sat bolt upright, in wonder and joy. And fear.

Teva had said *when*! *When* he calls, go to him. And she must know! Was it not her business to read the future?

In the days that followed, Gyva thought often upon the words of the witch-woman, lying awake long into the night, her mind and heart fixed upon the image of Torch, wondering when he could call her to him. By day, in spite of the fact that she groomed herself most carefully, and always made certain that her garments were clean and mended, that her headband was of a bright color, he rarely seemed to notice her. It was true that in those days he had been preparing for his first raid against the whites, the first time he was to be allowed to accompany the older braves. But was that of such importance that it should close from his mind the very thought of her, save for a glance now and again, and his reserved, almost haughty greeting? He was aware of his strength, of the eyes of the villagers upon him. He knew his worth.

In the nights, Gyva despaired. And then a suspicion
came to her: Perhaps the witch-woman had told her
those things in order that she might suffer. Anticipation can be the worst torture of all. But why? What
had Gyva ever done to harm the seeress? And despite
the harshness with which the words had been spoken,
the meaning behind them was not ungentle. Or—just
perhaps—Torch was leery of Gyva's mixed blood. The
young maiden suffered a moment of doubt, as she
sometimes did when she thought about her parentage.

But, as always, the doubt dissolved when she imagined the parents she had never known. How they must
have loved! Her father, the son of a chief! And her
mother must have been as bold as any brave, if the
stories were true. To attack Chula Harjo with a common pitchfork, to give the Chickasaw war cry, and to
fight until the death in a flaming town! No. Whatever
her doubts about her ability to make Torch pay more
attention to her, Gyva had no misgivings about the
blood that ran in her veins, or of her own uniqueness.
What did it matter, truly, if some of the women
yammered about her at the well, or while pounding
laundry on the rocks down by the river? What did it
matter if Little Swallow smirked and whispered to
the other maidens when Gyva approached, and then
greeted her so sweetly when she joined them?

Gyva had learned early to be strong, to go her own
way when necessary, to be proud of what she was. But
the new surging ecstasy that she had begun to feel
toward the young brave altered everything, threw her
whole being into tumult.

Then one morning warriors gathered before the
wigwam of Four Bears to embark upon yet another
mission. Most of them bore the wounds of previous
battles, and on their iron arms were rows of tiny scars,
each scar the result of a ritual cut, signifying a man
killed in battle. Many of the warriors had scars from
wrist to shoulder, and some had scars on both arms.

Many more warriors had gone out to fight the pale jackals and had never returned. Such might be the fate of Torch, who waited with the others for the blessing of their chief. Suddenly Gyva did not want him to go, although she knew how proud he was. She wanted to cry out, to stop him before it was too late. But there had been nothing she could say.

The warriors waited, and their horses pranced and nickered, eager to be off. Then the buckskin covering at the entrance to the chieftain's wigwam was pushed aside, and Four Bears appeared. He was old now, bent and bound for the end of his days, having seen the circling of eighty suns. But his spirit remained commanding, and he would be indomitable until death took him. He stood in the sunshine and gazed at the warriors who had gone forth so many times before, to win victory after victory that, somehow, had always turned into defeat. Slowly he moved toward his tribesmen, placing his hand upon the shoulder of each of the braves in turn. He did not speak, but the meeting of eyes was a message in itself. Then he came to the young men—Hawk, Torch, and a few others. Upon them, too, he bestowed the benediction of his touch.

"It is not for men to live without hope," he said, addressing the young men, the seasoned warriors, and the gathered tribe, "although sometimes it seems that such is our fate. And today, after we have already fought so long, so bravely, after we have already lost countless warriors, who watch us now from the sacred hunting lands of the Great Spirit, we are sending a new generation into battle. The white men come. The white men keep coming. Soon they will be upon us, even here in these sacred hills of home, upon which, once, Ababinili came to earth, and dwelt, and made us out of the living clay beneath the pine, and breathed life into our nation. If the tide is to be turned, it must be turned soon, by the bravery of these young warriors, combined with the wisdom and cunning of the old. According to our custom, I shall now ask these sons of ours, who go forth for the first time today, to tell us what wisdom is in their hearts."

The old chief's gaze fell upon Strong Badger, a saturnine, powerfully muscled youth, somewhat shorter than the others.

"I shall drink the blood of the jackal and spit it upon the earth he has tainted," Strong Badger declared, lifting his chin.

Four Bears nodded. This he had heard before. Often. Too often, and to so little avail. But he gave his approval nonetheless, and looked at Raven, who, though somewhat lamed by a hunting mishap in his youth, had overcome his curse, made himself strong and swift.

"The bones inside me are Red Sticks, every one."

A murmur of approval arose from the gathered tribe, and even hardened warriors nodded. Raven had been gifted with a telling thought.

"And you, Hawk, what say you?" demanded Four Bears.

Hawk, whose absolute fearlessness transformed his natural courage into something even more formidable, did not hesitate.

"The path of war is dearer than the path of plenty," he said. It was the kind of remark that the Chickasaw had come to expect of this bold, almost reckless youth. But it was right, true, well chosen on the morning of battle. "There shall be cuts from my wrist to my elbow before nightfall," Hawk added, for good measure.

"And what is on your mind, our young Torch?" inquired the chief, facing the brave upon whom Gyva's heart was set.

In the crowd Gyva strained to hear. Hawk had spoken well, eliciting much approval. There was little doubt that he would stand high among prospects when it came time to choose a new chief. But she wished that Torch would speak even more boldly, and surpass with his words and his wisdom the striking impression Hawk had made.

Torch, however, hesitated, or at least gave the appearance of hesitating, before he spoke.

"If courage is blood," he said slowly, "then wisdom must be death. But if wisdom is life, then courage must be peace."

No one spoke. No one moved. Gyva took the words, weighed them, and let them pass once more through her mind. Never had she heard such words before, or a thought phrased in such a manner. What did Torch mean? The braves, young and old, turned to study this young man, whom they thought they had known these many years of his youth. Four Bears himself squinted against the sun, even showed a faint trace of surprise.

Torch stood there among them, conscious of their perplexity, but unmoved by it. He seemed for an instant to stand above them, possessed of a strong yet delicate luminosity that was rare, if not unknown, among his people.

"The bird knows when to fly, and the bear when to sleep," he added, speaking as slowly as before. "So the Chickasaw must read what is written on the wind."

Old Four Bears looked sharply at the younger man. "From whom have you heard these things?" he demanded. "They are of great weight for one of few moons."

Again Torch did not waver, merely spoke, as if from his heart, to Four Bears and to the people of the tribe.

"My thoughts come to me when I think of the fate of my people," he said. "And from such a source can any but wise thoughts come?"

The people understood this thought, and a certain tension that had been growing now began to diminish.

"Mount now," ordered Four Bears. And after the warriors had done so, he said, "May your arrows be as true as the will of the Great Spirit. The strength of our people is with you."

Then the braves wheeled their horses in the dust

and rode down between the rows of wigwams. The morning was beautiful, sunny and blue, and smoke from cooking fires rose upward to the sky, like pillars upon which rested the canopy of heaven, to shelter the Chickasaw nation forever from the dark, hard rain of fate. Gyva watched her secretly beloved as he sat upon his horse. The surprise and mystery of the words he had spoken faded as he rode past her. He seemed, mounted and ready, to be like the rest of them, as fierce in his war paint, headdress, and golden arm bands as Hawk, who rode beside him. Gyva had a feeling, much like a premonition, that he was more than a warrior, more than what the people had thought and what she herself had thought. Torch's body moved with the stallion on which he was mounted, a strong gentle rocking motion that made her oddly weak as she watched it. He did not look at her. None of the braves looked at anyone. Their minds were on the journey and, beyond it, the battle. They thought of their duty as warriors, and about how valiant they would be. Then, with the braves gone into the forest, the Indians turned to their daily tasks.

"Do not tell me that a soft heart has gone with one of our warriors!"

Gyva turned to see Little Swallow.

"I saw you bend forward," Little Swallow smirked, pleased with her knowledge. "I saw you lean toward the words of Torch."

"I listened well to the words of all," Gyva responded coldly, "and all spoke well."

"But two spoke with extreme brilliance, did they not?"

Gyva herself was not certain of this. Hawk had indeed made a strong impression, but he had merely said—albeit more boldly and in better words—what all the warriors said. Torch, on the other hand, had touched upon something new. That the response to his words had been muted simply indicated—at least to Gyva—a form of wisdom whose existence might be real, but which was unfamiliar to her.

"All spoke well," she said again, feeling simultaneously proud and disconcerted. If she could find a way to get back to the wigwam and steal away down toward the river, she would be able to think about it . . . .

"And which warrior's arms shall have the most kill-cuts when our men return?" prodded Little Swallow.

"My prayer is first that all return safely. Then we shall count the kill-cuts."

Little Swallow gave her a hard, almost challenging look. "What means it to you?" she snapped contemptuously. "After the manhood ritual, I shall have whomever I want, and he shall be the best!"

Gyva was startled. To speak openly of what might transpire after a chieftain's death was a violation of tribal ways; to imply that Ababinili's will was capable of being read, insofar as it applied to the private wishes of an individual Chickasaw, was sacrilege. Little Swallow, it seemed, was tempting fate. Or else she was so sure of herself that fate no longer had a hand in what was to be.

"Our new chief will be the best," responded Gyva noncommittally.

"And he will be mine," smiled Little Swallow, who turned away, walking with a sensuous arrogance she had gained so quickly, wore so well. Then she turned around, saying, "The daughter of her who robbed a warrior from his people shall not become the bride of a chieftain."

Never before had Gyva been spoken to in that manner; never before had she been so badly hurt. Little Swallow walked away, pleased and amused, proud of her sharp stroke. But Gyva turned toward the forest, into which the braves had disappeared. Her eyes burned, and the mountains seemed veiled in haze.

"Are you not a Chickasaw?"

It was an accusation, curt and cold, from Mark-of-the-Cave. The old woman, who must have heard the exchange between the maidens, stood before Gyva. Not a trace of sympathy was revealed in her face or in her stance. The mark upon her face was pale in sunlight.

"I am a Chickasaw."

"Then why are you weeping? The Chickasaws do not weep, and certainly not for the pleasure of their enemies."

"Is Little Swallow my enemy?"

"I did not say that. We may not always agree with those in our tribe. But they are never enemies, because they are we and we are they."

Embarrassed, Gyva felt the welling tears come into the corners of her eyes. The old woman's voice, when it came, was just as grating as always, but her tone was subtly changed.

"You are not about to weep because you are Indian or not," she said, "or because you are white or not. Your tears come to you because you are a woman. So stop them. They are of no avail. Now go and think upon what I have said, and think upon the words of the young man."

"Will he return safely?" Gyva asked eagerly.

"All things are possible."

"But I thought you said . . . I thought you told me . . ."

"Did I? What did I tell you?"

Confounded, Gyva stood there in the village dust and stared at the ancient seeress.

"You said he would call for me. Remember the day you came to my wigwam? You said 'when he calls for you.' Those were your exact words." She was beginning to wonder if, indeed, Mark-of-the-Cave had been inside her wigwam at all that day.

But the old woman had. She smiled grimly. "You are still very young," she said. "Weeping—forming private meanings out of wind. Be ready for what comes to you. *That* was my meaning. Now go and think. And remember, the blood of chieftains flows in your veins. You must not flinch, or waver, when the time comes."

"When the time comes for what? Oh, you speak in riddles! I do not understand."

Old Teva gave an abrupt, cackling laugh. "There are naught *but* riddles, child, and life is the biggest of them all. In all my life, I have been able to read but a few of them. Yet the ability to read one or two, when compared to the blindness of most people, makes one appear to be wise, even when one is not."

"Then you do not know what will happen to us? To our nation?"

Teva considered the question. "I fear that I know," she answered slowly. "If Ababinili sends wise men to us, we may yet be saved."

"Yes!" Gyva agreed, caught up in the possibility of release from the encroachment of white settlers. "Bold warriors whose spears and arrows fly straight and true!"

About her, on all sides, loomed the rich blue mountains in whose embrace she had grown up, beneath whose rocky impregnability she had thus far defined what life meant to her.

"As you say," grunted the witch-woman. "Just as you say."

She went away; and soon Gyva, hopeful and puzzled and still sad, went back to the center of the village, joining the women at the well. They had seen many warriors go off before, and there was nothing to be said. Some would return, and some would not. That was all. Gyva now understood their quiet wisdom. What else could a woman do, in a nation of warriors? Life and death, love and joy, triumph or disaster—all these things depended on the men and sprang from them. Women alone, however, could fashion from the blood and fibers of their bodies the material of life, from which all else followed. So Gyva began to learn patience, patience of an ancient kind.

* * *

In this, her first lesson, she did not have to wait
long. Three days later the braves returned—or rather
some of them did. As always, the members of the tribe
began to gather quietly in the center of the village.
No words were spoken, but as if by some mysterious
form of communication, women left the meals they
had been preparing, or the sewing, or the tanning of
hides. Young boys appeared from the fringes of the
forest where they had been gathering firewood. Girls
came up the slope from the river bank, where they
were engaged in the washing or dyeing of clothing.
And each of them counted the number of returning
braves, marking that number against the total of the
original war party. Old Four Bears emerged from his
wigwam and held his face taut, that not a flicker of
sadness or fear be readable upon him.

There was much cause for sadness, and fear as well.
Of the thirty-seven braves who had set forth three days
before, only eighteen rode back into the village. Some
of them were riding double, which meant that their
horses had been killed or captured by the white men.
Many of the braves were wounded. Gyva, one of the
first to join the anxious but intrepid observers, thought
at first that her heart would stop. She could not see
Torch among the survivors! And then she thought her
joyous, pounding blood would burst the tiny veins
through which it coursed, so great was her relief.

But, like the rest of them, she showed nothing.

The beaten braves rode back into the village, bloody
themselves, some leading lame and bloody mounts.
They were not conquering warriors, as in the legends
of old that were repeated and repeated around winter
fires.

The women watched for their men. Those who
found a favorite or a husband among the remnants
of the war party touched eyes with them, as was the
expression in the tribe. Those who did not find that
special one showed no outward emotion, and tried
mightily not to think of loneliness and loss. There

would be many nights around slow fires to think about such things.

Gyva, having satisfied herself that Torch was alive and safe—although a gash had been opened over his right shoulder—scanned the rest of the men. Strong Badger was not among them. Raven must also be numbered among the dead, another name in a list of names that seemed to grow and grow, a name that would now be added to the war tales told in the council hall. Hawk was gloriously alive. He had been unmarked by conflict, and as he rode into the village and pulled his horse to a stop before the eyes of Four Bears, he raised his right arm above his head. First he let the chief count the number of his kill-cuts, and then he turned to show the people. Gyva numbered nine slashes. Nine white men had perished at the hands of this bold Hawk. A murmur of admiration rose among the Indians, but just as quickly faded. White men had been killed, true. But again the braves had suffered great punishment, and the battle, it seemed, had been lost.

Such speculations were not meant for a public gathering but for the great council wigwam. Four Bears, showing no emotion, ordered the braves to join him there, and ordered the women to bring meat and bread, berries and broth, that the braves might take nourishment. Gyva watched Torch dismount his horse, as young boys scuffled for the honor of grasping the bridle.

"You, Gyva, come with me," called one of the older women to whom Four Bears had spoken. "You must help us serve the men."

While she would always have obeyed such a command, her acquiescence would ordinarily have come from a sense of duty. But today she leapt at the chance to be near Torch, whom battle had spared. Of the women selected to help in preparing and carrying food and drink into the council wigwam, none surpassed Gyva in care or industry, and she herself saw to it that honey was spread thick and sweet upon the crusty wedges of bread.

The great council wigwam—as large as five common dwellings—was constructed of saplings, bent into a horseshoe shape at the roof, and shingled with pine bark. Tall shafts of pine and oak served as beams and braces, a framework covered by boughs and animal skins. The earthen floor of the hall was carpeted with the largest pelts, those of the bear and the elk; and in the place at which Four Bears presided, soft, rare skins of mink and ermine cushioned him.

Normally the braves would have ceased speaking when the women entered, bringing the food. But the battle had been so savage and the losses so heavy that they barely noticed the women at all.

"There is a new fort now, on the lake of Chickamauga," one of the older warriors was telling Four Bears. "Last year it did not exist and all those lands were ours. But in one moon—two—it has been built. And that means soldiers, many whites."

Some of the women were ladling a porridge of ground barley and beef into earthenware bowls. Two poured squirrel broth into small cups. Gyva passed from brave to brave, offering bread and honey. She saw Torch directly across the circle of seated braves, facing the chief across a small fire. He seemed at once exhausted and strangely alert, as if he could either sink into sleep or ride once more to battle, whichever was required. And, it occurred to her, his position in the circle was also significant. If judged by distance, he was farthest from the position of authority. But if the focus of the circle were reversed, he would be already in the chieftain's position. She drew closer and closer to him, offering bread, turning and turning the tray to make sure he would have the largest, sweetest wedge.

"But you did not attack the fort?" Four Bears was asking.

There was a moment of sheepish silence in the

council wigwam. Then Great Thunder spoke up. "It was not we who attacked," he admitted. "It was we who were attacked."

He did not meet his chief's eyes, this old and canny brave. He could not bear to do so.

"An ambush?" asked Four Bears, incredulous.

The aura of shame and defeat was almost palpable. It was to the Indian that the Great Spirit had gifted cunning in battle, communion with the forest. It was to the Chickasaw and the Choctaw and the Sac that He-Who-Dwells-in-the-Clear-Sky had given the nerveless touch, the preternatural acumen necessary to ambush and attack. And these were *Indian* lands! If the white soldiers were capable of surprising a band of braves well within the borders of their own territory, if they were able to construct a fort in the space of few moons, then the situation was graver even than anyone had dreamed it might be. Gyva felt a shiver work its way up her spine, and the heavy tray trembled in her hand.

"We were fording the Sequatchie," muttered Owl, not only to inform Four Bears, it seemed, but to convince himself that such a disaster had truly occurred. "We had come to the place—you know it?—where the fallen trees bridge the cavern of the wild boars."

"I do know it," replied the chief, who would take with him into death knowledge of the smallest ravine in north Georgia, the slope of each mountain in far Kentucky, from whence had come great legends of a man called The Boone. "But did you not proceed with care?"

"Yes, we did proceed in such a manner. But there was no sign."

"But we fell upon the jackals and fought with tooth and knife, and lance and spear. We did wreak many deaths upon them."

The tone of this voice was fresh and defiant. All turned to Hawk. He sat with his legs crossed, and his arm was turned in such a manner that all could see the nine cuts, into which he had rubbed coarse sand to raise a better scar. At that moment Gyva approached him and offered bread. Grinning, he caught her free hand in his own and pressed her fingers down upon the wounds of honor.

"Now I am blessed indeed," he said, and for the first time there was a quiver of good feeling in the council wigwam.

Surprised and discomfited—there was something about Hawk she had never liked, not even when they were children—Gyva dropped her eyes. The incident—no, it was not even that, it was but a gesture—passed quickly away, and the men turned back to grave talk. But when the maiden looked up, she felt other eyes upon her. Torch seemed to be studying her, in a manner she had not seen before. What good fortune it had been for Hawk to take her hand and press it so hard against his flesh! It had been a gesture to open Torch's eyes, to see her as she was, to see her as desirable to other men. Nor did he press her with his gaze, but turned his attention once again to the deliberations.

"I am proud of the scalps you have taken," Four Bears managed to say. "And for a young brave to be blooded is a great thing, of which to be most proud. But . . ." he seemed to choose his words carefully ". . . but we must now contrive a new approach for the future. The raids upon which we have embarked for the past years have not made us safe. With each, we are left more and more in jeopardy, and with fewer warriors to protect us. I must take counsel with you on these matters. What are your thoughts?"

"Perhaps," suggested one brave, "if we were to bind our Red Sticks to our bodies. Those who are killed are always found to have dropped their instrument of invulnerability."

"But the Great Spirit has revealed that the Red Stick must be held in the hand!" another disagreed.

"Then let us find a way to bind it to a hand, so that

it will not fall during attack. A bullet can find the heart in but an instant."

"No, no," demurred Brittle Serpent. "We must not speak of these things. They are not for us. Let us consult the one who bears the fiery hand."

"She has spoken on this many times before. The law is clear as a winter night upon this matter."

"The Red Stick is not at question. It is the fire stick. We must have fire sticks like the white man. Then we shall triumph."

"No! We must have a great war!"

Once again Hawk had seized the moment. In an atmosphere of defeat and disillusion he had struck out boldly, and all eyes were upon him. "We are failing," he said, looking around the circle and meeting the eyes of each warrior in turn. "We are failing, and it is because, since my mind grew to know and observe and remember, we have never really made war."

"What?" An angry cry.

"Never made war?"

"Hah! The pup should not bite until his teeth are hard! *Never made war!*"

Gyva was shocked. This time, truly, brash Hawk had overstepped the boundaries of acceptability. The other women were moving about, serving the men, but she stopped to have the satisfaction of hearing him upbraided. This was not to be. Hawk had nine kill-cuts in his first battle, had added nine scalps to the war pole in front of the council hall. He was not about to relinquish a chance to be heard, whether they ridiculed him or not.

"We have made *raids*," he explained. "Raids alone do not constitute war, no matter how many, and notwithstanding the number of years over which they are executed. Have all the warriors gone at once, together, to make battle? No! We send twenty, thirty, maybe forty. We burn a small village. We terrorize a lone farmer who has not been able to reach the nearest fort. We shout and shriek in the hills, alarming deer,

puzzling the black bear. In the past, yes, we have overcome forts. But the forts are bigger now, and more
soldiers with exploding fire sticks stand in our way.
Forty braves cannot match one of these new forts, such
as we have seen on the shores of what was once our
own Lake Chickamauga. Not even a hundred braves
could win that site."

His tone was powerful, authoritative. He spoke to
Four Bears as if he were himself the chieftain, young
though he was. Gyva, listening, was dumbfounded.
She began to wonder if Hawk was not indeed correct.

Four Bears interrupted. "These things I have long
considered," he said wearily. "But the women and
children who are left behind must have protection.
We cannot all foray at once against the white men.
That is the folly Jacksa Chula awaits."

The name cast an even deeper pall within the
council wigwam. Andrew Jackson, since the year 1803,
when Four Bears had rescued Gyva, had acquired more
and more power. His name was legend to the white
westerners, anathema to the red men. He had, it was
said, defeated a king whose empire spanned the globe,
beaten trained warriors at a place called New Orleans.
And he was, it was said, seeking to become the Father
of His People, the Great White Chief. Should such a
thing happen, all would be lost, and the Chickasaw
would know that Ababinili had forgotten them utterly.

"But we must take the risk," protested Hawk. "Our
warriors must go, all together, and drive the white
hyenas from these sacred lands once and for all."

"It is too late for that."

This new voice was as quiet as Hawk's was loud.
All turned to face Torch.

"It is too late for that of which you speak," Torch
said to the brassy Hawk.

Four Bears, who seemed to have drifted deeply into
thought at the mention of Jackson's name, now roused
himself. "The policy of our tribe is not yet decided

by either of you," he growled. "We have heard you both, and now we shall proceed."

"But we have never yet massed all the nations against the white man," Hawk attempted.

"Because," interjected Torch, glorious now in the eyes of Gyva, "because we have fought too much among ourselves. The Fox wait for us to be devoured by Chula Harjo and his soldiers, and they will cheer on the day we succumb, even though they will be the next to slake his thirst for blood. Or the Choctaw will be. Or the—"

"*Silence!*" Four Bears cried. "If the manhood ritual gains for some young brave this place I hold, then he may speak, because then his words will carry the weight of heaven. But until that time, you are allowed only to counsel. As all know, the counsel of a young man is too often bold"—he looked at Hawk—"or shaped in strange ways"—he looked at Torch. "So now listen as your elders continue these deliberations."

The conversations drifted back to Red Sticks and fire sticks and some strange weapon called cannon that could shake the earth, propelling balls of iron through the air.

Gyva reached the far end of the seated circle of braves and offered her tray to Torch. The largest piece of honeyed bread was there for him. He looked at the bread, and then at her. She met his eyes, which were strong and unyielding, yet troubled. The battle must have affected him in some deep manner that he was now contemplating. Then he moved his hand over the wedge of bread and gestured with his fingers, stretching them out to indicate his understanding and appreciation of her favor. Gyva thought that she would tremble; she prayed the tray would not fall from her hand. He did not look at her again, but took the bread and raised it to his mouth and partook of it, concentrating now upon the words of the older men, none of which contained any wisdom not known to the tribe a hundred years before.

When Torch took bread, Gyva saw that his strong arm, which was encircled by a bronze serpent, bore twenty-one kill-cuts. He had not displayed them boastfully, as had Hawk and the others. He did not have to boast. He knew his power. But did he also know how much Gyva wished to be encircled in his strong arms?

When the warriors had ended their palaver and gone in search of rest, Gyva helped the women clear away the meal, and then she, too, sought her wigwam. She was lying upon her panther skins, grieving over the outcome of the battle, and recalling Torch's troubled eyes. How she wished to ease his burden of concern, to soothe him in disappointment, comfort him in fatigue. Then a young voice called her name from outside the wigwam, rousing Gyva from her reverie of commingled lethargy and desire.

"Gyva? Gyva?"

She rose and pushed aside the tanned skins that covered the wigwam's entrance. A little boy stood before her, grinning innocently. He held a small branch, barely more than a twig from a willow tree, in one hand, and in the other hand he clutched something Gyva could not see.

"You are Gyva?"

"I am. Is there something I can help you with, or . . . ?"

He didn't reply, just kept grinning, pleased with a secret she could not begin to decipher. He handed her the willow twig and two small white pebbles—they were a little sticky from his chubby, soiled hands—and then raced away, back to the field behind the village where the children played.

Gyva stood there looking at the gifts. She smiled, remembering how she had felt as a child about Four Bears and a few other adults, how she would bring them flowers, or traipse after them every day, lovingly and worshipfully. So without knowing why, and without knowing who he was, she herself had evinced such innocent passion in that little boy. She tossed the pebbles into the dust, but soon thought the better of it. Should the child return, he might be wounded at the sight of his proffered treasure discarded beside the wigwam. So she picked the pebbles up, took them inside, and deposited them in the leather pouch that hung from a post beside her sleeping place, in which she kept the bracelets and necklaces and beaded head-bands with which she adorned herself.

That evening the tribe gathered to partake of roasted boar, eating together to welcome home the warriors, all of them seated around a great fire. In years past such feasts were joyous, triumphant occasions. This gathering was different, subdued and lugu-brious. No bold speeches were made, and the silent gratitude that any of the warriors had returned at all far outweighed whatever impulse might have been present to speak of new forays in the future. The meal was interesting to Gyva in but one respect. When she finished eating and took the serving bowl to be scoured and washed, as was her responsibility, she saw on the earth where the bowl had rested a curious yet oddly familiar configuration:

Clearly the markings were not random, and she peered down at them with curiosity. For some reason that she could not yet fathom, she had the impression that the symbol was meant for her eyes alone. But what did it mean?

"Gyva! Do not tarry there. Much work must be done before sundown!"

She put the puzzle out of her mind and went about her work. Each person must perform his tasks faithfully for the well-being of the tribe; it was as Teva had said, over and over and over again, a litany long since understood and now a part of Gyva's soul: "The nation can remain strong and of one spirit only as long as every Chickasaw places the good of all before his own wishes and dreams."

It was dark in the wigwam as Gyva prepared for sleep. She slipped out of her daily attire—beaded buckskin, bright calico—and felt her body cool and alive in the night air. The only light came from a rind of pale moon hanging above the mountains to the west. She sat down upon her panther skins, cross-legged, and felt the pelts lush and sleek against her bare skin. Around her the older women were drifting into sleep, if sleep had not already embraced them. Gyva brushed her hair, brushed it with long, flowing strokes, until it was radiant and silky, almost shining in the night, in spite of its blackness. Then she unclasped the necklace she had worn today, pieces of silver hammered flat and cut into the figures of animals, and fumbled for her jewelry pouch, unlooped the drawstring, and reached carefully inside to deposit the necklace.

She had very few items in the pouch, the simple treasures of a young maiden. Thus she knew the instant her fingers touched it that something new had been added to her collection. Had the little boy been bold enough to give her something else? To put it inside her pouch? How would he have known?

Amused, she wrapped her fingers around the object and pulled it out. It seemed to be a bracelet, but she could not see clearly. So, stepping carefully over the sleeping forms of the other women, Gyva, still naked, went to the entryway and drew aside the skins. In her hand, moonlit and sparkling, she held the war bracelet of a Chickasaw brave. A bronze serpent.

She shivered as with fever, and every nerve in her body was alive. She felt simultaneously very weak and very strong, as if she might run like the wind all night, take the wind to her glorious body like a lover, or sink down now and forever in her sleeping place, life and the world forever forgotten, her young dream answered so soon.

The bronze serpent revealed who her lover was: Torch-of-the-Sun, exactly as the seeress had hinted.

The white pebbles and willow sprig revealed the place at which she was to meet him: where the tall grass ran down to a shore of bright stones, and the tender willows bent, weeping, over the flowing river.

The strange hieroglyphic pattern beneath the bowl indicated the time at which she must go to him. Even now she looked up and saw the scythe of moon floating between the peaks of the Twin Mountains, west of the village.

Trembling with excitement and joy, she almost stumbled over one of the women, who stirred and grunted in her sleep. Sleep! Whatever possessed those who believed the night to be for sleep? How could they think such a thing? Did they not know that Ababinili had created the night for love, that man and woman be young and wild and free for one another? The brave must wait with yearning at a secret place, having devised a summons complicated enough to display his cleverness, and sufficiently original to reveal the intelligence of her whom he desires. The brave must wait, and the maiden must fly to him on the wings of the night.

Gyva reached for her buckskins, which hung from a peg on the pole, and then felt faintly sad. These were common garments, worn through days of work, somehow not fitting to wear in answer to this summons which—she was sure—would change her life from this hour forward. But the garment in which she was attired on festive days, or days of tribal prayer, was stored along with similar clothing for the other members of the tribe in a special structure near Teva's wigwam on the far side of the village. What should she do? Go now to the river bank in drab buckskin? Or risk traversing the sleeping village to dress herself in ceremonial cloth, with its fringes and woven designs and silver belt?

The answer was not difficult. She threw a blanket over her shoulders, stepped outside the wigwam, and peered into the night, letting her eyes adjust to the moon's pale luster. All over the village it was very quiet, fires banked for the night, the spirit of sleep riding in the heavens, upon a mount of silence. Silently, too, would she hasten to Torch.

Haste made her careless. She did not pause at the corner of Four Bears' wigwam to check whether anyone was about, but rather raced from its shadow into the moonlit center of the village. By the time she reached the shadows across the way, close to the witch-woman's dwelling and the hut in which the ceremonial garments were stored, it was too late. Following her, soundlessly but at a full run, was a fierce brave. He caught up to her, took her arm between elbow and shoulder, and turned her around.

"Beloved-of-Earth has become Lover-of-Night?" asked Hawk, his tone combining curiosity and insinuation. His grip on her arm was so hard that she felt each of his strong fingers through the quilted blanket that she held together over her breasts. Hawk studied her from head to toe. "And barefoot, too?" he wondered with a grin. "Beware the cold dew of the night does not invade your young body." Then he became serious. "I stand sentinel this night. Why are you about, unclothed, at this hour? It is not fitting. I bid you speak."

Gyva, who could not give the true reason, began to conceive a series of possible answers, one as inadequate and unbelievable as the next.

"Or do you go to meet a lover?" Hawk persisted. She could see his lazy grin in the moonlight. He leaned forward and spoke with arrogant familiarity. "Ah, no, you would not do such a thing. You come to me, isn't that right?"

She dropped her eyes in furious embarrassment. The warrior considered the gesture to be one of humility and acceptance. "When I am chief," he said, "perhaps I shall take you to wife. Perhaps not." He grinned.

Never, she thought. Anger freed her tongue. "I am out in the night," she said, surprised at how steady her voice sounded, "I am out because I have had a great dream, and must now go and ask the seeress what portent it has."

Hawk was interested. "A dream? What form of dream, Gyva?" He released his grip on her arm and dropped his hand. She pulled the blanket more tightly about her nakedness.

"I must not tell it to you."

He laughed quietly, indolently. "And why not?"

"There are those permitted to read dreams and there are those to whom it is forbidden. Such is the law, as you must know."

"But chieftains are permitted, and I am to be—"

"You are very certain of the future," Gyva responded, with some heat. "How comes this wisdom to you?"

Hawk was not offended by her manner, nor dissuaded in the indulgence of his own conceit. "Some are born to rule, and some are born to follow. Did you not feel it today in the council hall? Do you know why I took your hand and touched your flesh to my kill-cuts?"

"That I would know the greatness of your prowess as a warrior?"

She could not but put an edge in her voice, listening to Hawk boast and posture, when she had seen Torch, who had far more kill-cuts, bear himself with the quiet certainty of a true chieftain.

"Yes, that is a part of it," he admitted. "But you must already know my strength and courage. No, I touched your fingers to my wounds in order to strengthen your blood."

Gyva was outraged. "To strengthen my—"

"Now, do not create a display here. Our tribe sleeps. But it is as I have said. You may become my wife, should I choose you, but there is the matter of your white mother . . . ."

"Then," she said, "I am sorry. My blood is most acceptable to me . . . ." She had to end this conversation quickly; Torch would be waiting at the river. "But I would not be able to accept wedding with one whose blood runs as pure as yours."

Her manner angered him. "When the time comes, you will do what you must."

"Now you speak the truth!" she retorted.

"A chieftain decides what must be done in such things, and who his wife is to be."

"You are hardly chieftain yet!" she snapped, which set him back upon his heels. It was an incontrovertible truth, but one that his high opinion of himself seldom allowed him to consider.

"You keep me from my rounds as sentinel," he said loftily. "Now tell me where you go, and then be off."

"As I have said, to the dwelling of Teva, who is permitted the deciphering of dreams."

Hawk grunted. "Tell me this, then. Was it a good dream or a bad dream?"

"It was a very good dream," she said, but she could not resist adding, "and you had no place in it."

These words angered him truly. "When the lesson is taught you," he said before moving off, "the pain of it will far surpass the pleasure you have taken in these haughty words."

Gyva was about to make a sharp retort—something

about the snares of vanity, and what constituted true bravery—but something in Hawk's tone, and the thought of where she must now go, gave her pause. As an enemy, Hawk would be as harmful as the plague.

Chilled now, as much by Hawk's manner as by the night, Gyva walked toward the witch-woman's wigwam, moving slowly and glancing around to make certain Hawk had really left her alone. When she saw that he had, she skirted the small dwelling, which was quiet and dark, and entered the hut where special garments were kept. It was gloomy within, and Gyva realized that finding her own gown would be impossible. Cursing herself for not having thought of that, she threw the blanket to the floor and began to search for apparel that would fit. How many minutes had gone by since she'd left the wigwam? How long had she been detained by Hawk? Would Torch, waiting among the weeping willows, conclude that she'd been unable to puzzle out his message, dismiss her as a dunce, and turn to another woman? Sorting through the garments, she came upon one that was clearly visible, even in the darkness. But Gyva hesitated to touch it. Almost a sacred object, this gown was not of Indian design, nor even of Chickasaw origin. According to campfire tales, it had been stitched together in a far country that rested like a small green jewel in the midst of the purple sea. From this place, many hundred moons ago, had come a mighty white man to a land now known as Vir-Gin-I-A. This man, who sailed on ships so huge that even Teva could not describe them, had fallen in love with an Indian girl, greatly angering her father, who was a chief. The chief decreed that the pale sailor be put to death, but just as the execution was about to take place, the girl threw herself between her lover and the blade of the headsman's axe, begging to die along with him. Seeing the true passion of his daughter, the chief relented, and for the wedding ceremony a fine gown was fashioned in the sailor's island home and brought to

Vir-Gin-I-A. Years later the Indian girl went with her husband to his homeland, and through some mischance the lovely dress remained behind, eventually traded by the Chesapeake tribe of the bride, Pocahontas, to the Chickasaw, who had then traveled freely from the mountains to the sea. Teva, as a young girl, had lived for years in the east, and it was she who had brought the holy gown back to the mountains, bringing as well knowledge of the English tongue, which she had taught the brightest and most curious of the young people, Gyva and Torch among them.

Now Gyva held the gown in front of her, hesitating. The girls of the tribe revered this dress and regarded it with awe, for it was believed to make its wearer lucky in love. Likewise, it was to be worn only on special occasions, and then only by maidens or women who had been chosen or designated for some special privilege or honor. To select it for herself this night would perhaps be sacrilege, a violation of some holy rule, for which there would be retribution. But oh, the dress was lovely, long and pale, beautiful as the moonlight that it reflected, and luscious to the touch. She touched it with her fingertips, then pressed it to her bare skin. Unlike Indian garments, which hung straight, this wondrous creation had been designed to display a woman's body from her throat to her breasts, where a delicate, bejeweled bodice sparkled in the dim light.

It is all right, Gyva decided. I, too, have the blood of chieftains in my veins. And thinking tenderly of the Indian princess for whom the gown had been fashioned, she slipped it on and arranged its silken folds about her nakedness. Then she was out into the night again, and running down into the high grass along the whispering river. She ran like a brave, soundlessly, surely; and he who waited saw flashing against the darkness a vision born of dreams, a piece of legend shaped within the trembling heart of time, magnificent and holy. For among the tender tales of his people there were hints and fragments of stories about a sacred eagle that lived in the lost caverns of these smoky mountains, an eagle that was as white as the snow and flew only under the crescent moon. And those who saw it once would never die.

Gyva could not see him in the darkness beneath the weeping willow, but her heart knew that he was there. As the wild pigeon seeks its nest, the fox its lair, the doe its sheltering thicket, so she went to him. There was not a word, not one. Torch-of-the-Sun held out his arms and accepted a portion of his own heart from moon and mother night. Gyva felt his arms about her and the hardness of his body against her and his lips sweet and hungry upon her own. If he took and she offered, that was as it was, and if he offered and she demanded, it did not matter; it was all the same, one, as the two of them sought to be one. But there was no hurry, for the moon was high. The village slept in the distance; the river murmured. Birds were silent, sleeping, and so, too, the tiny animals of the night. The lovers kissed and embraced, violently at first, then more gently, lingeringly, when they realized, almost against the evidence of their senses, that they were indeed together. He wrapped his hand in the glossy hair at the back of her neck, bent her to a kiss as long as the night that lay ahead. Her arms went around him; her hands caressed his wide, strong back. Her fingers found the ridge of his spine and traced it, followed it down. Her hands were hungry. Lost in the sweetness of her kiss, enchanted as if by magic under her touch, he reverently drew down, slipped off the ancient vestment. Fighting an urgency that might have overcome them both, he drew her onto the soft mat of grass beneath the willow and reverently placed the holy garment aside. She found the knot in his drawstring, a knot loose to supple, easy fingers. Delicately, slowly, did they give and take of one another. Soft and knowing did he bend over her, to work kisses of mercy upon her tingling breasts, soft hands up and down her inner thighs, yet never touching—not yet—the fragile pearl that was herself, that was more and more herself as he caressed. He kissed her body, in the place where her heart was beating, and down along the lean beautiful length of her. He kissed and slowed to kiss and lingered to kiss the tiny pearl that now held all the world, but he did not release the world for her. Knowing that she was unversed in the ways of this magic, yet knowing, too, that all who love carry secrets of magic in their very souls, he then lay down beside her. He did not ask, because he did not need to ask. He knew. And as he knew, so did she, kneeling at first beside him, and then over him, kissing from his lips to the place at his throat where the blood beat like a signal drum. Now he was the one who waited, hungry, and she the sorceress, possessor of rare knowledge, purveyor of delight. She knew by instinct all there was to do, knew that giving all too soon would be to damp the flame before it was yet sweet as it could be. She kissed his great wound, and the kill-cuts that marked first blooding, and all down along his body she kissed him as he had kissed her. She sensed on her lips his triumphant delight, and in the center of herself she knew a soft and yielding rush that was a hundred times more powerful than that which she felt sometimes lying upon her panther skins alone, thinking in the night.

Enflamed and opened by his kisses, she accepted him without cry; he took her with slight cry, and of a moment the glow of the fire began to build again. She remembered the morning in the village when he had ridden his stallion off to battle, remembered how his body had moved upon the horse, at one with it. Now did he move upon her, the stallion upon the mare, but gently, gently, a careful tread upon holy ground. In this manner did he love her, speaking to her emptiness which would never be empty again, creating in her the overwhelming desire for a pleasure that must

ever be satiated, but could be satiated by none but
himself. The lance of him, which she had loved and
kissed, by which she was so sweetly impaled, stung
her to cries of delicious agony, and with all of herself
did she embrace him and take him and take him again.
His kiss and his body were everywhere upon her.

Delight radiated from them like the warmth of a
ceremonial fire burning before the eternal wigwam
of Ababinili, before which all worthy lovers would
one day gather. Torch loved her, each thrust an
attempt to have her utterly, and she moved about him,
to hold him until the end of all time. She felt her mind
dim, fade away for moments on end, only to be dazzled
then by bright new starbursts of pleasure, and then a
breathless hollowness seemed to spread beneath her
breasts, to spread downward, until she was all gone,
and her mind, too, until nothing was left of her but
the vivid, living pearl of sensation, which Torch
possessed at the price of his living body. They left the
weary earth behind, and heaven itself lay just beyond
the pillowed clouds of time; and they slowed to survey
the kingdom that lay within easy reach. Gyva could
not wait and did not want to wait, and she spoke
the first word that had been spoken between them.
"Home," she said, barely conscious now, and scarcely
conscious of her meaning, except that it had something
to do with fullness, dwelling, safety, rest, and peace.
All vistas were open to them there, and as far as ever
could she see the colored winds of time, the grace of
spinning earth. A gorgeous rush came to her, a gem
of wonder, and from him unto her burst tide and tide
and tide.

Then a long time passed when neither earth nor
heaven existed, when there was nothing at all but his
kiss, stirring her back to life.

"Ixchay, Gyva," he said, lying down beside her.

"Ixchay," she sighed.

"You knew my messages."

She came close next to him and pressed herself to his long body, one animal against another, curled against the night.

"The little boy brought pebbles and flowers, so I knew the place. But how did you come to make the figure of moon and mountain? How did you carry your bracelet to my sleeping place?"

"A true brave is silent upon the matter of his skills," he said, teasing her.

Immediately she thought of Hawk, whose heart held no such wisdom. "I was seen by one in the village," she said, "before I came to you."

He said nothing, but waited for her to go on.

"Hawk," she said.

He did not speak for a time, and seemed to be debating whether to speak at all. Then: "Hawk is a great fighter."

"I am sure that he is. I—"

"No, do not apologize for feeling about him as you do. I said that he is a great fighter, for such is the truth. But in these times, and in the times that are approaching, he will not be good for the tribe."

"Oh, yes—you will be a far better chief."

"Let us not speak of who shall become the new chief. That is not in our hands, and Four Bears yet lives. At one time Hawk would have made a great chief, just as he is already a great warrior. But we are upon new times, and new conditions. His strength is not the kind to see us safely along the trail that leads into the future."

"I know. I sense the same. But you—"

"Let us not speak of that. The Great Spirit will decide. We play in life the role for which he has chosen us."

Gyva felt vaguely confused. Did Torch resist the idea of becoming chief? Or was it something else?

"The good of the nation is most important," she said.

"The good of the nation is everything," he amended.

"And I have pledged myself to do whatever should be necessary to ensure our safety."

Gyva was proud of him for these words. How unlike Hawk he was. But she did not wish to pursue such grave matters. Touching him, she asked, "Did I not please you?"

"As greatly as ever I experienced. What you feel is not want of satisfaction, but the desire for more of such delight."

And so they shared it again, and yet again, until the time of dawn was coming. The moon, which had observed them through the night, and the falling willows which had sheltered them, were now greatly changed in the aspect of predawn light.

"You must return to your sleeping place," he said, kissing her for the thousandth time. "Now you know the person who sends for you, and the place that beckons. In future, when I call you, only the time need be signaled."

"And how shall that be done?"

"You will know," was all he said.

Gyva encountered no one, and returned safely to her wigwam. She removed the gown and, folding it carefully, slipped it beneath the pelts on which she slept. Then she lay down and contrived to appear asleep as the other women in the wigwam, one after another, came slowly awake. She heard them muttering about the "sluggard," and one of them said, "Look at that glow upon her skin! Surely she is dreaming of a lover. Perhaps a chieftain lover. We shall let her sleep until she awakens. It is not an easy life ahead of her."

"A sweet girl and a good worker," whispered another. "It is tragic that she is of mixed blood."

"Yes. What can we do of it, though?"

But Gyva did not care. She was new now, whole with love. Blood could not matter at all. The women left the wigwam to go about preparing the morning meal. Gyva tarried in her sleeping place. She did not feel at all fatigued. She felt alive in every nerve of her body; and she remembered, with a mixture of joy and sadness, how much delight her body had known. She was sad because the pleasure of the night was over; certain places of her body thrilled, but that was not the same thing as the actual moment of *having* delight. Still, she was joyous because he said that he would send for her again.

Then she fell to thinking.

They had spoken very little. He had said nothing at all about love. And neither had she! How could she not have? How stupid she had been! Certainly he had said nothing about a wedding, a melding of themselves in the eyes of heaven. The only thing about which he had spoken with feeling was Hawk, and the fate of the Chickasaw people!

Gyva lay there and began to wonder. A shadow fell upon her, and she turned to see old Teva at the wigwam's entrance. From the folds of her buckskin cloak she took out the quilted blanket, neatly folded, with which Gyva had covered herself on the previous night.

"You must have forgotten your dream," said the old lady.

Gyva was startled. "Hawk spoke to you?"

A nod.

"What . . . what did you tell him?"

"I said that all dreams are private."

Relieved, Gyva sighed.

"And how was it, child?"

"What? Ah . . ." The memory of pleasure surged. "It was better than any delight I could have dreamed."

Instead of smiling, or showing any approval whatever, the ancient soothsayer frowned. "You are a prisoner of it now," she said, "of the sensation."

"But . . . but you said to go to him when the message came."

"That I did say. But I also counseled wisdom. Carefully did I explain the distinction between love and attraction. Did you not hold it in your mind?"

"Hold it in my mind? How could I? I did not *have* a mind, I . . ."

"So. It is that way. Well, there is nothing to be done about it. Here is your blanket. Now give me back the fateful gown, and I shall—"

"Fateful? The legends say that it is full of love and fortune."

Teva cackled. "That is what the legends say."

"What is wrong? Luck in love comes to her who wears this gown."

"Certainly. Certainly. But she who wore it first died in a land far from her people and her nation."

"Yet she had love. The love she wished."

Teva cackled again, a grating croak full of wisdom. "You are far too young to know that there exist many things as great as love, and the nation is one such thing."

But that made no sense, no sense whatever, to Gyva. Not on the day of this bursting dawn. Not after the night she had spent enjoying the magic of Torch. She spoke no more. The old seeress took the gown of Pocahontas, placed it out of sight beneath her cloak, and departed. Time would tell which maiden might come to wear it on the day of tribal wedding.

Gyva lay upon her panther skins, thinking for a long, long time, waiting with all of herself to receive Torch's summons again. Time has a way with itself, and a maid has her own.

CHAPTER II

Gyva walked slowly from the village that day, watching the women who were at work down by the well. None of them seemed to notice her, and she was soon out of sight, hurrying toward the river bank. It was all she could do to keep from running; something different was in the air today. Never had Torch summoned her before nightfall. And never had his message come to her as it had this time. It is because of the great approaching war raid, she told herself uncertainly. After two years of recommendations, debates, protests, and blatant cajoleries, young Hawk had finally convinced the old chieftain to mount larger forces against the white men, and later today the Chickasaw braves would ride to join a body of Fox warriors and another party of Choctaw for a joint raid against Harrisville. The fort at Chickamauga was all but impregnable now; but Harrisville, a newly settled farming village just to the north of Gyva's home mountains, was considered vulnerable. Hawk and his hot-blooded compatriots believed that if this new town could be obliterated from the face of the earth, more great battles might be mounted, battles that would drive the white man out of Tennessee, back into Georgia. Indeed, should the red men gain sufficient momentum, perhaps the jackals might be forced all the way back to the coast of great water.

Torch did not believe this, and he had said so many times. Different opinions rose and clashed over the fire in the council wigwam, and divergent courses of action were proposed, to be decided upon by Four Bears, or to have their portent gauged by old Teva. The fact that Torch counseled care and caution was not held against him, save by hotheads like Hawk. Kill-cuts swarmed up Torch's mighty arms like angry bees; Gyva could feel the scars in the night when she lay in his embrace. Torch, too, had become legend. After one particular foray, a warrior brought back from Burnsville something he had ripped from a tree. It was a poster placed by the white men, and on it was a description of a certain vicious Indian. His feats in battle were noted, and his appearance. The concluding words sought to encourage mercenary instincts among the white settlers:

> The tribal name of this Indian is Torch-of-the-Sun, and we call him "Firebrand" for his habit of setting fire to our villages and farms. For his death, proof of which must be evidenced by display of body, or the severed head thereof, the citizens of Harrisville do hereby offer a bounty of one thousand dollars.
>
> Rupert Harris
> Magistrate

Gyva had shuddered while reading the poster, and she wished old Teva had not taught her the white man's tongue. What if, on this great raid to Harrisville, Torch were killed? What would she do then?

Firebrand, she thought angrily. It is not true.

On the grassy bank above the river, she glanced around. Finding herself unobserved, she raced down to the river, her moccasins stirring the white pebbles there, and rushed into the sheltering embrace of the weeping willows.

Torch was not there.

Had she made a mistake? Had he been delayed? Gyva let out a short, involuntary murmur of disappointment, almost a moan. Already her body was

flowing for him; already her breasts were tingling for
his kiss. The summons had been clear enough, had it
not? She had been in her wigwam, sewing patterns of
stars into her best buckskin, when she heard the sound
of someone outside the wigwam, on the side that faced
the forest.

"Gyva?" A man's whispered voice.

"It is I," she had replied.

"To the usual place. Now. And hurry."

The usual place? There was only one such place,
and urgently she had come to it; but now Gyva stood
beneath the willows and did not know what to think.
He had to have been delayed; perhaps someone had
detained him in the village on a tribal matter. She
waited for several moments, thought she heard someone approaching, decided she hadn't, and finally
stepped out into the sunlight. The day was warm, the
river bright, and a timeless penumbra of shimmering
haze hung over the mountains. White pebbles gleamed
like snow beside the blue, rippling waters; the brilliant
green of the grass almost sparkled against the darker
green of the forest.

Yet as Gyva stood by the river, wrapping about her
the warmth of day, the beauty of throbbing earth, she
felt a strange chill, as if some appalling creature,
familiar but unknowable, had flown down upon these
hills. The perception was so startlingly clear, so uncanny, that she looked again, long, at all the beloved
things around her, assuring herself that they were still
with her. And they were; but she felt it still—a tension,
a premonition—and she thought she heard the beating
of terrible wings in the distance.

Hoping to discard this formless flicker of woe, she
began to walk along the river, downstream from the
willows. She kept the willows in sight, and certainly
did not intend to go far, since Torch might appear
at any time. But she went a little too far, nonetheless.
Because standing quite brazenly before a hedge of
radiant wild honeysuckle were Torch and Little Swal-

low. The girl had allowed her shirt to slip away from
her shoulders as she circled her arms around the
warrior. She was pressing her breasts against his bare
chest, and her body moved, barely moved, serpentlike
and insinuating against his. They would not have seen
her had she been able to suppress the gasp of agony
and heartbreak that rose from her heart to her tongue.

Never, in spite of all that was later to happen,
would Gyva ever catch the smell of fragrant honeysuckle on the wind without feeling sharp violation, a
sense of tragedy and loss. Now she thought she knew
what it was she had felt moments before by the
willows. The sound of wings had been an omen.

"*Gyva!*" Torch exclaimed, hearing her anguished
cry, and raised his lips from Little Swallow's tender
mouth, which formed a sweet smile for the maiden
betrayed.

Broken and humiliated, Gyva found herself racing
upriver, past the willows, up the green grassy slope
toward her wigwam. She did not sob; Teva had said
it did no good to cry, and besides, Gyva was Chickasaw. But if she could only go into the dark silence of
her wigwam, and lay down upon and among and
within her panther skins, and lose herself forever
within their soft embrace . . .

But people were running toward her from the
village, many people, shouting, trying to tell her something. What was it? She could not understand because
she could not hear, and she could not hear because
her wounded heart thundered and thundered in her
ears. Several women intercepted her, and then a brave,
who put his big arm around her waist, almost as if to
keep her from plunging off some unseen precipice.

"Four Bears," they were saying, "Four Bears . . ."

What? What was this of the chief? Not now, not
now. Her heart had room for thought of but one
person now.

"Four Bears is . . ."

Then she managed to pull herself together, and the

brave who held her spoke clearly above the nattering of the others.

"Four Bears is dying, and he calls for you."

The shock of the news sobered her somewhat, and pulled her mind from the other sorrow, at least for the time being. Four Bears was more than chieftain to her, and more than grandfather. He had been her father as well, and her protector and guardian.

"Where is he?" she asked. "How did the end approach him?"

"It was but minutes ago. He was on his way from council hall to the wigwam of Teva when suddenly he fell upon the earth and did not move. He has been carried to his own wigwam, and lies there now."

Without delay Gyva rushed to the chief; and the others followed her, sadly but stoically. This death, now imminent, had been a long time coming, but it would be greatly felt, because the man was great.

The wigwam was gloomy and chill. Two women were building a fire. Four Bears lay on his back, wrapped in bearskins. The chief had received his name because at the hour of his birth four great black bears had appeared at the corners of the village, sentinels of the life force, bringing him into the world. The witch-woman knelt beside the chief. She motioned Gyva closer.

"He is very close to death," she said.

The old chief was pale, and already his skin seemed to be falling in toward bone, tight on the high cheekbones and black in his eye sockets. But he saw Gyva there and was able to gesture with a tiny movement of one hand: Down. Come down to me.

She obeyed, and he tried once, without success, to speak.

The fire was burning now, with faint heat. "Bring water," grunted Teva to one of the women. When she did, the witch-woman took from a pouch at her belt a small brown root, called for bowl and pestle, and ground the root into a fine powder. This she

mixed with the water, then lifted the chief's head and
bade him drink. The potion's effect was temporary,
but immediate. Four Bears smiled weakly.

"Grandfather . . ." Gyva began, a sound of desola-
tion in her voice. In a short while this man would be
no more. This man who had saved her life, or at least
brought her back for a life among her true people.
She had heard the tales around winter fires so often
that it seemed, through the darkness, beyond the shadows, that she could actually see Four Bears thrusting
at Jackson, and Chula Harjo slashing back with his
long mean white man's killing-knife; that she could
see Four Bears opening a huge gash in Jackson's forehead. But why had he not died? Did he possess en-
chantment of some kind?

"You were on your way to my wigwam?" prodded
Teva. "Can you tell me why? Was it important?"

Four Bears managed a nod. "Dream," he muttered,
on feeble lips.

His voice seemed already to come from far away,
as if his spirit were already departing the village and
the mountains, leaving his body to collapse here under
their eyes, a discarded husk of nature and time.

"Tell me," Teva urged.

Four Bears gathered what was left of his plummeting strength.

"I saw . . . Chula Harjo . . ."

"In the dream?"

He nodded. "As if . . . he were here."

Gyva placed her hand on her grandfather's forehead,
which was clammy and cold. She felt no pulse at his
temple.

"Chula is nemesis . . . of . . ."

"Of the Chickasaw?" asked the witch.

"And . . . more . . . ."

"Shall we all perish, then?" scoffed the old woman.
"What is this tale you leave with us? Our braves, our
women, our children need *hope*."

"Perhaps . . . not all perish. One with . . . strange name . . . may yet save us . . . ."

Gyva thought that she knew the portent. "Firebrand!" she cried excitedly. "He shall become chief and—"

Four Bears moved his head a little from side to side. "Not Torch. Strange name, not of our people. Unclear . . . to me."

"What did it sound like in your mind?" demanded Teva, seeking clues, signs. "Of what image was it conveyed in your dream?"

But the effort had already exhausted the old warrior. His eyes closed, his head tilted sideways. He still breathed, but sporadically, with a rattle that made Gyva shiver. All through the afternoon Gyva and the seeress stood vigil, and when the young maiden would ask "yet?" with her eyes, the soothsayer grunted and muttered, "Soon."

"Will he speak again?"

"If the Great Spirit wills it. Hush. Heaven and earth are about to mate now, as they do for every birth, for every death, and the wings of the warrior of death shadow these mountains and tremble the air."

Startled, and cold anew, Gyva remembered the unearthly feeling she had had down by the river, the unheard but perceptible flutter of shivering wings. The thought brought back that terrible image of Torch embracing Little Swallow, and the ache in her heart, already savage from death, doubled and tripled her pain. Why had Torch done such a thing? To send for her, that she might witness his faithlessness firsthand?

If he did not love her, even after all the pleasure she had so happily given him, why could he not have *told* her? He did not have to end their love by breaking her heart. Or perhaps he thought some heartless shock would drive her love away, that she would recover more quickly if she grew to hate him.

No, that would never be . . . .

But imminent death drew Gyva's attention away
from her own sorrow. Four Bears faded through the
afternoon, and Gyva grieved for him; yet she was
happy, too. He would know no more suffering; he was
soon to become immortal. All during the long day, as
Four Bears traveled toward another world, the tribe
gathered outside his wigwam, holding vigil. The sun
descended behind the purple mountains, and dusk
came to envelop the village like fog. A wild strange-
ness came into the air. So long had Four Bears lived,
so long had he fought to guide the destiny of his
people, that it seemed almost unimaginable that he
should die. The moon was up and the stars were
flickering when the soothsayer studied Four Bears,
lifted her head, and turned to Gyva.

"Go out now," she said, "and choose the youngest
and strongest among the blooded warriors, for our
new chief shall come from their number, and bid them
come here."

The maiden rose and left the wigwam and stood in
the open air, where all eyes were upon her. The question, unspoken, was "Death?"

She gave neither sign nor answer, but passed among
the assembled throng, proud of bearing, possessed of
great outer calm. Yet her heart thundered more and
more as she passed from Hawk, giving him the order,
to the others—Long Talon, Swift River, Arrow-in-the-
Oak. Finally she reached Torch, whom the jackals
called Firebrand. She stood before him, with all the
others watching, and betrayed not a flicker of the
feelings with which she was at that moment besieged.
She tried to block from her mind the image of Torch
embracing Little Swallow.

He looked down at her, with eyes full of pain and
. . . something else. Bitterly did it please her to see
the pain, and well did he deserve it!

"Teva bids you enter," was all she said, turning
away from him as a proud princess would, yet as he

stepped forward he might as well have trod upon her heart, which had fallen from her breast and lay now in the dust before him.

When the young braves were inside, Teva spoke.

"Take him up now," she ordered, "and his bearskins, too, and carry him out beneath the stars, that his spirit might more quickly find the direction of heaven, and that our people might know that one era has ended and another has begun."

Gyva did not fail to see the eager look upon the brash visage of Hawk. Well had he prepared for this day, and perhaps he had even prayed that it come soon. The great raid that had been planned for today against Harrisville had been put in abeyance due to Four Bears' condition. But Gyva knew that Hawk had in mind a yet more ferocious foray, with, if possible, all the nations commingled in blood.

Warriors, three on each side, stretched the bearskins taut beneath the chief's dying form and carried him from the wigwam out into the night air. No one spoke; even the little children were still. The warriors lowered Four Bears to the earth, then stepped back a pace, looking down at him. Teva knelt at his head. She took his cold hand. All watched the mark of the hand upon her face, for if blood flowed into it now, perhaps some saving wisdom might be possessed by the tribe.

The breath of Four Bears came, a horrible, racking gasp, then did not come for a long time. Gyva leaned forward, between the broad shoulders of Hawk and Torch. She thought her own heart had ceased.

But the great chief was not yet quit of life. He grabbed for air again, lungs clutching, and then again, and again. Gyva experienced the horror of watching suffering without being able to assuage pain. The mark did not grow scarlet upon Teva's face, and gloom as well as sadness rose and rode on the air above the tribe.

Then Four Bears' eyes flickered open, and the six standing warriors were reflected in them. Four Bears blinked, and coughed. His gaze turned to Teva, and on his mouth appeared a grimace that might have been a smile.

"*Ixchay*," he gasped, giving the greeting. "Now I believe it is time. . . ."

And together did the Indians, all of them, look toward the sky. Into the air came the quick, sharp chill that Gyva had known beside the river, and from the sides of dark mountains swooped the implacable wings of the warrior of death. The half-moon hung in the sky, a sphere of both darkness and light. Gravely the old people of the tribe studied the moon and the sky, nodding to one another, pushing forward now to glimpse Teva, who still held the hand of Four Bears. The chief's eyes were on the stars, and he seemed to be listening intently to a distant voice. He was beyond speech now, and only the dull glow in his eyes indicated a frail, tenuous connection to this village in the hills.

The soothsayer looked up and let her gaze swing to the west, and at that moment a flash of blood began to pour beneath her skin, outlining the print of the sacred hand upon her face. The villagers saw it and exhaled as one. Good omen or bad? Small children, gifted with the keen, innocent apperception that is the lodestone of childhood, now sensed an excitement in the air. A few began to sniffle in fear of the unknown, but they were quickly enjoined to silence by their elders.

Blood poured into the mysterious mark by which the Great Spirit had made Teva holy. Even Four Bears saw it, but he was too far gone into night to make a response. *A portent? A prophecy? Pray let it be good for the people of our nation.* Perhaps now they would learn more of this one with the strange name whom Four Bears had found in his dream.

But that was not to be—not then. Suddenly, although there was no true sound, the vault of heaven, the stars, the moon, seemed for an instant overlaid with a canopy of velvet blackness, so dark did the earth become. The people of the tribe looked toward one another, but for that single instant they saw nothing, saw no one. Four Bears shivered upon his death pallet of bearskins and opened his eyes wide. He alone saw what had come for him out of the sky. Over his withered features came a sudden, glowing burst of ineffable joy, a glorious acceptance of that which all the others feared but could not see. And with a final effort he turned slightly and reached toward his granddaughter, Gyva, who stretched out her hand. He seized her wrist and held it tightly. She was all but pulled forward by his last burst of strength, and sank to her knees, facing the chief's pallet, upon the earth between the feet of Torch and Hawk. The mark was brilliant on the face of Teva, and together did the old woman and the young maiden touch the chief as he passed over. The world hushed, time flickered, and then Four Bears was beyond them all, forever, mounted upon a steed of wind, the warrior of death his brother now, the two of them galloping in glory, bound for a hunting ground far beyond the North Star, where a dazzling necklace of light stretched on forever.

"*Look!*" shrieked a child.

The canopy of velvet receded; the moon and stars burned bright.

And all of them turned to see, standing in the shadows at the corners of the village, four great black bears silently watching.

Another moment and they were gone. Their task was completed.

"What was the omen, old woman?" demanded Hawk. The body of Four Bears was not yet cold, and already the young brave lusted for a future of power.

Teva shook her head. "I have told you the words that I heard. One with a strange name may save us, if we are very fortunate."

Hawk frowned. Hawk-of-the-Sky was not a name strange to the tribe.

"Perhaps I shall change my name," he said. "But we did all observe that upon the moment of the old man's passing"—Gyva noted that Hawk avoided the word *Chief*—"the mark of sooth on your face glowed like a coal in the hearth."

"Ah! Is that so?" asked Teva. "Now you would do best to see to the safety of the village tonight, you and the other young braves. We women must wash and dress and pray upon the body of our chief."

Hawk seemed inclined to contradict the soothsayer's choice of words, and clearly he did not believe that she had not sensed wisdom at the moment of death. But there would be time enough to make a stand regarding these things on another day. The death had finally come, the death he had been waiting for; and beautiful, rolling vistas of power stretched out before him.

"Come," said Torch, "let us meet briefly at the council wigwam, and decide upon the posting of sentinels for the night. Then we must turn to the matter of the Choctaw and the Fox."

"The Choctaw and the Fox? Why, what of them?" asked Hawk with some heat, as if he had been challenged.

"Because," Torch explained calmly, "we were to rendezvous with them for the attack against Harrisville. We could not do so because of Four Bears. They must be apprised of what has happened here, and mollified if they have been angered or offended by our absence."

"Cater to the Choctaw?" spat Hawk. "Why ought we humble ourselves before them? They will think it weakness, and—"

"It is but courtesy and good sense to be frank with allies," Torch explained.

Hawk curled his lips contemptuously. "You are not chief yet," he sneered.

"Neither of you is chief yet," interrupted Teva.

"And perhaps neither of you will be. The manhood ritual will test everything you have to give, and all you have to offer. So let us bury Four Bears on the morrow and proceed to the selection of whomever Ababinili wishes to be chief."

She spoke with some anger. It seemed to her that the young men were scrambling for hegemony over the very body of a great chief. Would that anyone in the tribe could become as splendid as Four Bears had been, or as brave, or as wise!

Somewhat chastened, the braves went off, leaving the women to tend the body of the dead chief. Because it was a task reserved for the older women, a privilege earned by long years, Gyva made a silent prayer over her dead grandfather. It seemed incredible that this still, cold, shrunken form on the bearskins had ever been a man at all, and she felt a mixture of deep love and deep sadness as she prayed that, for him, the eternal hunt be always fine. The blood in her veins was his, and she was proud.

"Go now, child, and sleep," muttered old Teva. "Much may be demanded of you. We will dress our chieftain in ceremonial robes, place him this night under the stars, on a pallet in the center of the village, and in the morning we shall bury him along the river."

Mention of the river upset Gyva.

"Why, child, what is the matter?"

It seemed unholy to speak of it here, with the old women already beginning to bathe Four Bears' body, but Gyva's hurt was too great to keep still.

"My chosen one," she said, as quietly as she could. "He has another."

Teva's baleful old eyes grew yellow, like a cat's. "This you have heard, or this you have seen?"

"I have seen it."

"Eyes may lie. Ask of your lover if it is indeed true."

Gyva lowered her eyes, remembering Torch and Little Swallow locked in embrace, Little Swallow's proud breasts against his chest. "I could not . . . face him with such words."

Teva grunted. "Youth," she shrugged. "Did you verily see a rival open herself to him, and he upon her?"

Gyva had to admit she had seen no such thing. She shook her head.

The soothsayer cackled. "Once I told you that you have become a prisoner of the pleasure your lover gives. You must be careful not to become so lost in the pleasure that you cannot think aright. What hold have you over any man, that another ought not challenge you? Do you not see? It is not only the brave who must be resourceful and unyielding in conflict, but also the maiden . . . ."

She let her voice trail off. Gyva felt a bit ashamed now, to have troubled Teva with this matter of the heart, especially at such a time. She began to apologize, but the old woman waved away the words. "Go," she said. "Sleep. For it is as I also told you, 'There are many things as important as love.' "

Gyva thought about those words as she walked toward her wigwam, and they were good words; but they did little to assuage her heartbreak and grief. How could they? Her love for Torch was—had been —the center of her life for two whole circlings of the sun. In spring and summer they had loved down on the grass beneath the willows; in autumn upon rustling, golden leaves that seemed to sigh, to whisper, as the lovers moved. Even in winter, the two of them wrapped tightly in blankets of fur, Torch turned her to fire in his embrace even as she embraced him with herself and, with her body, stroked him to delight.

Was that now over? How could he have wounded her so?

"I do offer you sad feelings on your grandfather's death."

Gyva looked up. She had been intercepted, just outside her lodge, by Little Swallow.

"It is without doubt a great pang to lose so much in one day," goaded Little Swallow.

The blood of warriors did indeed course in Gyva's veins. Her first impulse was to fling herself upon this evil-swallow-who-nests-in-perfidy and scratch out her lovely black eyes. But she did not.

"I thank you for your sympathy," Gyva replied, evading the provocation, and attempting to walk around the other girl.

But Swallow, her victory so utterly glorious today, so complete, wished to detail her triumph.

"Do you know what it feels like?" she hissed.

Gyva spun toward her, fighting for control.

"Do you know the feeling of those kill-cut scars when his arms are around you?"

Blood rose in Gyva's face.

"And do you know how it is with his kiss, and his body hard and wanting next to you?"

Heat flooded Gyva's body.

"Deep inside yourself, do you remember how it feels—way deep?" Swallow was taunting. "Do you remember? When both of you know that the moment has come?"

"*Stop!*" Gyva wanted to scream. But she would not let herself. She would let herself show defeat as little as she would permit herself to accept it. If only to save Torch from a maiden as mendacious and savage as Swallow, Gyva would move heaven and earth.

"It was my belief that you favored Hawk," she said, approximating but not quite duplicating Swallow's highly practiced gift for honeyed venom.

"I favor whomsoever will become the new chieftain," sniffed the other.

"Then you are giving yourself to both of them upon a time, are you not?" asked Gyva.

Little Swallow was a bit startled at the precision of Gyva's attack. "Whomsoever I love," she said, with just a hint of uncertainty, "then him I love."

"And you just told me that you favor whoever becomes the new chief. So do you also embrace Arrow-in-the-Oak, and Long Talon, and Two Paws?"

Her spirit somewhat restored by this attack, Gyva began to wonder. It was well-known in the village that Hawk and Little Swallow had eyes for one another. Perhaps Hawk was himself too hot-headed, too impulsive, to judge Little Swallow for what she was. *Unless* there was something else at the base of all this.

Swallow attacked. "A maiden who has lost her man is a bitter maiden," she said. "What truth can one expect her to speak? No one will take seriously anything you say."

"You are the one whose tongue craves my ears," Gyva shot back. "I wish but to know why."

Again, more perceptibly this time, Swallow hesitated, and Gyva began to wonder what was happening. Just how intricate and involved does the matter of love and jealousy become? If it *was* merely love and jealousy. Gyva knew, of course, that a victor claims every right under the clear sky to humiliate the vanquished, to make him grovel and suffer and plead. That was how things were. But, in the past, she had believed that this law of heaven applied only to relationships or encounters between the tribe and its enemies. Perhaps she had missed a lesson. Well, if it also applied to affairs of the heart *within* the tribe, so be it.

"You have not told me," she demanded. "Why will no one take my words seriously?"

"Hawk has said it!" declared Swallow, with a kind of nervous triumph. "You are not true Chickasaw!"

Again, the same thing. Always Swallow returned to it, when the two maidens spoke to one another. Does it truly matter so much? Gyva wondered. I have lived here all my years. My grandfather is chief—

Not any more.

She no longer had a protector, and the wolves were circling. How much they must have envied and hated her, all those years! Hated her for the power and protection conveyed by a great chief. Envied her for exotic, compelling looks: flawless ivory skin, perfect female body, and face framed by gleaming black hair, eyes like black bits of heaven beyond the stars.

"Good night," she said to Little Swallow, and began to walk away from her.

"Where do you go?"

"To sleep," Gyva called back.

"And alone," replied Swallow, with a tone in her voice that was contemptuous, yet not altogether so.

Gyva returned to her lodging, her mind somewhat cleared by anger. She removed her garments and sank down upon her sleeping place. The wigwam was dark. She could see a few sleeping forms: the women who had not been sufficiently old to prepare Four Bears' body for tomorrow's burial. She lay down; and her bare skin, as always, thrilled to the panther pelts, a sensuous experience she could compare only to Torch's sleek body upon her own. But she could only compare it, never equate it. There are at least two worlds in every heart.

When she leaned back, she felt something under her head, something hard under her rolled blanket. She took it up in her hand. A necklace. Had one of the other women dropped it? She explored it with her fingers. No, the necklace was one of claws, which women did not wear. Large claws they were, too. Very large . . . bear claws. It was the necklace of Torch!

Another message or signal? Another summons? So! It was too dark now to send her the usual diagram of moon and mountains, just as earlier his need for her to see him with Swallow had led him to hissing outside the wigwam! No longer did he show a shred of grace!

Bear claws indeed! she thought. I have been ravaged for the last time!

And yet, as she tried to fall into sleep, and tried, and then began to drift away, her resolve, her very honor, began to dissipate. Was not he *the one?* What of Teva's words—and two years of unremitting delight?

Am I right in not meeting him tonight? was her final thought, but then it was too late to think anymore. Her spirit was borne upon the blue haze over the mountains, and breathlessly she saw the beauty that was her homeland, far below. Far away, in the outer reaches of heaven, receding from her with speed akin to the flashing light of the sun, Gyva saw Four Bears astride a horse of lightning. Skillfully did he wheel his great mount, somewhere moonward of the mighty dipper of stars, and with great love did he lift his farewell hand to her. The world belongs to the living, but if they are lucky there is much love and courage left them by the dead, to love and cherish, upon which to build. Gliding like a hawk into the land of sleep, Dey-Lor-Gyva saw the face of her grandfather imaged in the stars. Softly did he gaze at her and send a kiss.

Then she was in sleep, in deep sleep, the canopy of heaven still within the circle of her skull. Very slowly, so that she did not know it, time moved and stars rearranged themselves into curious, monstrous formations, until a new face was emblazoned in the sky. Gyva, in her sleep, tried to turn from it; but the visage pursued her, even in nightmare, even in dream. A long, lean face, hard as stone—harder. The eyes were like sun dogs in a most violent winter, and some great galaxy a million journeys from earth formed upon the forehead of this face a scar as remorseless as memory itself.

The blasting of guns and war cries awakened her. Jacksa Chula, she thought, and closed her arms upon her breasts.

Any brave who speaks truly will tell you: There is no intelligence in battle.

There is only frenzy. And for some there is fear.

For Gyva, at first, there was only confusion.

Nothing in the world seemed to exist, save the explosions of fire sticks, and howling, and the pounding of horses' hooves. Outside the wigwam a rider flashed by. Gyva heard an ominous, crackling sound, and immediately the roof of the wigwam leaped into flames. Why had there been no warning? What had become of the sentinels?

Gyva grabbed her clothing, and slipped the leather pouch from its place on the pole, the small receptacle in which she kept her few treasures, and in which, with some misgivings, she had deposited Torch's bear-claw necklace. Then, with the other women, she dashed outside, as the fire edged down into the walls of the wigwam, and the roof collapsed.

Many other wigwams were afire, eerily illuminating the village. The attackers had ridden in from the north and were crashing through the village, firing their horrible sticklike weapons of flash and thunder, throwing torches onto wigwams, swinging hatchets and axes. Blue Crocus, a gnarled, fearless old woman of seventy years, rushed out into their path, flailing at an attacker with a long stick. The rider's knife flashed, and Blue Crocus's stick lay in the dirt, her hand and bloody forearm still holding it. Gyva fell backward, narrowly escaping the trampling hooves of another attacker. She could feel the heat of the horse as it pounded by; she smelled the strong, raw sweat of the excited man. Clouds of dust rose in the air; the thunder of hooves filled the village; pools of red blood spread in the dust. The attackers galloped through the village once, wheeled at the south end, and prepared to make another charge.

In the event of an attack, every member of the tribe had an assigned duty. Braves were to take up their weapons and fight. Older women would rush the children to shelter in the surrounding forest. And young women like Gyva were to fight fires or, should the fires burn out of control, assist in battling the attackers.

Gyva threw on her buckskins, slipped the leather pouch into a pocket, and raced to the wigwam where weapons were stored. The attackers were forming for another charge as she grabbed a bow and a quiver of arrows from the squaw who was passing them out. Gyva thought she saw Torch racing toward the enemy position, but she could not be sure.

The village was burning—at least ten wigwams were afire, including the council hall—and people raced about, screaming and crying. The assault had come so suddenly, so surprisingly. Who *were* the attackers, in fact?

One of the marauders howled something to his compatriots, horses were spurred, and the second wave of the assault began. The torches had done their evil work in the first attack, and now the nameless enemy galloped down upon the Chickasaw, firesticks blasting. As she had been instructed so many times, Gyva went down upon her right knee, her left knee bent at a ninety-degree angle, and pointed in the direction of the charge. Her left arm, which held the bow, was straight, parallel to her left leg. She slipped an arrow from the quiver and fit it with sure fingers onto the bowstring. With neither fear nor excitement—there was no time for either emotion—she drew back the bowstring and concentrated on the attackers, who were hurtling forward now, the hooves of their horses raising clods of earth. Gyva saw, without having time even to be astonished, that the enemy wore not the military uniforms she had expected, but rather the broad-brimmed hats and cloaks of farmers.

But farmers or soldiers, there was only one thing to do. She picked a rider toward the left of the charging line and drew aim. He was riding fast, but riding almost straight in her direction, so there was little problem in drawing a bead on her target. The bow bent, the bowstring was taut as could be, the attacker came pounding down on her.

But she could not release the arrow!

For a terrible moment all time seemed to cease. The village was suspended somewhere between heaven and earth, motionless, and all within it motionless; even the licking curls of flame around the wigwams were still, like fire that has been painted in a picture, forever burning yet not consuming. Gyva saw clearly now the man at whom she aimed, astride a mighty roan, the reins in one fist, fire stick crooked in his free arm. The dark brim of a hat shadowed his face, a cloak flew out behind him as he rode. Then slowly, slowly, she saw the round hollow end of the fire stick swinging toward her, moving dreamlessly to circle her in its depths. Beneath the hat brim, eyes had found her, and she was as much a target as he was.

Time began again, and Gyva released the arrow.

The fire stick exploded.

The horse passed close enough for Gyva to smell the sweat of it, the odor of hot saddle leather.

The man plunged to earth, scant yards away from her, rolled a time or two in the dust, and then lay still. His fire stick came to rest nearby, like a dead serpent, stretched out to be counted after a hunt.

Then the attackers passed through the village, hooting and shouting, and were gone. It was a long time before any semblance of order could be restored. The wigwams that had been set ablaze burned to the ground; it had been too late to save them. Mercifully, no children had been hurt; but three women were dead—one by fire, two by fire sticks—and eleven braves lay wounded, four dead. The attackers, of whom there had been perhaps a score, lost but two of their number; and many had seen Dey-Lor-Gyva bring one down with her arrow.

It would have been inappropriate to make display over her act, but members of the tribe gathered around, proud of her, as she approached the body of the first man she had ever killed. The death had been necessary. It had been her responsibility. And she had done it. She saw Torch approaching, his silhouette outlined against the embers of a ruined lodge.

"Take the scalp," people were urging her. "It is yours, and you must take it."

But how could she bring herself to do that? It was a thing for braves—the quick, brutal hack of a knife to remove a circle of skull from an enemy, his hair along with it. Her victim lay on his face in the dark dust, the wide hat still on his head. One of the peaceful farmers! she thought contemptuously. Always they came "to farm, to live in peace," and always they brought death in their wake.

The people were asking her to take the scalp. Torch joined the group. In the shadows Gyva saw Hawk and Little Swallow, huddled together in a pose that reminded her of something, some guise she did not like.

"Take it!" the people were saying, with more urgency now. "Add it to the trophies of our people!"

Among those, like Teva, who were wise and ancient, there was an expression: The heart knows its nature. These ambiguous words meant simply that certain people were born with inclinations or aversions about which nothing could be done, and so it was with Gyva. Often had she stood before the council wigwam to cheer and applaud some young brave come back from battle with scalps at his belt. She had been proud of him, too, and of what he had done for the safety of the tribe. But imagining the actual taking of the scalp, she shrank away. Yet it would be unseemly, and reveal a lack of courage, not to take the scalp of an enemy she had felled.

Slowly she approached her victim and knelt down beside him.

"Roll him over!" cried someone. "Let us see the gape of a white jackal quit of life!"

The man was limp and heavy in death. Gyva put

her arms beneath him and tried to force him onto his back. Then Torch was there beside her.

"Take the scalp!" The cry rose louder still. Her delay in doing so had already aroused a suspicion that perhaps she would not—or could not—do it.

In spite of what had happened between them, she sensed that Torch was there to help her, to give her comfort beyond mere aid. After the hurt she had been dealt by him, Gyva wanted to scream him away. Yet, oddly, she sensed kindness and not hostility in him. It was his trick, of course! Such are the ruses of men.

"You must do it," he whispered, as they struggled with the dead body, "or you shall be held in great scorn."

"Am I not already?" Gyva snapped, meeting his eyes.

"There are things you do not know."

"And many that I do!"

"Did you not find my necklace?"

"Do not worry. You may have it back, although you are the one who lurks outside the walls of wigwams, and makes love by the honeysuckle bush."

"You do not know the half of what you speak!"

"Scalp him! Scalp the white man!"

Torch rolled the body over and yanked away the hat.

Gyva was astounded, and a little afraid.

"Evil portent!" swore Torch, standing up.

For the body of the victim was not a white man's at all, but an Indian's. Even in disguise, no brave would venture into battle without the distinctive war markings peculiar to his tribe, and these were visible on the dead man's face. A *Choctaw!* The wide hats had been used to conceal the truth and mislead the Chickasaw.

"They have attempted to foment great bitterness between us and the whites at Harrisville," Torch concluded. "They wish to set us and the white settlers against one another, that we both perish. Or, as I have already surmised, they did not take kindly to our absence at the raid today."

He looked directly at Hawk.

"You would have gone upon that raid yourself," swaggered the other brave. "So what does it matter if the Choctaw stir us against the jackals? Is it not our will to drive them back to the great sea?"

"I go upon all raids because I am a member of the tribe and do what I am ordered, whether I agree with certain decisions or not."

The people stirred and murmured. Now the conflict between these powerful young men was clearly visible for all to see.

"Then what is your point?" Hawk demanded.

"My point is one for all to ponder. We must be far more subtle than we have been. Just as all white men may not be our enemies, equally so has it been proven that all Indians are not our friends."

He gestured toward the man Gyva had killed. She herself was confounded.

"You are foolish—and a dreamer, too," declared Hawk. "When the white men are all dead, every problem will be solved. This matter of the Choctaw raid can be readily attended to. Let us form up now, ride, and kill some of their women and children. Let us burn *their* villages now."

He paused, believing that he would hear cheers in his favor, and bloodthirsty calls for attack. He had miscalculated. There were many who would ordinarily have followed him; but the people were without a chief, and it was not right to form battle parties without a chosen leader. Hawk understood and fell silent, although he did not retreat from his position.

"Take the scalp," Torch whispered to Gyva. "It will distract the people from this unfortunate clash." He thrust a knife into her hand.

"I cannot," she pleaded.

"What? You are neither fool nor weakling. You must. So do it!"

He tossed away the broad-brimmed hat, grabbed a handful of the dead man's hair, and jerked the lolling head from the dust.

"Be quick. One swift slash. You need only show a small amount of blood. It will suffice."

"But I cannot."

Torch looked at her for a long moment. In the background villagers were clamoring for the scalp. Gyva saw her beloved's eyes, and her own image reflected in them. But she saw also his mouth, his lips, which just yesterday Little Swallow had kissed. How was it, then, that Torch's eyes showed no sign of infidelity? In spite of what had happened between Torch and Swallow, Gyva would gladly forgive him if only he would show contrition.

His voice pulled her from the reverie. "I will help you through it. Raise the knife."

Little Swallow and Hawk had edged closer. "Do you not think a true Chickasaw would readily take scalp?" the maiden asked, so that many could hear.

"Raise the knife!" Torch hissed urgently. "This does no good for any of us. You should be proud!"

The dead Choctaw filled her vision, her mind, the whole world. Gyva saw his long black braided hair, the low flat forehead, a sharp jutting nose. His mouth, thin and cruel in life, seemed lax and comic in death. His eyes were open, fixed upon nothing.

"When the Choctaw rode out of the village," Torch was telling her, "one of them deliberately upset the bier upon which Four Bears lay beneath the stars."

Gyva looked at him. Defilement of her grandfather's body? As soon as she realized the heinous import of Torch's words, she hesitated no longer. The great knife flashed in her hand, and lopped off a circled chunk of skull and hair. The dead man's head slammed back down into the dust, and Torch held aloft the scalp, for all to see.

A cry of revenge and triumph rose on the night air, to blend uneasily with the smell of scorched wood, and the terrible stench of the squaw who had been burned. Gyva stood up, staring at the blood upon her knife. *This shall be the last time I kill,* she vowed. *I could not have been born for such a thing.*

The members of the tribe were already walking toward the body of the other dead Choctaw, killed by a spear at the hands of Arrow-in-the-Oak, who might himself become chieftain. On the fringes of the crowd walked Hawk and Little Swallow, still very close to one another, and Gyva understood what their aspect signified: Somehow, they were conspirators.

But to what end, and by however many intricate byways, she did not know.

Teva presided.

The body of Four Bears, which, restored to its place on the bier, had lain for the night in the center of the village, was lifted by six braves—Torch was one of them, Hawk another—and borne down to the river bank. There, where the water was shallow, Four Bears was carried across to the burial ground at the edge of the pine forest. Tribesmen, their women and children, gathered in silence along the glittering river. Some of the children, half-expectant and half-fearful, studied the shadows where the trees were, looking for the black beasts that had appeared at death's hour.

The braves placed the body on the earth next to an open grave, and Teva stepped forward.

"We gather here," she said, "to place within the embrace of the earth we love, a man whom we have also loved and whose life was spent in leading us. Already, as we believe, his spirit is hunting the fields of far heaven. But he has remained with us in memory, to love and cherish, and thus do we inter with honor his body, whose strength in life was our protection. So let us lower him now into the earth beside the river, whose waters run to the sea, that in time our love for him and our memory of him will encircle the great globe."

Gyva felt grief wrap a cold hand about her heart, but she stood straight and true as a hickory tree, and did not flinch or weep or waver. Carefully the braves eased Four Bears down into his final sleeping place. His body was wrapped in the bearskins that had been his possessions during life, and his face was visible to the tribe. Then the braves moved back several paces, and Teva came forward. She settled her old bones on the ground at the grave's edge, and cast down into it a long war bow, a quiver of arrows, a cup and bowl, and lastly bread and barley seeds in a birch-bark container. Then she took a handful of earth from the piled dirt, held it over the open grave, and opened her fingers.

Torch and the other braves did the rest. They worked quickly and well together on this morning. Each of them knew—and so did every member of the tribe, right down to the smallest child—that one of them would surely become chieftain.

Gyva had hoped that, following the burial, she would somehow be able to speak to her lover, but that was not to be. A village waited to be rebuilt; there were wounded to be tended and, as always, people to be fed. The men, for their part, had to deal with political matters of great importance: future posture toward the white men in Harrisville, plans for responding to the Choctaw attack. Then, too, there was much quiet speculation in the village as to why the sentinels had failed so miserably on the previous night, speculation that might readily lead to accusations and denials and grievous ill-feeling. Over and above those things, the manhood ritual must be planned immediately. Bereft of the council wigwam, which lay now in a mound of smoking cinders, the braves went down to the edge of the village, seated themselves cross-legged upon the ground before Teva's hut, and, under her eyes, began to debate and discuss. Gyva saw them there when she came up from the river, and for the first time she felt the vast emptiness in the village which Four Bears had filled for so long.

Gyva's own wigwam was gone, but she had her clothing and her little leather pouch of treasures. She had something more, too: the watchful scrutiny of the people. All day, as she went about her work, the voices whispered.

"It was upon Gyva that Four Bears placed his final touch."

"The dying do strange things. His touch was but a last gesture, of little meaning."

"No. I think otherwise. Because in the final moments of our chief, the bloody hand glowed upon the face of Teva."

"But have you not heard? The soothsayer maintains that no omen came to her mind at that time."

"Ah! But has it ever been known that blood in Teva's mark signified *nothing*? One knows that is untrue. There is always meaning. She herself will tell you this.

"Why did Four Bears not beckon one of the warriors forward? According to the ancient tales, this was often done by dying chiefs."

"Perhaps his touch on Gyva meant that he had knowledge of how she was later to kill the Choctaw. Perhaps he meant to give her a measure of his final strength."

Much nodding and clucking followed this interpretation. Indeed, Gyva heard much appreciation of her marksmanship and courage. Some comments did not fail to note her hesitation at the moment of the scalping, but this was generally overlooked. What remained in the light of the subdued, buzzing talk was this: How would Gyva fare now, without Four Bears to protect her?

"She is a maiden of exceptional beauty, and courage, as we now know."

"But there may be something unknowable about her, to which Four Bears' final touch attests."

"In the end, she is a mixed-blood, and who can know what will become of such a one?"

There it was again. Mixed-blood. The heritage she could not escape, and which no one else ever completely forgot. Gyva heard these last comments as she carried the tanned skins of oxen from the tanning lodge to the playing field. Temporary wigwams were to be erected there, in which would sleep those whose dwellings had been destroyed by fire. All day she had worked hard, trying to put the sadness out of her mind, trying not to think of Torch. It was impossible. One moment she resolved never to speak to him again. Next moment she was planning how to prepare a message, summoning him this very night. But what if, again, he preferred Little Swallow?

"You do not know the half of what you speak!" he had said to her, in anger and exasperation. Was that the pose of a man who is caught in compromise? Or was that the justifiable anger of someone who is innocent, whom circumstance has played for a fool?

"Do you remember how it feels, way deep?" Little Swallow had taunted.

Such words conveyed little innocence. Wearily Gyva placed the hides on the ground, where young boys were at work tying poles and saplings into a frame for the wigwam. They were unprepared as yet to drape the hides over their framework. For a few moments Gyva could rest. She looked out across the village, down toward the soothsayer's wigwam, in front of which the braves were still conversing. She could see the seeress seated there, too. Gladly would they welcome her counsel today, given the sorry state of affairs among the Chickasaw. What would they be speaking of now?

In the history of the village, of the people, with its long tradition of leadership by braves, it is doubtful whether another maiden had ever possessed the impulse that now came to Gyva. Why should any woman even bother to think of it? She would know, in due course, whatever was necessary for her to know. But Gyva did not wish to wait. The playing field was on the slope above the river, but if one were simply to traverse the field, steal behind a section of squatting lodges, and enter the forest—well, such a person, quite discreetly, might find herself behind Teva's wigwam, able to hear everything that transpired.

Gyva picked up several pieces of firewood as she walked along, for convenient explanation should she be observed. The voices were indecipherable, although quite heated, as she came near the old woman's dwelling. Quietly she made her way closer and closer to the broad-leaved bushes where the trees ended and the village began.

". . . must have a meaning," Hawk was asserting, with his usual combination of arrogance and malice. "You yourself have spoken these words, Torch. I believe it is the right of all of us to know your meaning. Sentiments alien to our people ought to be grounds for disqualifying one who holds such sentiments from competing in the manhood ritual."

So that was it! Gyva, holding her breath, was instantly furious.

"And what were these damning words of mine?" Torch asked, with excessive politeness.

"On the raid of our first blooding, you did say to all assembled, *'If courage is blood, then wisdom must be death. But if wisdom is life, then courage must be peace.'* "

"True. I did say that. And you did say, 'The path of war is dearer than the path of plenty.' And so?"

"I wish to know your meaning, lest a deficiency of fighting spirit, by some mischance of destiny, become characteristic of a Chickasaw chieftain."

From the assembled braves came a rumble of response, and from the sound Gyva deduced that about half were in support of Hawk, the rest sympathetic to Torch-of-the-Sun.

"Perhaps we ought to compare kill-cuts," rejoined Torch, with an edge in his voice.

"Aha!" Hawk shot back. "You also stated, but a short time ago, that you have gone on raids because it was your duty. I say that such is *more* than duty. War is something that must be pursued with a spirit even greater than that which a man feels when he is in search of a fine woman."

This time the edge was in Hawk's voice, and Gyva realized that the two might be thinking of her. Or was it Little Swallow who filled their minds? Gyva crept out of the sheltering bushes and crawled over the grass, huddled behind Teva's wigwam.

"If we speak of duty," Torch averred, "let us discuss the matter of the sentinels last evening."

"We have been over this already!" Hawk cried, in hurtful rage. "I sent them to their posts, just as I have a hundred times. Choctaw crept upon them and cut their throats, and so we were not warned of the attack.

"Teva!" he demanded. "I asked a question regarding the meaning of Torch's words, and he is evading me."

The soothsayer was acting to facilitate the business of the council. She spoke dispassionately. "Perhaps it would be appropriate for you to speak about those words, Torch."

"Gladly shall I do so, then, that all may have it right in their minds. What I meant then, and what I repeat now, is this: If we must shed blood in order to be considered brave, then killing becomes a way of life. Even the blood of our own people will suffice to meet this definition of courage. But if we seek life for our people and an end to bloodshed, peace is not only the correct goal, but a courageous one as well."

"Hah!" Hawk scoffed. "You are forgetting that the jackals do not know the meaning of the word *peace!*"

"Nor do we, I think, who have made raid after raid all these many years."

"We shall destroy them. The path of war *is* dearer than the path of plenty. And nobler than the path of peace."

"Then they shall destroy us!" Torch said. "I did also say, at the time of which you speak, 'The Chickasaw must read what is written on the wind.'"

"Perhaps you would like to be seeress instead of chief," Hawk responded with an evil laugh. Some other braves, too, echoed him in mockery.

But Torch held his temper, calmly explaining himself. "It is too late to drive the white man away." His words were met by an ominous silence, and Gyva herself was gravely unsettled by them. *Too late* is as absolute as *forever*, like loss or death or an arrow gone from the bowstring. "In a full-scale war, even with all the nations combined, we would still be the losers. There are simply too many of them. Moreover, just as we are fearful of them—"

"I am unafraid!" Hawk cried.

"—so are they fearful of us. So always there are misunderstandings and battles. I speak as a warrior with a price upon his head."

Hawk was silent this time. He possessed no such distinction.

"But we ought not raid Harrisville. There is no fort in the place. It is a farming community. Perhaps if we were to demonstrate by restraint that we can live in peace—we in our mountains, they on their farms—we will be allowed to remain here in our ancestral homeland."

A great howl arose from the assembled braves. "*Allowed* to remain? What is this madness of which you speak?"

Torch held his ground. "It is not difficult to see what is to come if we are not wise."

"The path of your wisdom is the path of disaster," mocked Hawk. "Should you become chief—which pray Ababinili will never be—you would be the ruin of us!"

From the people there was considerable assent to this conclusion.

"As chief," Torch said, his voice rising just a bit now in the face of much opposition, "I would fight harder and more fiercely than any man if we should be attacked. *If* we should be attacked."

"And what is the precise meaning of this *if?*"

"If we are not attacked, there is no need for us to go to war. War is a folly now. As I have said, we are vastly outnumbered."

Once more great commotion broke out, and discussion became voluble and uncontrolled.

"One Chickasaw brave is worth fifty white jackals!" Hawk was yelling.

"You have it wrong," Gyva heard Torch reply. "The cost of fifty dead jackals is one dead Chickasaw, and that is a price we can no longer afford to pay."

For long moments Gyva could hear no words clearly. Accusations were apparently made, and denied; there was much shouting. She thought she heard Teva's voice a time or two, the old woman's attempt to regain order. Curious, and a little worried, Gyva peeked around the edge of the wigwam.

Even as she moved, Long Eel spotted her; and, springing up, he seized her before she could get to her feet. With a great cry, as surely befitted an old warrior with not one kill-cut in fifty circlings of the sun, he dragged her around Teva's lodging and thrust her before everybody.

"An eavesdropper," he grunted, proud of himself. "Huddling behind the wigwam."

"I was only collecting firewood," said Gyva defiantly, using the story she had contrived.

"Children collect firewood!"

All eyes were upon her now, and no one spoke.

"They are busy today," Gyva persisted, "and many must do work that is not their usual . . ."

Her voice trailed off. She could not bear to meet the eyes of Torch.

"Oh, Gyva," said the seeress, sadly.

Hawk stepped forward. "I think this woman is a spy," he proclaimed, laying his hand rudely upon her shoulder.

She pushed it off in anger, in rage, and was shaken to hear not one protest in her behalf.

"Now I know!" cried Hawk, remembering. "I was myself on guard one night and spied this maiden running beneath the moon. Even then she sought knowledge as to the number and location of our nighttime sentinels." He paused, that all might give him complete attention. "I believe it is she who conspired with the Choctaw to kill our sentinels so that we would be left without warning."

An angry mutter from the crowd. Gyva could not meet Torch's eyes, but she felt his upon her.

"It is not true!" she cried.

"A mixed-blood, too," he said, in a tone that signified "that is all I need to say. And what pure maiden runs beneath the moon, naked beneath a blanket?"

"Do you speak the truth?" cried the bold braves.

"Could it be?"

"Naked? And only a blanket?"

It was too much to bear. Gyva lifted her head, and looked at all of them, all these braves who just moments before had been fighting among themselves. Then she looked Hawk straight in the eye. "I am the daughter of a noble Chickasaw and a brave woman who died at Chula Harjo's hands," she said, "as well you know. I am no spy, I who killed a Choctaw brave—"

"But hesitated to take his scalp!"

"*I was savoring the moment!*" she retorted.

The braves gave a low hum of approval. Most of them had felt just such an ecstasy. Except for the ridiculous Long Eel, of course, who stood there now not looking so triumphant. His abjection, and the reaction to her retort, nerved her further.

"On the night of which you speak," she went on, again to Hawk, "I was rushing toward the dwelling of Teva. I told you as much, if you remember. I had had a dream that had to be deciphered before I could sleep again."

Everyone turned to the old woman, who had been watching with an expression of rue that Gyva could understand, although she thought it deeper than even this unfortunate situation warranted.

"Is it true?" inquired Torch coldly, his eyes moving from Gyva to the soothsayer.

"It is true," answered Teva boldly, immediately, but without spirit. "The maiden did indeed have a dream."

"And what was this dream?" asked Hawk, trying once again to stir the antipathy that had been his to mold just moments ago.

Teva looked at him. "There are tribal dreams, and there are personal dreams. The former are the possession of all; the latter have meaning but to the dreamer. This you should know."

"But a mixed-blood . . ." Hawk tried, "and the dead sentinels . . ."

"It is over," said Torch, in a voice Gyva had never heard him use, but that clearly meant—to Hawk and to anyone else—*If you do not think it is over, take the knife from your belt.*

Teva ushered Gyva into the wigwam, while outside the men settled upon the time for the beginning of the manhood ritual, days hence, and then dispersed. Trembling with anger and humiliation, Gyva sought to calm herself by examining the strange artifacts spread about Teva's wigwam. There were ragged beads sewn onto the hides of animals, making strange patterns, and misshapen arrowheads, and unusual, asymmetric lances of various designs. Teva slept on a wolf skin, she noted, and a large pipe rested in a bowl beside her sleeping place.

When the old woman entered, Gyva apologized. "You had to lie for me. I am sorry. How may I make recompense?"

Teva grimaced. "I did not lie. You had a dream, though not one for telling. But you cannot make recompense for your act of folly today. It may cost you much, very much. What possessed you to eavesdrop?"

"I wished to know what was being said."

"You would have been told."

"But I did not wish to wait."

"That is your error, and because you did not wish to, now you may have to wait a long, long time—perhaps forever."

"What do you mean?"

Teva looked at her coldly. "You are not much thicker than a mountain rock, are you?"

Gyva felt herself blush. The dream to which the witch-woman referred, of course, was Torch. But by stealing upon the council here today, Gyva had compromised herself before everyone. Evil charges had been hurled by Hawk, yet just because few had taken them seriously did not mean they would not be bruited about. The granddaughter of Four Bears had eavesdropped on the council and been caught, thus making herself doubly the fool! Memories are long, and among a people who feel themselves persecuted, long memories are like black soil in which flowers of malice might spring up overnight.

"Have I lost him?" Gyva asked after a while.

"Who is to say?" Teva said. "You must return now to your work, lest neglect of that, too, be held against you."

At the entrance of the wigwam Gyva turned. "But what am I to do now?" she asked, almost pleading.

The old woman was not helpful.

"You must live," was all she said.

CHAPTER III

Rabbit is not panther. The softness is true of the rabbit, but it is a softness of spirit as well as fur. Gyva felt the difference, and dearly felt the loss by fire of her panther skins. Now she lay upon a blanket of rabbit fur, looking up at the stars that she could see between open spaces in the makeshift wigwam's haphazard roof.

She looked up at the sky, with Torch on her mind. Today she had erred grievously by attempting to hear what the braves were discussing. But, however much she had violated tradition, the consequences seemed minor when compared to what Torch must think of her now. True, his willingness to fight Hawk for her sake had saved her from further interrogation and ridicule. But that he had had to make a show of force at all, when there was already great tension in the tribe, could not have pleased him.

That is his burden, she thought, trying to make herself think harshly of him.

The alien thought brought no more comfort than she had expected. And rabbit fur was really too thick, too warm, so late in the spring.

She tossed and turned in her sleeping place, trying to make it cooler, and accidentally rolled upon her leather pouch. Picking it up to move it, she remembered that the bear-claw necklace was still inside. Just moments before, she had been nearly immobilized, unable to decide upon a course of action. Now ideas fairly leapt to her head. At the scalping last evening

Torch had helped her; his eyes had been full of sympathy. And men were known to try the charms of many a maiden, if they could. Perhaps she ought not to have blamed him at all; surely the fault lay with Little Swallow. And she really ought to apologize to him for this afternoon, and thank him. Maybe he had summoned her tonight, and she had failed to locate the diagram. It could have happened. Certainly it could have.

As often occurs when one wants to believe, doubt wavered into conviction, which progressed to strong conviction, and onward to absolute certainty. When Gyva touched in her pouch the tiny white pebbles Torch had used to send for her the very first time, she knew without doubt that he was waiting for her now. She would return the necklace to him, and return herself to him as well.

Outside it was cool, and the night was lovely. Dew wet her bare feet and the hem of her buckskin skirt as she crossed the grass. Carefully she watched for sentinels, holding the necklace tightly, so that the claws would not clack against one another. Soon she could see the white pebbles glowing in starshine, and the white bubbling of rapids downriver. The willows swooped in the distance, ready to take her into their embrace, and Torch's, too. . . .

Gyva stopped, dead still.

Close, very close to her, she had heard someone moan.

She swept the area with her eyes and heard another cry, off to her left, then almost cried out herself. Oblivious to her, yet only scant yards away, a brave and a maiden were making love. Gyva saw Little Swallow's face, rapt with ecstasy, and the strong back of her lover. She assumed it was Torch.

Heartsick, Gyva sank down quietly into the grass. She had not been sent for because he had someone else. Over the bent, dew-heavy grass Gyva saw what she did not want to see or even dream. Little Swallow lay upon her back, her clothing spread out on the grass beneath her, her arms wrapped about her lover's wide back, legs drawn far up along his sides to allow him the full depth of her delight. Little Swallow's eyes were closed, and on her face was a twisted aspect, almost of pain; but it was not pain that she was feeling. Her lover buried his face in the tender place, lined with fine hair, at which Swallow's neck and shoulder met, and rocked upon her, slowly, slowly as time, again and again. He and Little Swallow had learned one another well, Gyva could see; they knew, without words, how to prolong pleasure and how to enhance it.

Gyva would have wept, but she was stricken beyond tears, beyond any reaction. She could not flee; she could not even bear to turn her eyes away. That heaven must look upon this thing! That stars should shine down upon it! Then Little Swallow—now she smiled, the vixen!—reached beneath to pleasure the man even more, and when he cried out and bucked urgently upon her, she matched his pace and crossed her slender legs upon his pulsing back. Exactly as Gyva had done for him, so Swallow was now doing!

Gyva could bear it not a moment more. There in the grass she stood up and hurled the bear-claw necklace at the pounding lovers.

It struck Hawk a glancing blow on the shoulder. With a strangled cry of rage and surprise he pulled himself from Little Swallow, and was on his feet in the manner of one set to wrestle or fight with a knife. The instrument of his manhood, exposed to the night, began slowly to recede. Little Swallow, astounded, lay open upon the earth.

"Gyva!" Hawk exclaimed. His eyes were hard on her.

She raised her hand halfway into the air, an abortive gesture whose meaning she could not guess. The glorious knowledge that it had not been Torch making love to Little Swallow was greatly mitigated by the demonic anger that gleamed in Hawk's eyes. On the ground Little Swallow hurriedly drew her garment around her naked body.

"Go," Hawk told Swallow, and as quickly as he spoke he was upon Gyva, holding her fast by the shoulders.

"How long have you been here?" he demanded, as Little Swallow, half-dressed, still pulling on her dew-laden attire, fled into the night.

"And what are you doing here?" he asked, before she could respond to his first question.

The afternoon's incident occurred to him. "This time I know fully and truly that you are a spy."

The word *spy* angered her, in spite of her embarrassment and confusion.

"And you are a liar," she said. "You would provoke our people, but you shall not provoke me."

"Ah!" he said, grinning, as if he had thought of yet another thing. "How come you to speak of provocation?"

"Do not taunt me," Gyva said, drawing herself up straight, so that the top of her head reached his jaw. "I shall tell all what I have seen here this night."

"And what will they say? They will ask, 'Gyva, what affair were you about, so late in the night?' "

True, she realized. That was exactly what people would say.

"I know," he was saying, "that you yourself have trysted in the evening time, and I know with whom. Your eyes tell it. That I have not discovered your rendezvous is but an oversight. Now it would seem to be somewhere hard by the river."

His big hands still gripped her tightly, but he began to move them up and down her arms and shoulders, like a rude caress.

"You did interrupt something of which I had great need," he said, in a different tone, which she understood with alarm at precisely the moment she felt him swelling upon her.

"No!" Gyva cried, struggling to get free of him.

His teeth were large and white as he gave her a knowing grin.

"Once, I told you that I would take you whenever I pleased," he gloated, sure of himself now, "and the Great Spirit seems to have provided me the opportunity."

She started to cry out, but he clamped a hand over her mouth.

"Fight? Ah, I like that. It will make everything better for the both of us." With his great strength it was all too easy to force her down upon the wet grass, to rip away her buckskins. She felt the cold grass against her skin, and then the hot naked weight of him upon her, fumbling for that which she had given Torch alone.

"And now you shall have your first chieftain," he laughed, and she felt him poised horribly above her, poised terribly for the plunging by which he would take her. His hand was over her face; she could not scream, and barely breathe. The weight of his body forced air from her lungs, which could not be replenished. Somewhere in the great vastness stars flickered, as mute and powerless in their beauty as she was helpless in her own. He held her wrists pinioned to the ground, and his mighty thighs had pushed her legs up in such a way that she was simultaneously open and helpless. She was lost now; all was over.

"Now it is our wedding night, maiden child," snickered Hawk, quivering to ram her with himself.

Suddenly she was free. Air rushed in at her, and she gasped for it. Against the stars loomed two men. Hawk, who had been ripped from her, whirled to face the other, Torch. But in his hand Torch held a hunting knife, blade gleaming dully in the night. Hawk had only his twice-disappointed instrument, which now failed him utterly.

But his will did not falter. "Use the knife, then, Torch."

Torch was calm. "I would not pierce a fellow Chickasaw, save I were first attacked."

"You would not pierce one with a knife, that is," Hawk sneered, lewdly now, knowing he would not be killed, naked and weaponless.

Gyva arranged her clothing, stood up, and stepped back a few paces. The men faced each other: Hawk naked, crouching as if to leap forward, Torch standing a bit more erect, knife poised in the event of attack.

"You have your victory, if victory you seek," Hawk offered.

"If we say there is no battle," Torch rejoined, "there is neither victor nor vanquished. I but aided the maiden, having observed that she did not seem to wish your favors. We need not fight upon this battleground. There is another, greater one which we approach."

Hawk dropped his hands, and Torch slipped the knife into his scabbard. "Go now," he said. "We will not speak of this."

"Wise of you, as ever," replied Hawk in a mocking tone, before he found his breechcloth in the grass and departed.

Torch and Gyva stood there in the matted grass, regarding each other. She felt confused and angry and embarrassed and crazily weak with love for him.

"Why . . . why did you not kill him?" she faltered.

His laugh was grim. "That all should know what has happened here? Of what good would that be? I am sure you know that he is not the first to meet a maiden by night."

"But he . . . he tried to . . ."

"And that I will settle with him at another time—that and many things. But in such a way that it does not further disquiet our people. A furor now over secret matters of love and lust would distract everyone, exactly as Hawk and Little Swallow conspired to distract me from the coming ritual."

"What do you mean?" Gyva asked, remembering the two huddled together, whispering, on the night of the raid.

He moved toward her, as if to speak more quietly, and she came to him, and suddenly they were in each other's arms, embracing not with passion this time—although there was that, too—but with relief, as people embrace after a battle, or after surviving some great ordeal.

"On the day you found me with Swallow," he asked, drawing away slightly, "how did you chance to come down to the river?"

"Because . . . because I heard you calling me from outside the wall of my dwelling! Who else would summon me to our special place? It was by accident I chanced to walk as far as the honeysuckle."

"Now it is clear," he said, frowning. "I myself found, scratched into pine bark, a message of great urgency that I assumed had come from you. And on my way to the willows, Little Swallow stepped forward, and bared her breasts, and took me into her embrace. You see, they must know we have been meeting by the river, but they are not sure precisely where. In any event, they wished to stir animosity between us, and would go to any lengths in order to do so."

"But why? If you do not love Little Swallow, and Hawk does not love me . . ." Swallow, she thought, lied about making love to Torch.

"Gyva, they wish to distract me, to sully my concentration, and thus to lessen my strength for the manhood ritual."

"But it was you who left the necklace in my sleeping place?"

"Yes. I wanted to see you, to explain how it was that I had come to be in Swallow's embrace. I did not wish you to grieve. But you did not appear. I was waiting by the willows when the Choctaw attacked."

She believed him, every word. Never had she loved him so much, possessed such faith in him. She offered her mouth to be kissed, and pressed her body against him, to do with whatever he willed, and anytime, and forever.

"No," he said, gently but firmly. He stepped away from her.

"Is something wrong? Are we not again as one person?" Gyva suppressed an impulse to panic. Had she done something so terrible?

"Are we not going to make love?" she blurted.

Torch smiled, bent down and retrieved his necklace from the grass, and fastened it behind his neck. "Gyva," he said, "you are young. And so you do not know that a woman is to be enjoyed when battle is over, not at a time when strength must be shepherded to win a forthcoming ordeal."

What? How could anything like that be true?

"The woes of love are even more draining than its pleasures. That is what Hawk and Little Swallow knew, and so they wished to stir trouble between us, that I should neglect to prepare for the trials of the contest."

"I think my love would make you stronger than ever," she answered bleakly.

"Do you understand?" he asked.

"No."

He put his arm around her waist, as a brother would do. "I must become chief," he said. "Hawk, as leader, will only bring war. Even if I do triumph, the hotheads who follow him will prove to be a constant source of dangerous agitation."

"I would not rob you of anything," she tried again.

"No," he said, with a tone of finality that left her disheartened. "Instead, we must sleep. There will be time for ecstasy when the struggle is won."

Gyva did as she was told. For a time, lying awake in her sleeping place, she almost believed what he had told her. But then she remembered all the times he had made love to her. Never had she felt so vibrantly alive as at those times, and afterward, when they lay together—their bodies savoring the glow, their minds still dizzy with living delight—she and Torch fairly trembling with bursting vitality.

No, what he had told her could not possibly be true. It must be one of those ancient tales passed along from generation to generation, invented by a misfit who did not wish men and women to enjoy that for which they were made!

Yes. That was it. Entirely.

Then she remembered that, once again, Torch had said nothing of marriage. Or of love.

Gyva did not sleep for a long time. She had been made for loving; she was sure of that. Perhaps the problem was simply that she had not been born for a bed of rabbit skin.

If Little Swallow had indeed taken Torch into herself, if she had not been lying with her insinuations of the deep pleasure she had experienced with him— well, then Gyva would find a way to take revenge. And, of course, if she *had* told a lie, it was a terrible one, and Gyva would get even for that, too.

She did not realize, that night, how perfectly she was playing into the hands of her enemies.

CHAPTER IV

"Let the contest begin," proclaimed Teva. "With these words do I summon the warriors forward."

Since sundown of the previous day, the six braves who wished to be considered as candidates to take up the mantle of Four Bears had been fasting and praying. And for three days to come they would be permitted, in spite of the rigors of the ordeal, to take only a small ladle of water at dawn, and another at nightfall, at which time they returned to special tents erected for the duration of the contest, one for each brave. During the day, eyes would follow them at all times, to make certain none of them weakened in will and tried to steal nourishment. At night, members of the tribe would watch over the tents.

Any brave who took food, or transgressed the rules of the manhood ritual in some other way, would be immediately disqualified. Violation of the rules was high disgrace; there were tales of warriors who, caught in perfidy, simply killed themselves, or went off into the mountains, never to be seen again. By the same token, a warrior might choose to drop out of the ritual at any time, in which case no stigma would be attached to him. That was the purpose of the ordeal: to sift the wheat from the chaff. Better for the Chickasaw nation to learn who its leaders were than, by misguided gentleness, to suffer any but the strongest as chieftain.

The seeress turned toward the row of tents, out of which emerged Arrow-in-Oak, Hawk-of-the-Sky, Dark

Eagle, Fleet Cloud, Brittle Serpent, and Torch-of-the-Sun, called Firebrand by the white men who had known his prowess. Each brave wore a simple breechcloth, undecorated, and none of them wore jewelry of any kind; they offered themselves without the accoutrements of position or reputation. Kill-cuts alone gave evidence of individual distinction, but they proved only that the Great Spirit had sent one brave more enemies than he had sent another.

Gyva watched along with the rest of the tribe as the contestants approached Teva and stood before her.

"Upon your honor," she demanded of them, "do you vow to offer all of your strength in the ordeal to come, and to obey the restrictions regarding sustenance?"

The men answered affirmatively, and quiet debate commenced among the spectators as to who had answered most fervently.

"And do you swear," Teva continued, "to accept with full heart, and to serve with lifelong fidelity, whomsoever among you shall emerge triumphant?"

There were many questions of this sort, to be followed by the joining of blood. Each brave would make a small slash on the palm of his hand and another on his forehead. Then, standing in a close circle, they would join hands and press their foreheads together, to witness by commingled blood their brotherhood and unity in spite of the competition on which they were poised to embark.

Nervous and excited, Gyva could not wait for the first event to begin, and at the same time she wished it never would. What if Torch lost? She would still love him then, as much as ever. But would he, with his great pride, be wounded in spirit? Be wounded so grievously as to avoid others, thinking himself unworthy? And what if he won? Would he then give himself so thoroughly to his responsibilities that he would have no time for Gyva?

And—lurking within the boundaries of her consciousness—there was the troubling question: Who is fit wife for a chieftain?

Gyva put the matter out of her mind and drifted to the edge of the crowd. The first event was to be a race on the playing field, and to this end hurdles had been positioned, and six running lanes marked with pennants for the competitors. At first she thought her eyes were playing tricks with her, but then—yes, she saw it clearly. Someone, whose identity Gyva could not ascertain at this distance, was bending down to the ground next to one of the wooden hurdles at the far end of the course. Even as Gyva watched, the figure arose. But rather than coming across the field to join the villagers, whoever it was ducked into the forest. How odd, thought Gyva, and almost shrugged the matter off.

Now the joining of blood was conducted, and all that remained was the distribution of the water, a pedestrian gesture that did not hold the interest of many. Children first, and then their elders, began to drift off in the direction of the playing field, the better to select choice positions from which to observe the race. Possessed by a niggling feeling that something was amiss, Gyva headed toward the far side of the course and eventually reached the hurdle at which she had seen the suspicious figure.

The course was over a mile in length, laid out in a semicircle, and in each of the six lanes, at various locations, were hurdles of different heights. Some were no higher than a man's knee; others would reach a woman's shoulders. The hurdle that interested Gyva was one of the latter, and she inspected it carefully. Why anyone would have tampered with it was beyond her imagination. Indeed, *how* anyone might have done so was equally obscure. The device consisted of two simple upright stakes of wood, notched at the top to accommodate a flat wooden crossbar that would disengage and fall to the ground should an unfortunate contestant fail to leap high enough.

But if the crossbar had been fastened hard, a contestant might be injured . . . .

She stepped to the hurdle and checked. No, the crossbar was loose, free.

Puzzled, Gyva circled the device; and as she did so, she felt something hard press against her moccasin. Bending down to look, she saw only the clay earth of the running lane. She pressed her foot down on the same spot, harder this time, and cried out. Instantly she was down on her knees, scratching away the dirt. And in a moment she had uncovered the pointed tips of five long wooden nails, buried headfirst into the ground, their mean points slanted toward the hurdle. A runner coming over the top would slam down into the earth. The nails would pierce his foot. Stunned and furious, Gyva leaped up, prepared to make known what had been done. Then she stopped, thinking it over. She had already removed the nails; and, as closely as she could tell, she had not been observed. What brave was to run in this lane? She didn't know. There would be time enough to reach the starting point and find out, but if she did that, the race would commence before she could get back here. And, Gyva was sure, whoever had caused these nails to be buried would be watching the race near this hurdle, the better to see the fruit of such handiwork.

Gyva sat down on the grass, keeping her eye on the people who gathered around. It was only when she heard the cry "Go!" far down at the other end of the field that she realized more nails—or other types of dangers—might have been contrived along the course. Then she was on her feet, like everyone else, watching the racers approach, watching the spectators around her.

None of them even so much as glanced at the hurdle; every eye was riveted on the contestants, who came now, pounding and panting and leaping along the lanes. This event favored neither Hawk nor Torch, who were fast men, but large; and approaching the halfway mark Fleet Cloud, true to his name, was in the lead. The brave ran like a demon, and when he leaped to clear a hurdle he left the earth like a deer in flight. He passed the hurdle at which Gyva watched, running with ease and authority, drawing away from the others. He continued to do so, and won easily, to a cascading burst of excited cheers. Hawk had been second, Torch third.

The nails had been in Fleet Cloud's running lane.

With the consummation of this first event, a mood of high-spirited good humor came over the tribespeople, just as happened at hunting festivals. And Gyva would have been caught up in it, too, except for the nails.

The next event was archery, and she hastened to the place where the targets had been set up. Arrow-in-Oak was the best archer in the tribe, and everyone expected him to win. Straws were drawn to determine the order of participation, and Hawk went first. Shooting from distances of fifty, a hundred, and two hundred yards, he did very well. When the scores were determined, Torch had done almost as well. Brittle Serpent and Dark Eagle were good, but not startlingly so. And then Arrow-in-Oak stepped confidently to the fifty-yard mark.

But this day had not dawned for him. It was not that he shot badly; he was too much an expert with the bow to offer a poor performance. But at each distance his efforts seemed slightly erratic, each shot just wide enough of the center of the target to lose valuable points in the competition. With a rueful smile he watched the flight of his final arrow and laid down the bow.

People explained his mediocre performance by attributing it to nervousness, or overconfidence, or to the wind, and moved off to congratulate Hawk, whose score had been best. Torch was second.

Gyva stayed behind for a moment as the others went on, puzzling the matter. First the nails in Fleet Cloud's lane. Now Arrow-in-Oak, the best archer . . .

She picked up his bow and inspected it carefully. Taller than Gyva, the instrument, shaped from a maple sapling and polished to a luster, was a beautiful, flawless thing, perfectly balanced and strung with cured, tempered catgut. This bow, and the brave's natural skill, ought to have won the contest for him.

Then she walked down toward the targets, where young boys were collecting the arrows, pulling them from targets and arranging them in neat piles. Making a show of interest, Gyva praised the boys and studied some of the arrows. It took some time, but here and again she found one whose feathers seemed to have been cut. Just slightly, ever so slightly cut, but nipped nonetheless, and enough to alter trajectory. Now she understood. In each contest, the brave who would normally be expected to win was being sabotaged.

When the candidates retired to their tents for rest at midday, Gyva sought out the old soothsayer. Teva listened without expression, then spoke: "At one time, before you were brought here to the village, there was an old wooden smokehouse where the playing field now lies. It was used for the curing of meat. The nails have been long in the earth, I think, and have finally worked themselves upward. In a matter as solemn as selecting our chief, I do not believe any Chickasaw would—"

"But don't you see? Whoever made use of the nails also knew where the smokehouse had been. That further proves my point, not detracts from it," Gyva said in exasperation. "And what of the arrows?"

"What of them? By notching the feathers, the braves attempt to gain the perfect flight. Whose arrows were they? How do you know?"

"I have but to ask Arrow-in-Oak."

"It is forbidden that any of the competing braves converse with the people."

"Well, then, *you* can ask."

"That I certainly can, but I do not intend to."

Gyva did not expect this attitude from the old woman. "Why not?" she asked, doubtfully.

"What proof is there?" Teva replied. "You have already removed the nails. The arrows tell nothing. And both contests are over."

"But I did see someone at the hurdle, someone who drifted into the forest in a most suspicious manner."

Teva rewarded this bit of information with a dry cackle. "Ah! I see. And do you know who this person was? And are you not exactly the one to go around making accusations and telling tales of those who skulk about, doing strange things!"

Gyva felt the color of shame rise in her face.

"No, you have compromised yourself most seriously, *most* seriously, and it will be painful for you to learn that trust, once lost, is exceedingly difficult to regain. Why, if you were now to tell your story about this mysterious figure by the hurdle, do you know what people would say?"

Gyva did not reply, but she knew. People would say, "Hah! The maiden conveys her own dismal mischief to shadows, thinking to lessen her folly."

"No, it is best you keep silent and be discreet in all things," advised Teva. "In any case, I do not see how the events of this afternoon, nor of tomorrow, can be changed from whatever course fate holds in store."

The soothsayer seemed secure in that assumption. Wrestling would occupy the afternoon, a demonstration of strength in physical combat; and a day-long mountain climb on the morrow would pit each brave against the south face of the twin mountains, a battle in which human endurance vied with the stony majesty of earth itself.

So that afternoon, when the time came, straws were drawn again; and Fleet Cloud was bested within minutes by the far sturdier Arrow-in-Oak. Hawk, matched against Brittle Serpent, fought ferociously, proving that the other brave was aptly named. Brittle Serpent, tossed viciously to the earth, found that he could not arise. His hip was broken in the fall, and suddenly but five contestants remained. Torch in his turn made short work of Dark Eagle. Fate then pitted Torch against Arrow-in-Oak, the winner to meet Hawk, who had won valuable time to rest. Teva herself held the straws; there was no doubting fairness.

Arrow could read the odds as well as Gyva. Brittle Serpent had been eliminated. Dark Eagle and Fleet Cloud were strong, but not exceptionally so; they would have trouble with the mountain course tomorrow. So if Arrow could whip Torch now—Torch, who had failed as yet to come first in any event—then Arrow would be Hawk's primary opponent in the struggle for supremacy. Of course, as everyone knew, the third day determined everything; but one must survive the first two days.

Arrow's strength was considerable, and desire for victory increased the fury of his assault. For long moments the two braves grappled, seeking an advantage, as the tribe held its breath. Then the wrestlers parted, panting and glistening with sweat, only to meet and grapple again. Gyva prayed that it would be over soon, so that Torch could conserve energy for the match with Hawk. But it was not to be. The match went on and on. Twice Torch had Arrow-in-Oak on the ground, his shoulders jammed into the dirt; but both times the wild blood of desperation allowed Arrow to kick free.

Finally, after more than an hour, the sun dropping now, superior strength made its mark. Torch pinned his opponent, then helped the crestfallen Arrow to his feet. Torch was pouring sweat, and Gyva saw that his hands were trembling slightly from the exertion. He reached down and picked up a pebble and put it in his mouth. But what little saliva he might engender thereby could not help him now. The ladle of sweet water was still hours away, and Hawk-of-the-Sky waited, rested and restless.

"You may, if you wish, drop from the contest," Hawk reminded his opponent. "You have fought much already. No one, and certainly not I, will hold it against you."

Torch neither spoke nor made gesture, but stepped slowly into the circle that had been drawn upon the ground.

The final battle called for the winner to subdue his opponent three times out of five chances. Hawk's hothead followers cheered him on as he swaggered out into conflict, crouched, ducked, feinted, and dove at Torch's mighty legs, bringing him down. From the first moments it was clear to everyone that this fight would be different, in tone and texture, from those that had already transpired, save possibly for Hawk's brutal dispatching of Brittle Serpent. Striking with the fist was not permitted, but open-handed slaps were; and while gouging with elbow or knee was not considered exactly honorable, who could tell, in the heat of struggle, whether or not such blows were merely accidental?

Gyva kept her eyes on Torch every minute, although as the fight went on, such devotion became harder and harder to maintain. For nearly an hour the two men rolled and grappled in the dust, too dehydrated now even to sweat. Blood ran from a cut near Torch's neck or ear—it was impossible to tell—and blood came now and again from one or the other of Hawk's nostrils. Again, no one could tell because of the dirt and the frenzy of the match, probably not even the combatants themselves. Dirt was their water, their food. Dirt was their clothing as well—the breechcloths had been long since ripped off in the fight. Two naked, powerful men stood toe to toe, grabbed one another, and went spinning onto the dusty ground, rolling and twisting and pummeling. Torch had suffered the first pin, but he came back and slammed an overconfident Hawk onto

his back with enough force to stun him. The after-
effects of that episode won Torch his second pin
shortly afterward; but Hawk came back, ripping and
grunting and snarling. As the sun touched the western
twin, the braves were tied at two and two. Teva reminded them that either could withdraw if he wished.
Neither had the strength to make a reply. They simply
stood in the circle, waiting for the call to begin again.

By now Hawk's men had learned not to count on
victory, and their earlier cheers, boastful and high-
spirited, had become mean. They snarled and urged
their champion to blaze away.

"Get him in the belly!" they called. "Get him! Use
your elbow on his biceps! Paralyze him, Hawk!"

Torch was exhausted; Hawk was not much better
off. Unable to rise, they fought on their knees. Every
movement came slowly, as if they were fighting underwater. Torch was dazed, groping forward, when Hawk
struck him a mighty blow on the side of his head. No
one could tell for certain, because it was beginning to
grow dark, but many were sure the blow had been
done with a balled fist—just as many were certain that
the opposite was true. There was much angry shouting
as Torch fell backward onto the earth, blinking dully.

Hawk crawled forward for the kill.

Barely moving, he groped toward the fallen Torch;
but there was joy in his eyes. His hand reached Torch's
shoulder, but from some last reserve—perhaps a buried
vein of rage so great it was not even born of earth
—Gyva's champion twisted aside. Hawk looked up,
stunned. He saw his rival up on his knees. He saw
Torch rise, sway, stand up. He saw Torch motion him:
Come up, come up. He blinked. How could this be?

But when Hawk proved unable to rise, Torch
reached down, put his arms beneath the other man's
armpits, and hauled him to his feet. Hawk stood, but
barely, too exhausted to lift his arms. No one who
watched ever forgot what came next. Hawk's earlier
blow must have been delivered by fist. That was the

only explanation anyone could contrive to account for Torch's rage. With a flat, open hand, he slammed Hawk halfway across the circle, caught him before he fell, and slammed him again. On the sidelines the hotheads went silent, strangling on their own bile. Again, again, and again, driven to the end of all effort, Torch blasted the luckless Hawk, not letting him escape, not letting him fall. Finally, with a last mighty blow, Hawk was knocked out of the circle itself, and came to rest flat on his back in the dust among the spectators. Torch lurched forward and dragged his unconscious opponent back into the circle for the last pin. Then he, too, collapsed.

The two men were carried to their tents and later were given their ration of water. Then they slept, unaware of the cool night, unaware of the quiet that had stolen peacefully into the mountains.

Brittle Serpent's tent had been removed, and only five remained when Gyva took her place at the midnight vigil. According to tradition every member of the tribe was given the opportunity to watch over the tents at least once during the course of the manhood ritual. In that way all might be assured that the prohibitions against food or excess water had been observed; but more importantly, each member of the tribe would become an actual participant in the event. There were in the village old men and older women who, if permitted, would ramble on about sitting in vigil one dim night in the trackless past over the tent of Tall Heron, the chief preceding Four Bears. And that was a long, long time ago.

The low-slung tents were pitched in a row, separated from one another by several yards of open space. Not a sound emerged from any of them; the warriors were seeking in sleep whatever sustenance there was. Eight men and three women had held vigil from sundown to midnight, seated in a quiet little group not far from the tents, and they rose a little stiffly from the damp

earth when Gyva, with the other members of the midnight vigil, approached. There were six men and four
women, one of whom was Little Swallow, who had
brought a blanket with her.

"They are all very quiet," observed a brave who left
now to enjoy his own sleep.

"They have reason to be," answered a man joining
Gyva's group. "And I surmise they will sleep even
more deeply another night from now."

Everyone stood for a time, looking at the tents and
deciding just how much personal meaning lay in the
potential power they symbolized. Then the men sat
down and lit a pipe to pass among themselves, talking
in low voices and smoking, and then just smoking. The
women, two squaws whose interest lay in bead stringing, sank to the earth next to Gyva and Swallow, some
small distance from the men. Swallow had not yet
unwrapped her blanket; and because the ground was
damp and cold at night, Gyva wished that she had
brought her own. But even if she were to stay here
forever, still she would not ask to share anything be-
longing to the wicked Swallow!

Time passed. The women muttered about the advantages of shell beads as opposed to the wonders of
stone beads, and the problems of stringing both. Swallow had not unrolled her blanket at all, but instead
rested against it as she sat on the ground. Now and
then she would glance at Gyva and smirk a little, but
when she saw that the only response was a contemptuous glare, even her smirks abated. At length boredom
and the cold ground got the better of her. She stood
up and stretched.

"The earth seems harder at night," she pronounced.

"It is a thing of which I am sure you have much
knowledge," Gyva observed, her voice like the edge
of a knife.

Swallow realized she had erred in giving Gyva a
chance to remark upon her tryst with Hawk in the

river grass. "And your soft back has known a bed of grass and ground as well," she shot back. "Indeed, perhaps the traces are still pressed upon the flesh of your underside."

Gyva glanced toward the other women. Fortunately they were not listening.

"Anyway, it matters not," Swallow was saying, "I shall be wife of whoever becomes chief."

Gyva's temper flared. This arrogance she could not bear. "Let us hope you are more certain of him whom you claim for husband than you are of those you claim for lover."

"What do you mean?"

Let us have it out, Gyva thought. "I mean that you have not enjoyed the manhood of Torch."

There was a pause, brief but telling. "You are pathetic in your jealousy," Swallow accused. "If you cannot hold a man, you need not attempt to attack a woman who can." Her tone, as always, was haughty, self-certain. Gyva was positive that Swallow had not been possessed by Torch. Positive. Almost positive.

"He told me that after the manhood ritual was concluded, I would be his choice," Swallow said.

Gyva considered this. Did it mean that Torch had not made love to Little Swallow only because he had wanted to "shepherd his strength," as he had phrased it? And did it mean that once the ritual was over he would call for her? No, that could not be true.

Swallow struck again, a bitter blow that she administered with relish. "A man will always choose a woman who knows her place in the tribe," she said. "You ought to have considered that before sneaking around the council meeting."

"I was only gathering firewood," Gyva maintained, knowing all the while how lame was her excuse. It was absurd. She was disgusted with herself. Why did she have to make such excuses, to feel ashamed? What was the point of it? "No, you might as well hear the truth," she heard her voice telling Swallow, "I did go to the place of the council with the intention of listening to the deliberations of the men."

Little Swallow, startled by this frank acknowledgment of guilt, and a bit stunned by the heedless audacity of the act itself, glanced toward Gyva with a look of curiosity. "Why?" she asked.

"Because I wished to know what the braves are planning."

"They would have told you. They always do."

"Yes. They always do. But after everything has been decided. It is too late to do anything about it then. There is nothing one can say."

Swallow's lovely mouth curled scornfully. "Ah! I recall the time you spoke up at the Meeting of Nations. Asking the Sac warrior how long it would be before the white men come into our homeland! Would that you had the power to stand outside yourself and observe your pretentious conceit! What do *you* know of affairs?"

Gyva was enraged, and tried to keep her voice even. She was not entirely successful. "I know more than you, and that is certain!"

Swallow just laughed. "So you think. Anyway, it matters not. The knowledge necessary to the wife of a chieftain lies in how to move her body, and when to caress, and how long, and where. The skill necessary to the wife of a chieftain encompasses the giving of a thousand kisses, each one different and each one in a different place. You will be gathering firewood as an old crone of ninety circlings of the sun, dried and withered as—"

"I know the things of which you speak so crudely!" Gyva retorted. "And better than you do I bestow them!"

The two maidens had grown quite heated in their exchange, and their voices had risen accordingly.

"You there," grunted one of the older braves. "Both

of you. We are here to watch over a new chief, not to decide who is to bed him!"

Embarrassed, both girls fell silent. Gyva could feel her fine skin burning with humiliation. How fortunate that it was night. Swallow, to put the brave's remark out of her mind, busied herself by unrolling the blanket. In spite of the darkness Gyva saw that the other girl had something wrapped within it, which she quickly slipped in back of her as she sat down.

"You may not sit here," she told Gyva.

"I would not, even if you asked me."

"There will come a time when you do all I say," Swallow hissed. They were both whispering now, but too angry with each other to cease speaking entirely.

"Hah!" Gyva spat. "There are not that many days even in the mind of the Great Spirit. There will come a time when you shall follow *me*."

"Do you know how the white jackals take black men as slaves? I believe, when I become wife of the chieftain, that I should like a slave of mixed blood, to fetch and carry for me. Yes, I think such a slave would suit me well."

"True chieftains do not hold slaves."

"Hawk has nothing against the practice. He told me. You see, I *do* have plans for you."

"Hawk will not become chief. Did you see today at the wrestling, how badly he was beaten?"

"It is but the first day. There is time." Having said this, Swallow smiled in a manner Gyva did not like at all. It reminded her of the expression on her face when Gyva had realized that Swallow was conspiring with Hawk, a secret grimace promising malicious delight. "Perhaps we shall simply send you forth from the nation, and you can go be slave of the white chieftain, Chula Harjo."

"It is as I thought. You are ignorant. The white chieftain is Moon-Row. Chula Harjo wishes to be chief—Four Bears told me so. But he is not chief now."

Uncomfortable that Gyva knew something she did not, Swallow returned to the personal level. "He has also killed one white woman, I have heard."

Gyva's mother. Gyva did not care for Swallow's tone. "And my mother fought him with a pitchfork. To this day Jacksa bears the scars."

"Hah! I do not believe that. Many of us do not believe that tale at all. Why, it may have been invented by Four Bears just for your sake, to make your blood appear richer than it is."

"It is rich enough!"

"We shall see."

The two girls were glaring at one another, and the rest of the vigil party was all but somnolent, when a moccasined brave raced silently down from the village. Gyva recognized him as one of Hawk's hotheads, and immediately her suspicions were aroused. But the brave was troubled. He brought an urgent message.

"There may be an attack party approaching," he whispered, as they rose and gathered around him. As they did, Gyva noticed Swallow pushing whatever it was she had been concealing under the edge of her blanket. It was a flask, for water or honeyed milk.

"What do you wish us to do?" the messenger was being asked. "We are charged with standing vigil here until the great dipper has spun halfway toward the horizon."

"Your responsibility to the new chief is indeed a sacred one, but so is duty toward your village. I have already spoken to Teva, and it is her advice that the contestants not be awakened, since we are not certain a raid is coming. One of the outlying sentinels has heard something, that is all. So what I propose is this: Just come up with me to the edge of the village, so you will be ready to help if needed. In that way, you can also look down here where the tents are, and fulfill your vigil, too."

It seemed a reasonable solution, and everyone rushed up to the edge of the village, to be ready to fight if necessary. The nefarious Choctaw raid was still on the minds of all, and the possibility of another attack was not to be discounted. Even the Harrisville white men might attack! In moments the sentinels passed along a comforting message. No intruders had been spotted; no attack was forthcoming. While waiting, however, Gyva and the others noted that, in the dark, it was very difficult to observe the tents, crouching back there on the grass.

All told, they had not been away from the vigil for more than ten minutes. Almost a fool's errand, and yet . . . and yet Gyva was upset. She had not lost her strong suspicion that, somehow, the manhood ritual was being sabotaged. And she believed it for certain when they came back to the place of the tents. Not caring what Swallow might think, Gyva drew back the corner of the blanket under which she had seen Swallow hide the flask. But the flask was gone. There was only one answer in Gyva's mind. The container—which had undoubtedly contained broth, or soup, or strong, invigorating drink—was in the tent of whichever brave had stolen out to take it.

Silence would mean dishonor now. The proof would be there for all to see in Hawk's tent. Gyva saw it clearly. Everything had been planned. The hothead brave rushing down to warn of a phony attack! Passing along Teva's "advice," too! The witch-woman had probably been asleep the whole time! And those assigned to the vigil had behaved predictably, had gone back up to the village, ready to defend the tribe.

"Where is the flask?" demanded Gyva of the other maiden.

"Swallow turned and blinked, as if puzzled, asking: "What? What flask?"

A cold silence fell upon the vigil party. Trouble.

Gyva explained what she had seen, every detail from the wrapped blanket to Swallow's hiding of the flask before they'd gone to defend the village against mythical attack.

"You are as the loon is!" Swallow jeered.

"Enough of this!" commanded the oldest brave present. "It is a fierce accusation. We must send for Teva immediately."

It was done, and within minutes the seeress came wavering down to the place of the tents. She had already been informed of the trouble by the messenger; she looked at Gyva with a gloomy eye. Yes, she had been told that an attack might be forthcoming. Yes, she had advised precisely the course of action taken by the hothead. But this matter of the flask was most serious.

"I swear it was there, and now it is gone," said Gyva.

"There was never a flask, nothing but my blanket," countered Swallow, with a most unsettling smile.

When she saw that smile, Gyva ought to have known. Somehow her enemies were far ahead of her. They had more ruses, knew more tricks. And with vicious skill they not only managed to use against Gyva her growing reputation for bizarre behavior—the killing of the Choctaw notwithstanding—but simultaneously augmented that reputation.

"What is this? She has done something else? She has truly implied that a future chief has dishonored the manhood ritual? Well, if she is wrong, that is one thing! But if she seeks to distract us from her folly at the council meeting by an accusation as serious as this one—well, that is quite another."

But this time Gyva was ready for them.

"We have but to look in the tents," she said. "I am sure one of the warriors has the flask."

An air of great foreboding settled upon the vigil, and upon Teva, too. The old woman drew Gyva to one side. "You are sure of this?" she asked, with a tone of extreme doubt.

"There was a flask and now it is gone. What else could have become of it?"

"If there *was* a flask," said Teva after a moment, "then I am in agreement with you." In the light of the stars the mark upon her face seemed to glow. "But if not . . . if not, you have made the most serious of all accusations. I hope for your sake that your words are true."

"What shall we do?"

"We shall wait until morning, and then inspect the tents of all, with everyone of the tribe in attendance."

The suggestion could not have given Gyva more satisfaction. At last everyone could see what manner of man Hawk was. She imagined him now, coming out of his tent, all the bluster gone, the tail of his arrogance tucked up between his legs, while at the same time the proud staff of manhood sought to curl into his flesh.

Gyva did not return to her sleeping place when the predawn vigil party arrived, nor did the witch-woman, nor did any of the others. In fact, word spread, and when dawn came over the blue mountains, most of the tribe had gathered around the tents.

Teva said not one word to Gyva during all the waiting.

Wise, Gyva thought. She does not wish to show favoritism.

Fleet Cloud was the first to appear, but he only pushed himself slightly out of his tent. "Help me," he pleaded. He could stand and he could hobble slightly, but he could not walk. Fleet Cloud would not be chief.

Only four candidates remained in competition, and they awoke now and emerged from their tents as Gyva reconsidered her accusation. She had believed that the flask contained some nutritious, sustaining substance, and that one of the braves—Hawk, almost certainly— had stolen out to acquire it, taking it back to his tent for consumption. But had it been a more complicated ploy? Perhaps Fleet Cloud had believed the contents of the flask to be good, while in fact a certain subtle poison was administered thereby?

She wondered over these matters while, one by one, the warriors awakened to the second day of the manhood ritual—and to the news of Gyva's accusation, which was conveyed to them by the soothsayer.

Gyva watched their faces as they heard the dark news.

Arrow-in-Oak looked faintly surprised, then angry.

Dark Eagle seemed disgusted.

Hawk did not seem to care one way or the other. He looked well rested, but his face was bruised by Torch's mighty blows.

Torch appeared anguished by the news, and doubly so when he learned the identity of the accuser. Never had Gyva felt the floor of the world drop away from her as it did now, and as it did moments later, when Teva caused the tents to be struck, pulled up from the pegs that held them to the ground, revealing under each nothing but a single rude blanket flat against the earth.

No flask. No sign of a flask. And absolutely no hiding place in which a flask, or anything else, might have been secreted.

"It is my duty," the old woman orated, "to ask the accuser if she is satisfied, that the ordeal may proceed."

"The ordeal may proceed," Gyva told her stubbornly. "My satisfaction is another matter, because I saw what I saw."

There were catcalls; there was ridicule and contempt.

"Hide yourself in the forest, why don't you?" smirked Little Swallow, as the tribe moved off to witness the beginning of the mountain trek. "Or take a knife and slit your throat in some trackless wood. You are disgraced now, and a troublemaker. We do not need such a one as you."

Gyva whirled, and seized Little Swallow by the neck. The wily maiden's mocking brightness faded more quickly than dew beneath the sun. "I know with my soul that you have sullied the ritual," she told Hawk's lover, "and I shall prove it if it be the last thing I do."

Swallow, deducing that she would be neither strangled nor struck, twisted away. "Why do you not simply climb the mountain with the men? Do you see that high peak, which they must reach? When you attain it, jump."

Then she moved off arrogantly to the starting place, where the contestants were savoring their ladles of water. She walked with an arrogant, suggestive motion, the movement of her hips a promise of how she would move for a mounted man.

Many watched her, but Hawk was not one of them this morning. His concentration was directed toward the twin mountains. He knew, as did everyone, that only those who ended this day in the first and second positions would be allowed to advance to the crucial exercise of the third day. In spite of his loss to Torch in wrestling, Hawk stood high in the other events, and he looked fitter than the others to make the day-long climb. The men had to race for miles up into the foothills, followed by a climb up the rocky south face of the mountain. Once there, they would present themselves, waving to watchers positioned all along the course, and return to the village by sundown. A brave returning after sundown was disqualified; and, as always, a contestant could legitimately give up the effort at any time. There would be great temptation to do so—men with water waited at various stations along the route. So easy would it be to stop and drink.

The race began. Dark Eagle, realizing that it was now or never were he to have any chance at all, dashed into the lead, scorning the advice given by well-wishers that he pace himself. For the early hours of the morning he was far out in front, straining with the zeal of desperation. Arrow-in-Oak made it his strategy to keep close upon the heels of Torch, who was strong, but obviously worn by the rigors of the previous day.

Hawk-of-the-Sky kept close on the heels of Dark Eagle, but was not so foolhardy as to spend his energy like the younger man.

Long before noon watchers passed the message back down the line: Dark Eagle had reached the rocky face of the mountain and had begun to climb. There was considerable surprise in the tribe; Eagle had not been expected to endure that far, at least not in first position. Several people remembered—or thought that they remembered—seeing him practicing on the cliffs in recent months. Soon a cheer went up from the spectators. They could not see the contestants running up the wooded foothills, but now they saw the tiny figure of Dark Eagle inching his way up the rocks. Perhaps this day would bring great surprises for the tribe. Minutes later another minuscule man-shape began to climb the rocky south face of the twins, and the word flashed back along the stations: "It is Hawk-of-the-Sky."

Gyva was grievously disspirited. No one spoke to her. Most did not notice her sufficiently even to bestow scorn. She was ignored. Yet she would not let herself weaken, not permit herself to seek privacy, or shelter from the silent contempt. In the short time since Four Bears' death, her world had turned. She had helped to change it—no sense denying that; but on the air she smelled disgrace, and its odor was the stomach-stopping whiff of human flesh in a fire, like the scent of the squaw whom the Choctaw had burned.

Gyva felt herself drifting along the edge of a precipice, beneath which waited the beckoning abyss of despair. But she would not go to it, she would not go to it now—and let Ababinili and whatever God there was damn her forever if she did!

Having thought such a thing, Gyva waited to tremble, but she did not. In fact she felt better.

Mixed blood? So they prate about mixed blood? Well, let them! It does not mean I am less than the Chickasaw. It means I have the capacity to be stronger

than they are. And as for the white men, I am stronger
than they are, too, and for the same reason. Mixed
blood! I am the best of both.

She felt very good for a little while, but the elation
did not last. It was not that she doubted her insight,
or lacked confidence that it was true. No, her sadness
was based upon the realization that whatever her
strengths were, she would never have an opportunity
to test them fully. She would always be little Dey-Lor-
Gyva, Beloved-of-Earth (if of no one else), the granddaughter of a man who had once been chief, making
hilarious conceits of wisdom, interfering laughably
in the affairs of the tribe.

Well, let them believe that, she thought, resolving
not to give way. When the new chief is named, we
shall see what life is like.

Four men were upon the mountain now, clinging
to the rocky cliff, and moving upward. Gyva herself
could not tell who was who; but when the word passed
down from the watchers along the stations, it was clear
that Dark Eagle had maintained his momentum. How
could it be? wondered Gyva. Eagle was a good brave,
but never outstanding. The men listened to him, but
did not heed his advice. The women treated him with
shattering equanimity. The children did not seem to
know he existed. The maidens, true, would not reject
the opportunity to wed him—he was courageous and
manly and fair—but neither would they swarm to bed
him before the ceremony.

Perhaps the contents of Swallow's flask had not
poisoned Fleet Cloud or shored up the vigor of Hawk.
Perhaps something had been conveyed in the flask to
Dark Eagle!

If that is the case, pondered Gyva, then I know less
than I thought I did. She turned toward the face of
the mountain, like all the others. Whatever one's
hopes or aspirations, whatever one's fears, there are
often times when one can only wait. And when waiting is the best thing to do.

High noon, and the brutal dance upon the mountain held the eyes of all assembled in the village below. Dark Eagle had begun to falter; the distance narrowed between Hawk and himself. Arrow-in-Oak and Torch climbed as if they were members of a team, neither one willing to break away, to make a move that would put him in a position to challenge the leaders. If anything, Torch had begun to fall back a little.

Gyva sent him a prayer of encouragement. The trick of the climb was to get to the top as soon as possible. The downhill trek, while not much easier, was faster, and the brave in the lead gained an enormous advantage. That lead still belonged to Dark Eagle; and now, perhaps a hundred rocky feet from the summit he seemed to increase his efforts, with Hawk coming up fast behind.

When it happened, no one cried out at first, or even made exclamation, so gracefully did the movement appear to be executed. Dark Eagle clambered to within inches of the top, reached out his hand for purchase of the halfway prize, and turned to look at Hawk—perhaps to grin at him, or goad the other brave to greater effort. The watchers on the mountain, later, were themselves unsure of just what had happened. Eagle had failed to grasp something strong enough to pull himself up, or he had been too fatigued to hold on, or he had slipped. Even Hawk, nearest him, was unsure. But Dark Eagle, his body bent like a bow, arched backward, seeming to push himself away from the mountain as a diver leaves his perch, and hung in the air, arms spread like wings, before he shot downward through the empty blue air to fall, broken and lost, upon the pine-needled floor of the forest below.

And so there were three.

Hawk managed to reach the top, and he could be seen looking down for a long, long moment into the abyss that had swallowed Dark Eagle. On the mountain, Torch and Arrow stopped climbing to ponder the finality of the contest that goaded their minds, tortured their flesh. When they recommenced, Arrow was clearly out in front; the second position was his.

There was no catching Hawk, however; and after watching for a while more, Gyva gave it up and drifted back toward her wigwam. She might sew; she might place extra skins on the makeshift roof. She might even sleep. No one would bother her today, absorbed in the contest as they were. But while heading toward the village, her eyes fell upon the five small tents; and the shameful events of last night and the morning bloomed in her mind.

There *had* been a flask, and it had to be somewhere!

Glancing around and finding herself unobserved, she walked down to the tents and examined the ground all around them. A man—Hawk, for example—might drink secret nourishment and then throw the container far away.

Gyva hunted in all directions as far as a man could throw a small container. Nothing. Then she walked back to the place where the tents stood in a neat row, little brown points of hide over stakes. She touched Torch's tent, feeling sad and tender. And here was Hawk's tent. Just looking at it made her angry. She knelt down, pulled the flap aside, and looked in. Nothing but the blanket, flat on the ground. No room to hide anything. Inch by inch she felt along the length and width of it, then lay down inside the tent to consider the puzzle. Now *think*. Swallow had the flask. Then it was gone. Assuming that no one but the contestants had remained in the area when the false rumor of the raid had drawn the rest of them away, there was no way the flask could have disappeared. So where was it?

All at once she knew.

Gyva pulled aside the blanket and saw a thousand tiny chips that flickered like mica. Hawk had broken the container into fragments, concealed them beneath his blanket. It was a great risk to have taken, for he and Little Swallow must have considered that the tents would be searched. Well, they certainly *would* be, and more thoroughly this time! She would go right now to the witch-woman and tell her what she'd found.

But she couldn't. The people would say, "See? See what she has done now? While all of us were watching the contest upon the twin mountains, bitter Gyva did place these chips under the blanket of Hawk. No, they would not believe her. And given her current reputation, why should they?

It seemed hopeless. Hawk and Little Swallow and their friends were obviously using every nefarious device to capture the leadership of the Chickasaw, and there was nothing Gyva could do about it, nothing that she could give Torch, no way to help him in his exhaustion. Even if he did manage to finish in second position today, a confident and better-rested Hawk would possess a keen advantage of imagination on the crucial third day. If there were only some way to convey to Torch an extra ladle of water, or food.

No, she discounted these impulses. She would not violate the code; and even if she suggested it, Torch would hold her in contempt. She could not even converse with him, to offer encouragement and consolation. Words, too, violated the code of the manhood ritual. Silence during the ordeal was a symbolic acceptance by the warriors that in positions of authority they would listen to the advice of others, and that if captured by an enemy, no secrets would ever leave their lips, in spite of whatever torment might be applied to them.

Gyva went to Torch's tent and lay there while the afternoon slipped into the fields of time. When she heard the first burst of raucous cheering, which certainly signaled Hawk's return as victor, she had decided what to do. There was something she could give Torch that would at once help him but not violate the rules of the ritual. Now she had only to pray that he would best Arrow-in-Oak.

* * *

She heard them approaching, all of them. The mutter of voices grew louder, and then old Teva was chanting as the ladles of water were given out. It did not take long. There were but two ladles to give. Torch and Hawk had endured to face the final day.

Torch crawled into his tent and sank down, too exhausted to do more than stare at Gyva in the sundown gloom. She put a finger over her lips, unnecessarily. He would not speak; it was a violation. Now if only he would think carefully, he would also know that her presence was not a violation of any rule. Never in all the moons of the Chickasaw had any chief or wise man or seeress sought to proscribe women in the tents of the candidates. Such an occurrence was almost unimaginable. Everyone knew that lovemaking during periods of high exertion was fraught with peril and would drain a man of his last quiver of resolve.

Gyva did not think so. From all that she had heard of the third day's task, it seemed that a man who knew he was well loved would have the best chance. But that was for later, the love. Torch blinked, tried to smile, failed, and dropped immediately into a sleep so deep it was almost frightening. At times he shivered, trembled, as the muscles in his exhausted body relaxed. Gyva pressed close against him, giving him warmth, giving him the wordless communion of her comfort and devotion. The third day might be long or short; only Ababinili knew, and only he could end it.

The last challenge in the manhood ritual was both physical and spiritual. Already having fasted and partaken of exertion to the point of collapse, the final two braves from the initial field of contestants rose on the morning of the third day, sipped their measure of water, and went off separately into the mountains. Once again neither food nor drink was permitted. Fasting and praying, the braves would remain in the wilderness until the Great Spirit came to them in a dream. He might appear in a vision, in daylight around the bright corona of the sun, like fire leaping from eternal fruit. But if he did not appear in the day, he must come at night, and if not the first night, then the second or the third or the fourth. But the manhood ritual was not considered complete until the Spirit did indeed come to one of the warriors, and all this time sustenance was forbidden. In the past it had often happened that a towering vision came to both braves; and when they returned to the village to tell the people of their dream, the tribe itself had to decide whose dream most befitted a chieftain.

Lying beside Torch in the tent, Gyva stroked his forehead, trying to impress her desire that he have a great vision, a splendid one, such as none had ever fashioned before. According to the tribal tales Four Bears had remained in the wilderness for two days, returning to tell of a "great growling God in the shape of a tornado-cone," who spoke to Four Bears, telling him, "In your lifetime, I shall spare the Chickasaw people." The message, when repeated to the tribe upon Four Bears' return, had caused great jubilation, and he had become chief. Gyva had heard the story more times than she could count, and always she had savored it, for by its import the Chickasaw were a chosen people. But now, quite suddenly, she saw it in another way.

"In your lifetime, I shall spare the Chickasaw people."

Four Bears was gone now!

Did that mean the nation was somehow vulnerable in the eyes of heaven? Had a blessed era finally come to an end? Would the black funnel sweep into these mountains, blasting away everything that had been, uprooting the Indians as it plucked tall trees from the very earth?

Gyva shivered and pressed closer to Torch, pulling the thin blanket around them both. She could hear the low mutter of the people keeping vigil outside. What if the tents were inspected in the morning, and

she were found there with Torch? Well, let it be.
There was nothing to prevent her from being with
him, save the scorn of the tribe, and *that* she already
bore. But would it not sully Torch in their eyes? Do
not think about that now. It is too late now to think
about that.

She thought instead of the dreams of kings. Everything, it seemed, had already been dreamed, every
mysterious vision had been granted to some chief in
the past. The legendary Gull Wing, who from the
veils of mist had brought the nation to these mountains: He had dreamed of golden rain that was rich
like wheat, sweet like honey, falling upon the flower
fields of home. Chief Salmon-of-the-River had been
given a vision in which ten pillars of fire bore up
silver clouds from the mountain tops. And Claw-of-
the-Panther had seen a warrior whose body glowed
like the sun, mounted on a steed of wind, bearing a
bow of light and a quiver with ten arrows of lightning,
one for each of the ten tribes in the nation.

Great dreams, visions. What remained for her beloved to see in his time of trial?

Gyva had another dark thought. What would Hawk
dream? She recalled the day both of them had gone
into battle, seeking their first blooding. Hawk had
spoken well that day, straight and true, and his words
had gone directly into the hearts of many. Torch had
been profound, but strangely obscure, almost mystical
in his words.

But she could do nothing about it. The vision must
be a gift, as must the dream. That was in the hands of
He-Who-Dwelt-in-the-Clear-Sky. Snuggling next to the
sleeping Torch, Gyva slept, too, but lightly, like a cat;
and when he stirred, she was awake before he was.
Dawn was very near.

She pressed her fingers against his lips and smiled.
He seemed faintly alarmed, and still tired, although
not so desperately tired as he had been on the previous
night. There was a question in his eyes, which trans-

formed itself into surprise when she kissed him deeply
—a kiss he knew and which had meaning between
them.

Torch shook his head.

Gyva nodded, and smiled, and kissed him again.

Deftly did she slip the garment from her shoulders
and slide it off her body; his eyes and body grew more
hungry than his belly had ever been.

One last time, with a suppressed groan and a twist
of his head, Torch tried to tell her no. But Gyva knew
what she was about, and knew it was true. If there was
any strength she might give him now, its source must
be love, and that she possessed in great abundance,
and knew how to give as well.

Pale waves of light flooded the valley as her supple
hands sought his readiness, to fondle and enhance.
Leaning on one elbow, she hovered above him, pressing her full, tender breasts upon his bronze chest, and
bringing her mouth down upon his. Giving strength
with her kiss, Gyva could fairly taste his hunger; feeling his hunger in her hands, she knew the blood-
throb of his strength. Mist rose, wavering on the
dawn; and she rose above him, carefully, gently, slowly, within the soft embrace of the little tent. She felt
her body all open and warm for him, felt herself flow
around him, came down and molded herself unto him.

Then it was with them as it had been since the first
time beneath the willows, but with greater meaning
and wonder, a consecration one to another for the
days ahead. Gyva felt the glow begin to build in her.
She knew once more the swelling tide that once possessed, can be but dimly remembered, which one must
have again in order to possess, yet even then cannot
remember, and so must possess again. Lying upon
him, laying with him, her body fitted every inch to
his, she moved as he did when he was upon her, the
sweet pull of her need matching his.

Light grew within the valley, casting rainbow colors

on the morning fog, and in the tent their melded bodies climbed a spectrum of delicious colors. In the back of her mind, which seemed now to be receding from her just as the very air was gone from her breast, Gyva remembered: *Do not cry out, do not cry out, do not cry out* . . . . Then his arms came around her like steel, like bronze serpents. He shuddered, a fountain of life, full life, flooding into her, and she trembled all along the length of her body as a current of ecstasy flooded her, crashing all the way up the length of her supple spine, and broke like a vast golden wave within her mind, upon the shores of her soul.

DO NOT CRY OUT, DO NOT CRY . . .

When at last she opened her eyes and looked into his, she knew she had been right. Torch was fully awake, alive in every fiber of his being. He understood, too, what it was that she had done for him, and kissed her once in gratitude. Moments later Teva called from outside the tent, and Torch went out to drink water and face the last of the challenges, the burden of the third day, the duration of which no one knew.

Gyva waited until she heard them leave, the warriors going into the wilderness, the tribespeople accompanying them to the edge of the forest. Cautiously, very cautiously, she peered out of the tentflap, emerged, and went to her wigwam.

There was much to pray for on that day, both in thanksgiving and in hope.

The people of the tribe were tense with expectation, a tension that grew as the day wore on. Torch, it was said, had drawn a straw from the soothsayer's hand that directed him into the west. Hawk departed toward the east, seeking his vision there. Hawk and Torch. Hawk *or* Torch. Somehow everyone seemed to have known always that the final choice would be between the two of them. Arrow-in-Oak said it best:

"I did not think Torch would be able to catch me during the race, since he was last to come down from the rocks. But all through the late afternoon I could hear him as I ran, his footsteps on the trail behind me like those of the spirit of death. I was as far ahead of him as Hawk was ahead of me, yet Torch would not fall back. The sound of his footsteps became a burden to me, and it seemed with each step the weight upon me was heavier."

Many grunted. Some sighed in casual sympathy.

"There was also the matter of your archery," someone suggested.

"It is a thing I still do not understand," muttered Arrow-in-Oak disconsolately. "Never was I prepared to shoot better."

The rest of the tribe went about performing daily chores, trying to keep their minds off the mystery that must now occur, in the mountains of home, within the hearts of two men. But it was difficult to concentrate. Most of the adults did well, losing themselves in the dull intricacies of labor; but on the field the children played with shrill agitation.

"Take them into the forest," Teva ordered. "It is chokecherry time. Let them pick until their excitement is diminished."

Gyva volunteered to go with them; she was uncomfortable in the village now, with almost everyone ignoring her. There were eight or nine boys and as many girls. Carrying wicker baskets, they followed her down along the river past the willows and the honeysuckle hedge, then across the shallow ford and into the trees beyond the grave of Four Bears.

Away from the river the earth swelled into gently rolling hills, covered with grass and bushes and small trees. There, in easy groves, were the delicate-looking but hardy chokecherry trees, hung heavily with the small black fruit. The berries were sweet yet dry (hence their name) and left a heavy aftertaste and a thirst for water. But the juice stained hard and was used in war paint. Gyva told the children to begin picking and sat down nearby to keep an eye on them.

An hour passed, perhaps a little more. The day was warm. She was drowsy. And there, in that dreamy state of half-sleep, she sensed it. The blood of hunters throbbed in her; the experience of a thousand ancestors nourished her wariness. The day was still as fine as it had been, and the children chattered, working happily; but Gyva sensed something alien and alarming in the chokecherry grove.

She did not move. As she had been taught so often, as she had done on the night Hawk and Little Swallow made love in the grass, Gyva swept the area with her eyes, taking everything in, missing nothing. There next to the edge of the grove, little Bright Badger was filling his basket with berries. He had wandered away from the others—not too far away, true, but he was definitely separated from them. Bright Badger was far from the cleverest boy in the tribe, a dull, stolid child who obeyed if he remembered what it was he had been told to do, but only if he remembered. Gyva was irritated with him, but at the same time she realized that it was not his carelessness that had caused her disquieting perception. Simultaneously she felt compelled to call him back to the others and to remain silent as well. For some buried reason she did not wish to give away the position in which she sat. Danger has its reasons.

The children were chattering and yelping.

The air was sweet and heavy. There was no breeze. Bees droned, and somewhere a snake slipped into a bed of wet leaves.

A moment passed, as quiet and natural as the day.

Then, unseen by the children but all too visible to Gyva, three men emerged from the underbrush. They moved stealthily, expertly, like men trained in ambush and attack. One of them—he had a great, red beard—seized Bright Badger, clamping a hand over the boy's mouth. The basket was shaken from his hands, and chokecherries filled the air for a moment, like a swarm of black bees, until they fell onto the earth. Red Beard was dragging Bright Badger into the bushes; the other two men—white men—advanced upon the happy, unsuspecting children.

As Gyva realized that the men thought the children were all alone, she screamed. It was as blood-chilling a scream as any Chickasaw had ever let loose.

The children looked up, startled. She saw the fear upon their faces as clearly as she saw the surprise on the hard visages of the jackals.

The children screamed.

The white men turned and fled, still not having seen her, she later believed.

Then everything, as in a battle, was madness and chaos. Gyva did not think the white men would pursue, but she was not sure, and brought up the rear to protect the children as best she could. Helter-skelter, stumbling, falling, they raced back toward the village.

Gyva was proud of the children now. After an initial display of fear, they remembered what they had been taught: Never cry out while in flight. Sink away into sanctuary or safety as water into the ground. They were not quite expert yet—too young for that—but the lesson had been learned. In minutes all of them, except for hapless little Badger, reached the outskirts of the village.

Gyva knew that her aid in saving the children could not make up for Bright Badger's abduction while he was in her care, and she felt the weight of further disapprobation upon her head. How should she explain it? What would she say? Who would ever have suspected that the white men would come so close to the village? And why in heaven did they want to steal a child?

Ransom? The boy was not even related to the family of a chieftain. And all the Indians had to give was land. Blood sacrifice? Perhaps. She would put nothing past the white men. Their religion—she had heard once in shuddering horror—had something to do with the body and blood of a man dead for thousands of years! If that was truly what they believed, it was quite clear that the white jackals were capable of anything.

Gyva was trying to decide how to phrase the terrible news about Bright Badger when she saw a big crowd gathering at the opposite end of the village.

Had Hawk or Torch returned with a vision already?

Children raced to mothers or fathers, spreading the awful news of what had happened in the woods. Gyva ran to the crowd of villagers, saw dark concern and even alarm written on their faces. Had they learned of Red Beard already? She tried to push her way into the center of the group, where Arrow-in-Oak stood listening to two agitated braves who had just returned from a scouting party. In the absence of a designated chief, and due to his creditable participation in the manhood ritual, Arrow was serving as temporary tribal head until a true chief was chosen.

"It is a very large party," one of the scouts was saying. "The men must number three full score, and women, children, animals—who could count how many!"

"They were skirting Lake Santeetlah, on the westward course for our homeland," added the other. "As soon as we observed them, we made like the wind to bring this news."

Arrow frowned.

"Please, I must get through," Gyva tried, but most attention was directed toward Arrow. On the fringes of the crowd, however, some of the children had found their parents, and the name Bright Badger was repeated now and again.

"It is likely they wish to join the Harrisville settlement, if they are farmers," Arrow-in-Oak surmised.

"In any case, it will be days before they reach our territory. We can wait and keep them under our eyes, to see what—"

"I have bad news," Gyva managed, slipping through the crowd.

Somewhere one of the squaws keened in sudden anguish. Bright Badger's mother.

Tell it fast, Gyva. "There were white men in the forest," she blurted. "One of them took a child from under our very eyes . . . chokeberry picking . . . there was nothing I could—"

"Bright Badger has been abducted by the white men!" someone cried. "Let us arm ourselves!"

The suggestion was met with blood-chilling enthusiasm, and braves turned away to seek their bows and knives. Arrow-in-Oak still evaluating what the scouts had told him, called them back.

"Let us consider these things," he ordered, his voice sharp and decisive. "How can we chase beneath the trees after a few men and one child when a jackal party of fearsome size bears down upon us from the east? Tell me," he demanded of a scout, "were there soldiers with the party?"

"Armed men there were," admitted a scout. "But no uniformed men with fire sticks."

"And you, Gyva? The men you saw? What was their apparel and appearance?"

She told them there had been very little time to notice. Everything had happened within the space of an instant. The man with the red beard had seized Bright Badger, and—"

"A red beard?" exclaimed Arrow, disturbed. Many in the crowd murmured darkly, some of them with a kind of awe, all of them with hatred.

Gyva affirmed it.

"That is the chief of the white men. He is named Roo-Pert by them, and it is he who gave our Torch the name Firebrand. The incident will show you what kind of bad blood beats in his foul heart.

"It was the time of our first foray on the village of Harris, and we had planned only to view it from without, and study the number and manner of its inhabitants. Torch, who led the party that day, had advised caution. But once we reached the village, we were observed, and one of the jackals turned his fire stick against us, alarming all the rest of their number. Hawk retaliated, as is his wont, and soon we were drawn into the fray.

"The Red Beard appeared then, one of the fiercest of their fighters, and killed several of our braves. Torch pursued him into a dwelling, but Red Beard, a man of incredible strength, threw upon him a blazing log from the hearth. Torch escaped, but the dwelling was set afire and destroyed. We did not learn until much later that this man Roo-Pert Harris told his fellows Torch had set the blaze, and so one of our own has been christened with a fearsome name and gold is offered for his head."

A frightening idea came to Gyva. Perhaps this man Red Beard Roo-Pert had abducted Bright Badger in order to hold him hostage in exchange for Torch! Never, she thought—uncertainly. Much as her heart feared for the welfare of the boy, no such trade in flesh must ever be made.

"And they did disappear back into the forest?" Arrow-in-Oak demanded of her.

She nodded. The eyes of the villagers were hard upon her, and in almost all of the faces she saw reproach. She did not know what to do, how to react. Since the death of Four Bears, both the things she had done and the things she had not done seemed to show her for a troublemaker or a fool, her honorable intentions transformed as if by some dark magic into the mocking perfection of folly.

"What shall we do, Arrow?" the braves were asking. "Pursue the Red Beard, or attack the oncoming white party?"

"You might wait until we have a chieftain," blurted Gyva before she could stop herself.

Bright Badger's mother—a squat, formidable woman whose initial wail of woe had become a character-istically bitter stoicism—stepped up and pushed her wide face forward. "So? You counsel the tribe to wait, do you? Shall we wait just as you waited, seated upon the earth, while the jackals made away with my son? A maiden who finds her backside of use only to take ease or attract pleasure ought not to speak at all!"

Many were forced to hide crude laughter, hearing these words.

Arrow-in-Oak made his decision. "The white settlers must be moving toward Harrisville, to join the village. If they reach it, we shall be greatly outnumbered. Thus it is my belief that we shall attack the approaching party first. Later we can turn to deal with Red Beard."

The eyes of Bright Badger's mother followed him.

"Even a white man," he told her, "would not make such effort to take one child, if killing were the only purpose. I believe your son will remain alive."

The decision made, the braves hurried to get their weapons and mounts. The long-familiar sense of im-pending battle settled on the village once again. Gyva, her senses dulled by what had happened, and by the ridicule to which she had been subjected, looked around to see Swallow smiling wickedly at her.

"Why do you not go from us and join your people in Harrisville?" Swallow suggested. "You are no In-dian. Hawk has told me that when he becomes chief-tain, he will banish you forever from our tribe."

There was no reason to doubt that Swallow was telling the truth, or that Hawk intended just such a thing. Thus he would have his revenge; and no one, least of all Gyva, could do anything about it. But the prospect terrified her. The tribe, the village, these mountains—they were all she knew, everything she loved.

"I said you are no Chickasaw!" Swallow tried again,

disappointed at not having received a response to her earlier thrust. "You will be cast out, never to come back."

For once Gyva's spirit failed her. Too many things had happened, too many worries bore down upon her.

"These are my people," she said quietly.

The fervor of her words conveyed a sincerity of belief so deep that even Little Swallow was silenced. She followed Gyva with wondering eyes as the wounded maiden walked away.

CHAPTER V

When the village came awake the following morning, Hawk stood waiting. Grave of mien, straight of back, even more confident of gaze than he had been, the warrior seemed in no doubt that he possessed the vision that would elevate him to power. When he was told that half the braves had gone on a war party against a train of white settlers, he replied: "I shall review all matters when I don the headdress and beads of Four Bears and his predecessors." When informed of Bright Badger's luckless fate, Hawk said, "Within this moon, the blood of the jackal shall be streaked like war paint on the face of the earth."

His own hothead braves—those who had not gone on the war party—stood a little apart from him now, and even Little Swallow did not approach. His bearing was that of one who has passed through fire, survived a great trial, and thus become more than a man. Hawk seemed to know that. The tribe sensed it. And so they kept their distance, waiting with increasing anticipation for Torch to return. The dream-visions must be told to the assembled tribe; the leader must be chosen.

All day Hawk stood motionless at the edge of the forest, taking neither nourishment nor water, although water would have been permitted him now. Once the gnarled witch-woman was seen to approach him, and brief words were exchanged; but no member of the tribe learned what they were. For her part Teva kept close to her wigwam. Gyva, who now had the feeling that the earth had forsaken her utterly, had also intended to keep to her lodging, but the restlessness of despair could not be borne in silence. She left her wigwam and began to walk, avoiding Hawk, avoiding whomever she could. At length she found herself near the small lodge of the soothsayer.

"It is Gyva, and I have need of you," she said, outside the hanging flaps of hide that covered the entrance.

"Then enter," croaked the old woman after a moment.

Inside, the wigwam was filled with a heavy smoke, heavier and more acrid than the smoke from the council pipes. It burned Gyva's nose and throat as she sat down near Teva; and as her lungs took in the smoke, the maiden felt an unfamiliar light-headedness.

The pipe was in the old woman's mouth, and great clouds of smoke rose from it, and continued to rise. Much of the smoke she pulled into herself, then expelled between the spaces of her yellow teeth. Her eyes appeared to be floating behind swirling veils of smoke; glittering, disembodied sparks of knowledge.

"What is your need then?"

"I . . . I cannot . . . breathe well here."

"Then go out. No, take a deep breath, and you will find breathing as easy as anything else."

Gyva did, and choked. The witch-woman cackled. Gyva inhaled again, and this time the smoke was sweet. How was it that the tent now seemed to be revolving slowly around her? And where were . . . ah, there were Teva's eyes, glinting far away, like a panther looking out from the forest and the night.

"So?" asked Teva once again. "What is it?"

The strange smoke from the pipe was sweet as elixir now, and Gyva fought to clear her mind. "Hawk has come down from the mountain with his dream-vision?"

"So he has told me."

"Did he tell what it was?"

"Not yet."

"Can you . . . can you see in your mind, now, at this moment, where Torch might be?"

"Why do you wish to know?"

"I fear . . . Hawk. He will banish me from the tribe, and put me away from my people."

Teva cackled. "That cannot be done."

To Gyva, though, it seemed all too simple to do; but somehow, with the smoke filling her body, her mind, the prospect did not seem as grave. She felt that she must leave, go out into air; yet a pleasant lethargy had hold of her, and she did not wish to move at all.

"No one can put another away from his people," Teva was saying. "That is a thing of the heart. You do have your own heart, do you not?"

"Yes, but that is not what I meant."

"And you wish to know if Torch has had a vision that will save you?"

Gyva nodded.

"Listen to him when he tells his tale."

"When will that be?"

"Now," said the soothsayer, and seemed to drift upward like the smoke until she was on her feet. "He will soon enter the village. Let us go."

The old woman and the young one left the lodge; and through the mist of her drugged senses Gyva was uncertain whether she saw or only imagined the figure of Torch coming out of the forest at the other end of the village. But as she walked, her head began to clear. It was Torch, true—yet how had Teva known he was coming? Sometimes she claimed powers, and seemed to possess them; other times she denied having power at all, just a touch more of intuition than most people had. Which was true?

But Torch was indisputably returned; and he took up a position facing Hawk across the length of the village, while the tribespeople ran from their wigwams or their work to hear and to judge the glimpses of

heaven brought back by these challengers. Always it
was the tribespeople who must pass final decision. If
the dream of a challenger was especially obscure, Teva
was called upon to interpret.

"Are you prepared to tell of what the Great Spirit
sent to you?" Teva called.

"I am," declared Hawk.

Torch looked about. "Many of the warriors are
missing," he observed. And upon learning what had
happened he said, "These are serious things. Would it
not be best to wait for the return of the war party?"

"No! No!" cried the people, who could not bear
to wait any longer.

"Why postpone this?" cried Hawk. "They will learn
it when they return. Do you wish to delay while you
fabricate some dream you have never possessed?"

The question itself was an insult, the very tone a
challenge. Truly Hawk must have been gifted with a
splendid dream.

"Let it be as you wish," Teva told the tribe. "That
is your custom, as it is mine."

"Now!" they cried. "Tell it now."

"One must be a servant of the tribe," Torch said in
acceptance, "before one can be its leader."

"Step forward to the center of our village," Teva
ordered. The two braves marched forward, neither of
them faltering in spite of the long ordeal. But Gyva
could not help noting that Torch seemed troubled,
deep in thought, while Hawk appeared stronger, more
vibrant than ever.

"Let us sit," Teva said, and held out two straws as
the tribe gathered to watch and listen.

Hawk drew the long straw, looked all about, and
began:

"I did walk east from this homeland of ours," he
said, "until at midday I could go no farther. Beneath
a ridge of pine and oak I paused to rest, and sleep,
and find my dream. But it did not come. When I
awoke, it was almost sundown. But my thirst had

gone, and my hunger, too, which I took as an omen that the Great Spirit was with me. At length, with the falling of night, I did sleep again and the dream came to me."

"Tell us! Tell us!"

Hawk smiled, savoring the moment. Gyva saw his eyes touch those of Little Swallow; she saw the certainty in his glance. Hawk knew he had brought home a gift for her as well as for the tribe, an offering of certainty and power. *You shall be a chieftain's wife,* he was telling her with his eyes.

"While deep in sleep," he began, "the image of a mighty bird came to me, and it was as if I at once saw the bird and was the bird, which was wide of wing and strong of talon, and in appearance did resemble the mountain hawk. The bird, too, was red of hue, red as the russet flowers in the fields in fall, red like the gloss on the flanks of a roan, brilliant as the oak leaves in the days of early frost. And this bird, which I both saw and was, sped fast and fleet above a gorgeous land, and protected the land and all who loved it and lived on it. Yet one day, in flight, the bird spied a white rabbit entering the land, eating and nibbling and defiling that which grew upon the land, and the bird knew this rabbit would reproduce and reproduce and reproduce until nothing would be left of the land or on the land. And so he did drop from the sky, fast and silent as an arrow, down and down upon the rabbit, and there below the bursting sky did the bird rend and tear the soft flesh of the rabbit, and he fed upon it, and what remained he took back to the mountains as food for his young!"

Hawk nodded somberly and crossed his arms. The people, much impressed, made quiet exclamations one to another. They were greatly pleased. Hawk's vision was so bold, so clear, touched so directly the emotion hidden within their own hearts, that no interpretation was necessary.

Gyva, unsettled by Hawk's cleverness, turned to re-

gard Torch. What had he seen? Would it be as striking as the vision of Hawk. At the same time she was
angry. She *knew* that Hawk and Swallow had conspired to gain unfair advantage thus far, and she certainly would not put it past Hawk to contrive now
a vision that he knew would evoke a response in the
people. A red bird like unto a hawk! Indeed! And a
white rabbit! Was that not a fine story to believe in,
and to repeat and repeat around the winter fires, all
down the days! She remembered her promise to prove
that Hawk and Swallow had cheated. Bold words. How
would she ever be able to do that?

Now attention focused on Torch. He was still quiet
and self-contained, and he seemed vaguely puzzled.
When he began to speak, it was with uncharacteristic
gentleness, ruminative in tone.

"According to the straws," he began, "I left our
village and went west into the forested parts of the
mountains. As I walked, I received a distinct feeling
that something was waiting for me in the west, or
calling me in that direction. At first, I believed it to
be the Great Spirit, with the dream I must possess.
This did prove to be true, but what I felt was born
of something else, as if a glimpse of another time were
being visited upon me, but whether past or future I
could not tell. It was almost as if I had lived before,
or perhaps would die and live again. I do not know,
for it was a very strange thing."

Gyva suppressed a shudder, and saw that the people
were exchanging glances. Had Torch become too fatigued during the ordeal? Certainly his manner of
speaking was not as it had been. She watched his face
closely, thinking he might be ill, as he continued.

"But disturbing perception or no, I did continue
into the west until the sun went down and the air
grew cool. I found a sleeping place within a stand of
hazelnut and hickory, fell into sleep; and while in the
land of dreams, my vision did come. I was walking
through a forest, along the banks of a mighty river.

I had never seen the river before, and yet, as with my earlier feeling, the river, too, was familiar to me. The thought came to me that, far ahead, around a bend in this great ribbon of water, I would discover something of incomparable meaning, both to me and to all of us as a nation. It seemed I marched and marched for many moons, took no rest, no food, drank no water from the river, although in my vision it sparkled like a liquid jewel. I was simultaneously driven on toward something of great significance, and attracted to it, as one is curious to learn the nature of a lover, or a secret."

He did not look at Gyva.

"And I saw no one during all this time. Finally, in a place where an arrow-shaped bluff jutted into the river, a bluff laden with pine trees so thick against one another a man could move but slowly upon it, the river itself swung into a great bend, and ran straight west into the eternal sun. And there, beneath the bluff, where the sand was red and soft and fine, Ababinili instructed me to lie down and sleep. Thus it was that I embraced a sleep within a sleep, and grew twice as close to the feral heartbeat of the wide universe."

What is this? the people were wondering. Never had they heard such a dream-vision, or one recounted in so strange a way. Some were recalling Torch's intricate words on the day of his first blooding. Old Teva had her eyes on him, watching, examining; and there were even a few among the crowd of listeners who seemed to step away from Torch, as if he, too, like the old crone, possessed dark gifts of knowledge.

"In my second sleep, Ababinili bade me rise, and so it was that within the scope of one trek I was ordered to embark upon another. Again, for many moons did I march, within the circle of the second sleep, and again did I move along a mighty river. In this dream, too, the river swung west around a pine-laden bluff, and on the banks where the sand was red and fine the Great Spirit ordered me to thrust my hand into the

red sand. This I did, as he commanded, and my
fingers closed upon a length of wood that had been
buried in the sand, and which I now withdrew. It
proved to be a stick, much like the Red Sticks warriors
carry into battle, but it was not a war stick. It was a
golden stick, and on it, in the letters of our nation,
delicately inscribed, was the secret of life."

Because Torch had been speaking so quietly, the
people, too, had listened with intense concentration.
Now they gasped aloud, an exhalation of wonder. The
secret of life! It was a wondrous thing. On Hawk's
dark features fear flickered, and savage resentment.
His look was one of a man who has suddenly learned
that he is not as intelligent as he had believed. Little
Swallow, Gyva observed, shared his stricken look. They
had planned so well and worked so hard, and now . . .

Too bad for them, thought Gyva spitefully. How
could she herself have doubted that evil would be
defeated!

"Tell us what it is! Tell us the secret of life!" implored the tribe.

"This is indeed the deepest vision ever to have been
granted one who sought the leadership of the Chickasaw," agreed Teva, "and well does it behoove you to
tell us this secret which has eluded men since time
began." Already the hand-shaped birthmark upon her
face was pulsing with buried blood, scarlet like wisdom or doom, however one was disposed to read its
gleaming portent.

Torch was silent for some time, and it seemed he
was permitting the suspense to grow, as Hawk had
done earlier in the telling of his own tale. But it
proved not to be so.

"In my second sleep," Torch went on after a while,
"I held the stick and read the words inscribed thereupon. Then Ababinili commanded me to bury the
stick once again in the sand, after committing the
words to my heart. This I did, with the thought that
the secret of life was as sweet and as simple and as

powerful as the love of an innocent child. And it was with great joy that I received the order to retrace my steps back along the river. This, too, I did, and I reached the place beneath the bluff where I lay in my first sleep, dreaming my first vision. I entered back within myself, lying there upon red sand, and I awoke into my first sleep as well.

"There Ababinili waited, and he bade me awaken from my first sleep, too, and with joy I obeyed, sitting up on the sand in the warm sun of the day. 'Now you may return to your people,' he said to me, and left me to join He-Who-Dwells-in-the-Clear-Sky. I started back along the river to the place where I lay sleeping in the hazelnut and hickory, soaring with a feeling of blessedness that I had never known before, or even imagined.

"But as I strode along, it seemed to me that something was missing. But what? I had only my bow and quiver to begin with, moccasins and breechcloth. All of these I still possessed. And then, in horror, did I know what was missing. The secret of life, which I had committed to memory, had fled the mystic caverns of my mind!

"No deer has ever raced as swiftly, nor eagle flown as fast, as I now ran back along the river bank to the bluff where the red sand was. Weeping, calling upon the Great Spirit, I crawled upon the sand, thrusting my hands into it, until I remembered that I had re-buried the sacred stick in the sand on the bank of the river of my second dream-sleep. Now I lay down on the shore and tried again to sleep, that I might go back and once again read the secret on the stick. But it was no use. At last, knowing futility, I arose and returned to myself in the hazel thicket of my true sleep, and came back into myself, awakening. And so did I return here to you, to tell you of the vision with which I was gifted, and which haunts me still, and which will live in my heart forever."

Torch fell silent. The very sky seemed dark. No one moved or spoke, and every eye was upon him.

Hawk was grinning. "A beautiful story," he mocked. "Where is the headdress and ornamentation of the chieftaincy? They belong to me now."

To his surprise, although there were some murmurs of assent, no outcry of support came from the people. Their gaze had passed from Torch to the soothsayer.

"It is indeed a mighty vision that you have had," she said slowly, "and I must decide what it means."

"Wait!" cried Hawk. "Before this thing is decided, why do we not wait until the war party returns? They also have a right to hear these things, and pass judgment upon them!"

Gyva did not fail to perceive the waver of fear in his voice as he saw the prospect of power slipping away. "It was you, Hawk," she cried, "who was in such haste to proceed, mere minutes ago. So now do you wish the support of your renegade roughnecks when Teva mulls the decision? Who knows when the braves will return?"

There were some who deplored her outspoken words, holding in their minds a memory of her behavior over the past days. But there were many, too, who remained silent.

"Teva must interpret the vision of Torch," many said. "It is something beyond our knowledge."

"Torch's dream is naught but a vision of failure," Hawk snorted, edging back into his usual manner of arrogant abrasiveness.

It was at that moment, when everyone was occupied with the conflict here and with Torch's strange tale, that Gyva spied Little Swallow ease away from the group and move off quickly toward her dwelling place. What did she have in mind now, this sneaky little bird who would bed many and deceive more to work her way toward power?

"I gave the vision to you as it was given to me,"

Torch said, calm and untroubled now after his recitation.

"Hah!" Hawk scoffed.

The people, however, were not half so brash. "It is not a thing for fast decision," they declared, repeating the judgment among themselves. "See how the blood has gone to Teva's mark of magic."

It was true. Torn between the desire to remain and listen to what the seeress would say, and to follow Swallow and see what she was about, Gyva could not decide what to do. Then she felt eyes upon her, and sought them out. Torch was looking at her. She touched eyes with him, giving her love. Then he glanced in the direction of Swallow's departure. Was he trying to tell her something? Yes. Quietly Gyva left the throng and slipped between wigwams, out of sight. She would keep a hard eye on a dangerous bird.

Gyva knew the wigwam in which Swallow slept and dreamed and spun her webs, and no brave would have stolen more stealthily than did Gyva now, advancing upon it. For a moment she hesitated outside the entrance, then quickly, boldly, she threw the skins aside.

No one was there.

Gyva looked around, surprised. She had expected to come upon the other maiden. But inside the wigwam there were but eight or nine sleeping places laid out on the floor, the skins and blankets neatly arranged. On the tent-poles hung various pouches for personal possessions, some large, some small, but basically just like Gyva's own little leather purse. She saw Swallow's hanging there, marked by a small bird outlined in beadwork on the leather. A dark temptation arrived within Gyva's soul.

Then she was pulling loose the drawstring and peering inside, trembling with excitement and rage. In the pouch, in addition to the bracelets and necklaces and earrings, were at least a half-dozen nails of the type that had been buried in the ground by the hurdle.

If Gyva had failed to show evidence of the drinking flask at Hawk's tent, here in the pouch was incontrovertible evidence of Swallow's perfidy in the earlier matter of the hurdle races! Gyva snatched the pouch from its peg and went to find the evil maiden.

She accosted Swallow at the edge of the village, and lifted the pouch. A look of fear passed over Swallow's lovely face. Then she steeled herself.

"What do you mean by taking my belongings?" she demanded.

"Come with me!" ordered Gyva, in a tone that brooked no refusal.

"Where?"

"Up to the village where our people are gathered."

"Hah! You speak presumptuously of *our* people, you of mixed blood."

"That will be of no importance, after what I am about to show."

"Have caution," smirked Swallow, not at all as afraid as Gyva had expected her to be.

But Gyva did not dwell upon it. She was determined once and for all to show how perfidious Hawk and Swallow had been, and to see Torch become the true, unquestionable chief.

Teva and the tribespeople were still in deliberation when Gyva pushed Swallow into their midst.

"And what is this?" cried Hawk, his eyes going from Swallow to the beaded pouch in Gyva's hand.

"I am about to display evidence—" Gyva declared, turning to meet the eyes of the people, "evidence that the manhood ritual has been tainted since the first event."

This was an accusation akin to one of sacrilege. A somber, almost threatening mood, with an undercurrent of alarm, came over the tribe.

"Are you certain of this?" Torch asked, most severely.

She was a little surprised that he was not more pleased with her strategem, but too excited to give his reaction much thought. She pressed on, opening the pouch, and drawing forth the handful of wooden nails. She held them aloft.

"The very same nails," she cried, "that were buried in the footpath at the hurdle, to injure the fastest of our runners, to sabotage his chances to become chieftain!"

She swept them all with her proud glance. "I daresay other events were also tainted."

Torch did not move. His face revealed nothing.

All Gyva could see, for an eternal moment, was Swallow's smooth smile.

"This is a most serious accusation," the old seeress said, her voice more sad than grave.

For the first time Gyva felt a quiver of doubt. The people were not responding as, in her excitement, she had expected. They were looking at the nails, true, but they did not see in them the indisputable evidence Gyva herself had seen.

"Swallow," spoke Teva, "what say you to this accusation?"

The crafty maiden answered confidently, and with a touch of anguished innocence. "I was asked to help in the clearing of the earth that is now our playing field. And I did take several of the nails as a remembrance. I pray that I did not give offense by so doing."

The people muttered darkly, watching Gyva with angry eyes. More trouble from the mixed-blood! And now Gyva knew the folly to which her desire for revenge had led her. She had disgraced herself utterly this time. And yet she had been so certain of her evidence.

"A pernicious and baseless accusation," Hawk declared, "requires the judgment of the tribe on the person who has made the calumny. A false accusation is a crime against the harmony of the tribe."

"Yes, it is so," called the people, speaking one to another.

"Banishment is the usual sentence," Hawk reminded them, helpfully.

"I shall not go," Gyva declared, containing her anger with an effort of will, and trying to hide humiliation behind a pride sorely wounded.

"There! You see!" cried Little Swallow gleefully. "She causes trouble and makes false accusations, and *then* does she yet possess the temerity to announce that the will of our people is not applicable to her. What gall has this one of mixed blood!"

It was clear, from the words spoken by the few as well as those unspoken by the many, that Gyva's position in the eyes of the people was deteriorating by the moment. Teva, to whom the people turned, possessor of knowledge and ancient law that she was, could not without a display of capricious favoritism ignore or overrule the right of Hawk and Little Swallow to bring Gyva to lawful sanction. Thus she could not ameliorate the situation with a quick judgment of dismissal, especially since the people were in a state of high agitation. Torch perceived the witch-woman's dilemma and sought at least to postpone whatever trial might be visited upon the girl whom he had loved so well.

"This is a grievous matter," he declared, "but it is not preeminent. We have other important concerns. One of our children languishes now in the hands of the white jackals. Our war party might even now be shedding blood to save our sacred homeland. And the matter of the chieftaincy awaits Teva's counsel with the spirits of the dark sky. Let us turn first to these important matters and—"

"Nay! The fair-skinned maiden of deception may flee the tribe and thus escape justice!" So shrieked Little Swallow.

"Is that not what you wished?" Torch replied coldly. "Banishment?"

"Not without the sanction! Not without the trial!"

"Ah!" said Torch. "I am soothed by your regard for the procedures of law."

But Swallow had erred in the passion of her speech. Members of the tribe began to perceive unseemly rancor in a maiden who claimed, in all innocence, to have been wronged.

"Torch is correct," the people were saying now. "Let us resolve the chieftaincy first, and from that all things shall follow."

Thus was it decided. Teva returned to her wigwam, to pray and meditate upon the dreams, seeking in them the hidden prophecy of good fortune for the Chickasaw. The tribespeople pursued their normal activities for the remainder of the day, but thought often upon the matter of the dreams. Tension simmered in the village by the time of the evening meal, a pervasive unease—almost distress—caused by many things. Gyva held to her wigwam, making do with a repast of bread and dried corn, not because she feared to go out amongst the people, but because she realized that her appearance would only exacerbate a dangerous situation.

Finally the sun fell behind the Twin Mountains, and from the doorway of her wigwam she watched it descend and disappear. It was not yet chill, but she shivered. She shivered because, whether Torch became chieftain or not, her own life—all that it had been, all that it would be—hung in the balance. If Hawk became the leader, Gyva would surely be cast out of the tribe. And even if her own lover should prevail, she might still be charged with lies and brought before the tribe for judgment. And then she might still be banished!

Watching the Twin Mountains blend into the purple sky, then shadow against it, then disappear, Gyva felt herself spinning upon a delicate point of time. More and more fragile became the beloved earth upon which she stood; darker and darker grew the surrounding abyss. Cloud cover came up this night, speeding in about the mountains, borne on a wind from the west. The west. From there the wind came, and there had Torch sojourned in his dream. There, far off, flowed Father-of-the-Waters, of which she had heard around the winter fires, but which she had never seen, believed she never would see. There, beyond the mighty river, must be a land of warmth and plenty, a place to which one might pass after death. It seemed so peaceful to think upon.

I shall not die, she thought, pulling herself together. *I shall not die until I am ready. Nor shall I suffer banishment*, she added defiantly.

Later, upon the soft but unbefitting rabbit skins, Gyva heard the sentries taking up their positions, calling softly to one another. Perhaps the war party would return by night; perhaps Roo-Pert Harris would come with his red beard and his jackals, thirsty for blood. Let them come.

Darkness drifted in slowly upon Gyva. She closed her eyes and saw behind them flashing patterns of colored light, gossamer filaments of sleep come to soothe her mind in the wrap and warmth of dreams. It came, sleep did, without her knowledge, and she was far out into the mountains where she had never been before. There was a sense of many people with her, behind her; but she could see no one, and she felt alone. Yet in spite of her solitude she was not distressed, nor did she feel isolation. She divined a great barrier somewhere ahead, a barrier that was at once as wide as time, as rich as a golden road . . . .

But dreams, to Indian maidens, are simply dreams, not portents, and even in sleep Gyva knew that images were only dreams. And so she vanished to a darker place, where everything and all she was curled softly and warmly and deep.

THE BOOK OF

EXILE

CHAPTER I

He could no longer walk, and so they dragged him into the village, behind horses. His hands were tied behind his back, a stout length of wood thrust through the knots. Twisted, the wood cut off circulation altogether, and the wood had been twisted many times. The man's wrists were cut to the bone, but he could not feel the pain. He was unconscious, near death.

"We have a prisoner," crowed Fast River, a young brave returned with the war party. "The only one strong enough to survive."

"A great victory has been given us!" cried the others. "The white men are dead in ravines and bushes and riverbeds."

"And this one will soon join them," said Arrow-in-Oak. "But not so quickly."

"He looks dead already," observed Teva, coming from her wigwam.

In truth the captive did look lifeless, slumped face-first in the dust. Villagers gathered around.

"See, he wears buckskins."

"It is true. A buckskinner. A killer."

"He shall pay. We shall see him die!" cried a young brave, eager to make entertainment with their helpless captive.

"He was a coward as well," one said. "When we attacked, he did not resist. Why, I believe he did not even carry a knife."

Gyva pushed through the crowd to take a look at this odd white jackal who was so timorous. Dirty,

bloody, and unconscious, he was not prepossessing;
but she saw that he was tall, with a strong, broad-
shouldered body, and that his hair was golden, like
corn silk or flax. Someone pushed him onto his back.
Gyva looked more closely. The captive was handsome,
at least for a white man. He looked very intelligent,
and not unkind.

"Let us get him to the gallows," someone urged.

"No," demurred Teva. "There are other affairs
which we must first consummate."

She began to explain what had transpired since the
war party had departed the village, and now the
braves looked around, saw that Torch and Hawk had
returned from their quests of the vision. A new wave
of excitement rose from the people, for clearly Teva
had spent the night in contemplation, and now must
render a judgment.

"Take the prisoner to a wigwam, and post a guard,"
ordered Arrow-in-Oak. "Later, after the chief is named,
we shall skin him alive, as a symbol of what we mean
to do to our white neighbors in Harrisville."

Spirited cries of affirmation met this suggestion, and
the buckskinned captive was dragged to a dwelling
and thrown unceremoniously inside. Gyva thought she
saw him open his eyes for a moment; she was certain
that she heard him moan in pain.

The braves had brought with them several bundles
of the white man's belongings, and eagerly the women
of the tribe set to examining them. Strange it was that
here among buckskin jackets and heavily woven shirts
were also the fine dresses of a white lady, and even the
clothing of a child! But there was little time to wonder
about the matter. A summons to council was heard.

Every member of the tribe gathered in the center
of the village. By this time those who had heard the
dreams on the previous day had related them to the
returned warriors, provoking much excited discussion.
Hawk and Torch took up positions on either side of
the old witch-woman, and she raised her arms to quiet

the tribe. All but ignored, Gyva hung about the fringes of the crowd. She saw that Hawk's hotheads were massed together near the two candidates, and also that all of them were armed. Little Swallow, her chest swelled today by much more than her proud breasts, turned her head this way and that, as if showing off, or practicing a posture worthy of a chieftain's wife.

Never had Gyva felt so lowered in the eyes of her tribespeople. To have permitted such a one as Little Swallow to beat her so badly . . .

"Sleep was no friend to me on the evening past," Teva began, "for my heart suffered beneath a burden weighty as the world."

A hum of anticipation rose from the assembled tribe.

"It was my fate from birth, either the blessing or the curse of He-Who-Dwells-in-the-Clear-Sky, that I be selected to ponder difficult things, as the blood-mark upon my face attests. I accept this responsibility because I cannot flee it, although many times throughout my life—and this is one such time—I would gladly have given up the duty, and been born instead a small creature happy beneath the green boughs of our forests, content to live from moon to glowing moon within the caverns of our hills."

The people nodded. Not many of them, today, would have wished to bear the responsibility of interpreting so crucial a matter as a chieftain's vision.

"Times have grown more and more difficult and threatening during the suns I have seen. In the old days, candidates returned from the forest with visions easily read, the meaning of which was clear to each and every one. But in these more trying times, complexity abounds. It is as if Ababinili wishes to try us in all things."

She paused for a long time, and the people regarded her. Hawk and Torch stood motionless, their eyes upon a far distance. Neither displayed the least tension, and yet what thoughts must be flashing through their minds! Power, glory, the long burden of responsibility . . .

Gyva tried to touch eyes with her lover, but it was useless. As she had speculated earlier, so did she again: Whether chieftain or no, a part of him was lost to her now, was above her now. But if only she could climb together with him to those places, share with him all that was or would be!

"You have heard the visions of Torch and Hawk," the seeress was saying. "And upon those visions I have spent the dark hours of the night. There was no moon, and thus even without heaven's light did I struggle."

Now, as one, the tribe gasped and then cried out. For beneath the flesh on the face of the withered crone, blood began to rise and course into the mark of the hand.

"*Aye!*" she cried, feeling the heat of the blood. "My hours were well spent, for now comes the sign to me —spectral or benevolent, only history will say—but it comes, and I shall ride it like a golden wind, and I shall tell the tale to thee!"

Even the mountains seemed to quiet now, and the colored birds, and the myriad animals that shared Chickasaw earth. Lush green wind-bent grass straightened in the silence, and the sky itself stilled in hush above this magnificent land that had been gifted to the nation for as long as the rivers flow.

"Hawk has brought back to us a vision as clear and direct as the point of an arrow piercing the heart of a man."

"Yes! Yes, he has!" cried the hotheads and many others.

"While Torch has been presented with, and has in turn presented us with, a strange vision at once soothing and disquieting."

Silence.

"And while I lay upon my pelts, I pondered this throughout the night. The clear vision as opposed to that which is more obscure, and in suffering and travail did I struggle to interpret what wisdom is and what life is."

The mark upon Teva's face was purple now, and the blood throbbed so powerfully beneath it that the handprint seemed to flex and relax upon her visage.

"And in the end it came to me," Teva said, "that life is neither clear nor direct. I believe there is, somewhere, buried in sand along a river upon this earth, or hidden among golden crystals along the paths of heaven, a stick upon which is indeed written the secret of life. I believe we shall one day know that secret. That we do not know it now is neither our defect nor that of Torch, but—"

At the sound of *but* the hotheads shrieked and wailed. They were certain Hawk had the power now.

"*But*," repeated the witch-woman, "to have been gifted with even a glimmer of such a deep mystery is a mark of special favor, both to our people and to Torch."

She put it to them simply, a decision of heaven.

"By his vision, as much as by his strength and example, Torch is our new chief!"

Gyva felt her heart flood with joy, and a great cry of gladness rose up from the people, or rather, from most of the people. The hotheads were silent at first, muttering to one another. Little Swallow, whom Gyva glimpsed, seemed simultaneously stricken with fever and possessed by rage. Hawk was frozen to his place on the earth, his face a mask of hurt and disbelief and anger.

Torch's expression did not change. He was as he had always been, and yet he had changed. All knew it. He was above them now, and would forever regard them as from a slight rise. No longer would he merely give his attention, offer his concern. No, in future he would bestow them as one would a gift, and in that wise, too, would his offerings be accepted . . .

"No!" Hawk screamed then, "I do not accept it!"

Before anyone could react, before most of the tribespeople even knew what was happening, he had seized the knife from his belt, vaulted over Teva, and thrown himself upon Torch.

If such sacrilege had ever before been committed, it was beyond the memory of the tribe. Even the hotheads were initially astounded, though not so much that they refrained from reaching for their own weapons. If power was indeed to be seized, then let it be. After all, Torch could not be chief if he was dead.

But Torch's vision, and Teva's interpretation, bore no trace of taint. Hawk's first thrust buried his knife in the ground, and while he struggled to draw it forth, Torch twisted free and leaped to his feet, drawing his own knife from its leather scabbard.

"Do not do this thing, Hawk," he warned. "I would be your friend as well as your chief, and the tribe has need of your courage."

But Hawk, having already commenced his assault, was not to be gainsaid, or dissuaded by words alone. Rising from the earth, he slashed forward, the knife in his hand meant for Torch's heart.

"Heaven and visions I curse," he roared, "the spilling of blood is what makes chief and man!"

Torch, with a deft flick of his hand, sent his knife through the air. It struck Hawk directly in the heart, stopped his forward plunge. Hawk's heart was already dead; his brain lived on for a fleeting moment. In that moment he seemed to remember what he had been, had hoped, seemed to recognize what he had become, and to realize the horror of what he had attempted to do. Still on his feet, and gripping the hilt of Torch's knife as if trying to pull it from his breast, Hawk looked at the man who had killed him and said, "So the tribe is yours. I go now to . . . seek . . . the golden stick . . . ."

He crashed down upon the earth, rolled over once, and lay still. Within the moment Swallow was howling over his body, trying to kiss life back into it.

"It is over," Torch told her, gently pulling her away.

Swallow stopped wailing. Gyva was unsettled by the way she let Torch comfort her.

Now Torch faced the tribe, especially the hotheads. "If there are any others who disagree with what fate has chosen, I invite you now to come forward," he said. "If such turmoil should have come to our people that now we must choose our leader by blood, then so be it. Step forward."

"No, no!" cried the people. "That is not as it is meant." And the hotheads, sobered by the dispatch with which Hawk had been destroyed, made quick to offer fealty to the new chief.

"Thus it has come to pass," cried Teva, "and thus it is to be."

"Let all the braves follow me to hold counsel," Torch commanded. "We have much to determine, and our destiny first of all."

"What of Hawk?" someone asked.

"Bury him like a dog!" came the response. "Bury him in a shallow grave at the edge of the forest, where rats and weasels and wild dogs can dig up and gorge upon his flesh."

"No," Torch decided quickly. "He had faults, as do we all, but he was first a warrior, and served the nation well. The women will prepare his body now, and we shall bury him as a brave. Let us go."

So the men went off to hold counsel, to discuss the captive, and Roo-Pert Harris, and the fate of Bright Badger, and tribal policy for the days ahead. Gyva sought to help the women who would bathe and dress the body of Hawk, but they sent her away.

"Hypocrite," one said, although Gyva had meant only to act in accordance with the spirit of reconciliation so recently proclaimed by Torch.

"We have had enough of you, white daughter," others said.

In the end, bereft and verging on heartbreak, Gyva was alone. She wandered about on the outside of the village, unable to feel much except her own pain and a vague joy for Torch. It seemed that a vast gulf separated them now, and that it always would. She seemed unable to focus her mind on that, however, and felt like disappearing into the trees. Then, walking behind a row of wigwams, she heard a soft moaning, and remembered the captive, who was at least as alone and abandoned as she was herself.

No one noticed Gyva when she entered the wigwam. The captive lay on his side on the floor of the dwelling, sweating profusely now, as if he had been taken by fever. Overcome by sympathy, despite the fact that this yellow-haired white man might well have killed some of her people in days past, Gyva knelt down and hesitantly touched his forehead. His eyes fluttered and she quickly drew back her hand. He moaned again and opened his eyes. Gyva was startled by their color, which was the clearest, palest blue, like ice in a winter lake. Yet their effect was not one of coldness but rather of directness, of honesty.

"Wa-ter . . ." he gasped. "Please."

Still kneeling beside him, Gyva debated with herself. He was a captured enemy and thus had no claim to comfort of any kind. On the other hand, the braves had said he had not fought during the battle, and certainly he did not have a knife. What harm could a measure of water do? A bucket rested at the base of the main pole that supported the wigwam's horseshoe-shaped roof, and a dipper hung from a nail on the pole. Gyva filled the dipper and carried it to Golden-Hair. Tied hand and foot and lying on his side, he could not drink properly. Without thinking about it, Gyva put her arm under his head, bracing him, and lifted the dipper to his lips. He drank, tentatively at first, the water spilling over his parched lips, down his fine, square chin. Then he began to gulp deeply. She withdrew the dipper.

"Not so fast," she said, using the English that Teva had taught her. "It is not good."

His eyes opened wide in surprise, and he peered at her from behind fevered lids.

"I speak your tongue," she said, "but I am Chickasaw."

It was as if this news discouraged him, just when he had felt a glimmer of hope. Perhaps he had thought Gyva was someone who might have helped him. Now he seemed to sag in resignation.

"Please. More water," he asked in a dull voice.

"Yes, but you must drink slowly. You will take cramps."

He looked up at her in startled surprise. "Am I not to die anyway?" he asked. Then he smiled. It was Gyva's turn to be startled. He had a lovely smile, for a white jackal.

She gave him some more water, then lowered his head to the earthen floor of the wigwam.

"Thank you," he said.

Gyva knew she ought to move away from him, leave the dwelling, but for some reason—perhaps simply the desire for some kind of companionship—she remained kneeling beside him.

"Are you in great pain?" she asked, after a little while.

"I cannot . . . feel my hands . . ." he said. "Are they still a part of me?"

"Yes," she said, glancing at the knots behind his back. Golden-Hair's hands were almost purple from lack of circulation. Impulsively she yanked from the knots the wooden stick that had been jammed into them, releasing the pressure somewhat. He could not escape anyway. What was the point of the added torment?

"You are kind," he said, feeling the pressure ease. "Will you not cause trouble for yourself?"

Again he had surprised her. He was thinking of *her* situation and safety. Was this not odd? Everyone knew that the white jackals cared not a thing for others, not even for those of their own kind. Was it some trick?

She drew away slightly, lest he have some ruse in store for her.

"What is the matter?" he asked. "Have I frightened you?"

"I told you I was a Chickasaw!" she declared, too passionately, and too quickly. "I am afraid of nothing."

He seemed to study her. "You look like an Indian," he said, after a moment, "and yet . . . no, I cannot see clearly. It is gloomy here, the light . . ."

"My mother was a white woman," Gyva heard herself tell him, wondering why she had done so. Was it because he seemed gentle? Was it because of his honest eyes?

"You have her beauty," he said. "Why are you here among these people?"

He was asking too much. "Why have you invaded our homelands?" she shot back.

His face darkened; he seemed sad. "I come to forget the past," he said, "and to farm in peace in the lands north of here."

"Harrisville?" she asked, thinking, peace indeed! Thinking of Bright Badger, abducted under her very eyes!

"Yes, that's the place. We were on our way there, by wagon train, when your braves attacked our party. We were not fighters. We were barely armed. And we were cut to ribbons." He gave her one of his piercing, direct looks. "Some of your people have little mercy," he declared. "I am glad to find, in you, an exception."

"Ah!" she said.

"Ah?" he repeated. "Your tone is puzzling."

"You seek by guile and flattery to turn me to your will."

His response was laughter, soft and immediate. "Would that I could, and then I should be free of this place."

"That will not be," she said, looking at him, feeling an unusual sadness come upon her.

"You are unhappy," he said. "Why? Certainly not because I am to be killed."

"Of course not! Every one of you white men deserves to die, for what you have done to us. Driven us from our hunting grounds, driven us back here into these mountains! Why—"

"Wait, I swear that I never—"

"—And the monster Jacksa Chula, who does not let us rest!"

"Wait—stop! Who is this monster?"

"The old and fierce one—Jacksa, who kills Indians."

"Do you mean Andrew Jackson?"

Gyva nodded decisively. "Aye! Jacksa," she repeated. "He who is called by the name of the hickory tree."

"He is no monster. He is friend to my family."

"But he has killed Chickasaw, and Cherokee, and Creek, and Fox, and—"

"And Indians have killed Floridians, and Georgians, and Carolinians, and Virginians, among which my family is numbered. We have lived there for two centuries, you know, and cultivate vast plantations."

Momentarily he seemed to grow very sad, thinking of something far and lost.

"Jackson is only defending white people here in the west from the depredations of savages."

Gyva considered his words. He was not speaking the truth, of course, could not be speaking the truth; but he apparently believed what he was saying, for in his voice was the ring of honesty. And he spoke formally —an educated man. Well, so he was misguided, not evil. It was unfortunate that he would have to die. No, he deserved to die. But—but if the white men felt the Indians were set upon killing *them*, and the Indians felt the white men were bent on the task of reciprocating . . .

Things were more complicated than she could at that moment decipher. Perhaps Torch's restraint in dealing with the white men was more salutary than she had once thought.

"We shall destroy Jacksa Chula," Gyva maintained, with more defiance than necessary.

"I doubt that," Golden-Hair replied. For the first time there was a touch of hardness, of steel, in his voice. "He is already a great leader of his people, and beloved here in Tennessee. One day he may well be—what do you call it? Great White Father?"

Gyva thought of the man who had killed her mother. She would not speak of this. He must not know of the terrible bond that connected her to Jackson, like a secret of the soul.

She stared coldly back at him.

"What is your name?" he asked after a moment.

"Why do you wish to know?"

"It is but a friendly question, an inquiry of courtesy among my people. I am Randolph, Jason Randolph. Of Virginia. I am a planter by heritage, and have read law and literature."

"And I am Dey-Lor-Gyva, and I make grain cakes, and know legends."

"Dey-la . . . *what*? Delia?"

"No, no. What? You cannot speak it? Dey-Lor-Gyva! Beloved-of-Earth, it means in my tongue."

"Ah, *Delia*!" he repeated, as if teasing her. "I believe I can pronounce it well enough."

"No, Dey-Lor-Gyva. My tribe calls me Gyva."

"No, I think Delia is much better. Have you a man, Delia? A husband?"

Gyva thought of Torch, felt Jason's eyes on her. Blood rose to her face.

"I see!" he cried.

"You see nothing," she said. "Have you a wife?"

Once more that look of sadness. "I did have," he replied. "I had a son as well. But they are . . . passed away."

The look of melancholy touched something in Gyva. She remembered the clothing in his baggage. "I am sorry," she said. "How?"

"They were killed," he answered, curtly but without

bitterness. "Killed and scalped in our house while I was away buying supplies. The house was burned, too," he added desolately.

Indians had killed his wife and child?

"Of what tribe were they?" she asked.

"What does it matter?"

"It matters a great deal. Were they Chickasaw?"

"It is all the same, is it not?"

"Nay. Not so. There are Chickasaws who are wicked, true, but . . ."

"So you are noble?" he asked, with a skeptical glance. "And the Choctaw, let us say, are savages?"

"The Choctaw are devious and unprincipled."

"That is a wondrous thing to know," Jason returned. "And I shall remember it tomorrow when I die on a Chickasaw gallows."

Startled to momentary silence, Gyva did not know how to answer him.

"Do you think you might be able to get me a bit of food?" she heard him asking.

"I do not know."

"A girl lovely as you? Certainly you must be able to have almost anything you desire among your people, just for the asking."

Now it was her turn to appear despondent. "I am not in favor."

Jason looked at her curiously. "What? Have you transgressed a code, Delia? Failed to keep your wigwam neat?"

"No, please do not jest. It is a serious thing to me."

He saw the seriousness of her concern, and asked to know the cause of her distress.

Perhaps it was his genuine interest, perhaps simply the fact that she had no other with whom to speak. But she told him everything, or almost everything. The conditions among her people, the manhood ritual, the struggle for the chieftaincy, Hawk and Little Swallow, and her own myriad blunders.

"And this Torch? He is the one called Firebrand, is he not?"

"Yes, but the appelation is most unjust, he—"

"And you love him, don't you?" Jason asked bluntly.

"Why, I . . . no . . . how did you . . . ?"

"Some things are the same in every land," he said quietly, "and among all people." He looked at her directly. "But had I your love, I would not treat it so."

"He . . . Torch . . . treats me . . . well. He has many complex matters before him."

"I expect that he does. But while he thinks of them, perhaps you could get me some food. I would be most grateful."

Thinking that perhaps she might be able to smuggle him at least a piece of barley cake, Gyva started to rise, when the sounds of voices and footsteps approached the wigwam.

"Oh, I must be—"

"Delia . . ."

"I ought not be here."

But it was too late. The hanging skins at the entryway were pushed aside, and several braves peered in.

"Gyva again!" one cried.

"Plotting with the captive!"

"Has she released him? I am sure she has released him."

"No, he is still here."

"But she *intended* to release him—that is certain. Else what is she doing here?"

"What is this?" demanded Torch, entering. He wore the headdress of a chieftain. He looked as somber, remote, and powerful as ancient law; he seemed to have aged ten years in the space of a day. "Gyva . . ."

"I but gave the prisoner water," Gyva said, standing before him, meeting his eyes. She did not shrink away. She was the one who had so many times given him ultimate delight. She knew his body and how it responded as well as—if not better than—she knew the way of the rapids in the river, the soft trails down among the forest trees. If by donning the portentous headdress, Torch had forgotten what she knew of him, had given him, then all was over, and the better to know it now.

But he had not forgotten. She saw it in his eyes, and she saw that he was vastly troubled now, torn between love and duty.

"You ought not to be here," he declared softly, but authoritatively, too.

"His wife and son were killed by Indians!" cried Gyva.

All eyes turned to her.

"How sad," exclaimed Tall Heron.

"I believe it is her white blood speaking," observed Arrow-in-Oak, his voice heavy with sarcasm. " 'His wife and son were killed by Indians!' How devastating for the unfortunate jackal."

"I am overcome," mourned Fast River, bending over the captive, reinserting the stick in the knot that bound Jason's hands, giving several brutal twists. Jason cried out.

"Will you not have sufficient opportunity to torment him tomorrow?" Gyva cried.

"He might practice screaming now," grunted Tall Heron.

Fast River twisted the wood some more.

"De-liaaa . . ." sighed Jason, and passed into unconsciousness.

"What was that he said?" asked Torch sharply.

"It is what he calls me. He cannot or will not speak my true name."

Torch frowned. The others grunted. "So you have spoken with him for a long period?"

"Not so long."

"You have exchanged names."

"What is that?"

"Much, when you are already—" Torch broke off and looked at the other braves. "See to preparations for the execution," he commanded. When they had departed, he looked sorrowfully at Gyva. "We must talk," he said.

"Then do so."

"Not here," he said. "I must meet you one last time in our special place."

Her heart went cold, but she suppressed a shudder. *One last time!* No, that was not true. That could never be true. She herself would change the will of heaven, and thus render false his thoughtless words. She would seek Teva's magic. She would invoke her own magic . . . .

"When the moon begins to hide behind the second mountain," he said, and strode through the door of the wigwam, rippling the skins that hung in the entryway.

Moments later Gyva left, too. But not before she removed the stick in the knots that bound Jason Randolph.

CHAPTER II

Clouds drifted in to cover the stars and the moon. Lying awake in her wigwam, Gyva tried to judge the time. Around her, women were tossing, snoring; children were muttering in their sleep. Torch was chief of the Chickasaw, but there was no great measure of peace among his people. Perhaps it was too soon for peace.

If I go too soon to the willows, Gyva was thinking, I will lose by the appearance of anxiety what hold I might yet maintain over him. But if I go too late, I may lose a last chance to be of influence to him.

She peered out of the wigwam and tried to judge where the moon might be. The village—her home village, which she had known forever—lay crouched against the darkness of the night, beneath the darkness of the mountains. For one long, excruciating moment it seemed suddenly remote, alien to her. Wigwams that had passed before her vision ten thousand times or more now loomed low upon the ancient Chickasaw earth, and Gyva had a shuddering premonition: *In the hearts of your people you are not wanted anymore.*

She thought with true sympathy of the white man who lay not far away, awaiting the dawn of his death day. Was there some comfort, whatever the agony might be, in knowing the day on which one was to die? He did not seem a dangerous or warlike man, this Jason Randolph. What had happened to him had been bad luck and accident, just as—with the timing, machinations, and good luck of Little Swallow, Gyva herself had been brought low by ill luck and accident. What would it be like, she wondered, to know you were going to die? That one morning hence, the sun would rise warm and shining upon the mountains, the fragrance of a thousand flowers would ride the blue air, and the living would eat and drink and laugh and steal away to know the keen delight of a lover's body. And you yourself would be dead.

Was it greater to hold a lover in your arms, to lose yourself in mortal ecstasy, or to ride the far hills of heaven, cold and alone, no longer capable of touching or of being touched?

The answer to that question came in a flash.

Gyva left her dwelling and fairly flew along the meadow to the place of the brooding willows. Yet she did not go forth with a glad heart. She knew already that the meeting toward which she sped was mournful in purpose and in spirit. Behind her, from the village, she seemed to hear a mysterious voice, like an echo, but stronger, and it called, *"Delia, Delia, Delia . . . ."*

Was she being sought out, named, rendered at once different and oddly substantial? It was almost as though a stranger's words had fragmented her identity, had caused her to become a conundrum unto herself.

"Dey-Lor-Gyva," Torch murmured, as she entered the veiled sanctuary of the living trees. But he did not come to her, or take her in his arms. Gyva sensed this even before her eyes perceived his stiff stance in the night. She stopped, and stood straight, too, and did not go to him.

Nor did she speak a word.

"Gyva? It is you?"

"No, it is Swallow, come to whore for the love of a chief!" Gyva replied bitterly.

"Do not say such."

She turned as if to leave, a movement born not of loss but of the knowledge of loss impending.

"Stay!" There was urgency in his voice, an urgency

not of physical need, but different, perhaps greater, if such a thing could be.

"You are my chieftain. I obey."

"Must it be so between the two of us?"

"Must it be? I am here again, as so many other nights I have been here."

A long pause, then: "Well do I recall those nights, and never shall time take the memory from me."

An ominous *but* hung unspoken on his words. She waited for it to come from his tongue, yet it did not.

"You did ask that I come here?" she said.

Tides of emotion—wordless, vexing, profound—swirled about them in the night.

He hesitated further, then nerved himself. "Do you wish to remain among our people?"

The tribe had cried "Banish her! Banish her!" but surely . . .

With a pain keener than she had ever known Gyva framed her reply: "Where I am not wanted, I shall not be. But where else can I go?"

The other tribes would not be overjoyed to take in a mixed-blood who had been expelled by her own people. And beyond them there were only the pale jackals, who would perceive in her not the white blood of her mother's heritage, but her raven-black hair, her onyx eyes, and the fact that she lived and dressed and acted and *was* a Chickasaw.

"We have held counsel upon many things," Torch was telling her. "And many words were spoken upon the things that you have done these past days."

She made bold to say what was in her heart. "You are the leader now. Why listen to the public gossip of fools?"

He spoke sadly. "That is true, I am the leader, and I both wished it to be and did not wish it so. As one brave, uncalled to leadership by Ababinili, I might have taken you upon my horse, and we two could have ridden where the sun sleeps, and worried for naught but ourselves. But—"

"Now you have spoken the *but*, that I have heard since I came here to you. Pray, do go on, and tell me what your heart holds."

"You are a strong woman, and I do respect it."

"And you a strong man—so say it."

"But I am no longer one brave, capable of cradling my own destiny, to be concerned with it alone. I have sought the chieftaincy, and I have won it."

Gyva's mind leaped ahead of Torch's words. "You are telling me that the nation is your lover now," she accused, not without hurt.

Torch went silent. Then: "In a manner, you speak truly. I must first think of the people, then of—"

"Me?"

"Yes. No—us."

"So there is still an 'us'?"

"In my heart and soul there will always be."

"You will forgive me, but again I hear a qualification in your words."

"We have held counsel, as I have said."

"You have said. It was about me. So tell me. But remember, among all these things I seem to have done to offend and alienate the tribe, I did also kill a raiding Choctaw, and I did take his lice-ridden scalp to hang upon the chieftain's glory pole!"

"Do not take anger. I have saved you among our people."

This news stunned her, and then it angered her.

"How is it that I need to be saved from my own kind?" she asked accusingly.

"Because you have seemed to be a troublemaker, bringing unfounded accusations, stirring turmoil in our midst."

Gyva was truly angry now. "The higher one rises, the farther behind is truth!" she snapped. "And the harder to find as well. Should one be even half-interested in locating it!"

"Do not speak thus to me, maiden," he said, softly but peremptorily. "There are things I must do. It may work out for us, and we may yet be as one, but only if you cease . . ."

The seriousness of his words, and of his responsibility—to say nothing of her own plight—came down upon Gyva with the weight of a burden.

"Tell me what I must do," she said, bowing her head slightly. "In your love I live and shine, but in the womb of the tribe also do I live and have my being. I am your loyal follower, too."

With that, Torch stepped forward, reached out in the darkness, and touched her face. The warmth and strength of him were transmitted to her, and she felt as well the seriousness and complexity with which he regarded his new position. It might never again be the same between them as it had been in the days of wild love and freedom, but she did not doubt that she was special to him, and would always be.

"You must cease to speak up," he said. "You must withdraw from the public life of the tribe. You must be, for some time, quite faceless in our midst, to earn back by obeisance and anonymity what you have squandered by willfulness."

"It was not willfulness!" she cried. "It was—"

"The council does not care what it was! I am telling you what is, and I am telling you that you must take heed, and take heed quickly. They would already have sent you alone into the forest, into exile, had I not pleaded for you, pleaded to give you one last chance to act as you ought."

Gyva felt shaky. That was how her own people felt about her, when all she had tried to do was bring to their attention evils being perpetrated in their midst . . . .

"And so you promised for me that I would be good?" she asked.

He seemed to shrink, there in the darkness. "Yes," he said. "I had to. It was the only way. I do not want to lose you," he added, "though it may well be some time before the two of us can, in public, go about . . . ."

"And what of this place of ours, here among the willows?"

Torch hesitated. "It may be . . . it may be some time for that again, too, but—"

"I have heard enough *but*s for one night," she cried, "and I thank you for all you have done for me. You may rest assured that I will do as I have been bidden!"

"Gyva!" he cried, anguish in his voice.

But she was already gone, back into the night, back to her wigwam, there to lie awake in angry sorrow until dawn.

CHAPTER III

Torch looked every inch a chief as he strode majestically before the tribe, which was gathered for the execution of Jason Randolph. Only on Gyva did his gaze linger, and in his eyes she saw an implicit accusation: *It was not I who ran away last night in anger.*

While she sensed that he forgave her, Gyva knew another thing: Once again she had acted impulsively, heeding only the advice of her soul. And once again, by having so acted, she had complicated everything still further.

But is not your soul the essence of all that you are? When your soul speaks, how can you not but act, without defiling yourself by omission?

Jason Randolph was dragged out in front of the tribe, where a raised scaffolding had been erected. The long trials of the nation, so vexing and protracted, were now to earn a measure of expiation; wrath and revenge for so many trials, so many wrongs, would fall upon the planter from Virginia. He wore the same buckskins in which he had been captured, but it seemed that he had slept some, for he appeared more alert than he had on the previous day. Listening to the people jabber, Gyva learned he had been given fruit and honey, to give him strength lest he succumb before the entertainment was fully commenced.

Jason was shoved through the jeering crowd and came before the raised stakes of the scaffold. Gyva saw his gaze rise to those beams and ropes, and upon his face she saw despair mixed with an effort of courage,

If this was the way he had to die, he would do it as bravely as he could. Perhaps because of the white blood in her veins, or perhaps because she had found him decent when conversing with him, Gyva felt great sympathy. Put an evil warrior, a Choctaw, a traitor to death by these horrible means, but not a man of peace!

"Secure the captive," ordered Arrow-in-Oak, who had begged to be in charge of the execution.

A dozen rough hands grabbed Jason Randolph, knives slashed loose his clothing, and he was bound naked, spread-eagled, between two uprights. There were murmurs of approval from the watching tribe: This man Randolph was fine and strong of body.

"See how pure and white is his body!" someone observed.

"Hah!" snorted Arrow. "In due course it shall be red with blood," which raised a shout of raucous laughter.

Jason closed his eyes as if in prayer. Perhaps he was calling on that white man's God, the one whose blood the jackals were supposed to drink. Then he seemed to resolve something for himself, and spoke.

"I say again," he told all the tribe, looking from one to another most fearlessly. "I am a man of peace and of the earth. I come here only to make bountiful the land. Never did I fight an Indian of any tribe or nation, nor do I wish to. I cannot believe such a life has earned me this most cruel of deaths."

"He begs!" Although many of the Chickasaw could not understand the white man's tongue, they knew that he sought to be spared.

Torch felt it necessary to clarify. "You were upon lands that have been ours since time began. We were not approached, even to grant permission that you might traverse the Chickasaw hunting grounds. That in itself is a violation of principle." His English was clear, but not as fluent as Gyva's.

Jason seemed to study the new chief, to decide that

here was an Indian who might at least listen to reason.

"Had we realized that was what you wished, we would indeed have sent an emissary to request such a favor. But—hear me—we took nothing from this land of yours, merely passed across its face. Does the bird require leave to wing through the free air? So it was with us on the way to Harrisville, which is a white man's land."

The people cried out in sudden anger.

"It, too, was once ours," Torch observed. In truth he was of two minds regarding this execution. The tribe demanded it, and the process had advanced so far that it could not be broken off. But the deaths of the members of Jason's party were almost certainly known in Harrisville by now, and this additional execution would add fuel to the fire of white rage.

"How came you to lose the land, then?" Jason was asking.

"In battle did you take it from us."

"Not I," Jason replied, quietly but without fear. "For never have I carried knife or gun. It is as I have already said: No man is my enemy. If you lost your land in war, it was not of my making. It takes two sides to make a war."

This time the cries of the people went on for some time, ominous with terrible anger as the prisoner's words were translated. Jason's words had goaded them, had placed upon them certain responsibility for their own plight.

"So you say that you have never fought," Torch observed, trying to find a way to lessen or eliminate the most brutal aspects of death by torture.

"That is true."

"Then what say you to this challenge? If I order you cut down from the scaffold, and place a knife in your hands, will you use it to defend your life against a warrior from our number?"

"No. No!" cried the people, who worried that they might be robbed of the spectacle of execution. Never had Gyva been more discouraged by the behavior of her own people, even though she understood what gave rise to it.

But Jason would have none of the suggestion. "If I agree to that which you propose, am I not myself cooperating in my own death? And is that not participation in murder, which I have never done in my life and have no intention of performing now? And even if, through some chance, I should succeed in defending myself, would that not also lead to my spilling the blood of another man?"

"Let us end this worthless talk!" cried Arrow. "Like all white men, this one has too many words. Words take time and time is a trick of the jackals. By the time he concludes his serpentine disputation, it may be tomorrow, and a rescue party will come for him."

The people applauded his words vigorously.

"Well may it be true," Torch stated, "that you are innocent of specific acts against us. But in war—and we are at war, as we have been for years—the rules are altered. You are a symbol of your people, and so you shall suffer—as at this very moment one of our own children, Bright Badger, may be lying in suffering at the hands of Roo-Pert Harris."

Jason showed surprise. "Harris? Is he not the leader of the settlement north of here?"

"That is the one. He is the man who gave me the evil name Firebrand, and put upon my head a price of gold."

"I have no personal knowledge of him. Word reached me in Virginia that he wished more settlers in his community. He is said to be shrewd and powerful, but also a peaceful man."

"Lies—more lies!" the people clamored. "Kill him now, as Arrow-in-Oak has advised."

Torch had reason enough to regard Harris with antipathy, and it seemed strange to him that a white man would not know the vicious predilections of one of his own kind. True, Jason claimed not to know

Harris personally; but such an excuse had little meaning now. The Red Beard was evil, and devious, and
a cheat of the lowest sort, who would resort without
conscience to the meanest of tricks. Anyone going to
join Harris's settlement must accept a burden of
culpability.

The discussion was over, and Torch stepped back.
Arrow advanced, taking from his belt a knife sharp
as a nettle weed. Gyva saw that there was no hope now.
Arrow, grinning, made a thin slash in the flesh of
Randolph's thigh. Jason groaned and twisted in bondage. Then Arrow made a second slash, parallel to the
first and about an inch apart. Deft flicks of the knife
joined the two longer slashes, and an elongated rec-
tangle, bloody bordered, stood out on Randolph's
white flesh. Then, still grinning, Arrow grasped a
shred of skin in his hands and ripped it away. Jason
screamed, and the tribe cried out in gleeful satisfaction.

"You ought to have chosen the knife fight," Arrow
mocked the Virginian. "It would have been much
faster than being skinned alive."

"I say . . . for the last time," Jason cried, gasping in
pain, "I am a peaceful man, who seeks only to cultivate the land and build a plantation. I have done
nothing . . . ."

"You are right," Arrow interrupted. "You have said
so for the last time."

The Chickasaw roared with laughter. Arrow made
a long slash across Randolph's abdomen.

Gyva moved up next to Torch as Jason howled
with the new pain. "Stop this, make it quick for him,"
Gyva whispered.

He did not look at her, but he did answer. "Perhaps
I will be able to do so in a while more. But I cannot
now."

"Why not? Are you not chieftain?"

"I am. And that is the reason. Affairs are not so
clear-cut and well defined as you might think. I must
walk a tightrope."

"Hah!" Gyva hissed, angrily. "What good is it to see that good man die so?"

"Do not speak such things. The people will begin again to call for your banishment."

Arrow ripped away another long length of skin, and Jason groaned like a dying horse and sagged upon the ropes that bound him, almost dropping into unconsciousness. The people themselves groaned, but in disappointment. "Give him strong wine," someone cried. "Revive him, that we may feast upon his misery!"

It was Little Swallow who stepped forward with an earthenware jug.

And it was Gyva who dashed out from Torch's side and struck the vessel to the ground, where it shattered into a hundred fragments, the spreading pool of berry wine soaking into the earth like Jason's blood.

A great silence fell upon them all, a silence that was partially of awe. Gyva felt the anger begin to smoulder, and she sought to cut it off with her words.

"What have we *become*?" she cried.

Torch regarded her with wonder. On the gallows Jason raised his head, astounded. A flicker of hope passed over his eyes.

"Are we all truly murderers," Gyva asked, "that we should howl like rabid wolves over one man's pain? If so, then we are exactly as Jacksa Chula and his kind believe us to be. We do such a thing as this upon the gallows today, and our enemies will say, 'See? See what they do? They are as crazed with blood lust as we have ever said they were!'"

Her words, she saw, had some effect, mostly due to the fact that she had stunned the people by the suddenness of her action.

Thus she gained their ears for a crucial moment before outrage and anger once again took hold.

She had, however inadvertently, given Torch an opportunity.

"There is truth in the maiden's words," he cried. "Perhaps not as much truth as she believes, and far less than will satisfy most of us, but truth nonetheless."

The people quieted. Torch was speaking. "It is a great matter," he went on, "and I shall call the seeress."

Teva was sent for. She did not deign to watch men die, and had not for decades attended an execution. "As one approaches age," she said, "one's own death begins to nod and wink in the night. Then death becomes less entertainment than friend. When you carry it with you, there is no need to witness it, or to cheer its presence."

But she came. Torch informed her of what had transpired. "It is my decision," he stated, aware of the risk he was taking in the judgment of the tribe, "that the planter be released to go his way."

In spite of his power there were protests. He had, after all, not been chief for very long. "Trust is a thing we cannot abandon, and I believe the words of the man when he says he is not a fighter. Also, he has suffered already."

From the gallows Jason sent Gyva a glance of gratitude. But she herself was now in trouble.

"Torch, our great chieftain," cried Arrow-in-Oak, his knife still dripping the Virginian's blood, "I am your loyal warrior and a true Chickasaw. But I cannot say otherwise. The maiden has, one time too many, affronted us all."

Acclamation came from the tribe at the sound of his words.

"Put the maiden on the gallows then!" cried a woman somewhere in back of the crowd. "Let the man go, but let her writhe for the trouble she has caused."

Gyva looked around, trying to suppress her fear.

"Ah, no," she heard Little Swallow say with menace, "our Torch has loved her, and he will play favorites now."

Swallow seemed to be seeking in Gyva's death a form of spiritual recompense for the death of Hawk, her lover.

"A Chickasaw chieftain has no favorites," said

Torch scornfully. But on his face Gyva could see that
he was well aware that his actions here would long
color his relationship with the tribe.

The tribe, she remembered him tell her. *The tribe
must come first for me now.*

A dull rumble of unrest rose from the people, some
of whom wished to see Gyva die with the man, some
of whom wished merely to see her perish in place of
Jason.

"They will both be sent forth!" Torch cried suddenly.

All stilled in hush, listening.

"Cut the man down, clothe him, give him back his
belongings. Within this hour he shall be sent from our
midst. He must seek his own fate now, and fulfill the
life we have given him. And also the maiden Gyva
shall be sent forth, to seek apart from us the happiness
and tranquillity she has not been able to find in our
midst."

Torch was saying these things? Gyva wondered,
stunned. *Her* Torch, under whom so many times, so
well, she had worked the magic of her body to bring
him the mystery of love.

And Teva was nodding dolefully. "It is a wise decision," the old witch-woman was saying, soothing the
tribe. "It is not a happy decision, but it is a wise one."

Because she knew it was the only decision that could
keep Gyva off the gallows.

They allowed her mere minutes to gather up a few
things. Her mind spun with sorrow and suffering as
she rummaged about the wigwam, collecting clothing,
a blanket of—rabbit skin? She looked down at the pale,
soft pelts upon which she had slept since her panther
skins had been destroyed by fire. No, she would not
take these of the rabbit, or run like a rabbit into the
forest. But Torch had rejected her and put her away
as easily as if that were what she was, a hapless rabbit,
fine for sacrifice!

On the peg next to her sleeping place hung her little leather pouch, and in it her few pathetic adornments, Torch's serpent-shaped war bracelet, and the white pebbles he had sent to summon her for the very first time. Oh, how she loathed them now, and what memories they stirred! She reached inside the pouch to draw them forth, to hurl them away, and the bracelet, too, but then she changed her mind.

The tribe was waiting when she emerged from her dwelling. It took every last effort of courage to hold her pride, but she held it and held her head up before them. Near the gallows Teva was applying some kind of ointment to Jason's wounds. He swayed at her touch, weakened as much by relief as by the ordeal.

Before the chieftain's wigwam Torch waited. He stood separated from the people, and she approached. Quietly, lest the others hear, he said: "I would that it were otherwise, Gyva."

She said nothing, but her eyes condemned him: *You could make it so.*

He read her thoughts. "No more. You have done too much for the people to abide. I must think of all now, not of—"

"To be banished is to die," she said.

Torch shook his head sadly. "It is not, and you will, I hope, learn this in time, and think of me—"

Gyva did not let him finish. "*This* is what I think of you!" she cried, and cast down in the dust before his feet the white pebbles and the bracelet.

Never had she seen such hurt upon his face. Never had she caused such hurt to anyone. Instantly she felt terror at having done this, a hurt of her own, now that they were parting, never to see each other again.

"Where will you travel?" he asked, making an effort to steady his composure. She did not at first know how to respond, or with what words. She looked down. There lay the symbols of his love. Symbols were much on her mind now, and what they meant, or what they seemed to mean.

"I go," she said, meeting his eyes, "to seek the golden stick of which you spoke in honeyed words. And *I* shall not forget the message written thereupon."

Then, giving him no chance to reply, no opportunity for fond farewell, she spun away from him and passed before the massed Chickasaw. Once they had been her people; now no more.

Little Swallow had contrived to stand near the path Gyva would take into the forest. "Shall I follow you now?" she mocked. "Shall I do your bidding?" A reminder of Gyva's boast to her, days earlier, about who would be a chieftain's wife, and who a queen.

"Whatever you choose," Gyva shot back crisply. There was a certain relief, she discovered, in having lost everything. There was no more need for restraint. "But remember this, should he take you to wife: I loved him first, and loved him best. Even when you are in his arms, you will know that I am always in his mind."

Swallow started in surprise: Gyva's words were true. She began to shape a retort, but none came. And Gyva was gone among the trees, cast out from the bosom of her people.

Hours passed, and Gyva trudged along through the forest, slowly climbing into the hills. Her first thought —her only thought—was to put distance between herself and the village of her youth. Then, through the grief-numbed darkness that encircled her, the exigencies of living need, beating blood, growling stomach, intruded upon her. She was hungry; she was alive. The stomach has no mind to ponder the pain of banishment and disgrace. Now, too late, she cursed herself. Food! She ought to have taken food with her. No one would have gainsaid a bag of meal, a chunk of dried venison, corn bread wrapped in bark. No, she had been feeding on her pride back there in the village, feeding upon her chin-lifted appearance, her strong demeanor. Much good pride did her now—and how

long and well would she feed upon her fiery retort to
Little Swallow, who this very night might entice Torch
down upon the loving earth, and offer her breasts to
him, open herself for him, and close herself around
him?

Involuntarily Gyva cried out in loss and anguish,
her sound carrying far off, rebounding from the wall
of the mountains.

Then she heard another cry, not her own. She
stopped, more surprised than fearful. Were Harris and
his men nearby?

For the first time the need for safety, a destination,
pressed itself upon her, as before the knowledge of
hunger had made itself known. Her clothing was
already torn by brambles and wild rose; her moccasins
were soaking wet and caked heavily with mud. Tonight
she must sleep somewhere upon wet grass, with wild
animals roaming about; the morrow would dawn, and
still she would have no place to go. The Choctaw
would kill her outright; she was Chickasaw, an enemy.
What of the Sac and the Fox? They would learn of
her banishment, even if they did not reject her for the
smooth ivory of her skin. Even among her own people,
the protection afforded by her grandfather's position
had been illusory.

Again came the far cry, sounding off the mountains:
"DEE-LEE-AAAAAAA!"

Jason Randolph. She had forgotten all about him.
For a long moment she debated whether or not to
answer. If she were captured in the company of a
white man, no tribe she knew would bother to listen
to explanations before putting an end to her life. But
the Virginian had seemed a good man, he was alone
like herself, and at night one of them might watch for
danger while the other slept.

"Here!" she cried. *"Here I am!"* She looked about,
to find a landmark for him to follow. *"Come toward
the hillock of windbent pines!"*

"Aye!" came his reply, rebounding from the rocky

cliffs of the Twin Mountains. She glanced up at them once, remembered the diagrams Torch had used to summon her, and turned away, waiting now for another man.

She sat in silence a long while before the Virginian appeared, stumbling through the underbrush. He looked very weak, but he smiled when he saw her, and collapsed on the earth beneath the tree where Gyva sat.

"Delia!" he panted. "Now there are two of us, at any rate."

"Such was my thought." She had meant to treat him somewhat coldly, lest he think banishment had broken her spirit; but he looked so tired, and was sweating so profusely, that she was immediately alarmed.

"Are you taken ill?"

"No . . . no, I think not. But I must rest for a time. The old woman with the strange mark upon her face treated my wounds, and that is something for which to be grateful. An odd woman indeed."

"Yes, she is magic."

He looked at her, then nodded, accepting the explanation, but obviously not believing it.

"She sent words for you."

"Yes?"

"She said that if I saw you I must tell you it was for the best. That exile spared your life. That things all change with time, and you will return someday."

"Hah!" cried the maiden, bitterly.

Randolph looked genuinely moved at her plight. "I am the one who caused you to be cast out, I know," he said. "There is no way I can thank you for saving my life—"

"Don't," she cut him off. "I was banished for many reasons, you the least of them."

He studied her. "Delia . . ."

"That is not my name!"

"No," he replied, quite seriously, "but I am no Chickasaw, and it is my name for you."

She glanced at him sharply, and saw his eyes fast upon her, and saw tenderness in them.

No. Not this. Not now. Not yet . . .

"I do not choose to mark you with the name that is used by the other one . . . ."

"What? What other one?"

With that, Jason took from his back the knapsack he had been carrying, opened it, and drew forth a serpent bracelet and the small white stones. "Your chieftain," he said, "asked me, for a favor, to give these to you, in the event that I found you."

For a long, long moment he held the relics of her love, offering them to her in his outstretched hand. She did not reach to take them; they were too painful to hold, and yet she could not pull her eyes away from them. Jason watched as wave upon wave of complicated emotion came to assault the Indian girl, until he was moved to sadness by the great sadness she felt.

It is all over, Gyva was thinking. Torch's love had been as true as her own, but circumstance had forced them apart. She wished to heaven that he had not sent these tokens with Jason. A Chickasaw did not weep, and never would she do so before a white man, it was unthinkable, but . . .

But then her tears came. Grief is a natural thing, and a dead love is as great as death, if not greater. The tears poured from her eyes. For a time she choked her sobs, but these, too, demanded relief, and soon she howled in loss and grief and despair beneath the pines. How it came about, she did not later recall, but by the time she fought her way up out of the throes of woe, Jason was holding her close, trying to soothe her, crooning to her wordlessly as if she were a child.

"I am so ashamed," she said, hiding her face from him, trying to get away. And she thought, I shall disappear into the forest, and die there like an animal whose time has come.

But Jason was bewildered. "Ashamed? Why are you ashamed?"

A white man. He knew nothing! "For I have shown tears before an en—"

She stopped herself. She had meant to say, instinctively, "enemy," because he was white.

He heard the word she did not speak. "No," he said, "I am not that. And no one need be ashamed of showing heartbreak. You must love him very much. It was a good thing, and there is no shame in grief for the end of a good thing. Do not violate the past by looking upon it with hard eyes now, lest in future years you have nights of painful memory."

She wiped away her tears and looked at him directly. There was much wisdom in what he spoke; her mind knew it, even though her heart was not yet ready to accept his truth.

"If it was good, let it die as such," he added. "Do not use your mind to deny what it was, or what it meant to you. I know that to do so is a natural impulse, and it seems to remove the pain, but that is only an illusion. Every loss brings pain with it, but pain dealt with honestly will sink away, like sweet water into the earth. Tears disappear into the soul, and if the tears are accepted, wisdom comes."

She said nothing, considering his words, grateful for the sincerity of the effort he was making in her behalf, and slightly astonished at the depth of sensitivity in a man who must be less than thirty circlings of the sun.

"Yes," he nodded. "I know grief. I have told you of the loss of my wife and child. That is why I understand what you have lost."

"Your loss . . ." she began, admitting it, and by so doing rejecting self-pity, "your loss was far greater. I thank you for the words you have spoken, for being kind to me."

"Delia . . ."

Whatever he meant to say then, he did not. She took from him the white stones and the bracelet and placed them inside her leather pouch. The great pain of loss was still upon her, but Jason's wisdom had made its mark in her soul. To reject her memory of Torch, to bury it, would mean that, for years, that memory would lie dormant within her, like an evil seed, to sprout one day, dark-flowered obscene, with thick black vines to entangle her soul and drag her down. No, she would not have that transpire. She would keep the tokens of her lost love, and someday, someday far in a future she could not now even dream, the bracelet and the stones would comfort her.

He smiled slowly, watching her place the items in her pouch.

"You will not be sorry for that," he said. "Though I might be," he added obscurely.

"Of what do you speak?"

"Nothing. Only a thought." He stood up. "You have not brought food?"

"I . . ." She shook her head, feeling inept. "I did not think . . ."

"It is all right. The old woman gave me water and a kind of bread. We shall share, and rest."

"What then?"

"I am going north to Harrisville. It is the only white settlement around. And you will seek another tribe?"

She explained why this would be impossible. "Then you are alone?" he asked, truly alarmed. "You shall come with me until you find a place, or make new plans."

"Do you not understand? I am Chickasaw. Harris will—"

"You are also a white woman. Don't worry. I will protect you. I am sure this man Harris is not as your braves have fearfully decreed him to be. He is a man like any other. And in any event, you need not worry. I will vouch for you. The word of a Virginian, of a Randolph, will hold good even here on the frontier. And to be doubly safe, you will wear my wife's— you will wear white woman's clothing. It is in my bundle. I could not bear to throw it away."

"You are of great family?"

"It is sufficient. Our ancestral lands are adjacent to those of the President's family."

"Moon-Row?"

He laughed. "*Mon*roe. He is our neighbor."

"I, too, am the daughter of high ones," she began, not wishing him to think that she was some vulgar little thing cast off by her people for unworthiness.

Jason Randolph's face turned serious. "Delia," he said, "I knew that as soon as I saw you. And," he added, "so will everyone else."

They ate, and then rested that day, to shore up their strength for the passage through the mountains to Harrisville. Evening came, and with it a cold wind. Jason had one tattered blanket, the maiden none at all, but she showed him how to fashion a windbreak shelter with saplings, leaves, and vines. "We shall share the blanket as we have shared the food," he offered. "I shall not trouble you in the night." So they nestled together down upon the earth, a bit awkwardly at first, but as darkness fell they curled close to each other for warmth and comfort, two animals alone in the wilderness.

"Good night, Delia," Jason said sometime later, and drifted into sleep.

But she stayed awake for a long time, listening to the wind, which howled down among the trees like a lost ghost seeking the trail toward home. Delia, she thought, as the moon rose, blasting the shuddering pines. Her past was gone. Dey-Lor-Gyva was an Indian name. Jason was right. Delia. If need be, it was a name fine enough for any white lady, and if she must pretend to be one for a time, so she would have to be. Delia.

This is a good man, and a wise one, she thought drowsily, feeling his heart beat slow and sure in the strong body that pressed against her own; and in spite of what had happened to her she felt grateful, and murmured a prayer of thanksgiving to Ababinili, up there among the stars. Grandfather, she implored, watch over me. And then she was gone to the living earth, taken and rocked and forever cradled in the velvet womb of mother night.

Owls called beneath the stars, and sleek animals moved beneath the trees, and the forest was eternal, at one with itself. The man and the woman slept, undisturbed by nature and the creatures of nature, peacefull allies in the night. Then all was still, and the ancient moon watched huge and brilliant behind the ghostly, wind-driven pines.

CHAPTER IV

"Curse these prissy scribblers!" growled the man. "Curse them all to hell, and their soft arses!"

A tall, lean man with a wild white mane of hair sat in his robe in a chair in his bedroom, reading the Washington newspapers that had arrived on the overnight stage. He was soaking his leg in an iron bucket filled with hot water, which he replenished from time to time from a kettle that hung over the flames of the bedroom fireplace. In weather like this his leg never failed to act up.

Outside his great white box of a house, the elms stood dismally, suffering the rain; and all down the long drive honeysuckle and narcissus sagged, wet and heavy, sodden and despondent. There would never be any sunshine again, his leg would never stop aching, and those petty, simpering, overeducated eastern newspaper liars would ruin the whole damn country if they had their way.

"The hell with that," he grunted to himself. "They ain't going to have their way!"

He snatched another rolled-up newspaper from the pile on the table next to him and opened it to the editorial page. His mouth tightened, his eyes darkened; with his strong, sharp nose he gave the aspect of a fierce, choleric hawk. The aspect was not softened when he read:

Under the civilizing influence of Mr. Monroe, great strides have been taken in the interests of

the common weal. But the President will leave
office after his second term, and unruly elements
may rise up to seek power. Particularly are the
western regions of our growing country to be
regarded with close attention, for in these lands
men have apparently chosen a champion well-
known for crudity, ill-temper, violence and many
such qualities that are less than well-respected in
gentler salons of learning . . .

"What in the hell is a *salon?*" he groused aloud. "Or
maybe it's a misprint. But who ever heard of a gentle
saloon?"

. . . Our choice in the election of 1824 would be
Mr. Webster. John Quincy Adams would be acceptable, but it seems the Adams family regards
the White House as a part of its patrimony.
Samuel C. Calhoun is too much a spokesman for
the southern slaveholding interests to stand much
chance in a natural contest, but even he would
be preferable to the egregious barbarian from
Tennessee . . .

"Rachel!" he roared. "Rachel, come in here, will
you?"
He poured some more hot water from the kettle into
the iron bucket and winced when the heat struck him.
Damn wound. Twenty years old and still throbbed
like the dickens. He lifted his leg from the water and
studied the deep blue marks where the punctures had
been.
A lovely, dark-eyed woman appeared in the doorway, and the man's face softened. Whatever else they
might say about him, they could never accuse him of
failing in chivalry toward the fairer sex.
"Yes, Andrew? Can I get you something?"
"Please. Have one of the darkies come here and
take out this water. Soaking's not doing any good.

Look"—he held out the newspaper—"what they're saying about me now."

"Oh, Andrew. Pay no attention. What can words do to you?"

"They can keep me out of the White House, that's what!" he declared. And he already knew what vicious talk was doing to her.

She came forward and handed him a thick towel to dry his leg. "The Hermitage is white, too," she told him, smiling tenderly. "And you're already here."

"Webster. Adams. Calhoun," he snarled, rising slowly from the chair and taking his leg from the bucket. *"Ouch,* damn . . . forgive my language. Webster's a pompous ass, and Adams is just an ass, and the only good thing about Calhoun is he knows how to treat the darkies!"

"I know," she said, teasing him. "And not one of them ever fought in an Indian war."

"I want the White House in 1824!" he declared.

Rachel sat down suddenly on a low couch next to the great bed; and although he did not let her see it, his glance was concerned. Her health was failing. If he had to wait until 1828 to make his move, she might not . . . She was weakening. She was being killed by the innuendos, the vile accusations . . . .

No, he did not want to think of it. He would try for the big prize in '24 and present her with it, as he had so many times before won victories—for his own glory, true enough, but as gifts for her as well. But would he be able to put the westerners together for a national effort in the few years that remained? He was a hero, sure, and he knew how to use being a hero for political gain—but was there enough unity yet? Were there enough people yet? There ought to be more here on the frontier, but those Indians still caused so much trouble, and people were afraid.

"Crude, ill-tempered, violent," he growled, drawing on his breeches.

"What's that?" his wife inquired.

"That's what that Washington rag says. Do you think I'm crude, ill-tempered, and violent?"

"Of course, darling," she said, "and everyone else thinks so, too. That's why you're the greatest man in Tennessee."

"In all America!" he amended with a growl, then paused and laughed at himself, went over to the couch, bent down, and kissed her gently on the mouth.

"Ummmmm!" she sighed happily. "So crude."

He smiled down at her indulgently. They had been through so much. He could take it, but the talk hurt her. Rachel had thought everything was settled and that the divorce had been finalized. And it was—now—but too late to stop the ceaseless wagging of scandal-loving tongues, or the more calculated maneuvers of tongues honed for politics.

Andrew Jackson knew politics. He was bound and determined to be president of the United States. A man with little formal education, he was strong and clear minded, even brilliant; and in the company of refined people he could speak as well as any of them. But he was a rough-and-ready frontiersman, who knew the harsh country language, and knew, too, that to win the votes of his fellow frontiersmen, it was necessary to speak their language. This he did with considerable enjoyment. It was his natural tongue. He had not become Old Hickory by aping "them mealy-mouthed pussyfooters" in the East.

He was drawing on his long, floppy boots now, and muttering about the pain.

"I wish you'd let someone polish those boots," Rachel said, glancing with dismay at the battered footwear.

"What's the point?" he said. "They'd just get scuffed again."

That was true, but it was not the real reason he did not keep his boots polished. When young Jackson was a captive of the British during the Revolutionary War, an enemy officer had demanded that he polish the

officer's boots. Andrew had refused, and for his defiance he had received a blow on his face that left a
scar he carried to this very day. He could chronicle
his life by the scars on his hard, lean body. And to
this day, too, he did not think it was right for one
man to shine another man's boots, not even a slave.
What difference did polished boots make anyway?
Them Indians would just see the shine in the trees,
and you'd wind up with an arrow in your gizzard.

He could see, he could just *imagine*, that feckless
Quincy Adams mincing around in mirrored boots!

"What will you be doing today?" Rachel asked.

"Oh, not too much. There's one of the darkies needs
flogging. He shoed a horse wrong, horse threw the
shoe, broke its leg, and had to be put down. I have
to watch the idiot get the lash, so the rest know I take
it serious. Then a man is coming up from southern
Tennessee. Indian trouble down there."

"Will you have to go out again?" Rachel asked, a
worried look on her face. She knew that her husband
was in charge of the militia, and that it was his duty
to protect the white settlers, but she always worried.

"I don't know yet. Have to hear the fellow out first.
Rupert Harris is his name. Hasn't come yet, has he?"

"I haven't heard anyone ride up today."

"Let's have some breakfast then."

"I . . . ah . . . you go ahead. I've . . . already eaten."

He sensed that she hadn't eaten, wasn't feeling well.
But he did not press the point. Instead he went down
to the long dining room. Servants appeared immediately, all of them darkies. The Lord knew what he was
doing when he made masters and servants, Jackson
thought. Darkies were the same as Indians, except you
could train them to do menial tasks. An Indian would
just spit in your eye and cut his own throat to spite
you. Hell, taken pound for pound, he actually liked
Indians better. Least they would fight. Caused him a
lot of trouble, though.

"Pot of coffee," he grumbled. "Stack of wheat cakes,

and don't forget to melt the butter. Fry me some ham, too, hey?"

The slaves rushed out to fulfill his commands, and he walked over to the oaken sideboard, took out a decanter, and swigged a couple of good slugs of bourbon. He felt better. Even his leg felt a little better. Outside, the clouds were moving fast, and it looked like the weather might clear up. Could turn out to be a halfway decent day.

He attacked a pile of wheat cakes and thought of the political situation. Not a learned man—they attacked him for *that*, too—he was remarkably intuitive. That, and a sure sense of timing, along with great personal courage, had always made him one to be reckoned with, and even those feckless easterners with their accents and their college degrees—hell, they knew it. They could study a problem to death, study their arses off, and come around the bend with some hare-brained solution, only to find Old Hickory sitting there by the side of the road, with the problem—whatever it was—already taken care of. That's the way he worked. And, wolfing his breakfast, his mind worked in precisely that manner.

Politically, how is the West to become powerful enough to elect its own president—me—over the opposition of the South and the East?

Answer: We need more people.

What's responsible for holding up a lot of people who might move on out and settle here? Who's responsible?

The goddamn red men!

What to do about it?

Run the devils out of the country. Hell, there must be someplace for them to go. Send them out west, beyond the Mississippi. There was a lot of empty land out there.

This, in fact, was what he'd suggested to Monroe: an Indian Removal policy. It was supposed to be policy, too; but it looked to Jackson as if diffident

James had scruples. He sure seemed to be dragging his feet on the implementation, anyway. And, damn it the whole thing was very touchy. Had to be done, though. If the Indians weren't relocated, there would be constant war, and eventually the Indians would be outnumbered, wiped out, obliterated.

Even Jackson couldn't see the sense of that.

The bastards were brave, you had to say that for them, and a brave people oughtn't be totally wiped out. 'Less, of course, they get around to thinking they can wipe *you* out.

He gulped some coffee, dumped some bourbon in the cup, added more coffee, and gulped it down, too. Then he put on his leather jacket and a wide-brimmed hat and went outside. The air was still pretty damp, but the rain had stopped. Jackson went down to the barns, and Rufus, the black overseer, ran to meet him.

"Mornin', Ginral."

"Let's get it over with," Jackson said. "Haul Floyd out of the smokehouse and stretch him up on the branch of that tree."

Floyd, who had been responsible for the horse's death, had been locked up overnight in the smokehouse, which was used for curing meat. Probably had eaten himself half a ham, too.

"Ginral, I . . ."

"Horse was worth more than *he* is. Summon all the darkies. They ought to see it. We'll use the cobbin first."

The cobbin was a flat board with holes drilled in its surface to raise blisters. First the victim was beaten with the cobbin, and then a whip was used to break the blisters. There was a lot of blood. The process served to discourage errant behavior among the other darkies.

"But Ginral—"

"Rufus, what *is* it?"

The overseer hung his head. "Ginral, Floyd's done gone an' busted out, an' run away . . ."

He let his voice trail off. Running away was punishable by death, according to statute, though often owners, not wishing to lose a slave, simply doubled the number of lashes they would usually have given. A hundred strokes was not uncommon.

"When?" Jackson demanded, cold with fury.

"Musta been sometime last night."

"Somebody must've let him out," Jackson decided. "That door is thick and that lock is strong. Take meat with him?"

Rufus nodded miserably. He might be blamed for Floyd's unauthorized departure. "Took him a half-side o' pork, Ginral."

"Well, we'd best mount up and find the trail. Shouldn't be hard. He's probably sleepin' with a full belly no more'n a mile away."

Jackson turned and started back toward the house. He would never think of leaving the Hermitage without telling his beloved Rachel where he was going, and why. Damn leg, riding would be no picnic today. After all these years he remembered the village of Talking Rock. A mess, it had been. Everything had gone wrong, everybody crazy, and then this woman, this *white* woman of all things, had come charging at him with that pitchfork. Would have killed him, too, no denying, and he knew it. If only it hadn't happened so fast, if he'd had time to feint, push her aside, *something* . . . .

Her face was burned into his memory; he would never forget it. A lovely thing, she had been, and fought him like a—

Like an Indian.

Why?

Jackson still didn't know, and he probably never would. Scowling, he looked across his yard at the big house he loved, and the rich lands beyond it. Maybe Rachel was right. Hell, she *was* right. Why did he want to be president anyway?

But the answer was easy. Because the people—*his*

people, soldiers and farmers and the rugged *real* men of the frontier—wanted him to be.

And he wanted to be, too. Show them easterners how much better the country would be if the common man had a crack at running it.

Then he saw the horseman coming up the drive. The fellow was coming pretty slow, and Jackson saw the reason. Stumbling along next to the horse, one end of a rope around his neck and the other end tied to the saddle horn, was Floyd, the runaway slave.

"Holy be!" Jackson said, and waited in the yard until the man rode up. A big-looking, mean-looking type, with a wild red beard, he leaped from his black horse and approached Jackson with a huge hand outstretched—a behemoth, with a sharp glint of authority in his gaze.

"General, sir, it's an honor. Rupert Harris at your service."

"Honor for me, too," Jackson grunted, shaking hands. He hated ceremony, or being made a fuss over. "What you got there?" He jerked his thumb at dismal Floyd, who stood head bowed, rope around his neck, like a lost soul. Rufus and some of the other slaves were peering around the corners of barns and sheds to see what would happen. For all they knew, Floyd was already a dead man.

"I was riding up, saw smoke from a fire not far off in the trees, and went to take a look. Saw this here nigger sitting there, happy as a pig on Sunday, stuffing his mouth with meat. Told me he'd been given a free day by his overseer, an' was just taking some ease."

"Hah!" Jackson said.

"So I subdued him, tied him up, an' brought him along. Who's he belong to?"

"Me," Jackson said.

A sense of advantage came immediately to Rupert Harris's hard face. *I have done a favor for an important man, now he'll have to reciprocate someday.* Jackson saw the expression and knew what it meant. He had seen it many times before on the faces of many others. It meant Harris was no less corrupt, and no more virtuous, than anybody else, and such a thing was comforting to know. Harris was not to be trusted totally. Pleased with this knowledge, Jackson explained about the horse he'd lost due to Floyd's stupidity.

"What's the penalty in these parts?"

"Hangin'," Jackson snapped, walking over to Floyd. "Or sometimes a hundred lashes and cut off an ear when it's over."

Floyd began to whimper. Harris came over and grabbed one of his ears. "How about this one?" Floyd's eyes were bouncing around like big brown marbles.

"I hate to hang anybody, unless it's necessary," Jackson said. "This darkie here, dumb as he is, can still chop cotton with a hoe."

"If there's punishment to be meted out, I'll be glad to have a hand in it," growled Harris with ominous eagerness.

Something about the man's alacrity, if not his presumption, startled Jackson slightly, but he gave no sign.

"No, no," he said. "You're my guest here. Rufus!" he called, "take Floyd here an' lock him up again. Put some chains on him this time, so he don't get away. We'll ventilate his back later on. I got a visitor now."

"So how are things down there in Harrisville?" Jackson asked his crude but imposing guest.

They'd gone out onto the verandah. On a table between the two low chairs in which they lounged was a silver pitcher filled almost to the brim with mint julep.

Rupert Harris took a hefty swallow of his drink, wiped his mouth on the back of a sleeve, and allowed as how things were going pretty well in his town, indeed, " 'ceptin' for the Chickasaw."

"Oh?"

"Murdered a party of farmers coming to join our

settlement, just a couple days ago. Only two managed to get through."

"Two survived?"

"Yup. Man and woman. He's from Virginia. Randolph's his name."

"What part of Virginia?"

"Charlottesville, he says."

"Well. The Randolphs are important people there. He could be related to Edmund Randolph. Mention anything about it?"

Harris seemed momentarily displeased that Randolph was of a family known and admired by Old Hickory. Rupert himself had apparently made a negative judgment about the man.

"Woman's a fine looker, Ginral. Says she comes from Georgia, originally."

"What was their story? About the raid against them?"

These were things Jackson had to know, as commandant of the Tennessee Militia. If you rode off on a mission of retaliation possessed of half-baked facts, you might stir up more trouble than you bargained for. There was always enough trouble to go around as it was.

"Not too exciting. They had 'em a wagon train, coming in toward my town . . ."

Jackson was beginning to note the man's constant proprietary references.

". . . an' they were attacked by a bunch of braves from old Four Bears' village. Ambush. Everybody but them two were wiped out."

Harris grunted on, telling how bad the attack had been, mentioning again, with a sly leer, how good-looking that Georgia girl was who'd come over the mountains with Jason Randolph. But Jackson was thinking back twenty years to a savage moment at dawn, on the banks of the river by the white falls of Roaring Gorge. In a sense he had been living on borrowed time ever since that day.

"What do you hear of old Four Bears?" Jackson demanded.

"He's dead."

"What?"

"Yup, he croaked, all right."

Andrew Jackson felt an odd tug somewhere down in his heart. The man who had spared his life all those years ago no longer breathed the living air. He felt as if he'd lost a strange kind of friend, or brother. No, that was ridiculous. Four Bears was—had been—like all the rest of them. A murderous savage.

"Where'd you learn this?" he asked Harris.

"Randolph told me."

"Well, then I guess he must have had time to take a little break during that ambush and sit down and palaver with one of the braves. How'd he know?"

A dull gleam showed far back in Harris's eyes. "He an' the wench tell me they got captured and taken to the village. Heard about Four Bears while they was there. They managed to get away. That grizzled old featherhead is dead, all right."

"Got them a new chief yet?"

Harris took a drink, leaned way back, and sort of grinned.

"That's why I come to see you, sir. Now's the time to go back in those mountains and wipe 'em out. Man, woman, and child. Now's the time. Every last godforsaken one of the miserable throat-slitting bastards."

"Sounds like you mean it," Jackson commented, watching the man closely.

"Their new chief is a buck called Firebrand, 'cause that's what he does when he comes to a white settlement. Puts the torch to it. Every time. Near lost half our settlement last time him and his shit-smelling red devils came around."

Jackson saw that Harris did not quite meet his eyes while rendering this enraged dissertation. Might mean nothing at all—some found it pretty hard to look direct into the hard hawk eyes of Old Hickory. Might also mean the man was lying, or not telling every last little inch of the truth.

"When did this Firebrand get to be the new chief?"

"Randolph said only a day or so ago. Let's see, took him an' the girl a day an' a half to come through the pass—would have been, let's see . . ."

"An' when was the raid that hit the wagon train?"

"Would have been . . ." Harris calculated, "four, five days ago."

"So," Jackson observed, "the raid was between Four Bears' demise an' the choosing of the new chief."

"So what?" Harris said.

"It's important. Might have been unauthorized. Just some jumpy braves going out on their own. Not that that's in any way excusable, but I just want to know the facts."

He felt his intuition throb and take over. Something was not quite right about this whole business.

"Nothing might have happened, did it, to stir up them braves? Any provocation you can think of?"

"No, sir, none at all!" declared Rupert Harris, staring Jackson straight in the eye—just a little too straight and a little too long.

Jackson sipped his drink, and wondered.

"So I just come up to suggest now's the time to wipe the bastards out, good and all."

"Well, Mr. Harris, I will certainly take that under advisement with my commanders, an' one of these times I'll ride on down to Harrisville and pay a call."

"That'd be great, Ginral," Harris oozed, although Jackson could see he was disappointed not to have won a decision for immediate battle with the Chickasaw. But no rank frontiersman debated military strategy with Old Hickory, nosiree, or leastways not directly to his face while swilling his liquor on the verandah of the Hermitage. Harris was crude, but he wasn't dumb. There's always another day, and more'n one way to skin a cat.

Talk turned to the national picture, and Harris

allowed that Jackson would pretty soon be moving to Washington.

"Maybe. Maybe. An' I'll tell you one thing. When we westerners finally do grab the big prize—an' we will—I'm going to throw the biggest, wildest, damn end-and-out *funnest* party Washington, D.C., has ever seen."

"I'll be there, Ginral. An' you can count on that!"

"I'm sure I can. I'm sure I can," responded Jackson, watching Harris polish off another mint julep. The man looked equipped to do everything to excess.

Rupert Harris spent the night in the Hermitage, sated with a huge dinner of roast beef, baked potatoes, corn bread and molasses, wild squash, and raspberries and cream. For entertainment there was the flogging of Floyd, which Harris enjoyed mightily, until the fainthearted darkie passed out on the eighteenth stroke, leaving eighty-two undelivered.

"Oh, hell," said Jackson, addressing Rufus, who stood there disconsolately, holding the bloody whip. He seemed embarrassed by Floyd's lack of endurance. "Cut off his ear an' lock him up again. Put him to cutting firewood in the morning. Tell him I'll expect a full cord by nightfall, or he'll get the rest of the lashes."

Walking back to the house, Harris observed: "Kind of gentle on the nigger, weren't you?"

"He's better off working than dead."

Harris thought that over. "Right there, Ginral. Right you are." Then, as an afterthought, "Too damn bad we can't make slaves of the red devils."

"They're not the type."

"I'm trying it out, though. Got me an Indian kid back home in my village. He's showin' some promise as a houseboy. When properly encouraged, that is. It's an experiment of mine, sort of."

"I see," said Jackson, who studied Harris out of the corner of his eye. A tough, brutal man, this one. He could be a big help here in the West, or he could bring disaster. You never could tell.

"Darling," Rachel said after Harris had ridden off the next morning, "I hate to say it but I didn't care for that man."

"I know what you mean," Jackson said. "But the man's determined to own a big chunk of Tennessee, and it'll be mighty dangerous for anybody who gets in his way."

CHAPTER V

Delia and Jason had stumbled down out of the mountains and entered Harrisville, hungry and in tatters. As they approached the town, Delia's fear grew by the moment. Rupert Harris, she knew, was a barbarian who abducted helpless children. And how often had she heard tales of the great threat posed to the Chickasaw by the very existence of Harrisville? Then, on a crude trail leading through the forest toward the village, she had seen nailed to a tree a poster offering money for the capture of "the murderous Indian, Firebrand, dead or alive." At the bottom was the name Rupert Harris.

"I am afraid," she admitted.

"Do not worry. Do not think about it," Jason had replied. "I'll take care of you."

She had not known what to expect of the village. She had not been out of her mountain home since Four Bears had carried her into it, so many years before. So when she glimpsed it for the first time, Delia was amazed. *This* was a war camp, a base of terror and bloodshed? This was Harrisville, the cause of so much worry and grief upon the part of the preoccupied Chickasaw braves?

"Why, it looks so quiet and peaceful!" she exclaimed, almost relieved.

"It is that," Jason smiled. "But remember, just as was true in your village, many things go on beneath the surface, and a wise person listens and waits."

His remark, meant to soothe her, served only to

increase her distress. Was she wise enough to know these subterranean things? Among her own people she had failed miserably and been cast out. If she failed here, or betrayed her origins, would they kill her?

On the trek through the mountains toward Harrisville, she had told Jason Randolph of her origins, and of the battle of Talking Rock. Indeed, as refugees will do, they had shared aspects of their lives with each other. But she had not told him that it was Andrew Jackson who had killed her parents. That he must not know, because Jason Randolph admired the general, and because—someday, somewhere—Gyva meant to kill the man. Jackson would pay with his life for the lives he had taken.

"When we meet the villagers," Jason was telling her, "they will want to know about us. I would advise you to stick as close to the facts of your life as you can. You are a native of Talking Rock, Georgia. Your parents were killed in a raid. Now you have come here to make a new life. All those things are true, and they will have a true sound when you tell them."

"But . . . but what about . . . ?"

"Do not hesitate. Tell me."

"But what about my eyes, my hair?"

"They are beautiful. What about them?"

"But surely they shall give me away, and brand me Indian before the white people."

"I think not. It was, perhaps, your fair complexion that caused you difficulties with the petty and the envious among your tribe. But here it will be your fine skin that marks you as a white woman. And a lovely white woman at that."

He looked at her in that way he had. She glanced away. It was not difficult at all to know when a man was falling in love with you. It did not matter to which race he belonged.

And so they walked into the village. What strange dwellings were there! Some were made of wood, but where did trees grow that were flat and long? And the houses made of stone had every stone the same, rectangles stacked one upon the other, up to a roofing of steeply slanting wooden slabs! How were these mysteries accomplished? Where were such trees, such stones found? Then a long, terrible shrieking pierced the air, and she pressed against Jason in fear.

"What is it?" he asked, seeing her alarm.

"Someone is dying!"

He actually laughed. "I do not think so," he said.

Fighting panic, she looked about the village. She could not see a soul.

Again, that long-drawn-out horrible sound.

"They *are* all dying!" she maintained, thinking of some disaster that had perhaps come upon this village. She was not especially sorry about the thought.

But Jason just laughed again. "They are probably down by the river. What you hear is the work of a sawmill."

She repeated the word, wonderingly.

"Let us go. It is as good a time as any. They will be very busy, and they will not stop their work long for us."

He led her through the village, which consisted of a long, dusty street, on either side of which were about ten or twelve of the strange wood and stone structures, none of them very large, but of many shapes, with lean-to additions on some of them, and on one an odd protrusion that Jason called a *porch.* These buildings were of great interest to Delia, but none astounded her as much as a spare wooden frame with horses living in it! She exclaimed about this bizarre thing in such incredulous tones that Jason laughed, explaining that it was called a *stable,* to keep horses, which were valuable, out of the weather, sheltered and fed so that they would be fit for riding or work in the fields. Delia accepted this, yet it seemed strange to her, as if the white jackals in some way worshiped animals, to house them as they did themselves.

Then she caught Jason studying her.

"What is it?" she asked.

"You know very little of our ways?"

"I have been in the village of my people since I was a tiny child."

He frowned, worried. She knew why. All of the simple, daily things in the life of white men were unknown to her. How could she hope to pretend to be a refined white lady when the most ordinary things were intricate mysteries to her?

"We will do one thing at a time," he said, reassuring her. "I shall speak for you as often as I can."

The trail down to the river was not difficult to find, being well marked by horses, wagon treads, and the deep gouges of logs that had been dragged to the mill.

Once more the terrible shriek arose. Jason and Delia came out of the trees along the river bank and into a clearing. Now she saw how the terrible noise was made! A great wheel, tall as five men, was turned by the flow of the river. By so doing, it turned also an axle attached to it, at the other end of which was a thin, silvery, jagged-tipped wheel, into which men— and women, too—were pushing a great log. The jagged tips of the spinning silver wheel ripped apart the logs into flat planes of wood such as Delia had seen on the houses in the village, and at the same time evoked from the wood that unearthly rending shriek. When the log had been pushed all the way through the ripping wheel—a *saw*, Jason called it—the direction was reversed, and another flat plane of wood was torn away from the log, until the log itself ceased to be. In a pit not far from the sawmill, Delia saw blocklike wooden forms being stuffed full of mud and straw by more women and children. "*Bricks*," said Jason, pronouncing it distinctly so that she would remember. "Bricks," she repeated, and recognized them as the odd stones forming some of the houses.

Say what one would about these white jackals, they did indeed perform some interesting skills!

Then the two of them were seen by the people.

A last length of lumber fell from the shrinking log. The axle was disengaged from the saw and silence descended for a moment, followed by a burst of babbling as everyone—men, women, children—rushed up to greet the newcomers.

The one who spoke first was a gigantic man with a great red beard. Delia subdued the trembling that momentarily threatened to dominate her. It was the man who had kidnapped Bright Badger!

"Hey, strangers," he said, in a suspicious but not altogether unfriendly voice, squinting at them against the sun. "What can we do for yuh?" He was the biggest man Delia had ever seen, not just in height but in bulk, too. None of it was fat, either. His shoulders measured at least two axe handles in width, and a massive torso tapered to a hard, rippling gut. To think that Torch had grappled with this man! But Delia looked him straight in the eye and did not flinch— not even when his eyes bored into her own, then dropped to follow the curves of her body. His eyes were bright with intelligence, she noted; but they also glittered with cunning, and arrogance, and appetite.

"What's your handle, man?" he asked, turning toward Jason.

Jason gave his name and began to explain what had happened.

"Randolph! Sure. Been expectin' yuh. Where's your party? Up there in town? We can use the new men, clear a lot more land—"

"No, wait," Jason said. And then he told of the raid, how he and Delia were the only survivors.

Everyone quieted.

"Damn!" muttered some of the men.

"Those foul redskins," Rupert Harris cursed. "We'll settle with them for good one of these days." He eyed Delia watchfully, and there was no doubt he desired her beauty, whether or not he suspected her of Indian blood. "Your wife?" he asked Jason pointedly.

For an instant she wished that he would say yes—
it seemed to afford added protection. But he had read
the situation well and, as promised, devised a solution
to increase her safety. "No, the daughter of a friend,"
he said. "I promised to look after her when he was
killed in the raid."

Even Rupert Harris seemed to accept this, at least
for the moment, though he gave Delia another long
glance, as if he might have seen her before, as if the
sight of her reminded him of something or someone.

"Well," he grunted, "you're safe, an' the important
thing is you're here. Got to clear a lot more land
around here, before we'll have plantations big enough
to support a crop of slaves to clear more of it for us."

Slaves, thought Delia, remembering the white man's
penchant for putting human beings into servitude.

"But don't worry. Plenty of land out there for us
all. Someday Harrisville will be the biggest, richest
center of life in all Tennessee!"

His people nodded and exclaimed in agreement.
Clearly Rupert Harris had the strength and vigor to
encourage their dreams.

But the land, Delia reflected, belongs to my people!

Harris went on to explain that for the time being,
due to the constant Indian threat, everyone lived in
the village. There were as yet no individual farms.
Men and women went out to clear and plant land
during the day, but in the evening returned to the
safety of numbers. "A couple of days a week," he
added, "we do community work—like lumbering, here,
or grinding flour—because that takes a lot of help. We
got several more logs to split now 'fore nightfall, but
then we'll break off an' get you and the lady"—his
eyes once again searched Delia—"situated and on track
for the future."

"Let me give you a hand here with those logs,"
offered Jason—a shrewd suggestion, honestly advanced,
which immediately won for him the esteem of the
people.

"I can work, too," Delia said.

"Come now," Harris demurred. "You've had a hell of a trek through the woods. There's no need."

"No, we belong here now," Jason insisted. "Just a drink of coffee or something and—" He stripped off his jacket and shirt, preparing to go to work.

The citizens of Harrisville let out a gasp of horror. They saw the great wound where the strip of flesh had been ripped from his abdomen.

"Get that in the raid?" inquired Rupert Harris.

Jason hesitated, but only for a moment. "I did not wish to make much of it," he said, "but, yes, Delia and I were captured and taken to the Chickasaw village."

Awed, fearful exclamations followed this announcement; and in spite of her anxiety Delia could not help but notice that the cries of these white people, when they spoke of Indians, were exactly like the sounds made by her own tribe when the depredations of the white men were anticipated or reported.

"They cut me some. But they did not bind her, and so at nighttime, she came, released me, and we fled."

Delia felt the approval of the people, though Harris seemed less willing to lend his immediate approbation. But he did not dwell on her then. Instead he asked a series of quick questions to determine the state of the Chickasaw and their leadership. Upon learning of Firebrand's ascendancy, he cursed bitterly.

"I've been meaning to go north for some time, to give news of our plight to General Jackson, and I think now the time has surely come to do it."

Mutters of agreement spread through the group.

But there were other things to do before they could consider the particulars. More logs remained to be turned into planking. In spite of continued protestations, Jason went to help the men. As for Delia, several women came forward with offers to give her dwelling. One of them—a fair-haired, pale-eyed girl with a very bright, persistent smile—pushed forward and said, "Oh, but you know Phil and I are going to add onto our house and make it an inn . . ."

This news seemed to take the other women by surprise.

". . . and I'm sure you wouldn't deny us our first guests."

The women looked at one another in a way that was both strange and familiar to Delia, glanced with measuring eyes at the fair-haired girl, and seemed to agree: Well, let her do it then, if it will make her happy.

So they returned to brick making, while the young woman led Delia back up the river bank to the village, talking nonstop.

"I'm so glad you're safely here. This is a fine place to live. A little rough yet, but with great promise. Just like Rupert says, wait until we get more land cleared, and get slaves. Slaves can make the difference. Oh, I'm sorry—" she laughed, very brightly—"I didn't even introduce myself. I'm Gale Foley. Mrs. Phil Foley. He's down there working with the men."

She lowered her voice slightly, but not much. "We're actually a little above a lot of the people here. In social station, I mean. But we try to manage. I'll explain everything to you later. So you're Delia. What a pretty name. From Georgia, did Mr. Randolph say?" It was all Delia could do to get in a quick nod. "Georgia is a fine place to be from. We're from Boston, though. Phil and me. I'm sort of the social leader here, you could say. Everyone defers to me because I've had more—well, I have to say it, I just do, it's the truth—more education and breeding. Phil's not really a common farmer, either, he's an advocate . . ."

Delia did not know what an advocate was, but the manner in which Gale pronounced the word made it seem portentous indeed, so she managed to inject a respectful nod, all the while wondering about this strange white girl.

". . . but he wasn't able to—oh, I'll save that for later, it's depressing. Now here's our place," she babbled on, showing Delia one of the buildings of wood, which looked just like all of the other wooden buildings, "and as you can see it's the biggest and best situated in town, that's why I had the idea and convinced Phil to let us have an inn. A lot of people will be stopping by, I'm sure, on the way to the West, and . . ."

She opened the door, and motioned Delia inside.

"We're sure to make loads and loads of money. Are you hungry? Would you like some tea?"

Delia had never heard of tea, but she was hungry, and perhaps tea was good to eat. She had just expressed her gratitude for the offer when she stopped in mid-step, her eyes riveted to the corner of the room she had just entered.

There, crouched like an animal, eyes half-crazed with fear, and a chain around his neck, was Bright Badger. The chain was attached to a rope that was tied to a bolt in the wall. Bright Badger wore only a breechcloth; his back was covered with welts and cuts. His eyes widened as he recognized her. But he said nothing.

Gale's tone, which had been friendly, changed abruptly in mid-sentence. "You!" she barked at Bright Badger. "Heat water for tea! This instant!"

The boy jumped up, knowing he had been commanded to do something, but he was not quite certain what it was. Delia remembered that Bright Badger, in spite of his name, had never been among the more intelligent children in the tribe, and this strange white woman barking at him must have verged on the incomprehensible. At any rate, he was not quick about heating the water.

"You ignorant savage!" cried Gale. "How many times have I explained the words to you?"

With that, she took up a length of rope and began striking Bright Badger over the back and shoulders, while he yelped and howled and tried to escape her fury.

"Stop!" Delia cried.

Surprised, Gale did so. "What?"

Quickly, in her own tongue, Delia explained to Bright Badger what it was he had been instructed to do, although she herself still did not know what tea was.

The boy did, however, and quickly made for the stove, half crouching, like an animal, and fed kindling into the place of the fire.

Gale put the rope down. "You know the savage tongue?"

"Yes," said Delia. "There were many friendly Indians in my part of Georgia."

"I see, I *see*," said Gale, contemplatively, and Delia thought the secret of her identity was lost now for sure. But it turned out that the white girl was thinking of something altogether different.

"You can help me!" she exclaimed with delight.

"Help you? Of course, but—"

"You can help me train this Indian boy to be a slave. You know how to talk to him."

This suggestion revolted Delia to the final degree.

"It's our Christian duty!" Gale was saying. "We must teach these pagan savages how to work!"

Duty was a word that Delia knew from her own life, and it was a good word. *Christian* she did not know. What could it be? Did it have something to do with slaves? She could think of nothing to say that would not further compromise herself, and so said not a word. In a moment she was motioned toward a strange-looking upright arrangement of wood balanced on four sticklike legs. Several of the same devices surrounded a flat piece of wood balanced on four thicker upright wooden supports. Delia had never seen anything like it.

"Sit down, sit down," Gale was saying.

Sit down? Delia wondered. On the flat wooden thing, or . . . ?

She hesitated, watching, and saw Gale pull away from the flat piece one of the four-legged upright pieces and sit down on it. Ah, so that was how one did it! She did likewise, and found it very odd, but not uncomfortable. It was not as pleasant a position as sitting cross-legged, but less tiring than squatting.

Bright Badger brought two tiny, hollow containers made of a glassy substance, a bowl with white powder in it, and the smallest pitcher Delia had ever seen, which contained something that looked reassuringly like milk. Gale smiled at her when Bright Badger put the pitcher on the table.

But what was to happen now? Was Delia supposed to drink from the pitcher? She smiled back at the white girl, and waited, wishing to all heaven that Jason were here with her. Bright Badger was not meeting her eyes, or even looking her way, and that unsettled Delia, too. It suddenly occurred to her that she herself might be made a slave, and chained to the wall. No, she would kill herself first!

Then the boy brought over a pitcherlike pot of some kind, from which Gale poured a dark liquid into the tiny containers. "Help yourself to sugar, please?" she said then, waiting.

Sugar? It must be the white powder. But what did one do with it? There was a miniature spoon in the white powder, true; but did one eat it, or what?

"No, thank you," she said.

"Oh, please. It's for special."

"You first," Delia said, buying time. "For being so kind to me."

Gale accepted the idea of being kind, and the principle that such a quality ought to be rewarded with favor. She spooned some of the white powder into the tea. Then she added milk. Delia followed suit, and sipped gingerly, as the white girl did. Tea was very good! She sipped some more.

"Rupert gave him to me," Gale was saying, with a nod toward Bright Badger, who had scuttled back to his corner. "Caught him out in the woods, the little beggar. No one else would take him, but I said to Phil, 'Let's.' It'll be a great advantage to have the first slave in Harrisville. Later, when we get darkies, we'll be even better off. It counts, it always counts, to be in the vanguard. That's how you get respect. I learned things like that growing up back east."

Back east must be a great place, thought Delia, from the way the white girl had said it, and a very important place. She wondered if it was as big as Harrisville, and if it was so great, why Gale had left it.

"Why doesn't he look at me?" Delia asked. "The boy?"

Gale was astounded. "Surely you know? A slave must never look into the eyes of his master—and never, absolutely never, must he look upon a woman! Oh, this boy has had some hard lessons, as you can see by his bruises, but he'll come around, don't you worry."

Right then Delia decided to plan something, anything, that would free the poor child of his torment.

"You have very striking features, do you know that?" Gale was asking, peering this way and that, examining Delia as if she were some exotic, newfound object of delight.

"Thank you."

"Are you interested in this"—she winked—"Mr. Randolph, who's supposed to be taking care of you?"

"He's . . . very kind. A friend of my father's," she remembered to add.

"If I were you, I might do a little taking care of him," said Gale with another wink. "Of course, Phil is a perfect husband," she saw fit to point out. "He does everything I want. That's because I—" she put her teacup down and leaned forward conspiratorially —"come from higher circles than him."

"Higher circles?" Delia asked, and fought an urge to look up at the top of this weird, square room.

"Yes," Gale went on, babbling again. "I could tell you things . . . . It's not easy for me, being way out here in the wilderness, even if it is a fine place, what with Mr. Harris and all. He's the real man around here. . . . Phil, of course . . ." Suddenly her bright look fell away, and something like a mean little glint came into her eyes.

Delia was startled. For that fleeting instant this Gale Foley woman reminded her of none other than Little Swallow: the same mixture of ambition and pride, insecurity and vengefulness.

But then the dark look was gone, as if it had never been there at all. The bright, optimistic face was back. "It was a good thing, really," she chattered, "that Phil couldn't get an advocate job in the East. Now we can get in on the ground floor here on the frontier. Back east, I would have just been one of many cultivated ladies, but here I'm . . ."

She made a gesture with her hand. Modesty would not permit her to describe the actual regard in which she was held.

"I'll tell you about the women," she said. "If we're going to be friends, there are things you should know. All of them are very nice, but none of them are too well educated. They all look up to me. Notice how they deferred immediately when I suggested you stay here? That's what I mean. They tell me all their problems. I'm very close to each of them. Just last week, for instance, I taught Mrs. Loftus how to improve her quilt making."

"Quilt mak—" Delia started to ask. "Yes." Oh, when would Jason get here?

Mercifully, she had not long to wait. The sounds of people coming up from their work by the river were heard, and Gale jumped to her feet with something like alarm. "Oh, my! Here it is almost supper time, and . . ." She picked up her rope and advanced on Bright Badger. "Up, up—and be quick about it now. I'm untying you, but only to go to the smokehouse—

smokehouse, understand? Fetch back a ham, and be quick about it!"

Delia saw the boy struggle to understand the strange words, and he seemed to, for as soon as the woman untied him, he raced from the house.

Then Jason came in, followed by a pleasant, nondescript white man.

"Phil!" Gale cried. "I'm so tired from making those bricks, and the slave has been so difficult!"

With an emotion very close to joy, Delia saw the look of astonishment and disgust that appeared on Jason's face when he heard the word *slave*. He said nothing, however.

After a moment of explanatory conversation—Phil seemed surprised that his wife's inn had been so soon established—Delia and Jason were led upstairs, the stairway itself hardly more than a rickety ladder that led to what had been a simple loft. Now, however, a thin wall divided the loft to form the rooms of the "inn."

"Now this is room one," Gale explained, "and this is room two. You may have your choice. Perhaps you'd like to rest while supper is prepared?"

Both Jason and Delia eagerly agreed.

"This time of year, cooking is done on the common range outside in the village. I must go over there now, if I can find that worthless boy, and cook up some ham. I'll call when I get back. Phil, would you help me?"

So the new guests at the inn were left alone.

Jason's glance was solicitous. "How are you finding life among the jackals?" he smiled.

"I do not understand this woman, Gale, and there are many things I do not understand. And Jason . . ." She lowered her voice urgently, glanced down into the small house to make certain they were alone. "She has a young boy here, an Indian boy, whom she has made into a slave. It is terrible."

"I know. It's one of the reasons I left Virginia. I

cannot abide such enforced subservience, but like it or not, our law states that—"

"But the boy is from my village! I saw Harris abduct him, right before my eyes!"

She saw him considering the problems, balancing her instincts and his own with their mutual need to survive, and his hope to make a life of farming in this land.

"How do you like the woman?" he asked, as if Delia might have found in Mrs. Foley some redemptive grace.

"She is strange. She frightens me. Like another whom I have known among my people, she makes great show of the teeth, but in her heart there is bile, and maybe terror, for a thing I know not."

"All right," he nodded. "I shall speak to her at our evening meal, and listen to her. If our staying here would be unpleasant because of her, we'll leave."

"But where will we stay?"

"I did not come here to put my comfort in the hands of others. I will act, and find a place. But if we are to leave this 'inn,' it should be immediate, lest we stir animosity in a woman with a small mind and facile tongue."

Delia agreed, and seeing Jason push aside a hanging curtain leading to his share of the loft, she did the same. Inside was a long, rectangular object on four wooden legs. It looked very much like the table downstairs, except that it was lower, and covered with a soft cloth. Wondering what it was, she lay down on the floor and dropped quickly into a nap, thinking about Bright Badger, running through the forest, picking berries.

CHAPTER VI

"Mr. Harris has decided to travel north to the Hermitage and speak with Andy Jackson," Phil Foley told them at supper, his mouth full of fried ham and squash.

Jason nodded, eating.

Delia was trying, painstakingly, to cut her piece of ham with a knife, as she had seen the others do. In her own village meat was eaten in chunks, with the fingers. Never did one have a great big hot slab of it on a plate, where it must be cut, and organized, and forever moved about. Fortunately Jason kept the Foleys occupied in conversation, giving her a chance to get accustomed to this strange new way of eating. Jason had spoken of the Randolphs, his family in Virginia, news of which Gale greeted with little yelps of delight. Her own family, in Boston, knew the Adamses very well and had entrée to the best of society, and consequently she and Jason were practically related—"in social class, anyway," Gale put it.

Jason smiled pleasantly and said nothing.

"And like yourself," Gale went on, "Phil and I sought greater challenge here in the West, where you can forge your own life . . ."

Her voice trailed off, and Phil ate, studying his ham and beans. It was clear even to Delia, who had but limited knowledge of her hostess, that Phil had disappointed Gale grievously by not having achieved some high position in the East.

In due course Jason courteously inquired as to Phil

Foley's interests, and was delighted to learn that, like himself, Phil had "read the law," which was the expression used to indicate that a man intended to practice as an attorney.

"But that was back east," Phil explained. "A lawyer will be needed out here someday, but for the time being I make a living by managing the grist mill. And I've also begun to clear some acres south of town. I want to farm as well."

"Progress would come faster, wouldn't it," Jason asked, "if people lived on their separate plots, instead of coming back here to town every night? Isn't considerable time wasted traveling to and from the various plots?"

"Yes," Phil agreed, "but like Mr. Harris said, no one has been bold enough to set up a house and live away from the village. To do so would be a certain target for an Indian raiding party."

Jason acknowledged this wisdom soberly, and said no more. In the corner, crouched against the wall, Bright Badger whined in hunger, his eyes still downcast. Phil rose to give him some meat. Gale touched his hand. "Not until we're through," she hissed. "He must learn to wait."

Phil's instincts were good, even if he lacked courage in the face of his wife's strong whims. "He's just a boy," Phil managed. "I wish you hadn't taken him from Harris."

Gale smiled sweetly at Delia and Jason, as if to say, "He doesn't really mean that."

Delia fought the impulse to leap forward and plunge this useless ham-cutting knife into Gale's pale breast.

"It seems to me," Jason offered judiciously, "that using Indians as bound slaves would tend to provoke the very attack you might wish to avoid."

Phil seemed pleased. "Why, that's what I—that's what I've tried to tell Mr. Harris."

"Oh, *Phil*, no, you *haven't*!" Gale cried. "I told you and I *told* you to go along with the majority."

He ignored her this once. "But Mr. Harris is gunning for a showdown. That's why he wants to persuade Jackson to bring the militia down here, go up into those mountains, and wipe out the Indian village."

Delia dropped the slippery silver fork.

"But some of us think the territory is big enough for everyone. If the new Chickasaw chief will make an effort to show peace, why, I think we can have peace."

"I don't think Andy Jackson will rush down here," Jason said, quite decisively.

"You know his mind?" Gale asked, after a moment's hesitation.

"I know him," Jason said. "That is, my father does."

Delia, already startled by the talk of wiping out her ancestral village, now shot an almost fearful glance at Jason. His people *knew* the terrible Chula Harjo? They could touch and see and know and converse with him, as some stupid innocent might drink with the devil?

"Jackson can be brutal, and he is certainly decisive," Jason was explaining, "but he is careful as well. With each year his chances for national power increase. And as those chances mount, he is less and less likely to undertake a sporadic or local conflict. The provocation would have to be great, and the justification for retaliation would have to be clear enough to explain to the liberal reformers back east. They have begun now to champion the fate of the Indian."

"And we may die, out here in the West, at the hands of the Indian," Gale said.

As if in counterpoint Bright Badger whimpered in his corner.

"That's enough—I'm feeding him," Phil declared, and this time Gale did not offer resistance. She was too busy, anyway, being impressed that Jason knew General Jackson.

"Tomorrow," she told Delia, "I'll take you around

to all the ladies. Once you know who's important and who's not, it'll be easier for you here."

Supper eventually reached its conclusion, with only one further moment of danger. Gale, leaning forward over her dessert, a serving of corn cake, asked Delia, "And where were you educated, dear?"

A flicker of alarm showed in Jason's eyes, and he made as if to speak for her. But Delia had taken her measure of this Gale, at least for the moment.

"At the school of Talking Rock," she said quietly, with perfect pretense of assurance. "It is a very well-known school in Georgia."

"Really?" cried Gale. "Of course! I know it well."

Not much later they sought their separate rooms in the loft, and Jason managed a few words with her.

"We must not stay here too long," he said. "I smell trouble. The man is not unintelligent, and he seems decent enough—or he might be if he had the chance. But the woman, Gale, is a born troublemaker. If she makes it appear to the townspeople that we are her fast friends, we shall be isolated."

He was whispering. Delia nodded. It was dark, and he leaned forward, waiting for her to speak. Their foreheads touched, just for a moment, just briefly. But a telling shock passed through them both, and although they did not know it yet—it was something to be considered later, as they waited for sleep—they had, in a short time, become more than two conspirators plotting their futures in the darkness. He is not Torch, Delia would think, but he is a man indeed. I wonder . . . no, he will wish a girl like himself, whose flaxen hair shines in the sun . . . .

She is lovely, and smart, thought Jason, in his turn, but her heart will be long in mourning for her chieftain lover.

Such thoughts were the companions of imminent sleep. Before the two parted, Delia had another worry.

"There is so little room," she complained. "I cannot move."

"In your part of the loft?"

"Yes."

He looked puzzled. "I know it is a small area, but mine is adequate. And I believe they are the same size, your space and mine."

"It would be well, if only the soft table were not present."

"The—what soft table?"

"I have no room to sleep," she whispered. "The space upon the floor is insufficient."

There was a long silence, and then he seemed to be choking. It was a moment before she realized that he was trying to hold back his laughter. What was so amusing? For a moment she felt ignorant and offended.

"That is a *bed*," he informed her. "One sleeps *upon* it, not beside it on the floor."

"For sleeping?" she wondered.

"Some of the time," Jason said, with an inflection she did not immediately interpret.

CHAPTER VII

The first few days in Harrisville were filled with constant activity, with so many new things to learn. And yet it seemed to Delia, as she first observed the activity and then began to participate in it, that the routine of these white jackals in their strange boxy village of stone and wood was not so greatly different from the daily exercises and observances of her own tribe, separated from her now by mountains, and much more.

Rupert Harris packed saddlebags, loaded his rifle, stuck a knife and a big pistol in his belt. Then the villagers gathered around as he mounted his horse and rode off to visit Chula Harjo, and the scene was quite like that among the Chickasaw when braves set forth upon a war party, or when the chieftain left to hold counsel with warriors of another tribe. Delia put it into perspective. Harris was a small chief, Jacksa a greater one. And Monroe, far away in Washington, was the greatest of all. But, as among her people, an old chief could depart and a new one take his place. Jacksa could become the great chief, so—her mind leaped ahead of her—so why could Jason not become chief here?

Maybe Harris would never come back. Maybe a mountain lion would leap from a tree, to rend and devour his pale, stinking flesh. Or perhaps a Choctaw would send an arrow into his hard heart. Or a crocodile might be sleeping on the river bank when Harris sought to ford a stream . . . .

Among the villagers, occupations, relationships, feuds and alliances, stresses and strains, grew more and more obvious. Jason went out into the country, to inspect parcels of land for the plantation he intended to mold, by effort of will as well as of muscle, from the surrounding wilderness. "Ten thousand years have made the earth rich," he told her. "It will grow cotton plants ten feet tall." While he was away from the village, she helped perform whatever tasks were necessary. At Gale's house she learned how to replace the soft covering of the bed after she awoke in the morning, and how to position what Gale called the silver on the table at which they ate. She also learned how to listen to Gale without saying anything of importance herself, because she had grasped quickly that anything she told the other girl was quickly repeated to everyone else who would listen, yet always with strange twists and turnings. At dinner that first night, to spare herself an inquisition, she had made it appear that Talking Rock had been a school, and a distinguished one at that, rather than the deadly place in memory where her parents had been killed by Chula. Gale had clearly never heard of the school at Talking Rock, but she had spoken of its renown to the women of the village.

"Of course I don't know much," said Mrs. Hawkes, the blacksmith's wife, when the women were at work hoeing the garden. "*I* haven't had a fine education."

And she gave Delia a stare that was like the shaft of an arrow with snake venom on the point.

Delia did not understand at first. Instead she was chagrined, and accused herself of not trying hard enough to contribute to the efforts of the community. Then, when they stopped working and took lunch, Mrs. Randall, a farmer's wife, handed the water dipper to Delia before anyone else had drunk. "I suppose you're used to being first," she said with an unsettling smile, "so we'd best coddle you."

Immediately Delia knew that her own instincts had

been correct, knew Jason had been right. Whatever it was in the awful soul of Gale Foley, she was born to scatter bitterness and strife upon the earth. From her mouth poured twisted words, like evil seeds, and they fell always upon the ever-present human soil of suspicion. Gale was at once pretending to be Delia's friend, then misrepresenting everything she said, thus giving the other women the idea that Delia thought herself better than all the rest. Which, in fact, was Gale's unfounded opinion of *herself*!

Humiliated, burning with anger, Delia took the dipper from Mrs. Randall. "I thank you," she said, "and I drink to the kindness of your offer." She drank. "But it is not necessary. I am in no way used to coming first."

There was among the rest of the women, Gale included, a subdued, satirical titter. Delia knew from experience among her own people—and certainly from her disastrous attempts to engage Little Swallow in open conflict—that shrewdness and discretion must serve her. Open anger would be the doom Gale seemed so eagerly to be awaiting. Why? Delia didn't know. Perhaps it was simply the way Gale was. Or maybe it was the way Delia looked, or acted, or spoke. There did not need to *be* a reason. Gale had to be countered, and quickly, in a manner all would understand. This was a thing in which Jason, gone into the country, could not help her.

So Delia drew upon her own past, her own strength.

All during lunch she did not speak, though the hot blood of her heritage surged often when she heard Gale say, "Yes, Mr. Randolph says he *knows* Andy Jackson, but we shall see!" and "Sure, everyone could come into Harrisville high and mighty if they pretended to be a Virginia Randolph. Virginia! Hah! Maybe he can spell the letters if he thinks about it long enough!" and "You all know I tell the truth, and this one truth is that we'd better be very careful whom we befriend around here!"

That made it seem almost as if Delia were being accused of thievery or some wrongdoing within Gale's own "inn." Or did it have something to do with Jason Randolph, and the two of them sleeping upstairs?

Yes! That must be it! Gale had said so many other things that she must have made insinuations about sex.

One part of Delia's nature pressed her to respond, but then—based upon her hard-earned wisdom from clashes with Little Swallow—she saw that such a response would be deadly, the end of everything before anything had begun.

In the moment of restraint that she forced upon herself, Delia saw, read, knew, divined, the feelings of the women. *They* knew in their hearts, whether or not they would fully admit it to themselves, exactly what Gale was and what she was doing to Delia. But they did nothing, because they were afraid Gale would, out of her bottomless supply of snide rancor, do the same to them! So Delia waited until lunch was over, rose with the rest of them, and calmly picked up her hoe.

The land, rich as it was, had taken each planted seed—corn, beans, peas, squash, turnips, beets, potatoes —and transformed it into rich and flowing fruit. But, curse of lost Eden, weeds grew, thrived, ran riot among the flowering plants. Between the rows of vegetables curled carpets of weeds that must be hacked to death by brutal labor if the harvest were to be good. After an hour of such chopping, the muscles of even the hardiest person cried for relief. To advance fifty feet in one hour, hoeing and chopping, was a feat for the best of these women, and some of them were very tough. They had not left their homes in the little white villages of New England, they had not left the big red barns, the rich red earth of Pennsylvania and the sweet old estates along the Tidewater, they had not left the raw, rugged life of Georgia and the Caro-linas because they were not strong, or followed venturous husbands because they were not bold! No, these were hard, strong people, brave as any, and Delia knew it. Thus it was doubly revolting that a simpering wisp of a girl, with poison on her brain and tongue, should cow them so.

Delia began to hoe. In an hour she was twenty feet in front of the rest. In two hours she had completed one row and started another. In three hours, not stopping, slacking, or even appearing to be making great effort, she was midway up her third row, while the others paused for water, barely beginning their second rows.

They had at first tried to keep up with Delia, and thus had further outpaced Gale, who could barely keep up with them on normal days. But this day was far from normal. Gasping with thirst, the women did not want to stop, lest Delia, whom they had at lunch conspired to defame, take the revenge of satisfaction. But how did she do it? Where did she get the strength, the endurance? Was there something in her heritage, her fiber, just as strong as in their own, or stronger?

Finally Mrs. Randall called out, "Delia—rest—water."

But Delia went on hoeing and did not appear to hear. The women were discomfited. This beautiful young slip of a girl was made of iron. Taking no water in the heat of the Tennessee afternoon was hard enough, but hoeing in the heat was even worse.

"She is just trying to show off!" gasped Gale, coming up from way behind. She received no answer from the other women. The dipper reached her last. She gulped pathetically and said nothing, though hatred burned in her eyes.

"Send that boy of yours," said Mrs. Randall after a time. "You, Gale, send that pathetic little redskin you call a servant. Have him take water out to Delia." Mrs. Randall glanced at the others. "I think Delia's tried to show us something here today—and, by God, I think she's done it!"

Mrs. Randall, nearly six feet tall and at least a hundred and eighty pounds, had borne six children, lost three more, outlived two husbands, more than kept up with a third, and had once, alone, managed a plantation in Mississippi. She knew well what she could do, but she knew that she could not do what Delia was doing out there under the sun this day.

"*That* is a woman!" she told the others with a kind of contained pride. "I don't care if she went to school with Marie Antoinette."

"Who's Marie Antoin—?" gulped Gale Foley, before she stopped. But before she stopped, she realized how totally she had been outdone.

The vicious, catty, mendacious chatter she had practiced so long, to give herself the appearance of superiority—well, she could no longer have recourse to it now. Talk and babble, however bitter, can never approach the proof of hard work and accomplishment. Gale had to learn the hard way.

And there out in the field was Delia, still without water, still chopping unceasingly, apparently without great effort.

The women tittered and snickered, but this time Delia was not the object.

"Boy!" gasped Gale, all but sagging down along a row of gloriously thriving cane stalks. "Boy!" she called to Bright Badger. "Bring that woman water. The one out there." She pointed to Delia. "Out there. She looks like you, you beggar. She looks like an Indian."

She did not plan to say it. She did not, then, consciously know it.

Delia paused and leaned on her hoe, looking down at the child. His eyes were on the ground. He did not look at her. His tongue was lolling. Gale had not given him water!

"Drink first," she told him in the Chickasaw tongue, when he proffered the dipper. "And do not be afraid to look at me."

Bright Badger raised his eyes, and remembered the fateful day in the forest by the berry bushes. He fought the tears, he was still a child, and no brave. Yet he had borne up well enough, here in these terrible surroundings. He had nothing to be ashamed of, much to be proud of, and she told him so. "Now drink."

He drank, then passed the dipper to her. She sipped, waited, sipped again. The other women were watching in the distance, but with interest and not animosity. Delia sensed that she had accomplished much this afternoon.

Then she spoke quickly to the boy. "If you left here, could you find your way back through the mountains to our home?"

She felt a thrill, saying "our home."

He answered immediately. "Just let me leave here, and that is enough."

"But you are young. I would not want—"

"Death is better than this. To the south I see the twin mountains. In our village I looked north and saw them. Do not worry for me. Get me away, and I will know in which direction to go."

"It may take some time."

"The Red Beard is gone now, for some days. No other time will be better."

"But if they catch you on the run, they will kill you."

"What matters? If I remain, I will die, too, and my heart first."

Delia looked at him. He stood there bleakly, close to defeat, the marks of beatings all about him. Some day Gale would pay for that, too.

"Can you untie the knot by which you are bound in the corner?"

"I have tried. My fingers are not strong enough."

"If you had a knife?"

"Those are kept where I cannot reach."

"Boy! Boy!" Gale was calling—afraid, perhaps, that Delia and Bright Badger were talking about her.

"If you had a knife to cut the rope?"

"Then I could do it, but the bar on the door is too heavy for me."

Delia thought of the inside of the Foleys' house. A thick oaken beam, set in iron brackets on the door frame, secured the house during the night. It was true. Bright Badger would not be able to lift it by himself. He would not even be able to reach it without standing on something. So he would need help.

But the Foleys slept in a small back room downstairs. If Delia came down from the loft to help Bright Badger, how could she do so without making a colossal noise on the rickety, creaking stairs?

"I will think about it," she told him.

"Boy! Get over here at once!"

"Do not lose heart and do not betray the fact that we know each other."

"I shall not."

With that, he ran off, and Delia once again picked up her hoe, her mind working furiously on the problem of Bright Badger's escape.

At supper that night conversation was desultory indeed, save for the fact that Jason had found a promising plot of land.

"It's very rich," he said, describing it, "and it won't be too hard to clear of trees. The only problem is that it lies down near the river. You know—where the bend is?"

"Sure, I know the place," Phil Foley said.

"I was worried about flooding, especially in spring."

"Didn't flood this spring. Didn't flood last spring either, far as I know." He glanced at his wife, and seemed to realize that she wasn't saying much this evening. "Feeling tired, dear?"

"Oh, no, no," replied Gale with forced gaiety.

"How do I go about making a claim on that land?" Jason asked.

"Just wait until Mr. Harris gets back. He makes the decisions about who gets what." He said it matter-offactly, but with a delicate undercurrent of disapproval.

"How did that—that *arrangement* come about?" Jason wanted to know.

Phil was a bit defensive. "Well, Rupert organized the original party that came out here from Wheeling, and in the beginning there were a lot of problems. With the redskins and such, and people wanting to leave. He held it together. When there was conflict among the group, we turned to him. It's rather an accepted practice now, as if he were a judge."

"I see," said Jason, but he did not pursue the matter. He had just arrived in Harrisville; it was no time to begin suggesting improvements, much less pointing out deficiencies.

After supper the men went out to feed and curry Phil's horse, shell corn to feed the chickens, and milk the two cows. Gale, in the kitchen, was trying to teach Bright Badger how to dry dishes. He had a hard time holding on to the slippery things.

"The boy is tired," Delia observed. "Here, let him rest, and I'll—"

"The job of a slave is to be tired!" snapped the innkeeper. "What do you think? Look, I'm getting mighty tired of—"

She seemed just on the verge of a terrific explosion of temper, but somehow she found the strength to hold herself in check. Delia knew for certain not only that she must leave this house quickly, but also that she would never be safe from the possibility that Gale would fashion some kind of revenge for her humiliation in the field. It might come tomorrow; it might come in a month or two. Or it might come in years— if, the heavens forbid, Delia had to stay here that long.

She went immediately up to the loft and lay down on the bed, waiting for nightfall. Tonight, at least Bright Badger would know free air, and the whispering leaves of the trees as he fled through them. If only she could go with him!

Someone sighed aloud, and it was a moment before

Delia realized that the sound had come from herself. Reasonably safe now here in Harrisville, with the moment-by-moment exigencies of survival no longer pressing, Delia was aware of her body's needs. She thought now, in the evening with the sun descending and the sky soft and many-colored, of a man's love— of Torch's love—and her body burned in all the places he had kissed. She put it out of her mind, that memory —or tried to. But it was no use. Even when she succeeded in making her mind blank and clear as the ice on a winter lake, yet did her body remember . . . .

The twin agonies of need and memory tormented her as nightfall slipped across the land, spreading its soft cloak from the river across the rich fields, the forests, and upon the far mountains that marked the borders of her vanished life.

Phil and Jason came inside, having completed the chores. As Gale retreated to her room in the back of the house, the two men lit pipes downstairs. One of them gave Bright Badger food and said kind words to him.

After a long time Jason's footsteps sounded on the rickety stairs.

Delia shuddered, breathing hard.

Jason paused outside her curtained place, then entered his own. She heard him removing his boots, his clothing. She could hear his breathing for a time as well; then everything was still.

She waited until midnight, and then she waited more. Finally, when night was high and sleep deepest, it was time. The stairs would be too dangerous, too noisy; so she rolled the soft blanket on the bed lengthwise, did likewise with the thin sheet, knotted them together, and knotted one end to the railing of the loft. Soundlessly she slid down to the kitchen floor, let her eyes adjust to the darkness, and looked toward Bright Badger's corner.

He wasn't there!

Approaching, she saw that the hook was still in the wall, the big rope still knotted in the hook. But the other end of the rope had been cut through, where it had been tied to the leather collar around his neck.

Had he managed to reach a knife after all?

Quickly she checked the big door, found it securely braced by the mighty oaken bolt. That must mean Bright Badger was still in the house. But where? Certainly he would not have gone back where Gale and Phil were sleeping. He was not under the table, or in the front section of the house. She would have heard him if he had gone upstairs.

Mystified and a little frightened, she climbed her blanketladder hand over hand, unknotted the device, and returned to her bed. But something about all of this seemed drastically wrong, and she could not contain her need to know what it was. The only one who might help her was Jason.

She slipped barefoot across the loft to his bed and paused beside it. His breathing was deep and regular, and in the small space he gave off a man-smell that was not at all unpleasant, although it was distracting.

She moved forward, accidentally brushed against his bed, and immediately felt herself pulled forward, flung through the air. Then she was on her back in the bed, and he was above her, in an attitude of attack, as if to strike her. His fist was raised for a blow.

"No!" she managed to gasp.

"Delia!" he whispered. "Don't ever do that again! I thought . . ."

The moment of instinct passed, and they were suddenly aware of each other. She wore a thin chemise Gale had given her; Jason wore nothing. She slid off the bed, half crouched, half kneeling beside it. He rested full-length on his elbow and drew a sheet halfway across his body, which in the darkness seemed all heights and hollows.

"What on earth is it?" he whispered.

"Bright Badger," she replied. Had that been a noise downstairs? The Foleys? The Indian boy himself? "Bright Badger seems to have gone."

"How do you know?"

"I went down there to—"

"Why?" His question was curt.

She decided to admit it. "I wanted to set him free."

"Perhaps he's gone on his own."

"No," she said, shaking her head in the darkness. "By himself, he could not manage the bar on the door."

There was a long silence in the darkness. Finally he made a decision of his own. "I lifted the bar for him," Jason told her. "I set him free."

They spoke no more; but her gratitude, in spite of the silence was evident, and did not require words. After a time she reached out and touched his face, gently, gently, and she felt his fingers seek her, and find the place where her neck and shoulder met, where her black hair fell and flowed upon her bare skin. Delia was reluctant to withdraw her touch, and Jason his; but, whatever his reasons, he did not quite curl his hand about her willing neck and draw her toward him, and she did not quite bend her head to him.

The moment passed, but it had been neither dream nor accident.

And they both knew it.

CHAPTER VIII

&

"So," grunted Rupert Harris, sliding a jug of corn whiskey across the rough wooden table, "it's time we talked business."

Jason nodded, pulled the cork from the thick neck of the jug, and stuck his thumb through the curved thumbhole on the base of the neck. Then, lifting the jug onto his shoulder, he half turned his head, tilted the jug a bit, and let several healthy gulps of the clear, strong liquor pour into his mouth. He swallowed it, gasped, and slid the jug back across the table. Harris grinned, wiped the neck with the palm of his hand, hoisted and gulped down twice as much as Jason had. The two men sat at a battered table in Harris's shack.

This was a frontier negotiation. One drank from a common jug, to show trust. One drank more than an adversary, to show endurance, if not necessarily wisdom. Just recently a cultured Frenchman named de Tocqueville had toured America, from the eastern seaports to the backwoods settlements, and had concluded: Whiskey is the wine of America, drunk daily and in quantity by all, including children.

Certainly Rupert Harris was a patron of the local still.

"Mentioned your name to Old Hickory when I was up there to the Hermitage," Harris was saying. There was a guarded shrewdness in his eyes. "He said he knows your folks back in Virginny. Asked to be remembered to you."

Jason said nothing, but he saw that Harris was not

entirely pleased about the fact. He also understood that, properly used, the family connection to the general might serve him in good stead.

"Yep, stayed overnight at the Hermitage," Harris felt compelled to add. "That wife of his, Rachel, is quite a woman, there."

Harris often spoke of women. No, he did not so much *speak* of them as make insinuations about them. Harris was, he said, a "self-admitted bachelor—leastways, so far."

"I think Rachel Jackson is a fine lady, from what I have heard," Jason said agreeably. "And one of the general's best characteristics has always been his love for her, in spite of the vicious talk. He is, I understand, gentle and civilized with all women."

"That's a mistake now, ain't it?" grunted Harris, taking another good belt of the liquor, and sliding the jug back to Jason.

Talking business required a certain mellowness, and if that pleasant state took time to achieve, so be it.

"How's that there dark-haired wench doin'?" Harris was asking, "since the two of you got booted out over at the Foleys'?"

Stunned, Jason looked at the cunning, red-bearded brawler. "What?"

"Come on, Randolph. You're a man like me. I don't blame you none."

"Blame me for what?" asked Jason, thoroughly mystified. Was this some devious ploy on Harris's part to get him unnerved?

Harris slapped his thigh. "That's the way," he chortled. "That's the way to be, all right. Don't even pay it no never mind."

"Look, would you please tell me . . ."

Even Harris, in spite of his gleeful thickness, seemed to realize that Jason didn't know what was going on. "It's all over town," he said. "How Gale had to kick the two of you out of her so-called inn there, on account of . . ." He made a loop with thumb and

forefinger and slid his other thumb back and forth
through the loop, chortling gleefully while doing so.

Jason went icy cold with anger. From the first he
had read Gale Foley correctly—a gabbling busybody
who felt, alternately, as if she owned the world, or
as if everyone in the world were dedicated to making
her life miserable. Talk like hers was difficult to combat, hard to stop. Old Hickory had learned the danger
of talk well enough himself, and he was not free of
it yet. Rachel had been married to a man named Lewis
Robards, but it had gone badly. Pursuant to Tennessee law, Robards petitioned the legislature for permission to seek a divorce, and it was granted. Robards,
however, did not immediately seek the actual divorce;
and Jackson, however unknowingly, wed a woman
who was still legally married to her first husband. Had
the general not been an already controversial public
figure with an obvious political future, the entire
affair might have been quietly set aright. But not even
the fact that Robards *did* eventually get the divorce,
and Rachel and Jackson took vows a second time,
stopped the talk. Rachel was loose, immoral, and
worse! And what was Jackson, to consort with such a
woman?

Talk, even the talk of a babbling nitwit like Gale
Foley, could be dangerous, Jason knew. He had heard
that the innuendos of smug moralists and vicious people were breaking Rachel Jackson's heart. He had no
intention of permitting either himself or Delia to be
destroyed by the flapping lips of a lightweight social
climber!

"Rupert, I've got to apologize for my ignorance,
but what exactly did the Foley woman say?"

"Huh? Why, that one mornin' you didn't come
down for breakfast right on time, so she sent Phil up
the stairs to wake you, an' that's when he saw it. You
an' that Delia wench, an' she was—you know, with
her mouth."

Surprised and upset, Jason held back his anger.

"It's not true, Rupert," he said. "Talk like that is not good for the community. Gale is just irritated because Delia and I moved out of her place."

Indeed, that was the most likely reason for Gale's pique, although Jason was also aware that the Foley woman envied Delia her beauty. Since leaving the Foleys' Delia had moved in with Mrs. Randall, helping with the Randalls' four children, and Jason had set up a lean-to shelter out in an area of woods he wished to claim and clear for farmland. That was the purpose for this meeting with Harris tonight: Jason had to get the man's permission to homestead the rich land down by the river bend.

"You'll notice," he said, handing the jug to Harris again, "that Gale put the accusation in her husband's mouth. How typically courageous of her. Anyway, there's not a word of truth in it."

"There isn't?" groaned Harris, clearly disappointed. But he could tell that Jason was not lying. Harris knew every trick but he also knew when a man was telling the truth.

"If you want my opinion, that Foley woman should be horsewhipped."

"Aw, Jason, forget it. Women will always be talking that way, I suppose. I'm a little put out that the story's not true, 'cause I was sorta lookin' forward to havin' a little of that Delia myself. Maybe I still will." He drank, and wiped his mouth. "Never can tell, can you?"

Jason said nothing.

"An' anyway, Gale ain't all bad. She volunteered to train that there Indian boy for us."

"How did that boy happen to get here?" Jason asked innocently.

"Aw, he got lost from his tribe," Rupert Harris lied casually. "I figured we'd take him in an' give him a home. Thought maybe, since we can't afford niggers yet, we might try Indians."

Wishing to avoid a discussion about slavery, which

would only rile Harris's less-than-humane instincts, Jason kept his mouth shut.

"An' how'd that boy bust out, anyway?" the village boss asked.

Jason had known the question would come up, but he had already answered it many times, explaining to the people of Harrisville that the boy must have secreted a knife, cut his bonds, and slipped out of the house in the darkness.

"Yeah, but on the inside of the house, the bar was still in place by the door. How could that be?"

"The boy was slight, and wiry. Also, I doubt he could have lifted more than one end of the bolt. So he did, eased out the small opening, and let the bolt fall to when he closed the door."

It was all very plausible.

"Indians. You know how sneaky they are. Even when they're young."

For some time after Bright Badger's departure the village braced itself for an assault by the Chickasaw. But none came. "It's some kind of a trick," the people kept saying, then gradually they relaxed a little. Not much, true, but a little.

Rupert Harris never relaxed, not about the danger of Indians, anyway; and the thought of Bright Badger reminded him of this preoccupation. His voice slightly slurred now, he grunted and confided to Jason, "You know, I sent word east again that we need more settlers out here, but news of what happened to that wagon train of your'n has done got there first. Ain't too many people who want to chance it."

"The people will come, though. Give them time, they'll come."

"Not until we go on up into those mountains and bring us that there Firebrand back down here on a rail. Why, that red bastard near burned us out when we first got here. Had to set up the village all over again." Harris took a pull on the jug, swallowed, stuck a wad of chewing tobacco in his cheek, looked over his shoulder as if someone might be eavesdropping, then said, "I got me a mind to get Firebrand, cut off his head, and send it to President James Monroe in Washington and say, 'Here's what Rupert Harris had to do hisself. Now why ain't Andy Jackson on the job'"

Harris was still angered at Jackson's reluctance to attack the Chickasaw.

Jason declined tobacco but took a short slug of whiskey. It was beginning to affect him, and they had not even gotten around to discussing the distribution of farmland.

Harris initiated the exchange. "So what's on yer mind?" he grunted, turning his head sideways, shooting a gleaming brown swash of tobacco juice onto the floor.

"Well, to be blunt, I'd like to have that land down along the river."

Harris's eyes narrowed. "Down there, eh?" He spit, wadded the tobacco far up inside his cheek, and took a drink. "Well, that's rich land—mighty fine land, mighty fine. What'll you offer?"

Jason had learned by now the secret of Harris's control over much of the land. According to Tennessee law, each man's claim, subsequent to surveying and boundary demarcation, was to be registered in Knoxville. But Harris knew that many of the settlers would endure one or two seasons in this rugged country, give up, and return back east. Some would be—and had already been—killed by Indians. Thus, plots of farmland or potential plantation acreage might theoretically be subject to resale. Only theoretically, though, because Harris had never filed the original claims! "We'll do that when we get settled," he told the people, who were in general agreement with him because the situation meant greater flexibility in land trading, and freedom from the onerous precision of deeds and titles and laws. "We'll work it all out here amongst ourselves," Harris told the people, "an' that way nobody but ourselves is gonna tell us what to do." But what it came down to was that Harris claimed ownership of considerable portions of land, and held effective control, on the basis of authority or force or both, over a lot more. Anyone making a claim for land on which to build and settle could count on pledging a significant portion of whatever his land might produce to Harris himself, who kept a share, but who was sufficiently shrewd to turn over to the community just enough to make the whole venture seem cooperative and idealistic.

Sometime in the future, Jason had decided, he would challenge this system, possibly in Knoxville. But he would make no challenge now. He had two reasons. One, he wanted the river-bend land, which, he saw, would be ideally located for taking crops to market by barge. Two, he did not wish to wake up some morning with a big gash in his throat. The frontier was not a gentle place, and law—stable, deliberate, civilized law—was far away.

"Well, it *is* pretty good land," he admitted to Harris bargaining himself now, "but I expect it has a tendency to flood."

"Flood? What are you saying? That there land ain't never flooded since that there guy in the big barge with two animals of every kind. Besides, it's a choice piece of property. Prob'ly' the best we got here."

"It's good, but not the best," Jason lied, sticking to his guns.

"Why dontcha try for something else then?"

"The river bend is all I can afford, I'm afraid."

"I ain't even named my price yet. Anyway, you're a Randolph. You got plenty."

"No reason to strike a bad bargain," Jason said.

Harris took another long draught of whiskey. He was clearly showing the effects of alcohol now, one of which is that the duller the brain becomes, the shrewder it thinks it is. He passed the jug to Jason, who mouthed it eagerly, but didn't swallow any of the booze.

"So what are you asking?" said Jason, making a show of wiping his mouth.

Harris added more tobacco juice to the dark, spreading pool on the plank floor. "For the river-bend property? I'll hold you to a thirda yer crop, to be turned over to the community granary, acourse."

Slowly, and with somber gravity, Jason shook his head. "A third is too much. A third wouldn't be worth my making the effort."

"Suit yerself."

"Well, how about the strip of land up there by the ridge."

"That land? That land is prime," pronounced Harris.

"That land is mediocre at best," Jason countered, and in truth he was right, but he was using it merely as a bargaining device.

"I'll parcel out that there land to you—" he hiccuped—"for . . . ah . . . let's say . . . *quarter* of yer crop. Give me that there jug."

"A quarter of the crop?" protested Jason, as Harris slopped back the jug yet again. "A quarter of the crop along the ridge land won't yield a full half of the crop down by the river."

"Yeah, but the river land is the best property."

"If it is, why hasn't it been claimed yet? Why hasn't it been cleared?"

Harris considered that, squinting owlishly. "Too many trees down there," he said. "Land's rich, but it'll take too much work to clear."

There were many trees, Jason knew, but the earth was softer than it was in areas away from the river, and the task of removal would not be as arduous as it appeared. He did not tell this to Harris, though.

"All right," Jason slurred, pretending to take another jolt of the corn liquor, and thinking that it was time to try for a deal. "Tell you what, let's put it this way; clearing's going to be hard work, and the land is only average."

"Only average!" Harris snorted.

"But the crop *will* be far better than I could get on the ridge. Just like I told you. A *fifth* of the river-bend crop would equal a *half* of the ridge crop. Take it or leave it. A fifth!"

He leaned forward across the table and attempted to approximate the fish-eyed, bleary look Rupert Harris was sending back to him. "A *fifth*!" he repeated with emphasis, striking the table.

"Not good enough."

"Thass my las' offer," coughed Jason, leaning back suddenly in his chair, blinking dully.

"Can't handle the juice, eh?" glowed Harris triumphantly, his booze-ridden brain run riot now on an opinion of itself as a masterful negotiator. "Okay, a fifth of the crop it is. But there's one more thing."

Jason went immediately on guard. "What's that?" he asked.

"Slaves!" Harris growled.

"Slaves," said Jason noncommittally.

"Right. When we start makin' money in this place, an' clearin' more land, there's gonna be a lot of us gonna go down to N'orlins an' Baton Rouge an' buy us up some. We worked hard enough. Now when that day comes, I got to know you ain't goin' to give us no Tilly Titmouse routine about them niggers bein' people just like us, are you? 'Cause they ain't *halfways* people just like us!"

"How soon will that be? This slave-purchasing business?"

Harris winked drunkenly. "Boy, I got me the money *now*. I'm jes' watin' for a few others to get ready. Don't want to be the only aristocrat, see what I mean? Share and share alike, I say. Ain't that right? Hate to pay for 'em, though. I thought for a bit Indians might work out, but, hell, you can't even do anything with the bastards when they're little, like that kid was. The hell with the red bastards, we'll kill 'em off in due course. But right now we got to have black nigger slaves . . ."

So Harris raved on. He had grown up in "Cah'lina," an' his daddy was a dirt farmer, didn't even own his land. Up the road a piece was the big house, an' fer God sure you better believe it there was nigger slaves livin' in that house eatin' more than Harris's whole family, an' owned 'em two shirts *each,* an' some of them niggers even looked down on Harris's daddy and little Rupert, so he swore when he got big he was gonna go way out west an' build him up the biggest plantation anybody did *evah* see, an' there would come a time when he wouldn't even lift a *finger,* not even his little *pinkie* finger, without a nigger there to help him do it!

"If a man works for me, I'll pay him," Jason said, truthfully, but trying to avoid arousing Harris any further.

But Harris barely heard him. The man was off on a long drunken recital of wrongs done him, blows delivered unjustly, promises unkept. Finally Jason got him back on track. They shook hands on the riverbend property, and they shook again on an annual payment of one fifth of the crop yield. With that, Harris's mood seemed to improve somewhat, at least enough for him to stand in the doorway of his shack when Jason left, to stand there swaying, and to say, "Hey! You say hello from me to that Delia lady now, y'hear? One of these days I might just slip her something she might like!"

There was a raucous burst of laughter and, moments later, a resounding crash, as Rupert Harris missed his bed, hit the floor, found he didn't care, and went to sleep.

But not before thinking, I won't file Randolph's claim in Knoxville, either.

CHAPTER IX

Torch-of-the-Sun, chief of the Chickasaw, rode out
early from his village that morning, and he rode alone.
Many things were on his mind, and he had to think
them through. Councils had their place in the grand
scheme of things, and certainly they were useful in
debating and deciding tribal policy; but in the land
of a man's heart solitude is often the best seeress.

The tribe—its women especially, but many men as
well—were beginning to wonder aloud when their
chief would take a maiden to wife. It must be done,
it was expected, because the chieftain, even more than
the common brave, must be strong in the loins as
well as fierce in battle.

Winter had passed, and it was spring again—almost
a year since Gyva had been cast out. During the course
of that year, Torch was pleased to reflect, he had
presided over no battles, no wars, no deaths.

Had his interpretation of the intents of the white
jackals been accurate? Did they truly wish peace, or
was this pause in the pursuit of hostility only a temporary respite, a time during which the settlers in Harrisville girded themselves for greater conflict?

Torch had to know.

Scouts had been sent out many times, to the town
and its environs, but their reports had been contra-
dictory, often unsettling. So he rode out that morning alone, to see for himself. War and peace were
great issues, not to be decided on the basis of information handed down by others.

And there was another matter too.

"Torch, I have seen her," confided Fast River, one day after a general council meeting disbanded. "I thought you would wish to know that she is still safe."

Torch did not have to inquire about the object of Fast River's words. The brave had just returned from reconnoitering Harrisville.

"I saw her in the fields, working," Fast River continued.

"Like a slave? Like Bright Badger?" Torch had demanded angrily. Late last summer, when the Indian boy had stumbled back into the village with his terrible tale, the entire tribe had wished for war. But Bright Badger had reported that a *white* man had helped him, had freed him. And he had reported that Gyva was alive and well. From his descriptions of the man's appearance, it became clear that he was the one whose life Gyva had spoken for, the man Randolph, whom Torch himself had set free. So Torch had spoken against war—that time.

"We gave him his life, and he has repaid us by freeing Bright Badger. So unless they mount an attack against us, my decision is to hold to our peace."

The decision seemed to have been a good one; but now, if Gyva was being forced to work as a slave in the fields . . . .

"No, it seems she does it of her own accord. She works alone," Fast River said.

"Alone?"

"Perhaps not totally alone," the brave amended. "She works with the sun-haired one."

At this news, something deep within Torch's breast turned over. He had to see it for himself. He had to know the conditions and surroundings, the life and the health and the changings, of his secretly mourned, unforgotten beloved.

And so he rode forth that spring day.

* * *

The sun beat down on the fields, and waves of heat shimmered dreamlike above the black and furrowed earth. This great field, river watered, river drained, was almost cleared of trees and brush. When it was cleared, crops would be planted, and it would be what Jason already called it: Riverbend Farm.

"Stop!" he ordered Delia. "You'll hurt yourself. Please, give me the axe."

"No!" she cried, panting with exertion, "I almost have it." And with those words she took another mighty swinging whack at the half-buried root, felt the tingling solid *thock* of the blow through her fingertips and up her arms to her shoulders. The last root was sliced through.

"Now get the horses," she commanded, smiling in triumph, "and we can pull away the stump."

"You did it!" he cried.

"I told you," she said, still panting, but happy. "Come. Get the horse. Two more trees and the field is done."

"*Our* field," Jason said, pointedly. He searched her with his eyes.

Delia did not respond.

The help she had given him in clearing land for his farm had been as valuable as it had been honestly proffered, and Delia's delight in the accomplishment was no less than Jason's. But the long days of working together had intensified their relationship. There were times when they joked and laughed, pausing in their work to rest beneath the shade of the trees and lunch on fried chicken or cold roast pork, with brown bread and butter and a tin of cold, pale beer. These times were glorious, and she all but forgot her past life amongst her tribespeople. But then there were other times, times marked by currents of tension, a tension all the more difficult to bear because Delia knew exactly what gave rise to it.

In one instance, several days previous, she and

Jason had been working down near the river, dragging stumps and torn, rotten logs from the mud at
the place where Jason intended to build a dock. The
day was abnormally hot, even for this humid summer
along the river; but suddenly a chill passed into the
air, and black clouds massed and piled and rolled
above the mountains, soon to be crowned by a purple
thunderhead that advanced across the valley, blotting
out the sun and plunging the earth into shadow. In
moments the first cold spatter of raindrops began to
fall.

"Hurry," Jason had said, grabbing the reins of the
horses, slapping their rumps and driving them into
the forest. Only among dense trees would there be
safety from lightning; to remain out under the few
scattered trees still standing on the farm site would
be to invite disaster. Delia threw a shawl over her
head and raced after him. By the time they reached
woods thick enough to keep some of the rain off them,
she was already half-soaked.

The horses stamped and chomped green foliage
with big stained teeth, their huge work-sweated bodies
steaming in the sudden coolness. Jason tied their
reins to the trunk of an ash tree, and leaned against
it, fanning himself with the brim of his hat, lifting
his face to the tender rain that filtered down through
the leaves.

Delia stood under the shelter of the shielding
branches, receiving immediately a flurry of potent
images and impressions: closeness; Jason's loving eyes
on her; sharp, tingling air; and a burning memory of
having been beneath other branches, other times. A
jagged streak of power passed from heaven to earth,
rending a tree to kindling with a blasting crack of
horror, and a long dread roll of thunder echoed
beneath the clouds.

Delia huddled against the tree trunk beside Jason,
and the rain that poured from the leaves of the ash

shut them away from the storm, and from all of the world that waited beneath the rain. They were not comrades here. She was aware of every nerve in her body, and a few of them flashed as brilliantly as the second lance of lightning that now cracked down upon a hillock just to the west. She started at the sound, and Jason turned toward her, his eyes filled with wanting and concern. She saw the need in his eyes, saw, too, the readiness of desire in his body. She did not know what to do, that moment; and had the moment not been broken, she truly did not know what she might have done, how she might have responded. The tension was left unresolved, because Rupert Harris and Phil Foley came crashing into the underbrush, leading their dripping mounts by the reins. Harris was cursing a storm of goddamns and Holy-Mother-soaked-through-to-my-gutstrings when he saw Jason and Delia there under the big tree.

"Hey, now," Rupert Harris said, his eyes passing from Delia to Jason and back to Delia again. "Nice little spot you've found for yourselves."

She felt his eyes pass down over her breasts, to linger where her legs met, a concavity clearly outlined beneath the wet buckskin skirt.

Phil Foley stumbled beneath the branches, leading his horse. More sensitive than Harris, he seemed to discern that he had somehow intruded upon a private, unresolved exchange. But he had the good sense not to mention it.

Harris pulled a yellow bottle from his saddlebag, dropped to his meaty haunches under the tree, and took himself a healthy drink. He held it out. The bottle passed from one to another, Delia, too.

"Yer goin' real good on this here land," Harris complimented. "When you reckon to have 'er cleared?"

"Couple more days."

"What then?"

"Put up a house. Put up a barn."

"This far from town? That's bold, ain't it? Red-skins can creep up here in the night and take your scalp off before you can blink an eye."

"They've been pretty quiet lately."

Harris took another drink. "Don't you believe it. That Firebrand is just a lot trickier and meaner than old Four Bears, that's all. He's just a'lyin' up there in the mountains, waitin' till we drop our guard, an' then he'll be down here burnin' and killin' like it's in his blood, which it is. You can't trust a redskin, let me tell you."

Delia looked away. Jason showed no emotion. Phil Foley wore a pained expression. Why? thought Delia. Did he know she was a Chickasaw?

"Only good redskin is a dead redskin," Harris guffawed. "Where you goin' to situate the house an' barn?"

Jason told him.

"Too close to the river," Harris pronounced. "You'll get flooded out."

"You said there haven't been any floods."

"Law of averages. Got to be, sometime, right?"

"I want the place to be near the dock."

"Dock, hey? Big plans? Glad to hear it." An acquisitive gleam came into his eyes, the cause of which Delia did not then understand, and which the men apparently did not see. Why would Harris display such mercantile enthusiasm over property that clearly belonged to another man?

"Yep," he was saying in a self-satisfied way, "looks to me like you're plannin' what might become the biggest plantation in these parts. You just build 'er up, hear, an' get you a mess of horses and a mess of niggers an' a heavy whip, an' you're in business, all right."

There was a moment of silence as the storm pounded down, and thunder rolled away toward the mountains. "Get you a wife, too," Harris added in quite another tone, with his eyes hard on Delia's body. He was not a man given to diplomatic exchange.

"You know," he said, "I swear you look like you got some Indian blood in you."

Phil Foley coughed. Delia faltered, but did not have time to reply. Nor did she have to, because Harris talked on.

"Sorry," he said. "Didn't mean t'offend you. How could you be an Indian, skin like you got, so . . ."

She did not like the way his eyes were, or the husky tone in his throat as his voice died out.

"Oh, I expect I'll marry sometime," Jason said, too casually, "but a man's got to offer a wife more than a half-cleared field full of tree stumps."

"Right you are," grunted Harris. He eyed Delia hungrily. "You know what I think? I think there comes a time when a man has to fish or cut bait, know what I mean?" He was speaking to Jason, but his eyes never left Delia, never ceased sweeping slowly up and down her body.

"Let me put it another way," he drawled, wetting his lips a time or two. "A man's got to make a decision or let it be known that he's not goin' to make a decision. Got to do it or get off the pot, ain't that right?"

He glanced at Phil and gave him a nudge.

"Some truth in that," agreed Phil nervously. He knew that Rupert Harris was speaking of Delia and Jason. He also knew that Rupert Harris was being as gallant as he would ever be about the subject. It was not difficult to see that he wished to possess Delia, one way or another.

"There's always a proper time to decide," said Jason evenly, catching and holding Harris's gaze. The men looked at each other for a long moment, until finally Harris glanced up at the sky and broke the tension. "Looks like the rain's easin' off a bit," he said. "Sooner you get that field cleared, sooner you'll get to that 'proper time' you was talkin' about."

After a few more squalls the thunderstorms swept

away from the valley. Gray, scudding clouds replaced
the black-and-purple veil of the storm; and presently
rays of sun—wan at first, then more powerful—slanted
down onto the steaming earth.

"Well, Phil," Harris grunted, "guess it's back to
town for the two of us, an' let these two get back to
clearing that field. Then we'll see how things go."

Harris was right, Delia reflected as she and Jason
returned to work. Something had to happen. The air
of irresolution was greater than ever. She examined
her feelings, her soul. If what she had had with Torch
was love, then she did not exactly love Jason; but it
would have been hard to say why she did not. Perhaps the difference was that Torch had been her first
love. Or perhaps that had been something else, more
mysterious, more profound—something that, in any
case, she would never have again.

Jason and Delia worked well together, and soon
but one tree stood where the field would be. (Jason
had left a thick grove where he wished to erect the
farmstead itself, the better for shade and for beauty.)
Now he clucked at the horses and eased them toward
the final pin oak. It was an ancient, massive thing,
easily seventy feet tall, a vast plume of foliage; and
its dark, rain-wet leaves gleamed like jade. Delia
came across the field carrying the axes and the shovels.
First they would have to dig all around the mighty
trunk, exposing the roots. Then the roots would be
cut, and the tree would come roaring down in a blast
of dust and leaves and branches, to be divided for
lumber or firewood. Sometimes the tree was cut down
first, and then the stump cut away from its roots, to
be pulled away by the horses, all the stumps piled
together at the edge of the field and put to the torch.
Jason meant to fell this tree first, and then rip out
the roots. Delia saw him sharpening the crosscut saw
as she came into the shade.

Placing the implements on the ground, she sat

down with her back to the tree and closed her eyes. The scraping of the whetstone on the jagged steel blades of the saw drowned out all other sounds; and when Delia looked up into the tree, the leaves fluttered, the branches moved soundlessly in easy wind, like plants under water. For long moments she was mesmerized by motion, and even the rasp of the whetstone did not intrude. Suddenly she left the reverie.

"Don't cut it," she told Jason.

He stopped sharpening and looked at her. "What?"

"Don't cut it down."

He looked puzzled.

"It doesn't have to be cut down," she said. "You can plant your field around it."

Jason was doubtful. It seemed odd to leave a tree standing alone. It might attract lightning. Worse, it would shelter birds who would gather to feast upon seeds planted in the earth. And wouldn't the effect itself appear to be slightly bizarre? Leave a cluster of trees, or a grove, or a windbreak, certainly. But one tree?

"Why?" he asked her.

"Because," Delia said, "I want you to. It is important to me."

Jason put down the whetstone. "A high wind, a storm, could smash this oak down on crops or cattle."

"I . . . I know that."

"Then why . . . ?"

Delia felt a touch of emotion in her voice, and her throat was tight and hot. "It is . . . it reminds me of something I want to remember."

He came near her and sat down beside her. "Of course," he said, "a tree is just a tree. If you like, I'll leave it standing for you, but . . ."

Delia felt that she owed him some form of explanation, but the reason for her request was difficult to put into words. The life she had known in her village was behind her now, forever, and Four Bears was dead. Torch-of-the-Sun was as remote to her now as the North Star. And here on the banks of the river, which was eternal, the white men were striking down trees Ababinili had meant to be eternal, else why had he caused them to live? These lands, which had been of her people, would never be the same.

"It is something I want to remember," was all that she could say.

Jason did not press her for further explanation; he simply sat beside her, thinking it over, now and then glancing at her as she gazed off down toward the river. He knew her well now, and sensed the ebb and flow of dark currents in her soul. Admiring her dignity, her bravery, and grateful to her for saving his life, he nonetheless sensed in her many things he would never know. This puzzled and saddened him, but he accepted it. Delia had been raised in a manner alien to him, and there were forces molded in the heart, infused in the blood, forces that could be neither translated nor transmitted to an outlander, however bright he was, however much he wanted to share.

He pondered her, sadly, lovingly, while Delia sat motionless, watching the slow silver slip of the river moving down among the trees, flowing at the bend there, out of sight.

A bend in the river.

She remembered Torch's vision, a golden stick in the sand at the bend in the river on which were inscribed the words of the secret of life. Why had he forgotten those words? How could he have forgotten them? If he had not, perhaps everything would have been different, and she would be with him now, and happy.

Perhaps not.

And no, she was not truly unhappy. She could not say that. One day, very soon, she would steal down where the river turned westward, and search the river-bank sand for the stick . . . .

"You are thinking of home, are you not?" Jason asked softly.

Delia turned to look at him, and he was there, close and gentle as he always was, strong and reassuring.

"And that is what the tree means? Home?"

Delia nodded, but could not find words. He had understood, and knew the depth of her heartbeat, knew also that her sorrow could not ever be fully shared.

"This land is still your home," he said. "And it can always be your home, if you wish it."

Time hushed. Silence was everywhere, shimmering like light. He was inches away from her, and her soul knew the gentle power of his love. Mysteriously, the tension between them was breaking down even as it was increasing. I should move away, she thought, her mind working slowly, the words of the thought coming in tatters: *I . . . should . . . move . . . away.* But she knew at the same time that she did not wish to move away, and knew, too, that he would not permit it. Not anymore.

Beneath the lone tree Jason reached for her, and Delia came to him. She did not simply acquiesce, but rather she came of her own accord into his embrace, and the two of them lay down upon the earth. Their kisses were tender at first, a reading of each other, but the kiss of love is like a burning spark destined by God or Ababinili to burst into flames, to rise blazing until all who lie beneath it are consumed.

And so it was with Jason and Delia, still Beloved-of-Earth, although she did not think of it just then. She could not think of it; she did not think. His caress upon her was like the living wind that fed the fire, and without thought she reached to pleasure him. The earth beneath them, which they together had prepared for planting seed and harvest, now cradled their fire and their love, making them rich as it was rich. Above them, sheltering, stood the great oak that Delia had saved, and beneath it Delia made love with the man she had saved, who gave himself to her now, and gave with himself a place on the land that was her birthright and possession.

Then they were bare upon that earth, and his lingering, hungry kiss touched points of fire, darts of liquid heat that quivered along the soft curves of her body, spinning down along the length of her like tiny pillars of flame. He would have kissed her there forever, it seemed, but behind the closed lids of her eyes even the leaves of the tree had burst into gorgeous tongues of blue-and-yellow fire, so she took him then, and gave him what she knew with an honest heart, a needful body, and he was to her, gladly, all that he was or could ever be.

The leaves were a beautiful green, no longer ablaze, as Jason and Delia lay in drowsy embrace. The pin oak lanced upward, strong, into the sun. In the distance the river murmured, flowing down toward the bend. Delia thought again of the golden stick. Perhaps there was no golden stick. Perhaps no secret of life, either, save this love upon the earth.

"You've given me great pleasure," Jason whispered hoarsely, "I cannot say how . . ."

"Then do not say, because the pleasure itself, and the love, may be enough, may be . . ."

". . . all there is," he finished.

I do not know, she thought, stroking him gently, soothing and dazzling his afterglow. I do not know. But if this love is all there is, it is for me more than enough.

Momentarily, disturbingly, a pale vision of Torch glowed in her memory. She started suddenly in Jason's embrace.

"What is it?" he murmured.

"Nothing," she soothed. "Nothing. Just rest with me here until the day is gone."

"There are many more days to come," he said. "Thank God."

"Ah!" sighed Delia. "Do we not so wish."

* * *

Torch rode through the mountains, following secret trails, dismounting many times to lead his pony down rocky embankments, across grassy clearings pitted with leg-breaking gopher holes. Finally, north of the Twin Mountains, he could smell the cooking fires of the Red-Beard's village, and urged his horse down toward the river. If he happened to be spotted, and tracked by dogs—the demon Harris thought of everything—then he might use the river to hide his trail.

Torch was filled with awe and sadness when he saw how the land along the river had been desecrated. Great patches of earth were bare and dry in the sun, all the trees gone, never to be again. What manner of vileness had created these white jackals, to strip the earth itself, when all knew that man could live best when he accepted the earth as it was? Maybe the skill of the hunt had not been given to the white man when Ababinili breathed life into his creation. That must be the reason they had such passion for filling the earth with seeds. Yes, they had great energy. Even Torch did not deny it. To cut down one tree was labor enough—ill-advised though it might be. But to cut down hundreds, thousands! It was an endeavor beyond imagining.

So it was with dull awe that Torch rode along the river and came to a great field upon which one lone tree still stood. What is this? he thought.

From behind deep folds of greenery he saw it, and a part of him died. Not because he saw what was happening, nor even because he knew to whom it was happening—and thus who was at once aggressor and recipient. No, his heart could no longer enjoy its full measure of life because there was undeniable love in the act of wonder and tenderness that he beheld; and the lovers wrapped together beneath the solitary tree, in their trembling communion, created a unity from which, forever, he would be excluded.

That much was clear.

It was clear, too, that he must now return to his people, and serve them, and lead them, and fulfill their expectations of him.

After what he had seen today, he was now free to take a wife. Someone, someone . . .

She would have soft skin, fine breasts, and know how to please him. She would have beauty; her breasts would be sweet. She would be comely of face, wise with children, judicious in trial, respectful of elders.

She would be all, everything necessary to the wife of a Chickasaw chieftain.

Torch did not expect more, and he deserved no less. Yet, as he rode back through the mountain passes on his way to the ancient town of his people, Torch knew one other thing: No matter how fine a wife he chose, always in the dark of night, when she could not see him, nor he her, even when they were locked in love together, that woman-to-be, that nameless wife, would always possess the beautiful face of Dey-Lor-Gyva.

CHAPTER X

In the beginning she dreamed at night that Torch had come for her. She heard the pounding of hooves, the wild, blood-curdling war cries, the hiss of arrows slashing through the air, finding their targets. She dreamed these things, and they were so real that she leaped up in the darkness and flew from bed to window.

But outside there was only the Tennessee night, filled in summer by the sounds of crickets, bullfrogs, the ominous whoosh of darting bats, and in winter by the rustle of dried leaves, the mournful wind in the branches of trees, and the slow mutter of dying cinders in the fireplace.

Time had passed. Torch did not come, and after a while he came not even in dreams. She would stand by the window for a time, looking out into the night.

And then Delia—Mrs. Jason Randolph—would return to her husband, and curl next to him in bed, as first she had done in the mountains of her homeland. In her other life.

"Andrew. Andrew?"

No answer.

Where could he have gone? One moment he had been at the kitchen table, then Delia had heard the door slam. But she'd been busy laying out the crystal, silver, and china for tonight's party—fine wares shipped all the way from Virginia—and the familiar screech and slap of the opening, closing screen door possessed no immediate meaning.

But when she was done with her task, Andrew was gone.

"An-drew!" she cried, trying to suppress a note of panic that had crept into her voice.

Festus Farson, the new overseer Jason had hired, ambled out of the big new barn and looked over to the house, where she stood calling and looking about. He ought to have been out in the fields this time of day, supervising the workmen, and she suspected he often holed up in the cool barn to drink corn liquor; but her suspicions were unimportant just now.

"Missus?" he asked, coming over. In spite of her anxiety she noticed that he stopped far enough from her so that she could not catch a smell of his breath.

"Fes, have you seen Andrew?"

"Nope, Missus. Can't say as I have. Anyway, he ain't been in the barn."

Fes stood there looking at her dully. He *had* been drinking. A well-built, sturdy fellow, he made an appearance of stolidity and even intelligence when he wanted to, which was why he'd been hired. But there was either more or less to him than appearances conveyed, revealed now and again by a sudden, ominous grin that crossed his face for no reason and just as quickly disappeared.

"Run away, did he?" asked Fes Farson, as the grin came and went.

"Hurry. We have to look for him. He might have wandered down by the river."

Delia raced off, as fast as she could go, down through the orchard and along the cattle path. She thought Fes was right behind her; but when she turned to look, she saw that he was trotting along quite a distance away.

"Fes! Please! Is the bull locked up?"

He stopped. "What, Missus Randolph?"

"The bull! Is he locked in the barn?"

"Geez, Missus, no. Mr. Randolph told me to turn him loose in the pasture. It's servicing time, you know, and . . ."

That, too. She did not want to think of it, began to run again toward the river bank. Jason had purchased a prize bull for his growing herd of cattle, and because of the danger posed by such a beast should he become enraged, Andrew was to be most carefully watched. Oh, what a fool she had been, thinking of her party! She knew her little son loved to go down to the river with her, for picnic lunches, or to hold a stick and a string out over the water and "fish." He had been cautioned innumerable times against going by himself, but what did he understand? He was barely two years old.

Jason would die if anything happened to the boy. *She* would die.

She reached the pasture fence, climbed up on the lengths of wooden railing that bordered the grazing area, and scanned it at a glance. There he was, toddling along in the tall hay, his sturdy little body wobbling when he tried to run. He had her fair skin and Jason's hair and eyes. As always he was eager for adventure, the burst of blond hair like a sunflower moving across the pasture.

"Fes!" she cried in anguish, as the foreman jogged up beside her. "We've got to do something."

"Yup," admitted Farson, squinting after little Andrew.

She caught the blast of his corn-fragrant breath.

"Fes!"

"Oh? Oh, yeah . . ."

The man climbed over the rail fence, none too quickly, and Delia saw the cows look up from their grazing. They had seen, or sensed, something unusual in their pasture. Festus Farson chugged along after Andrew; the cows scattered a little when they saw him coming.

"*Andrew!*" cried Delia at the top of her lungs.

Her call was loud and full of panic. But it was the wrong thing to have done. Because, down among the cows, the big black bull ceased grazing, too, jerked up his massive block of a head, and sniffed the wind belligerently.

Andrew stopped and looked back, saw his mother at the fence. He waved. The bull caught the hint of movement there in the grass.

Fes Farson saw the bull, too, stopped, looked back, measuring the distance between himself and the fence, as opposed to the open space between himself and the bull.

The bull stomped a bit and pranced from side to side, turning his head. The bull's bloody eyes reflected Festus, and then the little boy's image gleamed in them.

"Fes, get him," pleaded Delia, over the fence herself now. "Get Andrew!"

The bull let out a great bellow, and the cows scattered, only to stop and turn a moment later, dumb observers of the scene. Fes drew upon whatever speed the corn liquor allowed and dashed toward the fence, and safety.

Although Delia was too angry and afraid to consider it at the time, Farson's panic decided Andrew's fate. The huge beast flipped the iron ring in his nose a couple of times and studied the thing that ran on two feet. He did not like it, not at all, but his brain was so small that it took a few moments before he decided to pursue. When he did, when the bulky, stiff-kneed trot turned into a full-fledged charge, the bull's momentum was unstoppable.

Delia could hear Farson's breathless, panting whine as he scrambled toward the fence, and she knew that her only chance had presented itself. Almost as fast as Fleet Cloud in the race on the day of the manhood ritual, she dashed across the pasture toward her son. He was alarmed by now, although he did not know exactly why, and began to stumble toward her. The bull, charging headlong after the fleeing Farson, caught a glimpse of her skirt flying, wanted to stop but could not, became confused, and stumbled.

Farson made it to the rail fence and had no trouble performing a one-armed vault over it.

The bull smashed once into the fence, then slammed it again with his brutal head in an effort to find the intruder.

Delia had Andrew now and was running with him toward another section of the fence.

"Run! Run!" Farson yelled. To his credit, he did rip off his work shirt and dangle it over the fence in an attempt to hold the beast's attention. But this ploy did not suffice. Doubly enraged now, the monster saw Delia carrying the child, and a new burst of hatred poured into his veins. He turned, paused only a moment as if to take aim, and charged at the woman and child.

Delia could hear the pounding of the cloven hooves, but she did not look. To look would slow her down. If she looked backward, she might fall. And if the bull hit her and Andrew, she did not want to see it coming.

Festus ran along the fence line, waving his shirt. "Come on," he urged, "come on."

Delia thought that she could feel the hot wet breath of the beast upon her, and the fence rose and fell before her eyes as she ran. She was crying. There was no more air for her lungs, but somehow she managed to reach the fence, to throw herself across it. Then she was sprawled on the other side, lying in the grass. Andrew had landed on top of her, screaming. And Fes Farson, standing over her, looked down from his white, pale face. Jackal! was her instinctive thought.

"Help me up," Delia said.

Fes did. Andrew was still howling. Jason had insisted on the name, as a mark of respect for his family's illustrious friend, Chula Harjo. Delia had not liked the choice, but had decided that it was unwise to protest. A man's firstborn was significant.

"You don't care for the name?" Jason had inquired, when he saw the frown on her face after he had proposed that the baby be christened Andrew Jackson Randolph.

Delia had come very close to telling him the complete truth that time, come close to telling him it had been Jackson who had killed her parents. She told him everything else; they kept nothing from each other. But instead she said, "It is your right to name your son, and what you choose will please me as well."

Jason had studied her then, for a long moment. He was very much attuned to her ways, her expressions, her sudden reticences, and traits of her that he did not fully understand were attributed to her tribal past.

"If you do not care for the name, is there a reason?" he'd asked.

Yes, Yes, Yes! Delia had wanted to scream. But she did not. She chose silence. If he knew how much she hated Jackson, and why, then his knowledge might at some future time hinder her or prevent her from killing the beast, should that propitious moment ever come.

"There's no reason. It is a name like any other," she had said.

The child upon whom it had been conferred now gasped and choked in his mother's arms. His arms were around her neck as hard as he could cling.

"There now," she soothed. "It's all right. It's over now."

Delia began to walk away from the fence, and Fes Farson followed. The bull bellowed a time or two and smacked into the wooden rails, which shivered and wobbled up and down the fence line, but did not give way. Then the beast just stood there for a moment, smelling grass, water, air, and remembered the cows. With an entirely different kind of bawling he trotted back to them, big head high, legs stiff, and tail flicking.

"We must do something about that bull," Delia said, holding Andrew's head to her breast, walking back toward the house.

Farson seemed remotely apologetic, but did not wish to commit himself, lest he be held culpable.

"Mr. Randolph told me to put it out with the cows," he whined. "And," he added, "I wasn't the one tendin' the boy."

Full knowledge of her own lapse galled Delia. "And what were you doing in the barn?" she snapped.

"Building stalls for the horses," he shot back.

"You? You were hired to supervise, not perform the work yourself."

He gave her a hard look, as if debating whether or not to say anything else. This was his boss's wife, and already he'd behaved with less-than-exemplary courage in the pasture.

"It's hard to get enough hired hands," was all he said, with a hangdog attitude.

Jason had gone into the village of Harrisville that afternoon to fetch four girls who would serve at the party. Almost three years had passed since the hot afternoon of love beneath the tree. Almost three years, and not a week had gone by when Jason did not vow, "When the house and the barns are up, when the fields are in flower, I'm going to throw an affair that people will remember for a generation."

He meant it, too.

To help her around the house, Delia had a young black girl called Tanya, whose freedom Jason had purchased. Tanya was comely and a hard worker, but she would not be able to take care of a hundred guests. So Delia had arranged to hire village girls for the task, and Jason had taken the carriage into Harrisville to bring the girls out to the farm. Tanya seemed somewhat distressed by this fact, as if the need for other help was somehow an indictment of her own capabilities; but she was a mournful girl, owing to her youthful enslavement, and said little.

Tanya was polishing silver and Delia was fussing over little Andrew when they heard the carriage roll into the farmyard.

"Papa!" cried the boy. With a child's resiliency he had already forgotten all about the pasture and the bull. Now he ran from the house again, letting the screen door slam behind him.

"That chile gonna get hisself killed yet," muttered Tanya, as she and Delia followed Andrew out into the yard.

Then the carriage rolled up, drawn by four gleaming black Arabians, imported from Spain and purchased in New Orleans. They were Jason's pride, and the envy of all the counties of east Tennessee. The carriage was new as well, and had been equipped with wheel springs to cushion the ride. In a very short time Jason had managed considerable prosperity, most of it by his energy and ingenuity, although in the town there were dark mutterings about "Virginia money."

"Whoa!" he called, and the horses drew up, prancing and jingling their harness buckles. He leaped down from the carriage seat and grabbed his son, hugged him. "Hey, young man, how's the fort holding?"

Andrew giggled.

Delia would not mention the bull just now. She turned to see the four young girls, none of them yet married, climb down from the carriage. Beth and Eloise, Prudence and . . . where was Deanna? Instead Delia recognized Melody Jasper, who worked as an all-purpose servant at Gale Foley's place. (It was considerably larger than it had once been, a true inn now.)

"Deanna was ill," Jason explained, "and when I

stopped at the inn for a beer, Gale volunteered Melody."

"That was kind of her," Delia said, but she felt a formless flicker of alarm. Melody was a hard girl, much like Gale Foley, and although Delia knew nothing about her at first hand, Melody Jasper seemed . . . devious.

"Please come in," Delia told them. "There are some refreshments for you, and then Tanya will show you what is to be done."

Eloise, Prudence, and Beth hurried happily into the big new house, which they'd never seen, but about which people talked a great deal in the town. But Melody held back a bit.

"Come in," Delia began.

"I ain't about to work with no niggers," Melody hissed, pointing at the black girl, who, fortunately, did not hear the comment.

But Jason did. He had not a few times been accused of undue compassion, and always met such calumnies head-on.

"Tanya is a free woman, and no slave," he said, with Andrew still in his arms.

"Still a nigger to me," Melody smirked.

"You offered to work for wages, and here you are," Jason declared. "I haven't time to take you back into town."

Melody thought of the long walk, and the wages, then glanced at the house with rude curiosity. At least she would get a chance to see it.

"Well, this one time, on account of you're such nice folks," she shrugged. Without waiting to be asked again, she went inside.

"Gale's girl?" Delia's question was almost a reproach. "I don't like it."

"Don't worry," he said. That was always his advice when something troubled her, and Delia had to admit that he was almost always—indeed, always—right.

Everything in their lives seemed to be proceeding splendidly. What was there to worry about?

"Well, young man," Jason asked his son. "Anything interesting happen while I was gone?"

Andrew chortled happily.

"He almost got killed," Delia said, quivering again with the memory.

She explained what had happened.

"The bull was out? Why, I told Fes to keep him locked up until next week."

"The beast was in the pasture today, and your son almost died because of it."

Jason's eyes darkened, and he gave Andrew a sudden hug. The boy was surprised, but accepted this, too, as no more than his due.

"There must have been some misunderstanding. I'll have to talk to Fes."

"I think you'll find him drinking in the barn. I think he's drinking pretty much all of the time."

"Oh, I doubt that."

"Jason, I . . . there's something about him . . ."

But her husband was used to Delia's suspicions. In the beginning she had good reason for them, but now that she was known and accepted by the people of the community, there was no cause for her uneasiness.

"Don't worry," he said again. "I'll talk to him. And meantime, we'll *all* have to be a little more vigilant about the young soldier here." He put Andrew down on the ground and tousled his hair.

Delia had not missed the way he'd said "all."

"I'm so sorry . . ." she began.

Jason saw her contrition, the hurt, and put his arm around her. "There, it could have happened to any—"

Just at that moment the little boy decided to go back inside the house, and darted in front of the horses. High-spirited and nervous by nature and surprised by the child's sudden movement, the two lead horses neighed and reared, and the wheel horses jerked forward. For one dazzling instant Andrew was beneath the pawing, iron-shod hooves.

Jason dived, grabbed his son, and rolled away in the dirt.

The hooves plunged down; for a moment it seemed that the horses might bolt.

Jason rolled away, still holding Andrew.

"Young man," he said severely to the boy, who seemed to think some kind of game had taken place, "you stay in the house for the rest of the day. You'll get yourself killed, do you know that?"

They went inside then, and Delia remembered that Tanya's words had been exactly like Jason's.

They would have to watch Andrew more carefully.

CHAPTER XI

The guests began to arrive well before dinner time. People from a few of the nearby farms and new plantations came on foot or on horseback; those from Harrisville itself or from more distant homesteads came in wagons or buggies. Rupert Harris, who had contrived to profit hugely over the years, pulled up in a carriage drawn by one of his many black slaves, both Harris and the slave dressed in magnificent swallow-tailed coats as red as Harris's brindly beard, which was as crudely cut as it had always been. Soon the yard was filled with vehicles and horses; guests milled on the green lawn in front of the house drinking mint julep, corn whiskey, beer, tea, or lemonade.

Delia and Jason greeted one and all as they left their horses in the care of Fes Farson and the hired men. Jason kept little Andrew in a firm grip, although the boy fidgeted and writhed with all the excitement taking place. Tanya and the four girls from town fetched drinks and tasty morsels, and everything was going smoothly. The tables were laid, and all that remained to finish preparations for dinner was to carve the beef now turning on spits over fires down in the orchard. Fes Farson would handle that task. He had volunteered, a big mug of beer in his hand, repeatedly flashing his weird grin.

"Jason, how are you?" bellowed Rupert Harris, thrusting out a hairy red paw. "Nice place you got here. Damn nice. My share of the crop ain't too bad, neither. Hey there, Delia, you look—" he scrutinized her for a moment—"you look even nicer than my share of the crop, if you don't mind my saying so."

She smiled and suggested a julep.

"That'd be blood to a vampire," he growled, moving off toward the lawn.

Phil and Gale Foley arrived. Phil and Jason had become fairly well acquainted. Jason respected the efficiency with which Phil managed the sawmill and the flour mill; and both men saw that Harrisville— if properly developed—could eventually become a leading center of trade in the region, due to the richness of the land and the proximity of a navigable river.

"I really needed Melody at the inn," Gale said, smiling to show how charitable she was, "but seeing as we're friends . . ."

"Thank you," Delia said.

Later, when most of the guests had arrived, Delia went to check on the progress of the party. Everything was proceeding well, and the girls, under Tanya's supervision, moved through the throng with trays and glasses and cups. Delia was just about to tell Fes Farson to start carving the barbecued beef, when she noticed Gale Foley whispering something to Melody, in a manner that seemed quick and sly.

It's your imagination, she told herself, recalling Jason's usual advice: Don't worry.

Yet shortly thereafter Delia noticed that Melody was no longer circulating with her tray. She waited a little, checked the kitchen and the parlor, and glanced out back, where the hired men were engaged in some serious drinking. Puzzled and wondering, she walked all about the house and noticed that the door to her and Jason's bedroom was closed. But she'd left all doors open, so that guests might see the entire house.

She paused outside the door, listening.

There was no sound, and yet . . .

Quietly she turned the knob, eased open the door, and slipped into the room. The closet door was open, and in the closet, digging far back among the folds of hanging coats and dresses, was Melody.

Delia knew instantly that she might already be too late.

"Get out of there!"

She *was* too late. Melody withdrew from the closet, a bit surprised to have been interrupted, but not at all shocked. In her hand she clutched the beaded leather pouch that contained Delia's few treasures and remembrances from her past life: a few pieces of jewelry, Torch's serpent bracelet, and the white stones with which he had first summoned her to the place of the willows. The pouch was unmistakably Indian, the contents even more so, save perhaps for the stones, which might mystify Melody.

"What are you doing in my closet?" Delia demanded, with as much anger as she could summon.

Melody just smiled. "I can't tell the tribe from the beadwork," she said. "Chickasaw, I suppose? Or Cherokee?"

Delia said nothing, though it pained her not to be able to shout, "Chickasaw, yes, Chickasaw," to spring forward and tear that weasely little smile from Melody's hard face.

"Gale always guessed," Melody said. "And now we know she is right."

With a supreme effort of will, Delia saw that her only chance lay in doubt, in the casting of doubt.

"What do you mean?" she demanded coldly.

"Why—why, this," Melody said, holding out the leather pouch as if for Delia's inspection.

"And did you try to place it in my house for some reason?"

"I—no, I was—"

"Attempting theft?" pressed Delia, knowing she had good ground now, and set upon gaining more.

"Are you a thief? Where did you get that pouch?"

"It was . . . I was . . ."

"I shall take you right out now before all the guests, and tell them of a thief in our midst!"

Melody was genuinely frightened now. "I didn't take it. I . . . was just . . ."

"Yes?"

"I just wanted to . . ."

"Who put you up to this? You mentioned Gale Foley."

Melody struggled to keep her wits, and kept them.

"Go ahead and do what you want," she said, lifting her chin. "Tell them of a thief in your house. Take me out before them and say anything you want. I *know* where I found this leather purse, and all will know where it came from."

That was true. Delia saw that, while she had Melody at bay, there was no clear purpose in publicly accusing the girl of theft. An imbroglio would result, of accusation and counteraccusation, and no good would come to Delia as a result.

"Give me the pouch," she commanded.

"What? Why?"

"Did you find it here?"

Suspicion. A trick? "Yes."

"Then it is mine and Jason's, until we find out to whom it belongs."

Melody was incredulous, but saw in the ploy a way to escape being marked a thief.

"As you wish," she said, smirking.

Delia took the purse and held it lightly, as if it were of absolutely no significance to her. "Now get out of here," she said.

"I'll . . . yes, I'll go back to my work now."

"No. Go home."

"But you hired me!"

"You are dismissed," Delia pronounced.

"Now? At this time of the evening? I shall never be able to walk back to the village before nightfall."

"Then wait in the barn and ride with Gale and Phil in their buggy. I believe you are in Gale's employ, is that not correct?"

Melody thought first to respond with arrogance, but she faltered. And because she did, Delia knew the truth.

Gale was hunting for revenge, and she had decided that to reveal Delia as Indian would cause great harm. She was right. And she knew where to strike Delia where she was most vulnerable.

Outside, the guests were looking about, wondering when mealtime would arrive. Delia wondered, too; and when she went to check on Festus Farson's progress at the barbecue spit, she discovered that no such progress had been made. Instead she found Farson drinking with the hired hands behind the house. While it was improper in the best of times for a supervisor to socialize with his subordinates, Fes had chosen the worst of times.

"Fes, why aren't you carving the meat?"

He was squatting against the house, in chortling conversation with a huge, one-eared, whip-scarred freedman and two Kentucky hill people whom Jason had hired. He turned his head slowly, regarded Delia with red eyes, and grinned his disquieting grin.

"You said to carve it when the people was ready to eat."

"I told you to start carving half an hour ago."

Grin. "Nope, you din'."

He was drunk! It was hopeless. Jason would have to do something about him. The man was looking at her, wondering what she would do.

Well, there was nothing *to* do here now. Without another word she sought out Jason. He was deep in discussion with three local farmers, who were explaining something to him. They seemed distressed.

"What is it?" he asked distractedly when she

touched his sleeve. Whatever they had been saying had had a most sobering effect upon him.

She explained about Fes Farson. "Drinking with the help?" he asked, confounded.

Then, with Phil Foley and Felix Wohl, who had set up a general store in the village, Jason went down to the barbecue spits. The three men set to work, and soon guests were at the table, feasting on the meat, enjoying the succulent sauce. Tanya and the three village girls served, and the meal proceeded efficiently.

"Why, where's my Melody?" Gale Foley asked.

"In the barn, I think," Delia whispered, leaning down.

Gale was startled. "What?"

"Yes. I found her rummaging through my closets. Did you know she was that kind of a girl?"

Gale Foley paled so suddenly that it seemed as if all blood in her face had drained away to some distant spring, and her eyes showed alarm, fear. Gale knew that Delia had guessed what Melody had been instructed to do: to look for something incriminating in the Randolph household. There was no doubt, either, that Delia knew who had put Melody up to it.

Gale recovered, though. "Well, if what you tell me is true, I wouldn't have her in your house, either. Of course, one must be fair. She's never given *me* cause for complaint."

"I suppose not," Delia rejoined.

The tables had been set up in the long dining room and also on the adjacent verandah, where the French doors had been opened to give the effect of one vast room. Delia took her place opposite Jason at the main table and found, to her chagrin, that Rupert Harris had seated himself on her right.

"There you be," he grunted, barbecue sauce dribbling down his chin. "Been waitin' fer yuh. I got tired of jawing with the men."

She smiled.

"Hey, I sure like it when you show them teeth,"

he grinned. "You're the best-lookin' woman Harris-ville's got, by God, if I do say so. Ain't that right?" he demanded of those nearest him. "I would've married her myself, if Jason'd waited any longer." He gave her a wet kiss on the cheek.

Then Harris decided to stand up. Mopping his mouth with the sleeve of his scarlet coat, he held a beer stein high and called for attention.

"All of us genteel folks know that fine dinners like this here one got to have a toast!"

People quieted and turned toward him. When Harris spoke, he was listened to. He had power. And knew how to use it. With his size, ruthlessness, and crude but keen intelligence, he was feared.

"First of all I'd just like to say this here farm is a fine place . . ."

A chorus of assents.

". . . an' that this here new house is a real wonderful place."

More agreement.

"It goes to show you what a man can make of himself in a well-run community. Now, we got our whiners, true, and our yellow-bellies. We got our fainthearts, and even a nigger-lover or two . . ."

There were some murmurs of assent to this, but most of the guests looked on quietly, hoping he wasn't referring to them.

"But I will say this," he continued, punctuating his main point with an energetic gesture that caused a small tide of beer to wash over the top of his stein. "I will say that, when the big battle comes, the chaff will be separated from the wheat, as the preacher says, and by God you better believe it."

Then he sat down, his lower lip thrust out pugnaciously, and took a long swallow of beer, banging the stein down on the oaken table to signal that his speech was over.

"Hear, hear!" some said, and there was a small round of applause. Many of the guests—and Delia herself—seemed confused about the meaning of "separating the chaff from the wheat." All knew that Harris was quite capable of rough trade, hard practice, and it was unsettling to hear him speak of "battle." Aside from a tavern brawl now and again in the village, or a dispute over fence lines or access to the river, the community had been quite peaceful. Nor had there been any incidents with Indians, save for an occasional alarm when a "redskin war party" was said to have been sighted in the hills.

The people returned to their meal, wondering whether they were chaff or wheat in Harris's estimation, and Delia asked him what he had meant by "battle."

"Coal," he said, chewing.

"Coal?"

"Them mountains south of here is chock full of coal," he expanded, as if that explained everything.

The mountains to the south sheltered Delia's people, and many other Indian villages.

"I don't understand," she said.

He had some more beer and gave her a shrewd wink. "You didn't think a big operator like me'd be satisfied for long with just a plantation and a town, did yuh? Nope, I aim to branch out. Coal is goin' to be the comin' thing in America, and everybody who knows anything knows that, too. Them big cities a'growin' out east is goin' to be the biggest and richest market you ever dreamed of. An', why, when I was up to Lexington t'other week, I heard talk that, by and by, ships ain't goin' to run on sails and wind no more, but big smoky engines. An' you know what them engines is goin' to need to run on?"

"Coal?"

"Coal," he repeated, triumphantly. "You bet your —you can bet on it. There's only one little problem."

Delia knew what was coming.

"Them Indians still living up there have got to be kicked out!"

She tried not to appear alarmed, and sipped some tea, not looking at him.

"Bothers you, don't it?" he pressed.

"Why should it bother me?"

He chuckled. "You're too much like old Jason, down there t'other end of the table."

Wheat and chaff? "In what way?" Delia asked.

"Too much heart. You got too much heart, both of you. Now look, I know all about how you went to that there fancy school in Georgia. Gale told me all about that. And I know a woman with looks like yours is generally protected and don't get to see much of the seamier side of life. And then your husband comes from that there fine family in Virginia, never had to sweat for a dime, and nose points northward from the time of poking out of his mama. But I been raised different. I know what the world's like from firsthand experience. There's plenty for the taking, an' I sure as hell—pardon my language—aim to get my share."

"I just wonder where the Indians will go," said Delia, trying to stay calm.

"Hell, who cares where they go? They could die for all I care. But I'm goin' to have those mountains an' the coal that's in 'em. I got my sights set on bein' the biggest man in the state of Tennessee, an' maybe, down the road a piece, I might even branch out."

"Branch out?"

"Sure," he boomed expansively. "Washington. If Andy Jackson can do it, so can I."

Delia nodded. Jason had told her that the man who murdered her parents was seeking what was called a "nomination" in this year of 1824. But Jason didn't think Jackson would win it yet. "We westerners aren't strong enough to put him over yet," Jason had said, "and God knows we're not united enough." She had been pleased to learn that her nemesis did not have a good chance, and now, in her desire to refute Harris's bombastic certainty, she spoke too quickly.

"Chula Harjo will not win," she said, using the Indian epithet that had been burned into her brain since girlhood.

He stopped chewing, his mouth open, and looked at her. "What was that you said?"

"I said I don't think Jackson will win this year." Her voice was lower. She sensed danger.

"No, there was something you said. Those words."

"I'm sorry, but you must be mistaken. Perhaps I did not speak clearly."

He looked at her with an odd expression, but decided not to pursue the matter further. *I have made a bad mistake,* Delia reflected.

"How're them hired men of your'n working out?" Harris wanted to know.

"Oh, quite well, thank you."

"That ain't what I hear."

She found nothing to reply, especially since she did not believe they *were* working out as well as they might.

Harris laughed. "Don't let me bother you none," he said. "I'm just needlin' a little bit. I already warned Jason about it. That's what I meant when I said before that you two got too much heart. You don't know how the world goes. Oh, sure, them ex-slaves and hillbillies will work for you, but how much? I told old Jason he could get twice the crop twice as quick with a bunch of niggers and a good driver. An' how's this Fes Farson coming along? He get the work out of those men?"

Before she had a chance to respond with some agreeable vagary, Harris read her thoughts.

"Now, come on. Fes is a good man. He's—like I was sayin' before, wheat and chaff. Fes is all wheat."

Harris considered Fes Farson part of the *wheat?*

"It's just he's into a bad situation here. That boy could drive niggers real good, give him a chance to do it. He'd get the work out of them or they'd be hangin' from a tree. You just can't waste a good hand like old Festus on hired help."

"Jason has decided how he wants the farm run, and certainly he's prospering. As are you," she added.

He drew back a bit and looked at her. "Loyalty," he cried. "I can tell you I sure as hell—pardon my language—like to see that in a woman. But don't worry, Jason is young yet. He'll come round yet to my way of thinking. He'll see the light. And so will you."

Harris seemed very certain of this, and dropped the subject.

"Anybody hear the rumor that Ginral Jackson'll be comin' down this way pretty soon?" called Felix Rafferty, who owned the village livery.

"Ain't no rumor," Harris shouted back. "He's comin', all right."

Delia felt a chill creeping around the walls of her heart.

"What for?" she asked.

"Hell, it's a political year, ain't you heard?" Harris chortled. "An' if you all will listen to me, I think we can make that fact work to our advantage."

At the other end of the table, Delia saw, a certain wariness appeared in Jason's eyes. He quickly masked it.

"I been thinkin'," Harris drawled, giving the assembly the benefit of his cunning. "If we was all to get together an' make sure Old Hickory knows he can count on us to the last man, politically and in any other way he wants—well, I think that'd be to our advantage."

"Do you have anything specific in mind?" Jason asked.

"Well, I might have, and then I might not have," Harris replied. "But you all know by now that if I have something in mind, it's goin' to be to everybody's benefit."

Delia heard something like a derisory snort midway down the table. Reuben Sills, a farmer who was not doing very well, seemed angry.

"How'd you all like to get rich?" Harris was asking. "An' I mean *real* rich."

Reuben Sills squirmed in his chair, his face growing red.

Everybody was listening, though. "What you got in mind this time, Rupert?"

"Oh, a little something," Harris said cagily.

But Delia believed she already knew what it was. Harris would not tell them about his coal scheme, though. He would keep that to himself, and maneuver the people of the community into a position where they would unknowingly help him. She knew Harris all too well. A few years ago he'd gone up to the Hermitage to try to get Jackson's militia to wipe the Chickasaw out of the mountains. He had failed, that time. But now conditions were altered. If Jackson needed support badly enough, and if he could now be persuaded to attack the Chickasaw, Harris would have access to the mountains and the coal.

If the Chickasaw were defeated!

Then and there, she vowed that if the white men decided to make war, she would warn her people somehow. Even if it meant trekking through the forest, taking the news herself. They would not be surprised by ambush; they would be warned.

"Seems to me," drawled Reuben Sills, in a manner that was at once obsequious and disrespectful, "that a lot of us been hearin' about gettin' rich for an awful long time, an' ain't too many actually been doin' it but a couple people I could name."

Harris laughed, too heartily. "Come on now, Reuben. Stop this here bellyachin'. Everybody in the whole valley knows you'd rather wrap your hand around a whiskey jug than a plow handle."

"That—that ain't the truth."

"Yeah, an' we all know you got your crop in late

three years running, an' so you got a paltry little harvest. That ain't nobody's fault but—"

"That ain't the real reason!" Reuben cried, leaping up, knocking over his chair.

Momentarily Harris looked stunned. He knew people muttered about the shares he took from each crop—hell, wouldn't be human if they didn't complain, right? But open defiance was quite another thing.

"Sit down, Reuben," advised Jason quietly. "It's neither the time nor the place . . . ."

He said it in such a way that those listening closely received the distinct impression that there *was* a time and place for some sort of complaint. But no one wanted a scene, least of all at a party celebrating a proud new farm. Reuben sat down again, and everyone conspired to forget the incident.

The hired men were none too quick about getting the guests' horses and buggies ready for the homeward trip, and Fes Farson wasn't much help. He stood in the lantern-lighted yard, trying to direct things, trying not to stagger, and saying as little as possible. Whenever he did have to issue an order, such as "Zeke, hitch the horse to the buggy" or "No, Paul, the dapple and the roan go to the hay wagon, not the charabanc," his words emerged like a pool of slurry consonants.

Jason, saying farewell to his guests, and recalling Delia's comment about Festus drinking with the men, walked over to him.

"What's the trouble, Farson?"

"Huh? Aw, ev'thing . . . ev'thin's fiiinnne . . ."

"I don't think so. You're embarrassing yourself, and the rest of us. Go to your quarters, and we'll discuss this when you sober up."

"Ain'gon' 'scuse nthnng, you—"

"This isn't the first time, either, is it? I've had

reports that you've been drinking in the barn when you ought to have been out in the fields."

Farson crinkled up his eyes, his alcohol-riddled brain working on the problem. *Reports?* Reports could have reached Jason from only one person, an' that was—

"Miz Randolph! The . . . I'lll . . ." and he made an ineffectual punching gesture that threw him off balance. He swayed, almost fell, recovered, and weaved his way across the yard, disappearing into the barn.

Rupert Harris, waiting for his carriage to be brought round, watched Farson go.

"Too bad. You're wastin' that boy's talents."

"I'm afraid I'll have to let him go," Jason replied. "You can't have the respect of your workers if you sit around drinking with them. Not only that, Fes is disgracefully drunk."

"Don't bother me none," Harris grinned. "He's out of his element, that's all. Like I was tellin' you, get darkies. Get about fifty darkies and give ol' Fes a whip, an' you won't ever see no happier or more productive man in your life. 'Cept me an' you, of course."

"Of course."

"But then, it is your farm."

"Is it?"

Something flickered in Harris's eyes, something quick and knowing, but he grinned readily and threw his big arm around Jason's shoulders. "Maybe you'd like to renegotiate that share of the crop you've been giving me. It *is* a little steep, I know, and I can afford to ease off on you some, on account of how big your harvests've been."

"I wouldn't turn that offer down," Jason said, not warmly.

"Heh heh. All right, couple of days or so, I'll drive out an' we'll jaw on it. Want to keep you happy. You're one of the best men in the community, an' I think that truly."

"Nice to know," Jason said.

Then Harris's big slave, gold buttons gleaming on his red coat, held open the carriage door, and the community's leading citizen got in. "Great dinner," he said, "great party. An' once again, say thanks to the Missus. An' by the way," he grinned, leaning out, his big, red-bearded face right in front of Jason's, "what do the words *Chula Harjo* mean to you?"

"Why," exclaimed Jason, not expecting the question, and distracted by all the activity in the yard, "that means 'Jackson, old and fierce.'" He'd heard Delia use the expression dozens of times.

"Indian term, ain't it," Harris drawled.

"Yes, it—yes, it is," Jason replied, a hint of caution in his voice.

"Thought so," said Harris. He gave a nod to the slave, who vaulted up into the driver's seat and took up the leather reins. "Ho! Giddyap!"

Rupert Harris rolled off into the night, with new things to ponder.

Down in the barn Fes Farson was likewise pondering things. Very drunk, but not drunk enough not to realize the portent of Jason's words in the yard, he also knew the raw humiliation of public chastisement. "Ainobdy do . . . do 'at to ol' Fes . . ."

Staggering to the horse trough, he picked up a five-gallon bucket, dipped it into the water, hoisted the bucket, and dumped the contents over his head and shoulders. The procedure was repeated, and the cold water effected a slight change for the better.

Or possibly for the worse. "Miz Randolph . . . she . . . becuzathe bull . . . the *bitch!*"

Of course; it was clear to Fes. The fact that he had a nip now and again throughout the day, from the jug concealed behind loose bricks in the milk shed, had never hindered his efficiency, not one iota. It was just because of that stupid kid going off into the pasture. She'd probably blamed that on ol' Fes, too, and combined it with a story about the drinking—which, in any case, how could she know about?—when she'd told Randolph.

Wait. Was he getting this straight? Was this right? "*Damn* right!"

Smoky-eyed bitch, strutting around like some kind of a queen! Like to take her up to the haymow some afternoon, an' put John Thomas through his paces. That'd show her.

Poor old Fes. Nothing had ever gone right for him, and this was another one of those times. One job after another. He could always get jobs, because he knew how to do it, and how to look responsible. But something always went wrong. That stupid nigger who had to go and die after Fes'd flogged him, plantation outside of Raleigh. The shyster brother of that warehouse owner in Charleston, who'd—Fes was sure—dipped into the till even more than Fes'd been doing, and then blamed it on him. That was the way things always went, and always Fes had had to take it, accept it, and move on. And the wife of the ship owner in New Orleans, who got mad because Fes had decided to experience the pleasures of her darkie slave girl. Well, what the hell was a slave girl *for*, except to work and give you her stuff when you wanted it?

"No . . . more," he muttered, running a hand through his wet, dirty-blond hair, squaring his shoulders. "No . . . more . . . to . . . old . . . Fes . . . ."

Having made that vow, he grabbed a pitchfork and lumbered out of the barn toward the house, ready to settle scores. Only one or two buggies remained in the yard. Good. Fes skirted the lantern-lighted area and headed for the back of the house. The field workers had long since gone drunk to their bunks, so Fes had no problem getting to the back door. He peered into the kitchen. The nigger girl was up to her elbows in dishwater, and them other town girls was scraping and cleaning and yammering. The handle of the pitchfork was hard in his hand. Let's see, if I go around and sneak in by the verandah, might be she's over on that side of the house. No, there would be people around, saying good night . . . .

Then he had an even better idea. What was the use of poking the tines of this fork in Missus Randolph's gut? Why not just do something to that dumb little kid, who was bound to get himself obliterated anyway, the way they let him run around. But where did the kid sleep?

"What are you doing back here?"

Fes jumped at the sound of the voice. The girls working in the kitchen screamed. Fes dropped the pitchfork, and somebody grabbed him by the shoulders and thrust him into the lighted kitchen. It was Phil Foley.

"Jes—I was jes . . ."

"You," Phil Foley ordered Tanya. "Get Mr. Randolph. Right away."

In moments Fes was looking into, and then trying to avoid, the inquiring eyes of Jason Randolph. Phil had produced the fork, and was explaining how he'd seen Fes lurking about the back door. To harm the servant girls?

"No, I don't think so," Jason reasoned, with a look of horror. He knew Fes Farson had been after a far more devastating kind of revenge.

"'Sall a lie," Fes tried; but this new defeat and the resurgent effects of fatigue and booze combined to rob him of his last defiant impulse.

"You've got ten minutes to get off my property," Jason was telling him. "If you're not, I'll lock you up and take you into Harrisville jail in the morning, and press charges, too."

Fes stumbled off, not too far gone to recognize a bargain when he got one.

"Phil, I won't forget this," he could hear Jason telling Foley.

"No," Fes vowed. "No, an' Fes Farson don't forget, neither."

When he stumbled back into the barn to retrieve his jug, he saw a girl come ass-swaying down the hay-mow ladder. He grunted in amazement, and, startled, she looked around.

"Is . . . is the dinner over?" she asked warily, noting his condition, and measuring the distance to the barn door.

"Yeah . . . yeah, it is. What're you. . . ?"

Melody decided that Fes was a kindred soul. "I wasn't *good* enough for Mrs. Randolph," she said bitterly. "I was sent to wait out here, fell asleep in the hayloft."

Then she was gone, trying to catch the Foleys and get a ride back to town, and Fes was standing there, swaying in the barn, comprehension dimly beginning to dawn on him that there had been—all the time—an actual, live, and probably agreeable woman right here in the barn all evening! If only he'd . . .

Then the thought slipped and spun away, diffused into a thousand pale threads amid the dull, gloomy lights of his brain.

"What the hell," he mumbled.

He staggered toward the place where he hid his jug. A jug was always better than a woman, when you got right down to it.

A jug lasted longer, at least if it was full to start with.

CHAPTER XII

Delia was already in bed when Jason slipped in beside her. She was anxious, for a number of reasons, two of the most important being Fes Farson's intended assault and Gale Foley's machinations. Three times she had checked to see if little Andrew was safe, and sleeping soundly. And yet each time she closed his door and tiptoed from the room, she was pressed by an impulse to ascertain his safety yet again.

Next to her Jason sighed.

"Anyway, it's over," she said, reached out, and found him there. He took her hand.

"No," he said, "I'm afraid it's only beginning."

She did not answer immediately, both wanting and not wanting to know news that promised not to be very good. "Something about us?" she managed. "About me?"

"Indirectly. Well, to tell the truth, quite directly. Do you recall, just before dinner you came and asked me to tend the barbecue, and I was talking to some men?"

She did. The men had looked worried, distressed, angry.

"And then Reuben Sills caused that little disturbance at table?"

"Yes. I wondered why."

He sighed again and turned toward her. "I've long suspected that a few things were amiss around Harrisville. Well, more than just a few things. But suspicions are one thing and hard evidence is quite another."

"You have this evidence now?"

"I haven't personally seen it, but I intend to. However, I don't doubt that it exists. Reuben Sills had to take his wife up to the hospital in Lexington last month, remember? While he was there, waiting for the doctors to examine her, he strolled over to the courthouse. That's where Rupert Harris was supposed to have—finally—filed the deeds and land claims for the folks around our area. Now, we all know Reuben isn't doing so well on his farm, but at least he owns the land. He knows that, too, and he thought it would give him a kick to go into that courthouse and tell the registrar of deeds and titles, 'Look here, my good man, I'm Reuben Sills and I own a piece of land down near Harrisville. I'd like to inspect my papers.' "

"So he did that?"

"Sure he did. Or he tried to. The clerk on duty rummaged around and took out the books for our county, and went on down the list and said, 'What was your name again?' 'Sills, Reuben Sills.' 'Nothin' listed here for you, Mr. Sills,' the clerk told him."

"How could that *be?*" Delia cried.

"Because Reuben's land is held under the name of Rupert Harris."

"What? How . . . ?"

A little over a year before, when it became clear that Harrisville was going to endure, was not going to fail or fade back into brush pine and wild grass, the people had grown restless over Rupert Harris's relaxed you-trust-me-and-I'll-trust-you land practices. They wanted regular titles, all legally signed and witnessed. Harris hadn't resisted. On the contrary, he had purchased new respect from his people by quickly hiring a Lexington lawyer, had brought the man down at his own expense to Harrisville; and there for three and a half days, morning and afternoon and into the evening, the lawyer had drawn up papers and summoned landowners and witnessed signatures, and when he was finished, everybody knew what was what and who owned what and who didn't.

Rather, they *believed* that they knew these things.

"How could that be?" Delia wanted to know. "Everyone here in town saw what was being done, and then Harris and the lawyer personally took the records to file them in Lexington, didn't they?"

"They filed papers, all right. But not the same ones that we prepared and signed here."

The realization of what had transpired was, to Delia, no less than astounding.

"So Reuben found it out," Jason was saying, speaking quietly, tiredly.

"And our land?" she managed.

"It's in his name, too."

"I might have guessed." She remembered his acquisitive, proprietary expressions, signals of an interest in their farm far beyond normal concern for a part of his community. "But how did he manage to do it?"

"My signature is on a piece of paper witnessing his title to our land. And the signatures of a lot of others, Reuben among them, attest to the same kind of arrangement."

"But you didn't sign—"

"No, the signatures are false. Rank forgeries."

"So? What is the problem? Is there no way to put the situation aright? Among my people—"

"These *are* your people," Jason corrected.

"Among the Chickasaw," she amended, "a matter such as this would not arise. The land belongs to all, and all partake of it. It's even sadder to think that Harris has tricked his own people out of land that is really ours—that belongs to the Indians."

"We have our law," Jason said.

"So, then, let it do its work. Let it take its course."

"It is not that simple a thing."

"What do you mean? Harris has cheated and—"

"Ah! Certainly he has. But it is his word against ours."

"His word against yours?" She could not believe some high form of white man's law would even listen to Rupert Harris.

"There are some serious problems."

Delia waited.

"It is a matter of time, and hiring lawyers. And more seriously, many of the people here do not believe Harris has actually done what Reuben claims. Reuben has a poor farm, a sick wife, and he is by no means the world's most intelligent man. Also, there is the element of fear. Harris runs the town, manipulates affairs, has signed agreements awarding him with various percentages of people's harvests. All of this is fact. We cannot change it, and neither can we alter the effect of the power it gives him. Moreover, the fact is that the papers on file in Lexington are legally drawn up."

"Legally?"

"Formally, then. The fact that they exist and are on file according to proper form means that it is us— those few of us in Harrisville who may chance a trial—who are the plaintiffs. *We,* not Harris, must shoulder the burden of proof."

Delia was outraged. "It is no surprise to me that you white people kill others and rend the land, with laws like that!"

Jason saw her point, but he was a little hurt nonetheless.

"Delia, you are part of me. We are *us!* You have white blood in your veins."

"There are times I wish not to think of it, nor even to admit it."

He was silent for a moment. "Then do not use Indian expressions at table. *Chula Harjo,*" he said, pronouncing it slowly.

"The old and fierce one," Delia said coldly.

In the darkness she could sense him thinking.

"Has he ever done anything to you? I do not mean to your people, that is a matter of war. But to you personally. Has he ever caused you harm?"

Delia recalled Harris's desire to invite Jackson here to Harrisville.

"How might he have done that?" she asked. "What are you talking about?"

Jason was silent again, then: "Darling, there is nothing you cannot tell me. You know how much I respect General Jackson, but you also know how completely I love you. If there is something—"

"There is nothing," she answered, too quickly.

"Was it Jackson in charge of the attack at Talking Rock?" he asked, too abruptly for her to evade his question effectively.

"That is absurd!" she said. "I was a baby. How would I have—"

"Let it be," he said, in a gentle voice. "Let it be. I have done my best to leave behind the bitterness of my wife and child's deaths. Let me try and help you do the same."

She reached out and touched him gently. If he only knew the entire story. Or did he? Had he guessed?

"But it is unwise to use Chickasaw expressions in front of Rupert Harris. He is always on the lookout for information that he could use to his advantage."

"I won't do it again."

Then she told him about finding Melody in her closet, and how Melody had discovered the leather pouch.

Quite suddenly he grew cold. The pouch. Torch-of-the-Sun. Delia's Indian lover seemed to appear, right there in the room with them.

"I . . . I did not mean it that way . . ." she faltered. He remained silent.

Delia explained how she had sent Melody out of the house.

"Gale is still willing to cause trouble," he said without inflection. He did not ask her where she had hidden the pouch this time. It was at the bottom of the flour barrel in the pantry.

Then she told Jason about the coal.

"Oh, God!" he exclaimed.

She thought he was responding angrily to this acquisitive trait in Harris's personality, which caused the man to seek and take and grasp and seek and take, to trick by smile or treachery, to gain and gain and gain. But Jason had reached another conclusion, an insight Delia herself had known at dinner.

"He's going to use Andy Jackson and fear of the Indians to get those mountains!"

They were quiet for a long time. Then Jason spoke. "I believe it would be beneficial for us to entertain again. General Jackson."

Delia's blood ran cold, so cold that she was no longer Delia, but rather Dey-Lor-Gyva, who had vowed to kill Jackson Chula. A ripple of sharp cunning came to her, and she could not, did not want to, hold it back. Jacksa would be here in her house!

"Whatever you wish," she said, neutrally. In her body, in her soul, was the quickening impulse that a brave enjoys with his enemy just about to die, targeted there down the length of the arrow, and the bowstring already loose in his fingers.

"You see," her husband explained, "if he stays with Harris, Jackson will receive only one side, one very limited interpretation of our situation here. But if he is here at Riverbend, I can to some extent control what information he receives—and you will learn he is not the ogre you think."

We shall see, Delia thought. We shall see.

"Perhaps I can turn him from this madness of starting up the Chickasaw wars again," Jason said. "Coal or no coal."

"Would Jackson want war, when he is now seeking power of another kind?"

"I doubt it. But if his people—we westerners—are threatened, he would be compelled to act. And action

of that kind is something with which he is not unfamiliar."

This Delia knew.

"Coal!" said Jason. "That too, now. Delia, Rupert
Harris is a great man."

"You cannot mean that!"

"Yes, he is. But a very dangerous one, as most
great men are. In a sense, he is like Andrew Jackson,
only less subtle."

Jason talked for a little while longer, about ambition and paradox, and about all the unknown
things that arise from both.

Chula Harjo will be under my roof, Delia was
thinking. *And, unknowingly, he will be at my mercy.*

But then she recalled a tale she'd heard: "Old
Hickory can smell a redskin twenty miles downwind."
And she no longer felt so confident.

Then the night was deep and dark, and all talk
ended, save for the speech of the flesh. Much time
had passed since that hot afternoon beneath the pin
oak; Delia and Jason had made love many times, in
many ways, many places. He had taken her in their
bed, in sweet hay, in soft, light-dappled bowers beneath summer trees, knowing her quickly, slowly, now
with breathlessness and urgent need, now as slow as
time, gently, deeply. Her soul and body he had kissed
countless times, and she his.

In the early days Torch had been a presence when
they made love, a silent companion to their meld-
ings. But time had passed. Jason seldom thought of
the chieftain who had at once given him both Delia
and his life. For Delia, the memory of Torch would
never, could never die; but because her love for Jason
was real, and because the pleasure she had with him
was so piercing, she always tried to put the thought
of Torch out of her mind when she felt Jason's touch
upon her body.

And so she tried to do tonight, as Jason moved

closer to her, touched his lips to her face, and with
knowing fingertips keyed delicately, and wooed, and
tantalized the living, pulsing pearl of all sensation.
She moved for him in all the many ways she knew;
and when she moved, his sound was like a joyful sob,
an inexpressible cry of wonder, as if the sensation
she gave offered, too, a glimmer of heaven, as if one
could actually *see* with the pleasure of flesh. And for
Delia, when ecstasy flirted with her, approached, and
finally, finally let itself be taken, the words that came
to her were cries of the Chickasaw tongue. Rapture
sent her back to find an earlier, purer, more primitive
self, fair and true and lovely.

She did not think these things during lovemaking;
there were no thoughts then, and none were possible.
But later, with Jason beside her, drifting into sleep,
herself filled and easy, the throbbing fading now,
fading, ebbing away until it should again be called
from the mysterious source of joy—yes, later she
would think of it, and wonder that ecstasy must be
a kind of death. Because one moment your body
belonged to you, and pleasure was an abstraction,
something to be considered from a distance, desired
and sought. But then there would be that one special
kiss, or a particular caress, or the subtle thrust of a
lover, or some shred of delicious memory, and then
your body belonged not to you but to the pleasure
itself, which could not be stopped or held at bay, and
you were then in a different state, about which nothing could be done until pleasure was done. And the
pleasure would not let you rest until it had exhausted
its own appetite on your tender flesh, which it held
in thrall, to enslave and feast upon, to dominate and
consume.

And so it was on this night, too, as Jason caressed
her with his body, and she responded, now above
him, now beneath, until the miraculous moment
came, and began, and was all about, and Delia could
do nothing to hold it back, did not want to. They

held each other and were in turn held by the enchanting surges for which man and woman were created.

Then Jason slept and Delia slept, too. The wind moved in the branches of the trees beside the house—or did she dream it?—and she awoke and went to the window. Torch was not there. He had not come for her, nor would he. But far out on the dark fields of night, she saw the horseman, a phantasm, like smoke or fog upon a mount of pale mist, riding toward her like the wind until he disappeared into the wind itself.

The face of her first lover was outlined in the stars.

CHAPTER XIII

Delia stood at the mirror in her bedroom, looking at her image over and over.

Will he know? Can he tell?

First she studied her face for a long time. Then she turned away from the glass for a moment, to glance back suddenly, surprising herself, trying to see herself as if for the first time, trying to decide what she saw there in the mirror.

Her complexion gave no cause for concern. It was as pure as it had always been. But her hair was so dark! And deep in her eyes, ineradicable and never to be hidden, was the heritage of her people, a slow smoky depthlessness that seemed to see everything, a quality of blackness that bespoke indomitability, and infinite patience. Delia could not lie with her eyes, and anyone who looked carefully would be able to read in them *I know* and *I have waited* and *All things shall come to pass.*

Would Andrew Jackson look carefully into her eyes, and see those thoughts within?

"Soon I shall know," she said to herself. There was nothing to be done about it now. She left the bedroom and went down onto the verandah, waiting. It seemed as if she could no longer endure waiting, and at the same time she wished Jackson would never arrive at all.

"It will be over before you know it," Jason had encouraged her. "He'll arrive in mid-afternoon, speak with the men here—just Harris and a few others—

stay the night, and then ride on to the villages west of us."

He would stay the night. Chula Harjo would be beneath Delia's roof.

The day was drowsy with midsummer heat. In the kitchen Tanya was busy preparing a great stone jug of lemonade. Jackson was said to be fond of lemonade, which he often drank mixed with whiskey, and he was also fond of elderberry pie. Six such pies, baked on the previous day, now rested on a pantry shelf, covered with a long strip of cotton cloth to keep off the flies. Across the yard Jason emerged from the stables, and with him, leading Jason's horse, came Paul, the big, one-eared ex-slave. Paul passed the reins to Jason, who swung easily into the saddle and made some comment to the black man, who laughed and returned to his work. Since the departure of Fes Farson, Jason had exercised personal supervision of the farmhands, and although it took more of his time than he would have liked, the farm was running far more smoothly.

Jason rode across the yard and reined in the horse next to the verandah.

"I'm going to ride down to the main road. He's due any time now, so I'll meet him out there."

She gave him a wan smile.

"Don't *worry*," he said, and rode off.

Tanya seemed to notice her mistress's agitation, quite unusual in Delia. "Now, looka here, young mastah," she said to little Andrew, who was eating blueberry cookies and drinking milk at the kitchen table. "Seems your mama's mighty vexed 'bout somefin. Le's you 'n' me cheer her up."

She took the little boy by the hand and led him out to the verandah, where Delia stood watching the roadway.

"Don' worry, Miz. We's all ready. Ev'thin's done been done to prepare foh Mista Jackson's visit."

Delia turned. The boy ran to her and she picked him up. "Oh, I know that, Tanya . . ." Her voice trailed off.

"Then what *is* it, Miz? I sweah I nevah have evah seed you in this kine of way. Anythin' I done or din' do?"

"Where sojer?" Andrew wanted to know.

"Coming. He's coming. You father went to meet him. No, Tanya, everything's all right. It must be the heat."

Tanya contrived to look relieved, although she was sure Delia's nervousness had to be the result of something more serious.

"Sho is hot, I'll agree," she said, and went back to the lemonade.

"Papa with sojer?" asked Andrew. He had been told of Jackson's imminent visit, and one of the field hands had elaborated upon Jackson's career for the little boy's benefit. "Sojer shoot Injuns!" he cried gleefully, making a little pistol with his fist and outstretched finger.

"Don't say things like that," Delia admonished him, but her heart was not in it. She was too distracted. "Here, you go play with your rocking horse."

"Chase Injuns!" Andrew cried, and scurried to the wooden horse on the grass beside the house. In a moment he was yelping and howling, caught up in some dangerous chase.

Sojer shoot injuns. Nothing but the words of an innocent child, and yet weighty with meaning to Delia. Watching him teeter back and forth on the toy, she shuddered. Someday he would learn of his mixed ancestry. She would tell him, and he would be proud of it. Or would he? Of course. He was the great-grandson of a mighty Chickasaw chief! But would that really mean anything to him? Perhaps he would reject the knowledge, spend his life hiding it, even ashamed of it. Thinking of such a possibility, she felt a pain beneath her breasts. How complicated everything was. One's home. One's blood. One's people.

Don't be absurd, she told herself. These people of Harrisville are yours now. Jason is your husband and Andrew is your son. You have a home and a great farm. Thus she sought to put her mind at ease.

What would old Teva say, Delia thought, if she saw me carrying on this way?

Thoughts of the old seeress, unbidden, brought the memories flooding back. The village in the mountains, the snug warmth of a wigwam in winter, ghostly tales around the fire. Delia thought of the meadow below her village, how it sloped down to the river, across which lay the grave of Four Bears, the graves of so many others fallen in battle. She thought of the willows that had seen and sheltered the tender, flaming love of a great young brave and a girl named Gyva; and her heart quickened when she knew that she could never deny a magical bond to the mountains of her homeland, to the forests of time over which Ababinili kept his sacred vigil, and to all her memories and dreams that were no more, yet could never be extinguished.

Oh, it was hopeless! How could an Indian-hunter, Indian-killer like Jacksa Chula not read her heart, not see in her dark and watchful eyes the indelible proof of her past?

Then thunder on the roadway lifted her from woeful introspection, as a party of riders at full gallop pounded up the drive. Delia felt something much like fear slip beneath her skin. She could see Jason on his black Arabian, and she knew these visitors were expected—indeed invited—but the speed and suddenness of their approach seemed the advent of a war party, not a group of guests.

Trees and hedges shut out her view then, and she walked quickly inside the house, to watch from her kitchen window. She had not seen Jackson, or anyone who looked like he was supposed to look. Maybe something had happened, plans had been changed?

Laughing with excitement, little Andrew slid off his hobbyhorse and toddled after her into the house.

"Land sakes!" Tanya was exclaiming, "mus' be the devil hisself on the warpath, all that racket."

Delia did not reply, but the black woman's choice of the word devil could not have been far from right.

Outside, the men were dismounting, with Paul and the other hired hands hurrying to take the horses. She could not see Chula Harjo in the group, though there were many riders. Then some of the men moved, horses shifted positions, and Delia saw Jason holding the bridle of a big gray horse, and she knew. It is he, she thought. Her mind flashed back to the terrible stories, to Talking Rock, the pitchfork her mother had used, and Four Bears creeping down the rocky walls of Roaring Gorge to rescue her. This tall man now dismounting the gray, this Jacksa Chula—he who had killed her parents, he who must once have held the baby Beloved-of-Earth in his arms, who must have intended to sell her as a slave—he not only lived and breathed, but stood there in the dust in the yard of her very home. Soon he would come near her hearth, to talk and drink and eat, as if he were a human being like everyone else!

"Miz, you all right?" Tanya was asking.

Delia realized her breath was coming in fast, short gasps.

"I'm all right," she said, trying to calm herself, studying Chula Harjo.

He was very tall, taller than Jason, and wore a wide-brimmed weather-beaten hat from which long, straight white hair hung to his shoulders. A faded-blue, waist-length jacket of the Spanish style, a relic of the Florida expeditions, accentuated his broad shoulders and the hard planes of his back. Two rows of gold buttons, irredeemably tarnished, ran down the front of the jacket. Jackson did not care for adorn-

ments; he never had. The accoutrements of haber-
dashery would only serve to distract from the main
attraction, which was what he wanted to be, and was.

Then the horses were taken to the stables, and
Jackson's outriders were directed to a cool keg of
beer set up in the orchard. Jason had planned things
so that he would have a chance to talk to the general
alone, prior to the arrival of Rupert Harris, Phil
Foley, Felix Wohl, and a few of the others who had
been selected as a delegation from Harrisville and the
outlying plantations and farms.

Jason and Chula Harjo were striding toward the
house now, side by side, and Delia's eyes were fastened
on the general. So lean he was, so hard, just like they
said in all the stories. He wore tan riding breeches
and high, unpolished boots, the loose tops of which
flopped around bony knees, and a long, white-man's
killing knife hung from his belt. Jackson held himself erect without seeming to, held himself with a
natural, overwhelming dignity, a strength weathered
and tempered and made tougher than anything that
had ever been foolhardy enough to challenge it.

Delia watched him come toward her, and her heart
was beating like a drum. But then she remembered
who she was.

She recalled the wisdom of the old seeress, she of
the sacred birthmark: Those who are true to what
they be have no need of fear.

That was the great secret of a warrior's heart. And
since Chula Harjo was a warrior, he must know the
secret, too.

And so do I, Delia vowed. With an effort of will
she brought herself under control. What had she been
permitting herself to do? A Chickasaw did not flinch
or quiver, nor let her heart grow faint and race away.

No, a Chickasaw, always in battle, ever in danger,
even in defeat, met the eyes of an enemy, and though
a Chickasaw might die, never would he yield.

Never would *she* yield!

Then the door opened, and Delia was as still as a mountain lake in winter. Her deep black eyes stared straight and true, locked on Andrew Jackson, fixed upon his sharp blue eyes. She saw curiosity grow in them. Perhaps she had overcompensated for her fear. Perhaps her glance was too bold.

But if he was surprised or offended, he gave no sign. She saw him attempt to gauge the significance of her long glance, and then he seemed to decide that she was only doing what so many others had done: Seeing him for the first time, they were compelled to measure what they saw against the stories they had heard. That did not bother him; he more than measured up.

Yet she saw something else in his eyes, too; and he seemed to study her face, trying to sort it out, separate her from the thousands of images in his mind.

"Lady Randolph," he said, very courteously, and a short bow followed. "Forgive me, but somehow you seem familiar. Have we met before?"

Beneath his hairline, near the temple, was a long scar, etched twenty years before by Four Bears during the raid at Roaring Gorge.

With her own hand she took up a glass from the pantry shelf and poured into it a measure of cool lemonade. She moved as if in a dream, and each shred of lemon pulp in the liquid seemed to spin like a shooting star, or like a grainy creature of the deep. Then her hand reached for the jug of whiskey, and she thought, He will take this from me and drink of it. *I could use poison, the magic herbs of Teva!* But she had none of them, and so she carried the drink to the verandah, where Jason sat talking with Chula Harjo, and handed her ultimate enemy a drink to quench his thirst. He thanked her, and sipped, and thanked her again, and lived on, breathing the air he had shut off from the lungs of Delia's mother and father.

Chula was even now bouncing little Andrew on his

bony knee, and the boy seemed not to mind at all. In fact he seemed very happy.

"Lemonade, Jason?" she asked.

"Please. Have Tanya bring it. You sit down with us."

"By all means," the general said, turning to her. It was odd. When he spoke of politics, policy, war, Jackson was rough and irreverent. Yet when a pretty woman came near, he softened, grew almost courtly. Delia saw this phenomenon now, as he motioned her to a seat beside him, and she saw no hint of falseness or of artifice.

This is a great man, she thought, recalling Jason's words. But what *was* a great man, and why did he become so? Must one kill to be great? Was that what had made Four Bears great?

"Mrs. Randolph," Chula Harjo was saying, his bright, fierce face so close to her, "I can't tell you how much I appreciate your hospitality and this lemonade on such a hot afternoon."

She told him that he was welcome to both.

"We're just pleased that you could give us some of your time," Jason put in. "The others will be along shortly."

Tanya brought more lemonade, whiskey, and thin-sliced pieces of elderberry pie. Jackson ate two pieces right away. Little Andrew was sent out with the servant, protesting as he went, and Jackson laughed sympathetically. "You just mind your ma, there, young man," he advised, then pulled from his belt a jagged arrowhead. "Here, son, you can have this."

Like any child, the boy accepted the gift appreciatively, even though he had no idea what it was.

"That arrow almost split my skull up near Boone-town, fifteen years ago. Choctaw, it is. Was one of those situations where it was him or me. It was him, that time."

"General," Jason protested, "that must mean a great deal to you. Here, Andy, give that back."

"Andy?"

"Well, General," grinned Jason, "we had to name him after somebody, now didn't we?"

"Well, well," Jackson said, truly pleased. "Then, by all means, keep that arrowhead, son, and run along now like your ma says."

Watching, listening, Delia ascribed a few minimal qualities of humanity to Jackson; but she would not let herself be moved, she would not let down her guard. The demons who walked upon the earth were always deceptive; that was one of the first things she had ever learned. Besides, he wore that long killing-knife.

"And where does your family come from, child?" Jackson was asking.

Delia started in some surprise. "Oh, I'm sorry—I was thinking. Georgia. They come from Georgia."

"Why, that's surely interesting. I've spent a lot of time in that state, and a great state it is, too. What part you from?"

Delia did not think about it, or consider her answer. His shrewd blue hawk's eyes were on her, and all the past stood between them. He must remember, or there was no meaning to anything at all.

"Talking Rock," she said. "The village of Talking Rock."

"That was quite a while back," Jason interjected, with a casualness that hovered on the air.

But Jackson seemed not to notice. His eyes darkened, and he nodded.

"Talking Rock," he said, patting his leg. "Got a souvenir from that one, too." He looked very closely at Delia.

He spoke no more of Georgia. Talk turned to the progress Tennesseeans were making in forging their state. And after not too long a time a carriage was seen coming up the drive.

"That'll be Phil Foley," Jason said.

He was half-correct. Delia could see, beside Phil

Foley on the carriage seat, a woman, whose bright scarf could only partly obscure her blond hair.

Gale had come along for the ride.

Gale did not restrain herself when she was presented to the famous general. Words of admiration—many of them repeated several times—poured from her quick-working mouth, and it seemed she would swoon (or at least pretend to). Then she saw, to her great surprise, that Jackson appeared to be almost pained at her display, and she lapsed into silence. But she could not understand why he would not like to listen to such praise.

Felix Wohl and Stan Loftis arrived, without their wives, and then—brilliant in his scarlet coat and gleaming coach—came Rupert Harris. Introductions were made, and Harris made a point of thanking Jackson for the fine hospitality he had enjoyed at the Hermitage. Then the men sat down on the verandah to talk business.

Delia took Gale to the parlor.

"Isn't there some way we can hear what they're saying?" Gale asked, her tone now friendly and conspiratorial, seeking Delia's help.

"I think not," Delia responded coldly; but as she did, an idea came to her, born of memory. Once she had crept close to a Chickasaw council meeting and listened behind Teva's tent, trying to learn what her fate would be. Was it possible to do the same thing now?

True, if she were to sit out on the verandah, the men might pay her little attention, but . . .

But there was something else. They were sure to talk about the Indian question. That was one of Rupert Harris's favorite topics. No, she could not be present, but she had to know what was being planned.

"I must tend to preparations for the meal," she told Gale. "Here are some books, and a portrait album. I hope you will find them diverting. I will have lemonade sent in, and join you as soon as I can."

Delia left the parlor, gave Tanya a few instructions, told little Andrew about arrowheads, and then managed to slip out of the house. Over in the orchard the men of Jackson's escort were resting or dozing beneath the apple trees. She turned the corner, went around in back of the house, and could not see or be seen by them.

She heard the mutter of the men talking on the verandah, and it became louder and more distinct as she crept along the house. Honeysuckle bloomed there, and sweet forsythia; morning glory vines climbed trellises all the way up to the eaves. Skillfully she slid behind the flowers and slipped silently closer to the sound, all the while thinking how little difference there was in red men's and white men's regard for women. Useful to give pleasure and comfort! Useful in the rearing of children! Useful in the work of servants! True, she was more than those things to Jason, but now other men had shown up to deliberate high matters, and where was she? She was creeping behind banks of flowers, eluding drowsy bees, in order to learn what her fate might be! It was precisely as it had been in the Chickasaw village, stealing up behind the witch-woman's wigwam!

"Now, Ginral, how can you say that?" Rupert Harris was asking, apparently slapping his thigh on a tabletop for added effect.

"I can say it because I ain't a damn fool," Jackson shot back. "I can't make it this year, and there's no way to change that fact. We westerners ain't strong enough yet. That limp-ass Quincy Adams got everything sewed up this time around, so we got to wait until 'twenty-eight." Jackson was using the vernacular of the frontier, which he knew so well.

"Adams is only planning one term?" This was Jason's question.

"I don't care what the hell he's planning," Jackson growled. "He's goin' to be a washout, a one-term washout like his old man."

"That's right," someone said.

"Sure is," said another.

"And, boys, in 1828 we are going to go on glory road all the way to Washington, D.C. Ain't nothin' goin' to stop us then, neither. Why, lookit that Adams, will you? How could he ever hope to run the country? I understand he went to this here Harvard college. I'd like to take that boy down here in these mountains when the redskins is acting up, put him behind a tree, an' tell him, 'Now, Quincy, soon as you see an Injun coming to scalp you, hold out your college degree there, an' that'll stop him dead!' "

A great burst of laughter followed, and it tore Delia's heart to hear Jason laughing right along with the others.

Chula Harjo! She had almost softened on the verandah earlier, when he'd given little Andrew the arrowhead. What a mistake that would have been. Jackson was, would always be, an enemy to her people. He would have to be destroyed.

"Speaking of redskins . . ." Rupert Harris said. "Now I been thinking this over . . ."

How to destroy Jackson, though. That was the question. Poison? Delia had none. A gun, a knife? Of course. But if she killed him here in her house, she would certainly be arrested and tried. People would ask questions, and all the suspicions would be confirmed: *She was an Injun all the time—we ought to've known.*

But Jackson was here, and he might never be again, and she could end his life now. How many more depredations would he wreak upon the Indian nations should he ever occupy the Great White Wigwam in the East?

And yet, had not Jason explained to her that Jackson did not favor senseless, random forays against the tribes?

"Ginral, we got to do it once and for all," Rupert Harris was advising, in a tone that said, Look here, this is clear to us all!

"And we have to settle some questions about land rights as well."

Delia's attention quickened the more. The voice was Phil Foley's. She knew that Phil and Jason were fairly close, but she had never trusted him, since Gale was his wife. And yet here was young Phil, bringing up before a powerful outsider an issue with which certain aggrieved citizens of Harrisville had not yet decided how to deal.

"Land rights?" Jackson drawled.

There was a long silence, during which time Delia imagined the men sipping drinks and looking at one another out of the corners of their eyes.

"Land rights," Phil Foley repeated.

"Apparently, things have been handled incorrectly in filing pertinent papers up at Lexington," Jason commented.

Delia understood. Phil and Jason were giving Harris an opportunity to go back and change the situation on his own! If a crisis could be avoided by the threat of Jackson's ascendant authority, all might be well.

But Jackson had to be alive if the ploy was to work. How could she kill him now?

What was she to do? Listening for the next remark, she saw Gale Foley steal around the corner of the house, heading for the edge of the verandah. Of course Gale would want to know what the men were discussing! Why hadn't Delia imagined what the blond woman might do? Had she underestimated her enemy, again?

Was Gale a Little Swallow with white skin?

And then she decided. Gale would be the one to suffer exposure. From the dirt beneath the flower bed Delia picked up a half-buried rock, and waited, as Gale came creeping alongside the house, half-bent, awkward, without Delia's stealth.

"Sure, in a new state like ours, there can be errors made about land claims," Jackson was saying judiciously, trying to guess why the subject had come up in his presence. "But we are men of Tennessee, men of good will, and these things can be settled without trouble. We westerners have got to stick together."

Gale did not bother to hide behind the flowers. A bee might sting her. She might dirty her dress. Instead she simply edged along the outside of the flower bushes and strained to hear what was being said on the verandah.

Delia threw the rock. She threw it hard, so that it struck the wooden wall of the porch with a sharp crack, and the men ceased talking abruptly.

"Hey!" exclaimed Felix Wohl.

Delia saw Gale stop, still as a stone, suspended there next to the flowers for one absurd, open-mouthed moment. The woman seemed incapable of deciding what to do, run or stay, and had insufficient time to fashion an artifice before Phil himself leaned out over the verandah railing and cried, "Gale!"

"I was just . . . I was just . . ."

Phil was chagrined. Gale was terribly embarrassed, and angry at having been caught. Had she thought faster, she might have invented some plausible reason for skulking along the side of the house. But she'd been too surprised by the strange, sudden sound to think that quickly.

"It's an enemy scout!" guffawed Rupert Harris.

Andrew Jackson politely said nothing.

"Would you care to come up here?" Phil Foley asked his wife; and, having no choice, Gale did so. While the men were having themselves a good time asking the mortified woman how the garden looked and how the flowers were, Delia stole back into the house, with none the wiser, and appeared calmly in the verandah doorway to ask when the gentlemen might wish to dine.

*　*　*

From Rupert Harris's point of view, Andrew Jackson's visit to Riverbend could not be recorded on the credit side of his ledger.

In the first place, Jackson was coldly realistic about his political chances in this year of 1824. He wanted support, of course, but he wanted it for 1828. Given that fact, he was not desperate, and had no wish to stir up a situation with the Chickasaw when, as Jason had pointed out, "over two years have gone by since the last violent incident."

"Only a clear-cut Indian attack will bring out my militia," the general said.

Delia glanced at Harris as the big red-bearded empire builder listened to Jackson. Harris chewed his dinner, drank ale, and seemed to be thinking hard about his coal. Certainly his eyes were as dark as coal, brightening only slightly when Jackson added, "Now, 'course we all know the Indian is a tricky, devious, absolutely unprincipled animal, and anything can happen. We got to be on constant guard. But there ain't no lack of wisdom in the saying 'Let sleeping dogs lie'—right, men? Who was it made up that one, anyway?"

"Quincy Adams?" drawled Felix Wohl laconically, drawing a laugh.

Secondly, Harris had been put on the defensive when Jason and Phil brought up the land deals. No more was said about the situation, but it had not been forgotten; and over elderberry pie, without prelude, Jackson alluded to the matter again by saying, "I'm sure you boys down here in an area ripe as Harrisville can get your territorial affairs settled without a lot of legalistic shenanigans."

Everyone nodded, quite soberly, but without any great hope or trust.

And finally, Harris was astute enough to be aware that the impression he was making on Jackson was by no means overwhelming. At first glance red-beard Rupert seemed the most powerful personality present,

an effect aided by his big body and blunt, peremptory
speech. But Jackson's presence was paramount in the
house, and in his aura Harris seemed—indeed *was*—
more tentative. Harris's rough-handed manner set off
more clearly the personalities of the other men.

Jason was clearly the best educated, and drawing
upon his fine Virginia breeding, he spoke very well.
Phil Foley, in spite of his youth, was sincere and
occasionally passionate in his belief that Harrisville
had a great future. Felix Wohl was every bit as tough
and no-nonsense as Rupert Harris had ever seemed
to be. Stan Loftis, a landowner, showed little interest
in political questions, but his grasp of market locations and river access to them was close to encyclo-
pedic.

So as these men spoke their various pieces, Harris's
crude luster dimmed a bit, though it was by no means
extinguished. Delia could not help being pleased by
this transition, however temporary it would prove to
be.

"Well," Jackson said, standing to end the evening—
which, as honored guest, it was his responsibility to
do—"let me put it this way. You've come a long way
toward a great community in a very short time. Don't
stir up the Indians. Settle whatever squabbles you
have among yourselves, if you can."

He seemed to think of something. "Rupert," he
asked, turning to the big man, "when you were up
to the Hermitage, didn't you tell me there was some
hotshot new chief of a tribe down this neck of the
woods?"

"That's right, General. Firebrand, we call him."

"S'posed to cause you a lot of trouble, wasn't he?"

"That's a fact," said Rupert Harris.

"Well, see, it didn't happen, did it? But if we'da
gone up into those mountains when you wanted, a
lot of people would have died. It wasn't necessary.
And I hope to hell it ain't ever gonna be."

"Well, we just had to plan on all the possibilities," Harris temporized.

Gale Foley, who had remained quiet and abashed throughout the meal, chose now to get in her two cents.

"Tell me, General," she cooed sweetly, "how can a person tell one tribe from another?"

Jackson, who'd fought almost every nation and tribe in the southeastern United States at one time or another, was not averse to sharing the knowledge he'd gained. And he'd been feeling a little sorry for Gale, who'd been so starkly embarrassed by the flower beds.

"There's lots of ways, lots of ways. Headpiece, for example. Style of hair. Style of dress. The Cherokee marks himself different from the Choctaw, and the Sac has an arrowhead different from the—"

"But," Gale interrupted, drawing closer and closer to what she wanted to know, "in what tribe do they wear bracelets in the form of serpents?"

Delia, who had grown almost relaxed, now tensed immediately, and she saw a startled look appear on Jason's face.

"Why, that'd be Chickasaw, of course," Jackson drawled, pleased with his knowledge, and with Gale's question, which had given him a little forum to demonstrate his expertise. "The Chickasaw warrior often wears that kind of ornament."

"How did you come to have one of those?" asked Gale, turning, with all the world's innocence, on Delia.

"Why, I'm sure you are mistaken," Delia managed quite smoothly, after just the briefest pause; and the unexpected confidence in her reply disconcerted Gale and left her in smiling silence, save for a faltering "Oh, that's odd, I thought . . ."

But had damage been done? Jackson was looking at Delia very closely, almost as he had regarded her

upon entering the house earlier this afternoon—
almost with a glimmering of familiarity, recognition.
Yes, his eyes had been full of memory! Did she resemble her mother? Did Jackson truly *know*?

Then the moment passed, the guests left, and Jackson remained to spend the night. His outriders and
escort troops, having eaten at the field kitchen with
the hired men, would now sleep outside under the
stars or inside the hayloft, depending upon their
preference. Haylofts, for many of those rough men,
were highly prized elements of country hospitality,
especially in winter.

"Do you think I might have a bath?" the general
asked, when Harris and the others had gone.

"Of course," said Delia, and ordered Tanya to start
heating the water.

"Used to be I didn't have but a bath a month," she
heard Jackson telling Jason. "Now I swear a day on
the road leads me to crave one. I must be getting old."

The general smoked his pipe in the parlor, and
Jason went out to check on the comfort of Jackson's
men. Tanya heated bathwater. And Delia's mind
worked furiously.

The bathtub was in a bare, wooden room just off
the kitchen, next to the bricks that backed the kitchen
fireplace, in order to ensure warmth. The room could
be entered from the kitchen, but also from outside,
through a wooden door. Ever since his arrival Jackson
had worn the knife. But he would not wear it in his
bath, would he?

Suppose she were to kill Jackson in the tub? Suppose she were to manage the deed with such stealth
that she would not be captured, or even identified?
He was a guest in her house. She had been most
hospitable. Everyone had seen that, hadn't they?

Many people, for many reasons, would like to have
Andrew Jackson out of the way. Many might pay to
have such a thing done. An assassin might have trailed

him here to Riverbend farm, waited until the general was having his bath, entered the bathroom, and then . . .

True, Jason would guess right away what had happened, who had done it—but would he betray her?

Even if he did, she had already decided to pay whatever price was necessary to fulfill her vow, to avenge her parents. The land, the deeds—surely they were minor matters compared to life and death.

She had seen Andrew Jackson's stabbing eyes on her, and she knew he could not but be engaging in deception when he made public remarks about "letting sleeping dogs lie." Words like that were said solely to delude victims. And neither Gyva nor the Chickasaw would be deluded ever again by Jacksa Chula Harjo. See how fierce he would be, bleeding to death in a warm bath on Riverbend farm!

So she waited for her moment to come.

Presently Tanya poured water into the tub, an elaborate receptacle of the latest style, which rested on four supports designed to look like the claws of a bear. The servant also laid out soft towels and soap and hung a lighted lantern from a nail on the wall.

"Your bath is waiting, General Jackson."

He walked slowly from the parlor after extinguishing his pipe and slouched through the kitchen. He was tired. Delia saw that and was glad.

There was no lock on the door, all locks having been removed in fear that little Andrew might contrive one day to shut himself behind some door. Jackson closed the door, and in moments Delia heard the water splashing.

"That is all, Tanya. Go have some sleep."

"All right, Miz."

"Are you still up?" asked Jason, coming in from his check on the men and the farm.

"You go up," she told him. "I'll wait to see if he wishes anything."

His glance was frank, and not without suspicion. He recalled their conversation in bed after the barbecue dinner.

"Delia, shall I stay here with you?"

"Haven't I behaved well? I shall do what is right, as I have always done."

Yes, that is true, she thought. She would do the right thing. She would kill Andrew Jackson.

She thought then, too, that this was the first time she had ever deceived Jason in anything.

The decision was very difficult. But she had to deceive Jason in this matter, or else Jackson would go on living. Jackson's death was necessary, since without his leadership white rampages against the Indians might falter, and thus the lives of many people, both Indian and white, would be spared. One deception, one death—both wrong in themselves— were nevertheless necessary to accomplish something good: a potential end to future bloodshed. Believing this utterly, Gyva steeled herself to lie and to kill.

"No harm will come to Chula," she told her husband.

He gave her a long, searching look, with something else in his glance that she did not immediately recognize. She remembered that time in bed, when she was certain he had guessed the full truth behind the battle of Talking Rock. "All right," he said, "I'll see you in bed."

After he had left the room, Delia realized with a sense of guilt that what she had seen in his eyes was trust. But she banished the guilt. No time for it now. She was in the kitchen. Chula Harjo was splashing in the four-clawed tub. Now was the moment that had, since Talking Rock, waited to raise up and strike, like some patient beast of vengeance, concealed behind dark trees in the forests of time. Delia was ready for the moment. The butcher knife would be best, and it was in the kitchen drawer. She had had Paul sharpen it for her yesterday. The glow of the kitchen lamp glinted on the instruments, and light flickered on the blades. Delia saw her hand reach out and take up the horn handle of the chosen knife, fully as long as a white man's killing-knife, and just as deadly.

Without a sound, precisely as she had been taught, Delia moved to the bathroom door, and without a sound she turned the handle and eased the door open.

Chula Harjo was bathing, slowly, drowsily soaping himself, using a small dipper now and then to spill water over his head and shoulders. Without clothes he looked even leaner, and in the dim light of the lantern, Delia saw mark after mark, scar after scar. All those wounds! All those battles! And he had not been felled.

For just a quiver of an instant her heart faltered. Was this animal before her of mere flesh or of some other substance, more divine?

Then he brushed back his hair, and she saw the scar inflicted by her grandfather, and it was a great scar indeed. The only problem was that Four Bears had weakened, had experienced compassion at the ultimate moment. Death. Four Bears ought to have dealt death on that last moment.

Delia eased the door open a few inches more, enough for her to squeeze inside. The general's back was half turned toward her, and she saw one strong, flat shoulder, the other being obscured by the tub. Then she stopped. On the table next to the tub, which held the fluffy towels, she saw something else— Jackson's knife.

He left nothing to chance.

She felt at once both contempt and respect for him. He left nothing to chance, and that was why he had outlived his wounds. That was why he was alive.

Pressed closely but not rigidly next to the wall, Delia ceased to move. She was fully inside the room now, and the door closed of its own weight, making no sound. The flame from the lantern, encased by isinglass, was not disturbed and did not flicker.

Delia felt the knife in her hand. Her heart was beating slowly, and her soul was very still. She was ready.

But inexplicably, out of the past, she saw another man before her, a Choctaw brave, lying in the dust. "Scalp him!" the people were howling at her, "scalp him!"

A feeling of depression mingled with the righteousness in her heart, and for just a moment she floundered.

"Mrs. Randolph?" Andrew Jackson asked, turning slowly toward her. He was not surprised, nor was he afraid. He did not even reach for his knife.

"Talking Rock," she said, not moving.

"I know," he replied. And, lifting his leg, he showed her the puncture marks that Delia's mother had inflicted with the pitchfork.

They looked at each other.

"I wish to God I had not had to do it," he said, his eyes not leaving hers. "The day has never left me, and the day is with me still. You are the child?"

"I am . . . . I was." She had not moved, but the distance between them was not great. If she leapt and struck, he would have time to reach for his knife. It would be a fair fight.

"Why," she heard herself asking, "were you taking me to Florida? Did you plan to sell me into slavery?"

"No," he said, quite calmly. "The only thing I could think to do, after the folly of Talking Rock, was to find Seminole who would take you in."

Another long moment passed. Against her will, in spite of all her planning and resolve, Delia believed him.

"Did you come to kill me?" he asked then.

She nodded.

"Four Bears didn't when he had the chance."

"Perhaps he should have."

"Perhaps, but he didn't."

The fact was there in the room with them. Four Bears was there in the room with them.

"Don't do it," he said, not pleading, simply advising. "You'll gain nothing, and bring a lot of pain to everybody."

"Your pain will be short."

"But yours will be long. Very long."

Their eyes were locked together. Delia saw no fear in his, and he none in hers. Then he reached out, very slowly, and pushed his knife to the floor, where it skidded across the boards, out of immediate reach.

"I bear you no malice of any kind," he said, and waited.

All of the past, every one of the stories, came back to her. The long hatred of Chula Harjo, every twinge of it, was with her in the room. But also with her was his presence, and the knowledge—which she could no longer deny or misinterpret—that he had once done the best he could for her, and tried to bring her to safety.

Delia nodded to him and went from the room. But it was Gyva who had let him live when she could have killed him with the knife. And it was Gyva who knew that Jackson was a warrior, and a worthy one. He was, as Jason had said, a great man.

"And the general?" asked Jason, as she came into bed beside him.

"He is safe," she said.

They both knew what she meant.

CHAPTER XIV

"Well, Jason, what are we going to do?" Phil Foley asked again. "We've been waiting on this Harris thing since last summer. If we don't get together and act soon, we might as well forget about it."

"No one is more aware of it than I am," Jason responded wearily. "After Jackson's visit, I had hoped we could get most of the nervous nellies together for a united stand. But Harris was smart. He went around the county and talked to them one at a time. Making deals and telling lies. He told Otto Ronsky, for example, that the two of us were troublemakers, and then increased Otto's share of the crop by 10 percent. The funny thing—if you'd call it funny—is that the *whol*e crop was Otto's in the first place—Harris had rooked him out of his land, the same as everyone else."

"If people don't want to believe, they won't."

"They've *got* to."

It was evening, mid-March, at Riverbend farm. A cold wind howled down from the mountains, and rain battered against the farmhouse, gusting sheets of rain that moved like ghostly curtains in the air. Phil and Jason were drinking coffee at the kitchen fireplace, talking over community matters, when Delia entered, having just put little Andrew to bed.

"Phil, I think you'd better spend the night. You'll catch your death, riding back to Harrisville in this rain. Let me have Tanya make up a bed for you."

Phil went to the window and looked out. The final

effect of twilight was nothing more than a dull patch
of gray behind black, wind-driven clouds. Sheets of
rain slanted in toward the window, blasting the pane.

"Atrocious weather," he said. "All right, Delia,
thanks. I'll take that offer of bed. I don't need any
more convincing."

Jason, too, observed the progress of the storm.
"Three days now," he was saying.

Further words were unnecessary. The river was rising, and everybody knew it.

"Maybe we ought to get some sleep now," Phil said,
letting his voice trail off. They might have to flee by
night.

"Not a bad idea. But first let's check the situation."

The two men pulled on hip boots and oilcloths,
which gave some protection from the storm, and made
their way outside. Riverbend farm, its house and
barns and outbuildings, was an assortment of dark
gray shapes outlined against the sky. The yard was a
quagmire, and it took ten minutes to advance as far
as the bunkhouse. It took the strength of both men
to open the door in the face of the slashing wind.

Inside, cold and dark—and no one there.

"What the . . . ?" Phil exclaimed.

"Let's try the barn."

The distance was not great, but by the time they
reached the big, rambling structure of stables, stalls,
and hayloft, both men were soaked to the skin, and
cursing. The heavy, warm smell of sheltered animals
was not at all unpleasant, but most of the hired hands
huddled there in the barn wore expressions that
belied the apparent security of the place. Some of
them seemed a bit abashed, caught by their employer
in such a situation.

"Bunkhouse was a little too close to the river,"
boomed big Paul, the freedman, in his resonant bass.

"You have a point there," Jason said.

"What are we gonna do, boss?"

"First I'm going to try to check the river. If it's over the pilings on the dock, we'd better do some quick thinking."

"We gonna have to get out, boss? If so, ain't it better to go now than wait around and have to wrestle with the horses at midnight?"

The other hands were nodding, and not a few of them looked fearful. They were good fellows, hard workers. Since the departure of Fes Farson, whose very presence had been a bad example, Jason had had few problems with any of the men. And he could understand their desire to leave before the river rose any further, before the access roads were flooded, too.

"Let me make one last check of the river before it gets full dark," he told them. "In the meantime, it probably wouldn't hurt any to get the horses harnessed."

"I sure as hell hope we're not too late," he told Phil when they were back outside again, struggling through the storm.

There was no answer. Phil had trouble enough stepping from one sticky patch of mud to another.

Jason had built the main section of the farmstead close to the river because, with the big dock he had also erected, crops could more easily be transported to Harrisville, downriver, or on to larger market towns. Supplies needed for the house or the farm could be delivered readily, too, quickly unloaded and used. One of the reasons the farm had been so expeditiously built was the fact that lumber from the sawmill did not have to be hauled long distances overland, merely taken from the river barge and used as required.

Jason stood on the slight promontory—it seemed slight indeed—and listened to the thunder of the river. Last summer, when the river had been low, this little rise of land behind the barn had seemed an immense cliff; it had been inconceivable that the river might ever rise so high. Jason watched the water,

gray and white and black and roaring, and recalled
Harris's original piece of advice: "Build that close to
the river, you might get flooded out." Well, Harris
had never been stupid, no matter what else he might
be.

"My God, will you look at that!" exclaimed Phil
Foley, howling into the wind. There was fear, as well
as awe in his voice. From the east, where the valley
lay wide and easy, to the west, where the river swept
into a bend and disappeared into the forest, there
seemed to be nothing but water, a vast, sweeping
channel of thunder. By the last rays of light, the men
saw whole trees washed along like pieces of tinder,
unmanned boats washed from their moorings upriver,
and flat, dark shapes that could only have been parts
of buildings, battered down by the river and carried
along.

Jason said nothing for a long time, just stood there
watching the colossal tide of destruction rip and rip
and rip his earth away. Finally Phil nudged him.
"It's not getting any lighter," he said.

Whether there were tears in Jason's eyes, he could
not say. It was too dark to tell, and there was too
much rain.

"See that bend down there?" he called into the
smashing roar of the wind and water. "Where the
river turns?"

Phil nodded.

"I named the farm for that bend. Delia told me
once about a certain place on a river, and a sacred
stick buried in the sand—" He broke off, shrugged. "I
guess it's just an In—I guess it's just a story."

They abandoned the farm that night, reached high
ground safely, and were in Harrisville by dawn. They
were guests at Gale Foley's inn, exactly as they had
been several years before. Days later, when the rain
ceased, they rode back out to the farm. Everything

had been swept away. All was as it had once been, except that the trees were gone now, too.

Even the lone pin oak Delia had convinced Jason to spare.

An evil omen, she thought, but she said nothing.

THE BOOK OF

EXODUS

CHAPTER I

The Choctaw chieftain, slashes of war-paint crimson on his blunt forehead and high cheekbones, leaned forward. The council fire danced in his canny, eager eyes, and he even allowed himself a flicker of a grimace that might have been a smile, had he ever learned how to smile.

"Torch," he said. "What malady has entered into the heart of the Chickasaw people?"

Torch held the other's eyes and frowned. "We suffer no malady of which I am aware."

Around them, squatting upon their haunches or sitting crosslegged in the dust, were many braves of both tribes, watching one another with wary malice. The Chickasaw recalled very well the Choctaw raid in the year of Four Bears' death, and the Choctaw had not forgotten the warriors who had fallen in that raid. Thus this meeting between Torch and Red Dagger, the Choctaw chief, attracted uncommon interest. Red Dagger had sought the meeting; Torch had agreed.

"Let him come to us and speak what is in him," Teva had counseled. "Be well armed and vigilant. There seems little danger in listening."

So the Choctaw had made their way from forest strongholds in the West, and the first council in many years had commenced between the two peoples.

"Harrisville has been allowed to grow unmolested," grunted Red Dagger. "Is that not a malady?"

"The village has not harmed us, and I do not

believe we are in any danger from them. The weary, devastating times of battle upon battle, with nothing to show for effort but death, has ended." He stared boldly at the Choctaw. "Once we had among us a brave who often said, 'The path of war is dearer than the path of plenty.' We had war then, much war, but little else. Now we have peace and plenty."

Slowly, ceremoniously, he filled a great hooked pipe with fragrant tobacco and lit it. Still watching Red Dagger, Torch drew deeply on the stem and blew a cloud of smoke from his mouth.

"He was a fine brave," said Torch, "the man who spoke so endearingly of war. But he is dead now."

Then he passed the pipe to Red Dagger, who took it, scowling. Red Dagger puffed slowly and long, mindful that his braves were waiting for a reply that would surpass the eloquence of this big, young Chickasaw. Red Dagger puffed for a long time. He was, in fact, impressed and a little startled by the bearing and authority of Torch. Red Dagger had long believed that the strange absence of the Chicka-saw from the battlefields of Tennessee was due to this new chief, whom he had never met, and to the new chief's timidity and unmanliness. On the journey here Red Dagger had been in high spirits, eager to sit down and make a fool of Torch before his own people. But now, smoking the pipe much longer than was required, Red Dagger had the sensation of a man who has allowed overconfidence to outplay wisdom, and suspects it might be too late to rectify the judg-ment.

"There are those who die in the glory of battle for their people," he said at length, "and there are those who die ingloriously, with full bellies."

Choctaw braves grunted in admiration, and not a few Chickasaw nodded with respect. Red Dagger had been a fiery presence in these mountains for almost thirty circlings of the sun; he was one of those rare men who, still living, had already bequeathed to their people the vibrant stuff of legend and wonder.

"It may also be rendered thus," Torch commented slowly. "Tragedy lies in wasteful death. The Great Spirit did not provide us with rich lands in order that we live in hunger and want."

Another chorus of respectful grunts rose in the council wigwam, and the pipe began to make its rounds among the braves.

"He-Who-Dwells-in-the-Clear-Sky," retorted Red Dagger, the very quickness of his reply betraying some heat, "has not deeded us this land that it be taken from us by the jackals."

Torch looked at the older man for a long time. Red Dagger had come here for some kind of show-down, that was clear. Exactly what was on the old chief's mind, Torch did not yet know. But judging from Red Dagger's opening thrusts, he meant to put Torch on the defensive, to make him seem weak, and thus to force him, in the end, to prove strength by supporting Red Dagger's position.

Torch decided upon an approach that might smoke out whatever Dagger's position was. If successful, such a ploy would conserve many words, and not a few tempers.

"Did Ababinili create the white man, too?" he asked bluntly.

He phrased the thought as a question; thus he could not be accused of entertaining base, ignoble, heretical beliefs. But, as he had expected, the question itself was enough to stun listeners to an attention all the more keen for its utter silence. Well did Torch know, too, that this question had never been answered, not by any of the wise ones who had shared fate with the Indian nations.

There was a legend to explain the existence of white men, of course. It said that once, before there were red braves and maidens upon the face of the

earth, before the sun was old and easy, Ababinili
himself had lived in the mountains of Tennessee.
There had he planned the universe he was to create,
and there did he ponder all of the things he would
quicken with life and beauty. One afternoon, in the
midst of euphoric contemplation, he drifted into
sleep, and while he slept, the wind grew chill. In his
mind Ababinili imagined wondrous things, and saw
himself creating them. But the cold wind chilled his
blood, sullied his dream; and from his brain sprang
a terrible serpent that glittered like ice, and his eyes
were the eyes of death, and his forked tongue was
cold fire that would freeze anything it touched. Ababinili felt the cold then, both the cold of the wind
and that of the serpent, and awakened. Realizing
what had transpired, he drove the serpent northward,
ever northward, and on the top of the world itself
he created for the serpent a prison of ice from which
the beast was never to depart. The primeval serpent
of evil remained locked beneath the top of the sky,
but it had possessed powers of its own, and from its
pale body had come eggs to hatch in the ice of the
north. And when they were hatched, the offspring
of the cold serpent spread out through the world to
defile everything the Great Spirit had created, and
to kill his true red children.

Everyone knew the legend. But it was not a popular
legend, nor a comfortable one. Because, even if accidentally and indirectly, those who followed the tale
to its logical conclusion had to admit that Ababinili
had created the white man. And—again accidentally
and indirectly—the white man's genesis via the serpent
could be said to have preceded creation of the red
man. Indeed, many subleties in the legend had
troubled soothsayers for generations: Could the Great
Spirit err? Could he make mistakes? Was He-Who-
Dwells-In-the-Clear-Sky sufficiently powerful to correct evil in the world he had created? And finally, if
Ababinili had created him, must there not be *some*

good in the white man, since, being all-good, how could the Great Spirit create total evil?

So when Torch asked Red Dagger, around the council fire, if Ababinili had also created the white man, he stunned the old man. Such a question lifted the discussion from a level of tactics and strategy, where Red Dagger had intended it to be, to another level, which was philosophical, and rare, and where the traps of ambiguity waited to be sprung.

Red Dagger had never been a man to sit beneath trees or around campfires and listen to the idle yammering of dreamy women and fools: They were the ones who wasted their days on ambiguous prattle.

No, Red Dagger had lived his long, illustrious life in the company of two basic questions: One, Shall I bring my battle-axe down upon my enemy's skull now? And two, If I do not bring down my battle-axe now, when shall I do so?

After all, Ababinili had also created battle-axes, was that not true?

"I am respectful of the depth of your great question," he told Torch now. "But it has been my experience that such great questions lead to others that are even greater, deeper, and we may still be discussing them when Harris marches into the villages of our two tribes."

Much acknowledgment of this wisdom came from the assembled braves.

Torch, however, smiled. "Talk may be ended quickly, and questions satisfied as well, by the correct answers. Such answers may not require great expanses of time, if the disputants be wise."

Red Dagger sat there looking very fierce and thoughtful, but in his soul he was quivering. He had no idea what this strange young chief had meant, nor could he not ask without revealing discomfiture.

"You speak a truth," he said instead. "I grant that. Now," he added hastily, attempting to turn the discussion back to specifics, "I have a question of my own. If Ababinili sends a sign that he has bowed your enemy's head to you, would you not strike?"

"With good reason, and if the sign were clear, striking one's enemy would not constitute improper leadership—not in the least. But how is our enemy's head bowed?"

"The rains of the last moon."

Torch's glance was inquisitive.

"The settlement of Harrisville lies stunned beneath the flood caused by those rains, and even now many are homeless, much land is yet underwater. The time to strike has never been better. Many—perhaps all— of the jackals are vulnerable now. Those we do not kill can be driven away, and the land made ours again."

"Do you want that land? The trees have been removed, cut down, the soil denuded and sparse now, so much of it having been washed away in the flood."

"It is the principle of the thing!" Red Dagger thundered, to a chorus of yips and cheers. "And it is *our* land, do not forget."

Torch sighed to himself. Always it came back to the same undeniable, inescapable conclusion, which so few could see. "But even if we raze what is left of Harrisville to the ground, and destroy there every living thing, the army of Chula Harjo, which causes us no harm today, which has been happily quiescent, will form again and come into our hills, and that will be the end of us. You, Red Dagger, are a great chief, and my elder, and I hold for you every respect. Our peoples have quarreled with each other, but let us forget that now. What matters is the future, and—"

The old chief sensed that Torch was preparing to confuse him again with words.

"And they call you Firebrand!" he said, not bothering to hide his contempt. "I fear you have been misnamed. A more fitting appelation ought to be found."

His voice indicated that he could readily invent several names, none of them allusive to strength in battle. Some of the braves choked on their laughter, and mocking mutters were heard.

But Torch was not distressed. He held his ground. "I do not care for the name," he said. "Harris gave me the name, and it is loathsome to me."

"And is Harris loathsome, too?"

"He is," Torch nodded.

"Then let us destroy him!" thundered the old warrior-chieftain.

A vast quiet hung beneath the curved ceiling of the wigwam. Torch evaluated the silence. He himself was brave in battle. That was known. And he was wise with words. That was known, too. But he had not been in battle for a long time; and now, in spite of his best efforts, old Red Dagger had maneuvered him into a corner.

"There will be no doubt of our victory, we Choctaw united with the Chickasaw," Red Dagger added. "With the white men so weak and distracted, how can we fail?"

During the past few years, Torch had calmed his young braves, calmed even the old contingent of Hawk's hotheads, by telling them, "Do not worry. Do not be too much of haste for blood. The lesson of history is that blood will come to you." But here in the wigwam, with a famous chief asking, *begging* Torch to join a battle that *could not be lost*, his own braves could heed him only with difficulty. Once, not long ago, he had heard a stripling of but fifteen circlings of the sun speaking to his fellows. "Look at this," the youth had said, showing his bare arm. "I have not yet one kill-cut. My father told me that by the time he was my age, he already had eleven."

That was untrue. Torch, of course, knew the boy's father, and he suspected that many of the kill-cuts now on his arms had been symbolic of little more than imagination. But Torch also knew that sentiment among his people ran against him now.

"I will take counsel with our seeress," he said, "and by messenger send you answer."

Some of the braves might have accepted this, but Red Dagger, who had earlier felt the sting of Torch's logic, did not now find it in his old heart to ease the pressure.

"Are you not chief?" he cried. "Is the seeress chief? Shall I speak with her?"

There were a few hoots in the wigwam, quickly silenced when Red Dagger raised his hand. "So," he said, "you need time to consider? So be it. Consider. I give you two days, no more."

Great in dignity, he rose from the fire and pulled his robes about him. Red Dagger did not have to appear magnificent. He *was* magnificent. And his abrupt, magisterial departure rendered Torch's deliberate nature ineffective, weak. And in the eyes of the Choctaw, even in the eyes of some of his own braves, Torch did indeed appear tentative and weak.

He seemed, to some, a false leader. And such a thing was very bad.

Torch lay that night in his wigwam, pondering the issues confronting the tribe. His bride, Bright Flower, lay beside him, sensing his preoccupation, and wondering how well the love she planned to give him would distract him from seriousness. Almost always her lovemaking succeeded in taking his mind from the problems of his people, and for this Bright Flower was grateful. And always her lovemaking delighted him. For this Bright Flower was ecstatic. She wished to be everything for him, that he might forget the other one, the one who had been banished.

Bright Flower was a sweet and gentle girl, whose intelligence and sensitive nature had not been appreciated by many of the coarser young braves. After Gyva had been forced from the tribe, there had been much speculation about whom Torch might take to wife. Few mentioned Bright Flower. She was a shy girl and did not put herself forward. And in those days members of the tribe gave their attention to the maneuverings of Little Swallow. *That* maiden was truly a marvel! Following Hawk's death, she immediately approached Torch, told him that Hawk had forced her into terrible actions, had threatened her with violence if she did not do his will. All along she had loved only Torch. When he had not listened to her, she became first angry and then guileful. If contrition did not suffice to win Torch, then perhaps magic would. "Help me," she beseeched old Teva. "Help me prepare a potion that will bring his eyes to me." The seeress laughed in derision. "Such potions work only when your heart is filled with love," she said, "and they are dangerous otherwise." "Oh, but truly my heart is love-filled," Swallow had protested, weeping sweetly and watching Teva from behind glistening lashes. "Please, please, tell me the secret of the potion."

In the end Teva relented. "Go into the woods," she said. "Take the bark of the ash, and the bark of the maple, grind them into powder along with clover, willow leaf, dandelion, two measures of moss, the stem of the purple mushroom, dew from tall grass in the meadow at dawn, and one petal of the lilac, plucked at night. Add to this water from the river, and drink while hearing the call of an owl on a moonless night. But remember, do not attempt this thing unless your heart is filled with love."

Swallow hurried away to gather the ingredients for the potion. In no time at all she was busy grinding them into powder. "What are you doing?" people asked her, as they saw her working near her wigwam. "I am winning the love of Torch," she said. They all laughed. It was no secret that Torch would have nothing to do with her. "You shall see!" Swallow told them. "And then let me hear your laughter!"

She eagerly awaited a cloudy night, that there should be no moon, and finally Ababinili did send her such a night. She took a gourd down to the river and caught water to aid her potion. When it was ready to drink, she walked into the forest, listening for an owl's cry. That, too, came to her, and she gulped down the potion, which had a most pleasant taste. Now I am ready, she thought happily, and started toward Torch's wigwam. She would steal naked beneath the pelts covering him, press her breasts against him, fondle and caress his manhood, and then take it unto herself. After that he would be hers, and she would be—as she had always vowed— wife of a chieftain.

But it was very late, and her task had been fraught with anxiety, and Swallow grew very tired as she walked from the forest and back into the village. By the time she reached Torch's wigwam, dawn was rising, and Swallow could barely walk. Nonetheless, she pushed aside the skins covering the entrance to the young chief's dwelling, and entered. The sun shone on Torch's face, and he awakened.

"Who goes there?" he asked, blinking in surprise. "Who are you? Why have you come?"

Did he not recognize her?

Puzzled, and possessed by a terrible fear, Swallow hobbled to the well, and looked down into the still water. The face she saw reflected there was pale and drawn and contorted into a hideous mask. And even as she watched, the disfigurement grew worse, as if a potent poison were coursing through her blood.

So Little Swallow, whose heart had held many things, among which love was not numbered, collapsed. Not long afterward death took her. And in time Torch chose shy, beautiful Bright Flower as his bride, and the tribe rejoiced.

Bright Flower rejoiced, too. Her only sadness over the years was that Torch's responsibilities as chieftain took so much of his time, weighed so heavily on his mind. She was proud that he took his position seriously, but sad that it was so difficult to tear his mind away from tribal matters. Tonight he was most deeply in thought, and she wondered what to do.

"You're somewhere else," Bright Flower said sadly. "Or someone else is on your mind."

"No," Torch responded comfortingly, for she truly pleased him as a wife and had in no way failed him since wedlock. "No, my moodiness arises from matters of the tribe."

"Tribal matters," she sniffed, trying to tease him, to lighten his mood. "Better were your mind on another woman. At least I could take your mind off her."

Torch kissed Bright Flower, then said, "I am serious. I cannot fight the thought that disaster lies in wait for us if, as the young braves wish, we should go to war now. Nor can I very much longer restrain those who want war."

"Nor," sighed Bright Flower, reaching for him, "can you much longer restrain those who want love."

So they had their love that night, and the Chickasaw nation knew another night of peace. But such nights were numbered. Every night that passed meant one night less, and in time the number would run down to zero.

CHAPTER II

The meeting occurred in the schoolhouse, a month after the flood. The school was new, a one-room, one-storey structure, with twenty double desks for the children, one square desk for a teacher who had not yet been found, and a round iron stove in the center of the floor. The walls were bare. There were two tall windows on either side, and one door at the rear. A stone water jug, set on a stool, stood next to the door. There were no books. Rupert Harris had agreed, reluctantly, to the construction of the school, but had specified that any books, papers, or pencils must be provided by those who sent their children to study.

There were no students as yet, but the school was jam-packed this afternoon. The fate of the community was being discussed. Rupert Harris had resisted the meeting, which had been called by Jason.

"Now what in hell is the point of all this?" Harris demanded, as soon as Jason had called the meeting to order. "We ought to be at work in town cleaning up the debris, plotting out new buildings."

"You have to ask for the floor, Mr. Harris," said Phil Foley had just returned from the capital.

"*What?*" bellowed the red-bearded entrepreneur.

"This is a formal meeting," Phil explained. "We're following parliamentary procedure, so everything's fair and everybody gets a chance."

"Everything's always been fair in Harrisville," Harris said, sitting down. "Did you pick up this parliamentary procedure on your trip up to Lexington?"

Phil Foley had just returned from the capital. Most people figured he'd gone there to try and get loans from some of the bankers.

"You're out of order," Phil told Harris now.

"All right," said Harris, subsiding for the moment. His eyes darted about the schoolroom. He did not like the tone of this meeting. If he couldn't control it . . .

Reuben Sills had his hand up.

"Floor's yours, Reuben," Jason said.

Reuben stood up.

"Hey!" Harris cried, his eyes darkening. "I want to know how—"

"Reuben's got the floor," Phil said, keeping his face absolutely expressionless.

"An' what if I say he doesn't!" Harris said, standing.

"Then you'll have to leave, Mr. Harris. Rules of order."

"Rules of what?"

But Harris took measure of the people, and most of them did not seem on his side. In that case they *might* just kick him out of the meeting. Lot of these folks was pretty antsy lately, after the flood. And he didn't want to miss out on whatever was goin' on amongst 'em.

"Go ahead, Reuben," Jason said encouragingly.

"Seems like now'd be a good time to straighten some things out around here," Reuben said, "what with the flood and all. An' I say"—he hit a wooden desk with the heel of his work-hardened hand—"let's do it fair this time."

Rupert Harris stiffened just a bit, but gave no other sign. He did not have to. Now he knew the purpose of the meeting, and it had very little to do with the flood.

"I been cheated!" Reuben declared. "I been cheated an' you been cheated." He pointed at Felix Wohl and some others, then swept the room with a swing of his arm. "An' by God, we all been cheated!"

"You're out of order, Reuben," warned Phil. "State your piece, but no accusations. This isn't a trial."

Harris figured this was a good place to jump in, so he stood up and got ready to take things over before they got way out of hand.

"Reuben's got the floor, Mr. Harris," said Phil.

I'll wait a little longer, Harris thought. In the packed schoolroom he caught the eyes of Ben Beumer, Jed Alhew, and Jeevis Johnson. He'd done right by them, an' they'd done right by him, an' not a few of the poorer plantation owners had been paid a visit by one or more of 'em if they didn't come across with Rupert's share of the harvest right on time. He saw in their startled expressions that the direction of this meeting was a surprise to them, too.

To the rest of the townspeople, though, it wasn't no surprise. Rupert could *tell.* And that meant . . .

That meant Jason and Phil and Reuben, and God only knew who else, had gone ahead and set this here business up, an' it wasn't goin' to do Rupert Harris no good, no sir. No good at all. He gave Ben and Jed and Jeevis a glance that said, Be ready, boys.

They would have to be. Reuben was telling a long, involved story about the time he took his sick wife up to Lexington to see the doc, and wandered on over to the courthouse to check on the land papers "that Mr. Harris said he took care of so downright real good for us."

Oh, shit! Rupert Harris thought. Then he recalled that Phil Foley had read the law out east. Boston, hadn't it been? Gale had boasted about it often enough.

"An' he took care of us, for sure," Reuben was howling, "an' he also did us in, an' I think we should go over this farm by farm, plot by plot, plantation by plantation, an' see just who in the hell owns what!"

The people muttered agreement as Jason pulled a

thick sheaf of papers from a drawer in the teacher's desk. *Legal* papers.

"Let's have some order here," Phil Foley complained. "You'll all get your chance to speak."

Harris was just about to give the high sign to Ben and Jed and Jeevis. He wished ol' Fes Farson owned land so he'd be eligible to attend this meeting. Instead he was runnin' things back at the plantation.

Jason was laying the incriminating evidence of forgery out on the desk. Delia, seated in the back row with many of the other wives, and keeping little Andrew quiet, was telling herself, It's going to work, it's going to work, it's going to work . . . .

The people were poised, hopefully, fearfully, for a long-delayed blow against Harris—

When the attack began.

CHAPTER III

After all these years of vigilance, the people of Harris-ville had let down their guard. Taut for the confrontation with Harris, fatigued by the turmoil of the flood and its demoralizing aftermath, they had succumbed to the oldest assurance there is: We've been through it all; what more can happen now?

More can always happen. And it did, but in a way no one expected, and thus they did not even recognize at first that an attack was under way.

There was a small sound against the outside of the wooden schoolhouse. Only a few people heard it, and their attention was on the proceedings. Their minds barely registered the sound, and did not begin to interpret what it meant.

Then came a faint crackling sound, like the rustle of fallen leaves in dry grass. Delia's senses responded to its soft, lulling encroachment; her memory flared to it. Autumn in the mountains outside her tribal village, and—

Autumn? But it was raw, cold, shabby spring. Still, she could smell the fire smoke of pine.

Then, like the rising mutter of angry voices swelling in argument, the sound increased until it became a dull rumble that the people could no longer ignore, then a sharp thunderclap that turned into a burgeoning roar. The smell of pine smoke was suddenly everywhere, and people were screaming. The schoolhouse was on fire.

A few men raced outside, Felix Wohl one of them.

382   *Vanessa Royall*

He flung open the door, reaching for the revolver at
his belt, and for an instant stood outlined against the
scudding gray clouds. For an instant. Then he was
smashed back into the school, driven as if by super-
natural power. Hysterical screams mingled with the
roar of the spreading fire. A war arrow, three feet
long, protruded from Wohl's forehead, eagle feathers
still quivering from the released tension of the bow.
Outside, cries of agony, quickly ended, rose from
Abner Barkley and Will Tenant, who had rushed
without thinking to their doom.

But doom was all about. A fire-arrow had ignited
the pine shingles of the school, and the flames had
spread. Now, waiting on horseback all around the
building were Indians, resting easily, bows taut and
arrows threaded. *Death to the jackals! The time had
come to pass!*

Jason crept to a window. "Surrounded, I think,"
he shouted, cursing himself for not bringing a rifle.
Indeed, the prospect of this formal, democratic meeting had moved many of the men to leave their
heavy weapons out on the wagons, or in gunsheaths
fastened to saddles on their horses.

Rupert Harris, to his credit, kept his head. He had
not come all the way from a dirt-poor sharecropper's
shack without a hard supply of guts, and there was
still all that coal in the blue ranges of Tennessee.
"Women and children under the desks!" he bellowed.

"But the fire!"

"Under the desks!" Jason ordered, too, united for
a moment, by simple logic, with the red-bearded
brawler. They needed time, and if cinders began to
fall from the ceiling, as seemed imminent, the desks
might lend some shelter.

"The men will have to pile out of windows and
doors, all together," Jason yelled. "Try to take cover
and return fire. Women, stay covered until after we're
out, then you go, too, and head for the horses and
wagons."

Delia remembered the position in which their buggy had been left, by the tree near the east side of the school. The village was toward the east, but half a mile away. It seemed impossible ever to reach it. How many Indians were out there? Was Torch one of them?

She held her son close to her. After the initial shock of watching his elders yell and run about, the boy seemed studiously interested in everything that was happening. The men broke window glass with the barrels of their pistols, feinting and ducking, trying to take aim at charging Indians without themselves being hit. The schoolroom was a horror of screaming. The smoke thickened. War whoops sounded outside, again and again, like cries from hell. There was no order, no reason, in the turmoil. There was no logic save that of preserving one's life. Was this how it had been at Talking Rock? Delia wondered, within the space of an instant, as she crouched beneath a desk and held little Andrew in her arms. Then an arrow shot through one of the ruined windowpanes and crashed into the picture of George Washington on the opposite wall. More arrows followed. Delia saw how the feathers rippled, how the arrows shook and quivered. She did not think of death. There was no time to think of death.

Beneath a desk with Andrew, she heard a wild howl like that of legend-devils, a howl such as she had not heard since her days in the tribe. The cry split the air, and it was a moment before she realized that this was the howl of *white* men. Yelling for blood, they crashed out of windows, out the door, and made their counterattack, firing their handguns, trying to reach their rifles. Delia heard the shots, and then the *whick-whick-whick* of bowstrings released.

Jeevis Johnson, Harris's friend, did not make it outside. Struck by an arrow as he crouched on a windowsill, ready to leap outside, he smashed backward instead, onto the desk under which Delia huddled, then rolled off and thudded to the floor. His pistol fell beside him; but Delia could not hear the clunk of metal on wood because of the fire's rolling roar. The heat was already fierce. Outside there were shots—a few of them rifle shots—and more yelling. She grabbed the gun, stood up, and saw that many of the other women were ready to flee, too. None of them spoke, but they went to the open doorway and made their break.

Running with Andrew twisting and bouncing beneath her arm, and the pistol in her free hand, Delia could not apprise herself of the whole battle. Only impressions stood out, enlarged or diminished by the vagaries of her beating brain. Men behind wagons, loading and firing. Men writhing on the ground, wounded and bloody. Fire leaping and wailing on the roof of the school, creeping down the walls like tongues of red and yellow ivory. The *whick* and *swish* of countless arrows, and the despairing howls of the men and women whom death had found this day. She knew the war cry that signaled a charge, and her time was very short. She reached the buggy, threw her son beneath the seat, and grabbed the horse's reins. She thought fleetingly to look for Jason, but she knew there was no time. In the distance tides of smoke rolled from the roofs of the village. This was no raid. This was a massive attack. *Firebrand!* she thought, but she had no time. The horse bolted. Its glistening flank flashed beside her. The buggy wheel leaped forward and Andrew screamed. She grabbed a piece of harness and pulled herself up on the back of the maddened beast, pressed herself into its racing back, terrified for her son, who jounced in the narrow space beneath the seat of the jolting buggy.

But, as it happened, she presented a poorer target stretched out on the horse than she would have while seated upright in the buggy. Arrows flew past her, and then no more. Behind her, other horses were running; women, men, and the Indians charged toward the fireball of the school. One brave gave chase for a short while, howled something unintelligible, then gave up and returned to easier killing.

The village was burning. Andrew was screaming in utmost terror.

Delia got the horse under control and turned it to the woods by the river.

CHAPTER IV

Delia ran the horse until it could run no more, until
even lashing the beast with the leather reins had
no effect. But she had reached the site upon which
Riverbend farm had stood, and she stopped on
the promontory where the barn had been. The animal stood with its legs spread, head down, sides
heaving. Delia leaped from its back and pulled
Andrew from his place beneath the carriage seat. He
was sobbing, close to hysteria, and seemed barely able
to recognize her.

"It's over, there now, it's all right," she crooned,
knowing that none of the soothing words bore truth.
But she held him and crooned to him, and he seemed
to grow quieter; and he looked around as if this
location were vaguely familiar, as if his house ought
to be just over there, where the uprooted windbreak
trees lay strewn across the earth like a rubble of
broken sticks. The house itself had been swept away,
leaving a yawning, water-filled excavation where the
cellar had been.

There was nothing left; and now, over the remaining trees, clouds of smoke rose billowing from the
besieged village.

"My people!" she cried, lifting her face to the
bleak gray sky. "What have you *done*? This shall be
the end of you!"

Now the white men would ride into the mountains,
thirsting for blood, bent upon a revenge so malicious,
so thorough, that not one living Chickasaw would be

unscarred by it, and not more than a few Chickasaw would be left alive. What had possessed Torch to do this thing now, after years of peace?

She turned then, still cradling the boy, and saw the marks of the wagon tracks that traced her flight, clear sign to any brave that someone had escaped the slaughter. She feared for herself, because they might kill her quite readily: the outcast maiden, taken to wife by a jackal. But for little Andrew she felt true horror: He was undeniably white and would be scalped without a moment's hesitation. Considering the matter, she unhitched the horse from the buggy.

"It's all right, it's all right," she said, both to her son and to the startled horse, which seemed to antici-pate that yet another wild trek was imminent. Then, bracing herself, she pushed the buggy with all her strength. Its wheels turned once, twice, and then the power of gravity took hold, the buggy began to roll down the slope, gathered momentum, and crashed into the fast-moving river, where it bobbed a time or two, then floated downstream, spinning slowly, easily, as in a dream.

"Now, now, just a little farther," she said to the poor horse, steadying it, stroking its sweaty, foaming neck. Then, placing the boy on the horse's back, she slowly pulled herself up, too. The beast quivered, almost staggered, and seemed to sink toward the ground; but from some wellspring of endurance, it did not fall, and Delia tapped its flanks gently with her heels. Guiding the horse, she rode down to the river, careful that the hoofprints were left between the marks of the buggy tracks. Once in the water, she eased the faltering beast along the river bank, leaving neither sign nor track that she had passed this way.

Riding, crooning to the horse and the boy, Delia experienced a momentary but piercing sadness. *No sign that I have passed this way* . . . Exiled by her own people, and now driven by them from the place that had adopted her, she could not divine the future.

There seemed neither fortune nor pattern in the course of her life, only scant periods of chance happiness, followed by wracking, brutal devastation, the crueler for its inexplicability. It seemed almost as if fate were a living thing, with malevolence in its heart, cunning in its brain, and Gyva as its victim.

Gyva! She had thought of herself by her Chickasaw name! That had not happened for a long time.

Andrew was rocking against her, and presently he fell asleep to the horse's slow gait. Delia rode, thinking what she would do. Ahead, the river swept around the bend for which the farm had been named. A thin finger of land stretched out into the water, littered now with jetsam and debris left by the receding high water, and sullied trunks of stripped trees bore lines ten feet above Delia's head, marking the place where the river had crested.

The horse stopped, and Delia felt a shudder pass through it, into herself. Gripping Andrew tightly, she leaped sideways from the animal's back and felt the cold, rushing water up to her knees, here in the shallows. Then a sheet of liquid ice drenched her as the horse dropped dead in the water, its big body raising a tremendous splash, and Andrew woke, startled and wailing. No time for pity. Do not leave tracks, she thought; and, her feet growing number by the minute, the boy shivering, she eased toward the shore, searching for rocky ground. If she could get to the woods, find shelter, try to build a fire . . .

"Mama!" Andrew wailed. "Cold. Me cold." He shook convulsively in her arms. Both of them were dripping wet, and the March wind slipped through the river valley, laying icy fingers down to their skin. She made her way onto a rocky ledge, climbed, and soon the river was below, a vast strip of power, deception, and death, moving around the great sweep of the bend. Once Torch had dreamed a river bend where promise and wonder lay buried in warm sand. But the dream had been illusion, and the promise a mockery. And now Riverbend farm was gone, too. Did Ababinili create men to play with them, to deceive them, to laugh at their very dreams? There was no secret of life, nor would there ever be, and the golden stick was but the thread of a hope, a hope more heartbreaking for its shimmering evanescence.

"Cold!" Andrew cried through chattering teeth. "Papa! Pa—"

Delia stumbled. A curved chunk of wood, half buried in the silt left by the flood, caught her foot and sent her sprawling. Andrew fell and lay stunned beside her, blood oozing from his fine, pale forehead.

"Oh, darling!"

She picked him up, held him, pressed her hand to his head, trying to stop the flow of blood.

She looked down where she had fallen and saw the rim of a barrel, half buried in the sand. FLOUR, it said, in water-ravaged letters. Could it be the barrel from her pantry where she'd hidden the . . .

She pried off the lid and looked inside. The barrel had been solidly built, allowing only slight moisture inside in spite of the flood. The flour was caked into clumps, doughy but not hard packed, and when Delia stuck her hand deep into it, her fingers closed around the leather pouch, safe and dry. She shook off the white film of flour and pressed the pouch to her breast, pressed Andrew to her breast; and, although she was a Chickasaw, who flinched or wavered never, who bore with defiance and equanimity the gaze of conquerors and the vanquishments of fate, Delia and Dey-Lor-Gyva cried tears of mingled bitterness and love.

Years later, those few who had been told by her of this tearful grief at the river's bend, those few who knew of it, would say that it was at that moment, that moment undeniably, that the separate rivers of her heritage, the distinct impulses of her mixed blood, did join together forever. Thereafter, she was what she had been, true, as all of us are what we were born.

But, oh—after that moment she was not the same, she was more than she had been . . . .

The flow of blood was ceasing, but Andrew was in a dangerous state when Delia spied the canoes. They came from upriver, where the village was, and the high hoots and cries of their passengers left no doubt that victory in battle had been accomplished. The current sped the canoes toward the bend, and Delia crouched down behind fallen logs. If she were to move now, or try to flee into the trees, she would be seen for certain, and she was grateful that the shouts and cries of the warriors blotted out Andrew's faint moans. Very soon the crafts were within easy sighting, and Delia saw the Chickasaw designs on the bark, saw the Chickasaw war markings in bright paint upon the faces of the braves. But . . .

The river ran west! And the Chickasaw lived to the south, beyond Twin Mountains!

Then she heard distinctly the calls of the triumphant braves, and knew their words and the sounds of their tongue.

Choctaw!

The brave lay in the dust, and she felt the cold knife in her hand. "You must do it," Torch was telling her . . . .

"AIIIIIEEEEEE YIPYIPYIP AHHHHHHHYAA-AAAAARRRRRRR!" howled the impostors, their canoes skimming now around the peninsula, sweeping them away to the west, fleeing the scene of their twin victories: one in battle, one in duplicity.

And Delia alone knew what had transpired. The Chickasaw were innocent, but the Chickasaw would be blamed.

CHAPTER V

The distance between Riverbend farm and Harrisville was slightly more than seven miles, an easy morning's ride in a buggy or on horseback. But the trip took much longer on foot, and if one had also to bear a burden of heartbreak, did time matter at all?

When the last of the disguised Choctaw war canoes had swung around the bend—a river bend that once again had played its promise false, had shielded illusion—Delia turned back toward the source of smoke and fire. She tried not to think of Jason's probable fate, and Andrew's desperate plight was soon preoccupation enough.

"Ma . . . . Ma," he managed to say, coughing and choking and shuddering. The hard ride in the buggy, the permeating cold, the fall upon stone: too much for the little body to bear.

To stop here in the woods or out in the fields was pointless. Rain had begun, and she had no flint. The whole earth was wet and deadly. Only Harrisville had fire, this day. If Delia had possessed an oil-soaked arrow, such as the Choctaw had used to fire the pine shingles on the schoolhouse roof, all might have been well . . . .

The little boy began to choke. His tiny, perfect body shook uncontrollably in her arms. She held him and she did not think about it, and she walked as fast as she could and she did not think.

Soon his breathing came in gagged and ragged gasps, and he grew still in her arms, only to shiver

and convulse again. The walking warmed her, but
for him, for her tiny son, all there was was the warmth
of her body.

It was not enough.

Light rain was falling when she stumbled back
into Harrisville, choking on the ugly smell of half-
smothered smoke and the smouldering embers of wet
wood. To her surprise, several buildings were still
standing—the livery, the general store, the sawmill
down by the river. Through the haze of rain and
drifting smoke that clung close to the damp earth she
saw the moving bodies of men working, carrying
things. And when she walked closer, Delia realized
they were carrying exactly what she was carrying: the
earthly remains of those who had been beloved in life.

She stood for a while, holding Andrew, taking in
the dismal scene, then did all that she could do. She
walked through the smouldering village and quietly
set down next to the rest of the dead the beautiful,
eerily unmoving body of her dead son.

"Jason?" was her first word.

People moved about her, lugging bodies. White
men and women were laid out neatly along Main
Street. Indians—and there were more than a few—
were unceremoniously dumped in a heap at the edge
of the village.

"Jason?" she asked again.

"If you're quick you might get to say good-bye."
A drawl.

Delia whirled around. Fes Farson, grinning.

"Surprised to see me?" he said goadingly.

She couldn't answer. Fes looked the same as ever,
half-drunk, arrogant, oddly triumphant. He grinned,
and the grin went away, as it always did, a reflex
that signaled not humor but danger.

Then Rupert Harris came slouching out of the
livery.

"Phil Foley just went to his great reward," he said

to a few women who were standing around, dazed and shocked. "Liver. Arrow in the liver. But better'n being scalped like Gale, an' now—*Delia!*" he exclaimed, seeing her. "Where you been?"

She told him. She told him of her son's death.

"Now is that the truth?" Fes Farson drawled. "Is that the real truth now—*redskin?*"

"Shut up, Fes," grunted Harris. "Not now."

"Jason?" Delia managed.

"Yup. C'mere with me. We got the wounded on straw in the livery. Best we could do."

He took her hand and led her toward the stables, practically pulling her along. "Lucky we drove off them Chickasaw bastards," he was saying. "'Course, you might not see it that way."

"What . . . what do you mean?"

"Yer Chickasaw, ain't ya? We know. Melody told us about that leather pouch."

With effort Delia managed not to touch between her breasts, where the leather pouch was concealed beneath the folds of her wet clothing.

"Melody!" she snapped, showing open contempt.

"Uppity, too, ain't ya?" Harris grinned, unperturbed, and all but pushed her into the livery stable. "How come you ain't showing more sorrow? I know. 'Cause killin' by Chickasaw don't bother you none, ain't that right?"

"They weren't Chickasaw," she replied.

But Rupert did not hear how calmly, coldly she said this. He did not read her will. He heard her words but did not believe them.

Jason lay on a pallet of bloody straw, very pale. But the light of life and love was still upon him.

"Delia . . ."

She knelt down beside him. "Don't talk." She could see that he'd been badly wounded—not the clean wound of an arrow, but rather that of a tomahawk, a wicked blow that had almost severed his arm from his shoulder. There was blood all over.

"Now that indeed do look like the same man who run me off his farm once," said Fes Farson, coming up and standing there, looking down at Jason.

"Get away from here," Delia told him.

Paul, the big, one-eared freedman, appeared, and Tanya. They looked terrified.

"You got to help us, Miz!" Tanya began.

Paul put a hand on her shoulder. "If Mista Randolph dies, Mista Harris an' Mista Farson done tole us—"

"You been needin' some real larnin', Paul," drawled Farson, "an' I reckon I can give it to you."

"Delia!" Jason gasped. She bent down close to his lips so that she could hear. "Andrew?"

She looked at his pale, lovely face, made blank by the absence of blood. Death trembled behind his eyes.

"He is all right," she told him. "Andrew is . . . he is out of danger."

"He's dead, Randolph," interrupted Fes Farson.

"Stop it!" Delia cried.

Farson looked sheepish, then defiant.

"Oh, Miz Randolph!" mourned Tanya. "What's to become of us?"

Down on the bloody straw Jason was sinking fast. Delia told him of the flight from the schoolhouse, of the ride in the river, the cold, the fall. "It is true," she said, holding his hand, watching him go far away from her, watching his eyes go far. "Our son is dead. I did as well as I could, and at least he did not suffer much."

Seeing the look in Delia's eyes, Jason accepted Andrew's death. With difficulty he moved his good hand and touched hers. "Try not to blame yourself," he gasped. "It seems that nothing has turned out as we had hoped."

Delia remembered the meeting at the school. Whatever might have been accomplished there would not come to pass. How could it? The men who wished to challenge Harris were dead, and the legal papers prepared so painstakingly by Phil Foley had been consumed in the holocaust.

"How many were left alive?" she asked, stroking Jason's white cheek, watching him drift away.

"Oh, enough," Harris grunted. "With the slaves we got left, and the people we got left, I reckon we can start over. And this time around I'll avoid some mistakes I made in the first try. Like bringin' in nigger lovers and half-breeds an' such."

"Harris," Jason managed, his breath coming thin and keen, "Tanya and Paul, and the other Negroes working for me, are free people. Their papers are on file in Lexington."

"Is that right?" Harris asked, grinning.

"They are free to go . . ." Jason said, his voice trailing off in weakness.

Big Paul took those words as an indication that his service to Jason was concluded, and he turned to leave the livery.

"Hold it, nigger!" Fes Farson stood there, pistol in his hand. Tanya pressed herself against a harness rack.

"I done heard Mista Randolph say—"

"I didn't done heard him say nothin'," Farson smirked. "Get your hands up. You too," he told Tanya. "What'll we do with 'em, Rupert?"

"Ah, well, there's a backroom to the general store. Ought to hold 'em for now, I'd say. Yeah, run 'em over there."

"Mista Randolph!" Paul was pleading, and Tanya was speechless with horror. Back to slavery now, and with a master as cruel as Harris, a driver as brutal as Fes Farson? Tanya did not know how to react, and so she did nothing, but Paul had vowed never to return to bondage, no matter what the price. He lunged forward, his big arm moving powerfully, and caught Fes Farson a massive blow on the side of the head. Farson spun around and went crashing into the harness rack, buried in horse collars and falling leather. Paul spun, too, and moved for the door.

Then the shot rang out like a whip crack in the livery, and big Paul plunged to the floor like a great black tree, rolled over once, and lay still. His eyes were open. He was bleeding from the mouth. But he had kept his vow; he would be a slave no more.

"What . . . happened?" gasped Jason, who was too weak to raise his head and see.

"Done lost us a prospective worker," Harris grunted, holstering his revolver.

"Don't speak, darling," Delia told him, cradling his head.

"Yep, Fes, we lost us one out of his own stupidity and because Randolph here didn't know how to make 'em obey a white man's orders. Who we goin' to get to replace Paul anyway, hey?"

Fes Farson's eyes flickered malevolently, icy and cunning. "How 'bout we get us a half-breed, Rupert?"

Tanya was crying. Delia heard "half-breed" and tensed, wondering how she might flee.

"Well, a half-breed ain't all one thing and she ain't all the other, but I expect we can figure out a few things for her to do."

"You seen any half-breeds around here lately, Rupert?"

Then Jason gave a vast, unearthly groan, and it was evident that his time had come. Delia forgot all about her plight and rushed to him again, kneeling down beside him. Even Harris and Fes Farson quieted in the presence of death, and stood away so that husband and wife might exchange last words.

"I'm . . . sorry . . ." he gasped, with the flicker of a wan grimace. "It's all come to . . . nothing . . . ."

A bubble of blood appeared in one nostril, expanding and diminishing as he breathed his last.

Delia cradled his head in her hands and held him to her breasts. Harris and Fes were forgotten, Tanya, too, and she was alone with Jason in a strange, terrible world where years were measured in heartbeats, hours in the blink of an eye.

"Nothing . . ." he repeated, with the tears of death already seeping from his eyes.

"No, no," Delia soothed, pressing her cheek to his. "Everything! You have loved me, cared for me, protected me. We have had so much together."

"It . . . is gone . . ."

No, she thought defiantly. He cannot go into death with this on his mind. And so thinking, she began to speak.

"Nothing is ever gone!" she said to him, looking deeply into his eyes now, speaking a bit more forcefully so that he might hear every word and sense belief behind them. "Nothing good is ever lost. You gave me the best things in life, freely and with love, and however long I shall live, those gifts will not be just a part of me, they will *be* me." She stroked his face and wiped away the flooding tears. "Yes, yes," she whispered now, smiling down at him. "In the darkest hours, one loving memory is enough to keep the spirit alive, and you have given me so many such memories, so many gifts . . . ."

Jason heard her, understood, and believed. His lips moved slightly, a last smile. Then he died.

"Jason!" Delia cried then, her composure spent in the effort of easing his death. "Jason! *No!*"

But he was gone from her now forever.

She held Jason's body to herself for a long time. To their credit, Harris and Fes Farson permitted her at least a short time in which to grieve. But night was coming on, and there was much to be done. At length, when Delia stood up and stepped away from the body, the two men coughed, kicked at the floor, and got back to business.

"Them was your people today, wasn't they?" Harris asked, after a cold, momentary glance that effectively measured Jason's recent departure from life. "Chickasaw, wasn't they?"

With a shock she recalled the Choctaw in the war

canoes, and their disguises. Odd. She had seen them
hours before, and yet it seemed that years had passed
since then.

Excitedly, grieving, she explained to Harris and
Fes Farson how the Choctaw had practiced their
malicious deceit, how they were trying to stir white
men against the Chickasaw nation. Surely Harris
would realize the meaning of such a trick.

But his look grew darker and darker as she spoke.

"Come now," she urged him. "Let us look at
some of the bodies of the Indians who were killed.
Beneath the Chickasaw war paint we shall see Choctaw braves."

"Is that right? How can you tell?"

"There is one sure way. The Choctaw do not mark
kill-cuts by slashing their arms with knives. Rather
they tattoo an eagle upon their biceps, and for each
death they have dealt, an additional feather is added
to the eagle's tail."

"You're sure about that?" Harris asked, looking
worried.

She nodded, and started outside to inspect a fallen
brave.

"Hold it. You ain't goin' nowhere," Harris said.

"But—"

"Fes, we got to bury them Indians. When Jackson
comes down here, he's got to think it was Firebrand
and them Chickasaw responsible. There ain't no coal
on Choctaw land, and if he wipes *them* out, that ain't
gonna do us no good."

It was no use. Harris was poised to act now. The
attack upon the village was provocation sufficient to
even the most judicious militia commander. Chula
Harjo would at last go into the mountains and deal
the death that had been so long stayed. That was what
Harris had always wanted.

That, and coal.

"Fes, take that black wench and Miz Randolph

here, an' lock 'em up in the general store. We got to get to work an' bury them Indians."

"Might be we ought to burn 'em, if this kill-cut business is like Miz Randolph says."

"Good idea, Fes. Good idea. I always knew you were a good man, an' maybe when the work's done I'll think of a little something to offer you as a reward."

He gave Delia a long, ugly look, taking her in from head to toe, then shoved her along in front of him, out the livery and toward the general store. Fes grabbed Tanya and pushed her along.

They left Jason on the straw.

Delia was unaware of time, locked in numbness and grief. She could hear survivors burying the dead—Jason and little Andrew would be among their number. And just at nightfall there came a sudden flash, as lantern oil was poured and ignited. Not long thereafter, the thick smell of burnt flesh came into the air, and Delia covered her nose with the sleeve of her dress.

"Lordy!" choked Tanya, coming for a moment out of her own panicky torpor. "What on earth is that bodacious stink?"

"Evidence being burned," murmured Delia, but Tanya did not understand. She asked again for an explanation, but Delia was too dispirited to give further interpretation.

Then it was nightfall, and the storeroom in which they were incarcerated became gloomy, then dark. The heavy plank door was locked securely. There was no escape, at least none that presented itself, but the two women were fortunate in that cider and foodstuffs, as well as other materials, were stored within. Delia did not know, then, why she did not want to die, as her husband and son had died. Perhaps it was that she knew they had not been killed by Harris or

Farson, in which case being held in captivity by those men would have immeasurably increased her sorrow. Yes, perhaps it was because she *knew* that the Choctaw had—directly and indirectly—killed her loved ones that she did not succumb to grief. Oh, yes, she had already dealt a death in her short life, and a cunning, canny Choctaw had died beneath her hand. More would die, too, when she got free of here . . . .

Imagining freedom, and enjoying the thought of it, Delia rallied.

"Tanya. Let us eat. Did you see tallow here? We ought to have paid attention before nightfall. Did you see candles? Here, can you find the cider jug? We must keep up our strength."

Her words served to encourage the poor girl, whose every thought was now given to conditions of enslavement, the tragedy of which she well knew.

"Was over here, Miz, I think," she said, and soon they had a lantern lighted, and were eating hardtack and beef jerky and drinking cider on the floor of the storeroom. They had also found heavy blankets piled on a shelf in the corner, and these served to hold off the chill. Delia chewed the hardtack, thinking. There seemed to be no way out of this room, and yet it was made of wood, and they had fire. If, somehow, they might *burn* their way out . . .

And be burned alive in the bargain?

But might it not work? If they splashed a little lantern oil on a small portion of wall?

No, that was insane.

Footsteps, getting louder. Delia doused the lantern. For the first time since midday, she had been feeling warm, and faintly safe, in spite of her predicament. Now she tensed again in the darkness. Tanya's fright was palpable. Delia felt the leather pouch between her breasts.

The footsteps ceased outside the plank door.

"Get ready, ladies," grunted a voice. Fes Farson? Rupert Harris? Delia couldn't be sure.

The door crashed open, and a torch, held high in the doorway, cast the storeroom into wavering lights and shadows. Two big figures behind the torch.

"Take the nigger an' haul her back out to the plantation," Harris told Farson. "I'm too tired to ride just now. Ride a horse, that is. I'll be spendin' the night in the livery hayloft."

Delia, crouching on the floor, began to move slowly toward the back of the room. Her eyes had adjusted to the torch now, and she saw the marks of blood and sweat and grime on Harris's clothes, the gun and the knife in his belt, and his knotted, bedraggled beard.

"Don't you move a muscle," he ordered her. "I've had a hard day, an' I don't aim to put up with any more. Fes! Go ahead."

Farson's eerie grin flickered in torchlight, then he came forward and seized the shuddering Tanya.

"Miz Randolph, help me!" the servant begged.

"She can't even help herself," Farson chortled. "Looks like we got things turned around in this town. 'Bout time, too."

Tanya whined and keened and cried as Farson dragged her out. In moments Delia heard the sound of hoofbeats.

"Ain't these niggers somethin'?" Harris drawled. "Fes's got a nice job for her an' a place for her to sleep an' even some secret delights, an' she's bawlin' like a sick calf. Oh, well"—his tone grew measurably harsher—"Get up now."

"Where?"

"Nice soft bed of hay. Only thing that Torch fellow didn't burn, practically. Guess he knew you'd be puttin' your talents to good use, an' would need a place to do it."

Delia stood up. "I'm not coming with you. Stand aside, and let me go."

The next instant she was on her back on the floor, pain exploding in her jaw. Harris had swung out from behind the torch, knocked her down. His voice was menacing.

"You got two seconds to get on your feet. When I want you off of 'em, you'll sure as hell know."

Trying to decide what to do, knowing that to let herself be beaten by Rupert was folly, Delia struggled to her feet.

"That's better," he grunted, standing aside to let her pass through the door.

The town—what was left of it—was dark and quiet. A lantern hung at the livery doorway, casting a gloomy light inside. No Paul. No Jason.

"Where—?" she began.

"Buried 'em all, just like I said. An' burned them Choctaw bastards. Guess they were Chickasaw, after all," he cackled.

He doused the torch in a horse trough and slipped the lantern off the nail on which it hung. "Up the ladder to the loft, little lady," he said. "You know, I've been lookin' forward to havin' some of you since—"

"Where are the graves?" she demanded.

"Up the ladder, now. Don't be thinkin' about graves."

She began to climb, but persisted. "Where are my husband and son buried?"

"Better not to know. C'mon. Look. Why be thinkin' of dreary things when they're all in the past? Look, we can have a good time an' a great future . . . ."

Great? Yes, once Jason had begrudgingly called this foul-mouthed barbarian great, in the sense that his instincts were not those of an ordinary person. Indeed, his instincts were not those of a human being at all, but rather of an animal, a dangerous animal possessed of multiple lusts, complicated hungers, which only rapacity, property, and pleasure could assuage. Without the iron exigencies of the frontier, would this type of man ever have gained renown?

As Delia thought of these things, she realized that she had been acting unwisely. Harris's strength and determination made resistance futile, made any form of direct attack upon him equally foolhardy.

"Just tell me where the graves are," she said, softening her voice with effort, "and then my mind will be at rest and I can face the future you suggest. It is the way among us," she added, more softly still.

"Hey!" he cried. "So you're finally admitting it, huh? Melody told me all about that beadwork pouch, of course. I always knew you was redskin anyway, but that sure don't make no difference now. I reckon a redskin is built pretty much the same as any other woman, ain't that right? Anyway, they're buried down near the river, in that grove next to the sawmill. Don't worry. It was all done proper, an' soon as that itinerant preacher comes circuit riding, we'll have him say the proper prayers. Indian like you wouldn't much care about our God anyway, eh?"

Delia did not answer. She stepped from the ladder into the clover-smelling loft. Mounds of hay rose into the cavern of the loft, and Harris held the lantern high. "Right over there's a likely place," he said, his voice thick and husky with lust. "Tell me, you Indian women do it some special kind of way I don't know about?"

Delia turned and saw him there at the top of the ladder, at the edge of the loft. If she rushed him just at the right moment, he might trip and fall to the floor below.

But he advanced on her. "Don't tell me," he grunted. "I guess I'll find out, eh?"

"It seems so," she started to say, still searching for some ploy, some tactic that would allow her escape.

But quickly he hung the lantern on a rafter and grabbed her, pulled her to him. She smelled his raw breath and felt his body hard against her, grinding into her. She cried out.

"What? Yelpin'? This ain't nothin'. I'll have you yelpin' to quite another tune!"

Reaching for her breasts, he felt the leather pouch. Some weapon? he thought instinctively, and ripped the buttons from her leather jacket, tore open her blouse. The pouch fell out onto the clover.

"What's that?" he asked suspiciously, holding her hard.

"Some . . . some jewelry of mine."

"Hey! So that's what old Melody found, is it?" Not letting her go for a moment, he pushed her down, grabbed the pouch and opened it. The lantern flickered, but gave sufficient light to reveal the contents of the pouch; Delia's treasures, relics, remembrances.

"Why you keep this kind of junk?" he asked, genuinely puzzled, turning a bead necklace in his fingers, then squinting at the white pebbles.

She shook her head. She could not bear to talk about it, or to have his rough hands on her possessions.

"An' here's that serpent bracelet, like Melody said. What was it Ginral Jackson said? Chickasaw braves wear this kind of thing? I thought they carried them Red Sticks."

"That, too," she said.

"Well, it don't do 'em much good now, do it? How'd you get this snake thing?"

Delia didn't answer. He guessed.

"Had you an Indian warrior of a lover once, didn't you?" The thought seemed a challenge to him. "Well, you look out now, hear? 'Cause he wasn't nothin' compared to—"

Abruptly he stood up, unbuckled his belt, and pulled his breeches down to his boot tops. That was all. Then he was down beside her on the hay again, reaching and pawing, ripping away her clothes. His beard burned her face, her lips; and the calluses on his hands savaged her breasts. Against her thigh, she felt him hot and hard and throbbing.

"I'll be a little rough this first time," he was panting. "Then we'll settle down an' do it right."

She tried to pull her mouth away from the horrible taste of his breath, which was like burning, which was like death.

"Here," he said, thrusting his manhood into her hand. "Don't you know how to do nothin'?"

Delia tried to think. If she seemed to cooperate with him, even to acquiesce to his brutal assault, perhaps he would drop his guard, perhaps she might reach his knife or gun.

No—too far away, at least right now. Down below his knees where his belt was. And she simply could not force herself to a semblance of complicity in this attack upon herself. The man was all over her, and every place he kissed or touched left pain, or the shadow of pain, or the feel of odoriferous dirt upon her skin.

"Squeeze it," he said. "Rub it. What's the matter with you, anyway? What kind of training did you get from that Virginian anyway?"

That insult to Jason was what she had needed to brace herself, to steel herself against Harris. His lower body was jerking in her hands, and he was moaning, trying to enjoy himself, even as a part of his mind kept vigilant against her. *You can never trust a redskin* . . . .

"I am sorry," she crooned. "But I shall please you." And shutting her mind away from the revulsion she felt, she gave him a long kiss on the mouth, a kiss to dazzle his brain, and she felt him relax, give way . . . .

She kissed him again and then shifted her position, trailing her mouth down across his hairy, stinking chest. "Ahhhhh . . ." he sighed, and ah, what dreams of pleasure did he imagine, as he lay down and spread himself upon the sweet clover, waiting for the gift to begin. He felt her breath upon him, close, tantalizing, and in a minute the magic kiss would come down around him, and he was thinking, I underestimated this here squaw, I surely did, when he felt an odd tugging around his boot tops—and in a frozen instant that lasted as long as eternity or as long as his life would last, he remembered how the hilt of his knife stuck out of the scabbard at his belt, and how the knife felt when it was pulled from the scabbard, exactly as the tugging felt now.

The delicious kiss for which he waited never came, but the knife did, down into his naked chest. He was surprised that it hurt so little, as if everything, all sensation, had ceased; and he knew, fading, falling, that the hot pool upon his chest was life slipping away, a fountain pouring gently out of himself.

The last thing Rupert Harris saw in life was a beautiful woman hovering above him, her body pure as an angel's must be, and her eyes dusky and depthless and triumphant, indomitable, fierce glints of coal far back in the folds of the mountains . . . .

Delia took up her leather pouch, tied the drawstring around her neck, and pulled on her clothes. She took Harris's belt and buckled it around her waist, pistol on her left, knife—wiped clean of blood— on her right. Taking the lantern from the rafter, she moved to the ladder and climbed down. Then she threw the lantern back up into the loft, waited an ominous moment, then heard the unmistakable crackle, saw the flash of light that meant lantern oil had ignited the clover. Under cover of darkness she made her way down toward the river as, behind her, the livery flared. She heard the commotion among the few survivors of the village, heard their sleepy, dispirited voices. "Ah, let it burn. Ain't nobody in it, anyway. Be screamin' like hell if they were."

The grove by the mill, Harris had said. Easy enough to find, soft beneath her feet where the spades had dug and turned the gentle earth that held the remains of her second life. She could not tell where Jason was buried, or where Andrew lay, but the stars did glow upon that night, and a scimitar of moon rode the sky beyond Twin Mountains. For a moment she stood there, beneath the stars, upon eternal earth, her head bowed; and anyone seeing her might have surmised that she was lost in prayer. Within her mind there were no words. Within her heart were many things, but most of all love and loss, and the promise that never again would disaster like this be visited upon those whom she loved. Indeed, that thought was a prayer, a prayer and a promise.

Then she pulled from her pouch her own necklace of beads, tore apart the strand by which it was bound, and let the beads spill into her cupped palm.

"This I leave to you both," she called softly, saying their names. "Jason. Andrew. Each of these beads is a memory, and a wish. If it is true, as Ababinili has promised, that we live again beyond the North Star, borne forever upon trails of windfall light, I shall see you there."

She cast the beads up on the tender earth.

"Delia is ended now, too," she told them, turning away.

It was Gyva who moved silently, fleet as a shadow, through the forest. She set a course toward the Twin Mountains, looming beneath the rind of moon, moving softly and unseen toward home. Her lungs were filled with the scent of pine. Her mind was as clear and inexorable as the winter river, slipping toward the falls. Her heart beat steadily, at one with an ancient world, as she raced homeward through darkness and the night.

CHAPTER VI

"You're certain of this? You're absolutely certain?" inquired Andrew Jackson gloomily.

"Even Mr. Harris is dead," replied Fes Farson, ducking his head in pretended grief, studying the great Jackson. Old Hickory didn't seem any too eager to go out on the warpath, and this fact surprised Farson considerably. He watched Jackson ponder the information about the Chickasaw raid that had all but destroyed the Harrisville community, and glanced around the Hermitage. By God, it was magnificent, best house ol' Fes had ever seen. I'll have me one just like it, 'cept bigger, he promised himself. Biggest house in Farsonville.

"You sure it was this Chief Firebrand who done it?" Jackson grunted.

"Ask the men with me," Fes said, putting on an aggrieved expression, as if hurt that his word had been doubted.

Fes had prepared well. He'd spent the night of the raid with Tanya, Randolph's nigger wench, and he'd put John Thomas through his paces many a time. In the morning, after assigning Tanya to a plow, where she was still at work preparing the fields for the cotton crop, news had reached him that Rupert died in a fire at the livery.

Fes knew two things the minute he received that news: one, that that half-breed Delia had tricked old Rupert, caught him with his breeches down, so to speak, and two, that if he played his cards right,

Harrisville and all that went with it—future coal included—could, without too much trouble, become
Farsonville.

Fes liked the sound of it.

So he'd gone immediately to some of the older, less
remote communities, which had not yet been attacked,
and spread the word of Chickasaw savagery, spread
the terrible news of Firebrand's attack. People in
those towns were horrified, terrified, and it took no
more than the merest suggestion to persuade them
that a delegation to Jackson at the Hermitage was
the best thing for them to do.

"Fes is right, Ginral," they were telling Jackson
now. "We got to go up there and clean house. Ain't
no village a'goin' to be safe till that renegade Firebrand and his Chickasaws are plumb swept right out
of there."

Jackson sat before them in his rocking chair and
considered. That a whole community had been ravaged was incontrovertible. That he had a responsibility to these settlers was beyond question. And, two
days before, he had received in the mail a dispatch
from Washington, D.C., informing him that the Indian removals program was going forward at full pace.
As he sat there rocking, all the points came together,
added up, and demanded action. 1828 gleamed before
him, and the White House, too, more brightly than
ever. Jackson knew what he had to do, and it seemed
that a provocation had presented itself that made his
decision inescapable.

"Boys," he said slowly, rising from the chair, "I
hear tell them mountains of east Tennessee make
mighty good hunting this time of year."

The sudden shouts of the men, Fes Farson among
them, fairly lifted the roof from Jackson's big house,
and Rachel appeared, a little frightened, at the top
of the main staircase.

"It's all right," Old Hickory told her, glancing up.
"Go back and get your rest."

She did return to bed, for she was feeling poorly again. Now she felt even worse. Because she sensed that nothing was right at all.

Torch went to the doorway of the wigwam and moved the heavy pelts aside, stepped out into the air. The chill of the morning invigorated him, and there was beauty in the way ice clung to the bare branches of the trees. His soul quickened and, as always at dawn, he felt strong. Yes, he had been correct in his heart; he had been correct all along. This quiet village, lost in misty morning, with his people safe, asleep, dreaming—perhaps some of them making the drowsy, tender love for which dawn is meant—this peaceful life was wise, was just, was all that had to be. He knew that he was right. He would hold to the path of peace that had, after so many long years of fighting, given the Chickasaw room to breathe. Why, in these past years, none but the sick and old had gone to graves along the river; and during daytime the cries of babes, the chortling yelps of toddlers, brought sounds of joy to the village. With peace, hope had returned, and with hope the future rose new again, like the sun returning now, and all the days lay bright upon the distant horizon.

If peace might just be kept.

Now in the matter of Red Dagger, Torch thought, walking toward the well for a drink of clear water, framing the response that his message would contain.

Then, soundlessly, moccasins soft on the earth, a sentinel ran from the forest, approached his chieftain, stopped, and made fast signs with his hands to ensure silence. Sound carried easily, even in winter trees. The sentinel's fingers moved as if he were at work upon a loom.

Torch interpreted. Someone in the forest—approach our village—very fast—apparently alone. This time of year? he wondered. What does it mean?

The instincts of a warrior sensing threat came immediately to Torch. This approaching person might be a scout, a runner, an advance guard of an attack. His mind worked, and his own hands flew.

From where? he asked.

Harrisville, the sentinel signaled.

Torch thought it over. Someone coming alone through the mountains could only have gotten this far if all the night had been spent in travel.

Armed? his hands inquired.

I was not close enough to observe. I felt the warning must be carried here immediately.

"You did well," Torch whispered, and at that moment the first fingers of dawn lanced from behind the eastern wall of clouds. Inexplicably, in a manner that was so natural that Torch later imagined Ababinili had placed the thought in his mind, he felt simultaneously a great tenderness and a terrible knowledge. But at the time he did not know why, nor did he have time to think of it, because the ancient seeress tottered out of her wigwam, still wrapped in her sleeping skins, her body and the bundled pelts steaming in the dawn.

Old Mark-of-the-Cave, handprint red against her skin, looked to the wall of the forest. So did Torch, and the sentinel, who reached back expertly and fingered an arrow that rested in the quiver upon his shoulder blades.

"Now it all begins. Now it all ends," muttered the witch-woman in mournful ambiguity. "The words of Four Bears are fulfilled."

Torch and the sentinel heard her words clearly, but neither had opportunity to reflect upon them. From the forest, bathed in the cold, hard light of dawn, strode such a sight as none of them had ever imagined. It was a figure dressed in the long skirts of the jackal women, but sullied with earth, bark, and the twigs of the forest. The strange apparition paused once, there by the edge of the trees, to shake more twigs and dry leaves from her long, raven-black hair. She saw the three of them standing there in the center of the village, chieftain and sentinel and seeress, and stood erect before them. Her coal-black eyes were alive and burning. The buttons of her jacket had been ripped off. Around her slim waist she wore a wide belt and from it hung a pistol and a killing-knife. She lifted her chin toward them and stood erect and unmoving. The effect was that of a great brave of whom tales are told, returning for an instant to earth.

I have been to far regions, Gyva told them with her eyes, her bearing. I have been to far places and have passed through the fires. Touch me now who dare.

Torch felt a fullness, a rapture, against which even the cold logic of leadership could not hold fast.

"I bring you warning," Gyva told them then. "Chula Harjo will be on the march. Let us prepare."

The villagers gathered to see and hear this apparition whom they had once known, then banished. "It is a trick. Remember all of her other deceptions, in the old times? This is one who has whored to the jackals, and we must not listen."

"Silence," said Torch. "Speak," he commanded Gyva. Many among the tribe observed with skeptical gaze the apparent indulgence with which their chief treated this banished troublemaker.

But Gyva surprised them all. She had truly been through the fires, and the pain had taught her much.

"I come here asking nothing, not even shelter, nor to remain," she said. "I come to you with a warning, that you may prepare yourselves against destruction, and by having brought this warning, I have repaid you, one and all, for having raised me in my childhood, and sheltered me. There is nothing more that I deserve of you, or that I ask of you."

She told them of Jacksa Chula's political position, succinctly, coldly, masterfully.

She informed them of the Choctaw treachery, and of the howls for revenge that, mistakenly, the white men would now bring upon Chickasaw heads.

And she told them an attack was inevitable, would come soon, and would indeed be the battle for which all men like Harris and Fes Farson and their ilk had long been waiting.

Lastly, she told them of the coal. "The soft black rock," she told them, "that comes outcropping from the earth, and which often dirties our clothing when we chance to brush against it. That chalky blackness is, to the white men, worth countless and innumerable and boundless caches of wampum, and for the black rock they will make these high hills red with Chickasaw blood."

Everyone was staring at her. She looked back at them, she turned slowly to look at all of them, and to meet the eyes of each.

"Do what you will," she said quietly. "I have done my duty by you, as once you did yours for me, and I shall trouble you no more."

With that, she turned—not herself aware of what she might do now, where she might go—and began to walk back toward the forest. Her head was high and her shoulders squared—a princess and ruler in every respect—and the knife and the gun accentuated the pride of her carriage, and the decisiveness of her stride.

"No!" growled the witch-woman.

"No!" cried Torch.

"No!" roared the tribe, as if all of their separate voices had been combined into one vast voice, a call of the Chickasaw nation.

Beloved-of-Earth, granddaughter of Four Bears, stopped in her tracks. She had not expected this moment, because she had not imagined it. But it was there, and it was hers.

Old Teva hobbled forward, the blood pulsing scarlet beneath her sacred mark.

"Stay," she muttered. "You are ours. You have

always been ours. Do not worry. It is true. Those who knew it not before know it now. And Chula Harjo is coming. I sense it."

"I know it," Delia said, thinking, This time, one or the other of us will die.

CHAPTER VII

Early April, grass growing, green buds of leaves thick and down-soft on the branches of trees, moss thick and rich on rocks and trunks of trees, crocus and violet alive on the earth. Underbrush shivered with the passage of small animals released from winter in den or burrow or hutch, and snow upon the Twin Mountains gleamed diamondlike in the newborn sun.

All of the sparkling blue air—all of the world—was filled with the sound of Chickasaw drums.

In the pass between the Twin Mountains Andrew Jackson raised his arm; and behind him, in fits and starts, the long, long column of well-armed men pulled the reins of their horses and halted.

"What is it, Ginral?" asked Fes Farson, who had, by claim to familiarity with these regions, secured a place in the lead party. He was afraid, truth to tell, but he would not admit it. Ol' Festus had not experienced direct warfare before, although he had told Jackson of many an imaginary battle. He thought that the thrill of approaching battle would be like the feeling he enjoyed just before laying lash upon the back of some bound slave. But it was not at all like that. Fes Farson was scared.

"What is it, Ginral?" he asked again, after clearing his throat.

Ba-roooom, br-oom-boom, the drums resounded, rolling down among the mountains, above and within the very trees. *Ba-roooom, br-ooom-boom.*

* * *

Torch clung easily to the high branches of a hickory tree, looking far off toward the pass. There were many who had counseled him: "Attack them while they are in the pass; they will have no room for maneuver, and we shall destroy them then." "No," he had grunted, "no."

Now he watched the distant thread of Chula Harjo and his men snaking between the Twin Mountains. The tree shook slightly in the wind, and then quivered a bit more as someone climbed up to a branch beside him.

"Now that they are in the pass," said Gyva, with a questioning note in her voice, "why not attack?"

"Because there are too many of them," Torch said. "We are outnumbered at least two to one."

The column halted, and Gyva saw what he meant. The head rider was barely through the pass leading toward the Indian village, but the jackals spread back between Twin Mountains as far as she could see, and, quite likely, far back down onto the plains, and perhaps even into the valley where Harrisville had been. Ambushing Jackson's militia when they were partially through the pass would, at best, incapacitate but a small number of them. She tried to gauge the numbers and measure them against the Chickasaw braves. Her heart grew cold, and her spirit sank.

"They are coming," she said.

"They are coming indeed," Torch replied, "prepared for the last battle against us. And our nearest neighbors, the Choctaw, are now seated around sage old Red Dagger, laughing at our fate."

"It will soon be theirs," Gyva said, watching the head of the column, knowing Chula Harjo was there. "That is what you have been saying for all of the time since you have been chieftain."

"Few have listened to me."

She reached out to touch him, stopped. She had no right to touch him. He belonged to Bright Flower.

Sensing the movement, he turned to see her hand outstretched in empty air. In his eyes was tenderness, regret. He turned back to watch Jackson's advance, and Gyva dropped her hand. Neither spoke.

"Ever been up there?" Jackson demanded of Fes.

The former overseer, greedy for all the land around Harrisville, forgot himself.

"Yep, Ginral, I sure have."

Jackson's eyes were cold. "When?" he snapped.

Farson caught himself. He had been about to brag of the time he and ol' Rupert'd sneaked up here and abducted that little Indian kid, the one who'd later escaped or been let loose from Gale Foley's place. But such an admission would open a whole 'nother jar of night crawlers, as his daddy'd used to say, not to mention compromising Fes's rectitude. So he improvised with the wit God'd—in His infinite wisdom—given him.

"Ginral, I ain't a bad hunter," Fes lied.

Jackson grunted. Farson was a fairly regular-looking fellow, and the light in his eyes proved he wasn't dumb, whatever else he might be. Perhaps he even was less crude than Harris had been, but still Jackson didn't like that quick grin that went on and off. He didn't know exactly what to make of Fes—hadn't known him that long—but the guy had asked for duty at the head of the column, and any solider had to respect guts like that.

So, in the end, Jackson attributed his misgivings about Fes Farson to his own feelings about the impending battle: excitement, hot blood, desire and regret. And ambivalence. He was getting too old for this. Yet how could he back out of it? These westerners were his people, and they expected protection. Harrisville was smoking like a grass fire after a rainstorm.

"Know how the village lies?" he grunted.

Farson was waiting and ready.

"We was out after deer once," the man replied, cleverly embellishing upon his previous lie, "an' we got a little closer than we had intended to. That was Rupert an' me, 'course. Nobody else would've—" he was about to say "had the guts," but instead he said "—allowed themselves to get that caught up in the hunt. You know how it is. Anyway, I did manage to get me a look at the lie of the land. Here," he said, "I'll draw 'er for you in the dirt."

So, while the soldiers waited, Fes and Jackson dismounted and squatted down at the side of the trail. Fes broke a stick off a bush and began to draw a sketch of the layout of the Chickasaw village.

"Now, Ginral, here's the way it is. Straight south of these mountains, there's woods and trails and wild country. Won't be too bad, this time of year. Underbrush hasn't grown in full, not yet. Likewise, wilderness east and west of the red devils. Trails seem to run into the village, but nothing like a road, nothing big. Now"—he began to sketch with more detail—"here's the village itself."

"You got awful close," said Jackson, squinting at Fes. Initially skeptical, he realized that the man knew what he was talking about.

Farson cackled. "*Mighty* close, an' ain't it lucky, too. I might be the only white man ever was that close." He conveniently omitted Jason Randolph, who was dead anyway. "At least was that close and then got out with my ass intact," he chuckled. "But as I was saying, here's how the village is situated, with forest on three sides. Now right about here there is a sort of big playing field, an' that gives way to a meadow, which runs us on down"—he drew with his stick—"to a river here. Cross the river, an' there's more woods, and that's about the size of 'er."

"The river?" Jackson wanted to know. "How wide? How deep?"

"Not much of either. I figure it might get a little

swollen in spring, but nothin' near like the one that just washed us out back in Harrisville."

"I was thinking—if they see us coming, they might easily retreat across that river and get lost in the woods, and we could spend from now to October looking for 'em and not find a one."

Jackson glanced up at the cliffs and peaks of the Twin Mountains. God, this was beautiful country, way back up here in these hills. He was thinking of that, and thinking how the Chickasaw must love it, and how they would hate to lose it, and with what ferocity they would fight to keep it. Jackson appreciated the magnificence of earth; and above the rattle of harness and hoof, above the tense murmuring of his soldiers, he heard the whisper of wind such as it is heard only in the high country, a ghost trying to say something that can almost be heard, but not quite. And Jackson heard, too, the sounds that were *not* there: the cry of the hawk, the bleat of the mountain goat, the rustle of wing, the scratch of claw, even the sudden, reflexive chittering of a living thing asleep in nest or burrow. These things he did not hear, which meant that everything in the forest was awake and waiting.

Involuntarily Jackson shivered. Farson did not notice.

"Tell me, Festus," Old Hickory asked. "What do you know, personal, about this Firebrand?"

Fes's eyes narrowed. "Tricky. Tricky and ruthless. Don't give a damn. Would scalp a kid just like he'd scalp old grandpa—and for women, scalpin' is the least of what Firebrand would do."

Jackson brushed off the implications of atrocity; those things were common enough. Frontiersmen would be disappointed to hear of an Indian who did *not* rape or scalp or burn.

"Tricky," he said, considering. "How tricky?"

"Oh, terrible tricky, Ginral. There probably ain't no feint or ruse he wouldn't think up to do."

Jackson looked up once again at the rising land, the enfoliaged hills, the cliffs on either side. Perfect ambush country. Without telling his men, who would have been either too reckless or too cautious had they known, Jackson had led his tremendous column directly into this pass, knowing that not even the best of ambushes could pin down more than a third of his number. Thus the rest of his forces could fan out, occupy positions on ground even higher than that held by the Chickasaw, and force them down into the pass to be killed. It was a perfect plan.

But there had been no ambush.

Jackson remounted, looked back at his troops, lifted his arm and swung it forward. The long column lurched ahead, gathered momentum, and began to move out of the pass and into the Tennessee forest. Jackson rode, considering his next moves, trying to hear the wind-words of the ghost of the high country.

Beneath the hickory from which Torch and Gyva watched the jackals come, several braves stood ready. These were messengers, poised to carry Torch's word to numerous battle parties waiting in the village and scattered throughout the forest. Torch planned to gauge the white men's advance, judge from it their possible plan of action, and then respond with the necessary commands of his own. Gyva, who had lived among the white men and knew something of their methods and ways of thinking, was to aid Torch in the interpretation of the enemy's movements. Her manner of return to the Chickasaw, her strength and bearing, and the fact she had survived so long in alien places, had immeasurably increased her standing in the tribe. There were still, of course, those who watched her with less than complete trust. Bright Flower was one such.

"Torch, my husband," she had said, on the night of Gyva's return, "am I not everything to you?"

They were alone in the darkness of the chieftain's

wigwam, preparing for sleep. Bright Flower let fall
her raiment, pressed her breasts against his bare chest,
and worked her body skillfully against him, feeling
his hardness grow. "Am I not everything a wife should
be, my darling?"

Ah, yes, she had been, and she was again that night.
Torch knew Bright Flower felt threatened by the re-
appearance of Gyva. He knew, too, his responsibilities
as husband, as chieftain. But having seen Gyva again,
having felt his heart jump and tremble when he gazed
upon her face, Torch also knew that the higher the
happiness, the greater the pain.

He treated Gyva, after that, with gentleness and
respect, and fought his own nature, which seemed to
demand that he possess her again, as so often, and
in such splendor, he had possessed her before. But
the cost to him was great. Lying at night in the wigwam beside his sleeping wife, Torch remained awake,
his body tossing and his mind turning, his entire
being bereft of both sleep and peace. Flower's soft
nakedness was against him, and on her fine skin dried
the sweet beads of perspiration raised by the ferocity
of their lovemaking. Even now his essence seeped
from her body, which—however joyously she received
him, however enchanting the pleasure she gave—had
not yet produced a child. Lying there beside his wife,
Torch could think of nothing and no one but Gyva,
who slept across the village in the wigwam of Teva.
Torch remembered how it was—not so long ago, but
seemingly forever—when Gyva would come to him in
openness and joy beneath the willows, and how she
felt trembling in his arms, and how her lips hungered
for him; and he knew in his mind, even these years
afterward, the shudder of sudden quickening in her
body that meant she wanted him, that she could wait
no longer. Most of all Torch remembered—with his
mind, his heart, his body, remembered with every
nerve and fiber of his being—how it felt to move upon
Gyva, how it felt to move into her, a slide into silken

honey that held his body as a sweet lake holds the swimmer, and rocked against his body in forever-rippling waves . . . .

Now the wind eased through the branches of the hickory tree. Torch and Gyva rode the high branches, swayed gently to the wind, not touching. They watched as, once more, Jackson's column advanced.

"Why do you think he stopped?" she asked.

"Has he stopped?" called a brave from below.

"He is moving again," Torch called down. To Gyva he said, "Chula Harjo was making calculations, that is all."

"What do you think he decided?"

The wind ebbed slightly, and the branches to which they clung became still, so that they were momentarily side by side.

"He was listening for the words in the wind," Torch said.

Gyva was shocked. "He is a jackal," she protested. "He does not know the earth or the sky. He cannot hear the wind, as we can, or the words in it."

"Do you hear those words?" he asked her sharply.

Among the people it had long been a tradition that, as dream-visions gifted their possessors with portents of the future, the force and timbre of the mountain wind could bring its hearer advice and wisdom during hours of crisis.

Gyva met his eyes, then looked away from him. "We do not hear because there is no need. We shall triumph."

"What is happening?" prodded a messenger at the base of the great tree. "What are your orders, Torch?"

Torch looked once more at the place on the horizon where Chula Harjo's men were melting into the forest, making their ceaseless progress toward the Chickasaw village. There were but two choices: one, to stand and fight once and for all, with the rich earth, the mountains, the lakes, and the rivers prizes in the contest; and two, to flee, to melt away into the

forest, into darker country—to wait. But Torch knew
the second choice was no choice at all. His people
would not run. They had been running now for too
many circlings of the sun, and there was nowhere
else to go, no refuge their pride would let them
accept. The fact, too, that the Choctaw had conspired to put them in this humiliating position served
further to gird up their courage, their defiance. Torch
could only fight, unless Jackson called off the attack.
Torch had hoped—albeit with small heart, knowing
how difficult it is to call back a tide of men—that
Jackson would interpret the absence of ambush in
the pass as a sign of peace. Small hope, indeed. For
such hopes there was little recompense.

"Saddle my horse," he said, calling down. "Place
upon it the great saddle Four Bears took from Chula
at Roaring Gorge."

Gyva knew the saddle to which Torch referred; it
was kept in the room of ceremonial garments, sacred
accoutrements. The saddle was marked with the white
man's symbols: *A. J.*

"And," Torch continued, telling the braves, "pass
the word that all warriors are now to pick up their
Red Sticks and take up their bows. The time for the
great battle draws near and the Great Spirit shall be
with us in our endeavor."

On the ground below the tree the braves greeted
his commands eagerly. At last, battle, blood, kill-cuts,
and glory. But Gyva, in the tree beside the young
chief, could not but hear in his voice a sadness, and
a premonition that some delicate, unspeakable fate
lay concealed in the sound of the wind, words they
could not hear.

When Andrew Jackson came through the pass and
rode down into the forest, he had decided. He had
decided to call together the captains of the various
companies of his militia and give them orders for the
battle. Everything would have been so simple had

this Firebrand chosen ambush. Now it would be more complicated, and there would be more deaths. Women and children would not have participated in the ambush. But assuming the Chickasaw did not flee their village, which Jackson doubted anyway, women and children would be there, would be fighting. And it was inevitable that in the heat of battle some of them would die.

Jackson remembered Talking Rock again, the village where the battle had gotten totally out of hand. He thought, with both respect and sadness, of the beautiful half-breed whose mother he had killed, who had let him live in her own house. Dead now, too, he supposed, like all the rest of them—most of the rest of them—in Harrisville. It was well-known that a full-blooded warrior thought scornfully of the mixed-bloods. Mrs. Randolph would have been recognized and killed.

"We're ready whenever you are, Ginral," Fes allowed, when the captains had ridden up to the head of the column for orders. "What's it goin' to be?"

The men sat on horseback, in a ragged circle around Jackson, who remained mounted.

"Well, boys," he said. "We're a'goin' to do it. This is the way. The village is directly south of us. Sam, you take your Boonesboro boys an' leave right now. Strike southwest, till you get to the river. Zeb, take your men and strike southeast, hit the river, go west. Fes and I will wait here with the main body. We'll give you until about mid-afternoon, then attack the village direct. We'll close them against the river by late afternoon."

"Ginral, ain't you forgettin' somethin'?" Fes said.

Jackson did not speak, but turned his hard eyes on the enterprising Farson.

"Shouldn't we have a contingent sweeping up from the south? To trap the bastards in their den."

No. Jackson had already decided that. Let the

Chickasaw run if they wanted to. Fewer would die that way. "I don't think we need it," he drawled, which was interpreted by those present to mean that no Indian would get away, no matter what.

The men were about to ride off, to convey the orders they had received. "There's one other thing," Jackson said.

They listened.

"We got very little reason to doubt that Firebrand and his people are goin' to fight back. If you start hearing sounds of battle, get to it as quick as you can. All right, we've done this before. I want to thank you for what you've been to me, and to say I appreciate what we've been through together. That's all."

Instinctively the men saluted, although it was a gesture Jackson did not encourage. Who in the hell needed a damn salute, unless he was some candy-ass nosewipe who thought being a soldier was to dress up like a peacock and strut around?

Jackson returned the salute. Some of them might die today. *He* might die today. The momentary thought distressed him, a lot more than it used to. Maybe that was how it went. The older you got, the closer you got to death; the closer you got to it, the less dramatic and glorious it seemed.

"Move 'em out, boys," he grunted. "It's their village for Harrisville, an' these Indians have got to pay for what they done."

The messengers raced away to pass on their chieftain's orders, and Torch was left alone with Gyva.

"So now it begins," he said, preparing to climb down from the tree.

"No," she answered suddenly. "It began a long time ago. Now it ends."

"What ends?"

"The waiting," replied Gyva. "It seems that all my life has been—"

The weight of their bodies on the high, thin

branches, combined with another sudden gust of wind from the mountains, caused them to swing together and touch, far above the ground. Colliding, Gyva started to lose her grip. She did not, but Torch's arm went around her, and she was conscious of his closeness, his concern for her safety, his great strength.

She released her grip entirely, of her own volition, and then was borne up utterly by him.

"It seems that all my life has been waiting," she said.

Later Gyva could not remember how they had gotten down from the tree, nor how long it had taken. But she knew that it had happened, because mysteriously they were on the earth, down on the new grass of spring, clinging to one another. For an instant of such small duration that it would have been impossible to measure, his kiss was tentative, and whether or not Torch himself had the power to resist the call of his heart was beyond determination. For then the moment was over, and his kiss was urgent and reverential, hungry and wild. No thought then of chieftaincy, or sacred duty, or the promises of wedlock. In life there are many honorable things, and many more deserving of respect, and even a few things that, if violated, carry the pain of retribution. But none of these things mattered to Torch then, or to Gyva, for she was with him, had come home to him, and no power on earth or in heaven could deny the magnet of their natures, of their love.

From the village, sounds of preparation for battle, shouts and cries. And down from the smoky mountains came the endless roll of the war drums, a wild, mesmerizing sound, a rhythm as old as doom and time. As old as love. No matter that Torch and Gyva were unsheltered, no matter that they were covered but by leaves and sun and sky. He stripped her and spread her bare and warm upon the warm, bare earth that had known their love in ages past. Gyva, after that first heart-stunning moment in his embrace, captured by his kiss, found that she could not kiss him enough, could not hold him enough, could not touch him enough. But one mouth for a kiss, one tongue? Too few, too few. And how had Ababinili been so blind that day as to award his children but two eyes to feast in love upon one another: the soft curves and supple body of Gyva, and Torch with his hard, swelling aspects, born for love and war? How had the Great Spirit not known that two hands would not suffice, in the high sweet heat of passion on the wing, or that words might be heard ten times as well as two? And why did not the tongue have power to write words forever on the very flesh of a beloved's yearning body, arched and breathless for the flashing lance, and for the nest that it is meant to seek?

But, ah! Pleasure sufficient unto itself, pleasure enough, for no more could be borne. He came upon her as he had beneath the willows. She was a woman now, and not a girl, and he a man and not a boy, and so it was better for them than it had ever been. The cunning of the flesh is that it grows sweeter with the years, and wiser, to know better the giving of delight, and better the enjoyment thereof. Gyva took him unto herself, and held him so tight for so long that he could not move, but only moan and beg to be released. No, no, she sobbed, not yet, not yet! But for a moment stay in me this way! But then she, too, could not hold back the bursting need, and loosened the embrace of her body, that he might caress with sweet and never-ending thrusts all that she was and had ever been.

That her mother had loved her father: This love was why. That Four Bears had rescued her at Roaring Gorge: This was the reason. That she had grown in years and in beauty: Now she knew the purpose. That she had fought Little Swallow, and unmasked Hawk and been banished; that she had struggled against Gale Foley, and loved Jason, and given birth to Andrew: At last, at long last this very day, she

knew that her entire life and everything in it had
led her to this embrace on the holy grounds of her
people, a union no less holy; that she should feel her
always and only lover, her always and forever love
pulsing within the vibrant honey of her body's tender
heat, and wait now as he came toward her, rise up,
push back, and feel him slip almost but not quite
away and come toward her, within her, once again,
so sweet, so agonizingly slow, rise up, push back, and
hold, and hear him say, No, no, release me, let me
go, and doing so but knowing he would almost but
not quite, never quite, go from her now, because their
natures had conspired that *this is the way it must be,*
as he came forward again and pressed with himself
the living womb, the stroked and tingling walls of
her desire, so bend yourself like a bow to take the
arrow, and rise up, and hold. It was perfect and
seemed to be forever, truly, but then their bodies
could take no more of waiting, no more delay, and
suddenly Gyva felt her entire being shuddering out
of control, felt herself writhing against him, and
Torch against her, and there seemed no way to stop
it, no way to cease. The air was gone from her lungs,
the light from behind her eyes, and there was nothing,
nothing, nothing but her being, her body, and what
it wanted, what it commanded her soul to attain.
Her soul obeyed; and so, at one with Torch, at the
exact same moment, there on the spinning, magnificent earth, Gyva knew more love than she had ever
known before, and more delight. And then Gyva held
and held and held and could not move, and somewhere far back in her pleasure-driven mind she was
curious to hear the cry of some wild woman lost
intolerably in pleasure.

The world, after the lovers had broken from their
embrace, was still where they had left it, but changed.

"No more shall we ever be apart," Torch murmured,
stroking her glistening black hair. "No more."

Beautiful words, thought Gyva, thinking sadly of

the imminent battle, and trying not to think of Bright
Flower. In spite of her love for Torch and his for
her, which was sacred in its way, yet was Torch wed
to another. What retribution might await the trans-
gression of that bond? How *could* there be retribution,
Gyva reasoned, when the approbation of all divinity
must have been granted by the pleasure she had
known while Torch was loving her? The love and
the pleasure were reason enough, were they not?

But Ababinili might have looked down upon them
with other eyes. After all, he had created but one
mouth to kiss, two hands to stroke and tease, two
eyes alone to feast . . . .

Suddenly Gyva felt cold, and shivered. She felt that
something terrible was about to happen. How could
it, no way to cease. The air was gone from her lungs,
not felt pleasure beyond that bequeathed to mere
mortals?

"What is it?" Torch asked with some alarm, feeling
her shudder in his arms.

"Nothing. It is nothing."

"Speak, Gyva. Your heart is my heart now, and
mine yours. Hold back no words, as you would not
hold back your love."

"Perhaps it is Chula Harjo and the battle," she
said, pulling on her buckskins.

"No, it was something else that caused you to go
cold. I can read it in your eyes."

He watched her as he, too, dressed; and because
she knew that the union of their hearts was real, and
had always been, she spoke.

"Your wife has been dishonored in this, has she
not?"

Torch came toward her and placed his hand
tenderly against her face. "Are you dishonored?"

"I? I? Why, how could that be?"

"Because in my heart, and in the heart of heaven,
you are my true wife, and have been since I summoned you for the first time."

They embraced once more; and even as Gyva knew
that he spoke the truth that was in his heart, and
which she shared, yet still was Torch married to
Bright Flower in the eyes of the people. She could
not rid herself entirely of that vague feeling, an
apprehension, almost a fear . . . .

A messenger raced toward them, winded and waving. Torch released Gyva from his embrace. If the
brave had noticed the embrace at all, he gave no
sign. Other news occupied him.

"My chief! A scout has returned from the region
of the Black Ravine!"

Gyva knew the location of that place, and now she
knew, too, that it was the color of coal that had given
the ravine its name. Since returning to the tribe, she
had mentioned the value of coal to several people,
most of whom had laughed at her. "The white jackals
are crazy!" they hooted. There had been no time to
try to explain matters to these doubters.

"Black Ravine?" Torch was saying. It was about
five miles to the north.

"Jacksa Chula's advance guard has reached that
point."

"And Chula himself?"

"He rides with them." The messenger then offered
the scout's estimate of the number of white troops
riding with the advance party. Torch made quick
calculations.

"That is hardly more than a third of the number
we have seen riding through the pass. So, they have
divided their attack."

The messenger looked on, waiting, and Gyva felt
currents of intelligence and power flow from her
lover.

"The river!" he cried suddenly. "They will come
at us from the forest, and from the river!"

"Which direction?"

Torch cursed himself inwardly. Although he had
retained a sizable group of braves to guard the village

itself and to serve as reserves should too many others be wounded or killed, he had expected to make his stand in the forest, along Salawaullee Creek, whose unusual feature was a low bank on one side and a high bank on the other, positioned so that Jacksa and his men would be forced to ride upward into the ranks of Chickasaw defenders. The Salawaullee was a natural barrier, and a good one, but now Torch saw that he had nearly been outsmarted.

"Send scouts immediately upriver and downriver. Command them to return with word as soon as any of the jackals are sighted."

"What of the braves along the Salawaullee? They are poised for combat."

Torch considered this. Jacksa would be marching slowly, not only because of the forest, but also to wait until his troops, approaching the village by river, got into position for attack. If Torch ordered his men forward, he would lose the natural fortification of the creek, but he might startle Jacksa enough to put the white men at considerable disadvantage. Sounds of the battle, moreover, would alarm the river parties, and disrupt their flanking attacks.

"Your orders?" requested the messenger, looking more nervous and harried by the minute.

"A moment," Torch said, still thinking. He *could* order the braves along the Salawaullee to fall back toward the village. Thus Jackson would continue his deliberate advance untroubled, perhaps even thinking that he and his army had not yet been observed. But in that case, Jackson's advance party and the two river parties might arrive in the village at the same time.

"Order the drummers to drop a beat," Torch commanded.

"What? But—"

"Yes, let Jacksa think we are relaxing our guard. Next, call back the men from the creek. Tall Oak must take his men west immediately to the river, and

Graven Elk must go east. Fleet Cloud and Gray Eagle are to fall back to the village, and take fire upon Chula Harjo when he reaches these new defenses. Understand?"

Listening, Gyva understood the combined ploys. While the village itself would be put in more immediate danger by staging the battle so close, a deception that caused Jackson to maintain his slow pace might give the Chickasaw enough time to decimate the river parties first, and then turn to confront Chula Harjo with their full strength.

Already the beat of the drums grew slower; and, even in the village, a thin core of tension vibrated once, twice, and seemed to fall away.

"Do you think it will work?" asked Gyva, looking up into his resolute face, his flaming eyes.

"Do you have a Red Stick?" he asked her in return. "I myself put faith in strong knife and long bow—but, in truth, a Red Stick cannot hurt. Belief gives power to an amulet, as belief gives courage to a brave."

"I believe in you," Gyva said softly. "And whatever happens here today, I will still believe in you, and always."

He smiled. "Always is a very long time."

"Not long enough," she said. "Now tell me where I am to fight."

Fes Farson felt his nerves tighten, then tighten some more, building toward a tension of fear he had never imagined. This was *deep* Indian country. He might never come out of here alive, for godsakes. When the beat of the drums changed suddenly, it was all Fes could do to keep from screaming. As it was, he jerked in his saddle, and turned sheepishly to see the general grinning at him. That goddamn Jackson! Didn't he ever show fear?

"How come they did that?" he asked, trying to

cover his discomfiture. "How come they altered the rhythm? They relaxin', maybe?"

"Nope, it's a redskin trick, that's all," Jackson said, as unperturbed and matter-of-fact as anything. "That there Firebrand fellow is aimin' to spring something on us."

"How's that?"

"Well, Festus, look at it this way. The human ear is connected to the human brain, and the human brain is connected, by a series of overlappings I ain't got the time to go into, to the human stomach. Feelin' a little queasy just about now, ain'tcha?"

Fes could see no way to deny this fact without provoking considerable merriment at his own expense, so he agreed with Jackson's anatomical estimate.

"Yep, you do," Jackson went on. "And Firebrand, he knows that."

"He knows that?" Fes repeated, glancing into the trees.

"He sure does. So he decides to relax you a little bit. He slows down the rhythm of the drums, which fact goes in your ear, to your brain, and down to your gut, which begins to relax. So pretty soon you're riding through these woods like you're in some promenade, and instead of thinking about keeping your eyes peeled for a seven-foot savage lookin' to give you a haircut or worse, you find yourself thinking about how nice a cold beer would taste right about now, or about how great it was last time you had a roll in the hay, the equipment for which that seven-foot savage would also enjoy removing from your carcass."

Fes felt queasier than ever.

"So don't relax. And don't worry. It's all right to be a little jittery. I'd be worried about you if you wasn't."

Fes gave a sick smile and shook his head.

"Okay," Jackson ordered, turning to the men riding

behind him. "Pass the word down the line. We're goin' to pick up the pace a little."

"Why?" Fes asked.

"Because he wants us to go slower, Firebrand does. An' I'm an ornery cuss. When somebody goes through all this trouble to make me go slower, well, I'm a'goin' to go faster just to show him who's boss."

"But," said Fes, as the column increased its rate of advance through the woods, "what if he's already thought of that? What if he *wants* us to go faster?"

Jackson just shrugged. "Well, then he's goin' to get what he wants, ain't he? Besides, I ain't got but two choices. Either we get this fight over with sooner, or later, right?"

"Yep," Fes gulped, trying to look bold. He was only slightly encouraged when they arrived at a huge ditch in the earth, with black coal, rich black outcroppings of coal, glistening in the daylight. God, if only Rupert Harris could have been here to see this! What the hell am I thinking of? Fes corrected himself. I'm glad he *ain't* here. He chortled silently.

That was small comfort when they reached the Salawaullee and Jackson dismounted to take a look around.

"Chickasaw been here but they're gone," he said, with a gloomy look. "I don't like it." Then, from long experience, he put himself in his enemy's position. He saw himself in the village, saw himself watching the pass, waiting. Heard himself giving the order to pull back from the Salawaullee. But why? Slow the drums. Why?

"Boys," he said, leaping back up into the saddle. "Get into battle formation, and let's move out. Them flank parties on the river is goin' to be in big trouble, if they ain't already."

Torch chose to wait in the village; and, from the command post of his wigwam, he received and relayed orders through scouts and messengers—calmly, always calmly, never raising his voice. He was dressed in the full regalia of a chieftain-warrior, from a resplendent headdress of blood-colored band, with beads and the feathers of a white heron, to a ceremonial breech-cloth, also red as the eternal Chickasaw blood, to moccasins upon which had been etched the sign of the one Torch must kill this day. *A. J.* Outside the wigwam waited Torch's white stallion, and upon it the saddle of Chula Harjo, a talisman, a symbol that he who rode the white stallion already possessed half of Jackson, and would by flight of arrow, slash of knife, thrust of lance, acquire the remainder today.

Torch sat bare-chested in the wigwam and listened to the news as it was brought by messengers. When the time came, when he knew where the center of the battle would be, thereto would he go. Of all the women in the tribe, only Teva the seeress was with him. The old crone remembered history, re-called the wisdom gained in long lost circlings of the sun, battles fought in lost canyons beyond the mist and shimmer of time. It was Teva's duty, during the coming struggle, to recount the cunning strategems of old, should the young chief have need of them.

"How is it in thy heart, old woman?" Torch asked, but he spoke affectionately, for during the early time of his chieftaincy Teva's counsel had invariably served him well. He could tell in her face and bearing that she had little time left upon the earth, and his bond with her was stronger for that reason. Not many of the Chickasaw people had given as much to the wel-fare of the tribe as had this tottering witch-woman.

"My heart beats," Teva growled from her place beside him at the fire. "What more could one ask?"

They were alone for the moment, the last order having been transmitted by messenger, and no re-turning scout having appeared with further news of Jacksa's advance.

"I see not the blood beneath the mark of the cave

upon thy face, ancient one. Does this bode well or ill for us?"

"In truth, I do not know. This bloody pawprint of mine, with which I have lived since first I drew breath, responds not to my will but to things beyond my own understanding." She paused and gave Torch a hard, searching look. "And truly," she added, "there are things to be known that do not require witchery."

"I hear in your words the hint of something important. And yet you do not reveal your thought. Am I to guess it?"

The old woman was silent for a while longer, her eyes still hard upon Torch. "I think you know that of which I speak," she said at length.

"Truly I do not. Is it of the battle to come, or of the past?"

She shook her head, gave a rueful, toothless grin. "It is meant for man and woman to be hot-blooded," she sighed. "But there is a time and place for all things, for the rites of the flesh are as sacred as any other—perhaps more sacred. But violations of the spirit, violations of vow and duty, do indeed cause a trembling in the heavens, for which recompense must be paid, lest lust shudder the tender precipice upon which our nation is poised."

So that was it. Teva knew that Torch had made love to Gyva, only an hour before. Torch remembered how Gyva had shivered in his arms after the loving, as if suddenly she were cold. And he remembered her fear that something bad would transpire, something to make them pay in suffering for what they had shared in illicit joy. Torch had not believed her. But now, regarding the soothsayer's black and knowing eyes, he wondered. Yet how could the Great Spirit even think to send retribution? Torch's life—his very soul—had always been joined to Gyva's. The duties of his leadership, to which he had been most faithful, could not require that he deny a love of vast significance. And of his promises to Bright Flower . . .

Torch looked away.

"Battle is will and blood," he said. "The greater the love in one's heart, the greater the courage. As you have said, the blood comes not to your mark, and you do not know the possible course of this day."

"I should know it," the woman returned. "I have always sensed triumph or tragedy in the past. But not today. Today I seem to see another vision, which inspires me not to prophecy but to woe."

"What is it?" he asked, concealing a growing sense of alarm.

Teva was silent for a long time. "Do you remember the dream you were given during the time of the manhood ritual?"

Of course Torch remembered. How could he ever forget? A dream within a dream, a river within a river, and buried in the sand at the bend of the river a golden stick, the words upon which he had seen but had not remembered. He felt the naked skin upon his back grow cold. Was Teva telling him that his failure to recall the words of the secret of life heralded failure in battle against Jacksa today? Looking upon himself, he saw his smooth, taut skin, his great strength, his iron-muscled arms, upon which the serpent bracelet seemed to move and writhe in the flickering firelight. Would his strength prove as faulty as his memory had been?

"I remember the dream," was all he said. "What of it?"

Teva leaned forward and placed her curled fingers on his arm. "I too have seen the river."

Shocked, he stared back at her. "But of what meaning is such a vision? Especially, what does it mean to us today?"

"That I do not know, but I surmise it is why the blood does not flow beneath my mark."

She spoke in riddles! "I am confused. You must enlighten me."

"I did not dream the river, nor the bend in the

river where lies the golden sand. I saw the river. I was there. It was more real than any vision, and far more true."

"But what—"

"It is a place where we shall one day be, and that is why . . . ."

Then Torch understood. Teva was speaking of another land, another place. The Chickasaw would go down to defeat today, would become yet another nation dispossessed and exiled by the white jackals. And Teva had visited a place to which they would be sent. He expressed this thought.

"I do not know," she muttered. "I do not know for sure. It did not seem home to me, neither old nor new. But, like the river, we were on our way, on our way to . . . somewhere."

Without accepting her implicit message of forth-coming defeat, Torch thought of the one he loved most.

"And Gyva?" he asked. "Was Gyva with us along the river?"

Teva's cackle was harsh. "You ask not of your wedded wife?"

"And Bright Flower, and all the rest," he added hastily.

Teva shrugged. "We see what we see. You saw a stick and forgot the message inscribed thereupon. I saw a river, and did not bring back its name."

"And you do not recall, either, where I was taking our people?"

With his words Teva sat bolt upright, as if struck by some element of her vision that she had incompletely understood before.

"What is it?" Torch asked sharply, thinking her body might have suffered some seizure or attack.

"Nothing," she said, without conviction, still wrapped in dark knowledge.

"You must tell me!" he demanded. "Where was I taking the people?"

"You . . . you . . ." She faltered.

"Go on. I demand to know it."

"You were not taking us anywhere," Teva murmured, not looking at him. "You were not leading us."

Torch felt the breath go out of him, and sensed that his lungs took in no more, but he did not care just then. It was as if, in Teva's words, he had been given irrefutable proof of his own death.

Retribution? For loving Gyva? How could it be?

"But I do not understand—" he started to say.

Then a brave burst into the wigwam. "Battle has commenced on the river to the west," the messenger cried excitedly.

Torch had no more time to contemplate his fate. He did not have to anymore; it waited outside. He mounted his stallion and went to meet it.

CHAPTER VIII

Gyva had been given the duty of organizing the women and children. In a battle such as the one envisioned, much of the fighting would be done some distance from the village, and this fighting was the responsibility of the braves. Should the braves falter and be driven back into the village—or, worse, should they be defeated in the forest, along the river—then the women themselves must fight Chula Harjo until they were victorious. Or until they were defeated.

For such they had vowed. There would be no more retreat.

Gyva remembered most of the women, and knew they would fight with arrow and knife, tooth and nail, as long as they were able, and so would the older children. It was the smaller children who presented the greater problem.

"I shall bear my son upon my back during battle," cried Two-Reeds, she of broad back and ample girth, out of whose fertile womb had come nine children, this boy-baby to whom she referred being her last. "If I should see there is no hope, I shall myself take him with me into death."

There was much nodding of heads at this.

"It is unnecessary," Gyva countered.

In spite of her authority, they hooted when Gyva said this. She had survived the jackals, true; but, after all, what did she know of children, and safety in battle?

"The littlest can be taken even now into the forest south of the river," Gyva tried again.

"No, no. They shall stay with us. We cannot chance them to fall into Chula's hands. He will torture them. He will sell them into slavery!"

There was no persuading them. It was as if they yearned for this final confrontation, to end once and for all the cloud hovering over the nation. Yet she tried again to safeguard the little ones.

"I myself stand here alive because once Jacksa Chula, for all his depravities and true malice, did not let me die."

"Yes, but he would have sold you into slavery!" cried one of the older women, who knew the old stories of Gyva's rescue at Cradle-of-the-Speaking-River.

"I do not believe so," Gyva said. "But listen! There is little time." She thought swiftly. "Let me offer this. Those mothers who are nursing, or have recently given birth, and those women who are with child—none of you will be able to offer furious battle. So you be the ones to take the youngest across the river. Indeed, your presence here would *hinder* our progress in battle."

There were a few nods and some murmurs of assent in support of such logic.

"And if we triumph, of which I am certain," Gyva continued, although she was not so certain, "then return to the village to gaze upon the head of Andrew Jackson. If we fail, which I do not for one moment countenance, not even as a possibility, then you may return, or you may melt away into the forest. Your closeness to us during the battle will be sufficient to fulfill your vow to be a part of this final struggle, and all know it. And most importantly, there need be no death, particularly not that of a child, unless it is utterly unavoidable."

"You speak as Torch speaks," commented an old squaw, not at all critically.

Others agreed, so in the end it was decided to take the small children to safety. Gyva loaded her pistol, the one she had taken from Rupert Harris, and was tightening her bowstring when Bright Flower appeared. Torch's wife was readied for battle herself, carrying a full quiver of arrows and a knife at the band of her buckskin skirt.

"You speak as Torch speaks," she said, bitterly repeating the words of the old squaw. Gyva heard both fear and sorrow in her voice.

There was no time for a quarrel. "Our chieftain has ever been wise," Gyva said quietly.

But Bright Flower felt threatened, and she felt compelled to point out, "He is *our* chieftain, but he is *my* man."

"Yes," said Gyva, feeling a stab of guilt, and the memory of the apprehension she had felt after loving Torch.

"I know," Flower continued, "that you are in his heart. Often in his eyes I seem to see your image, even when he is looking at me."

"He is married to you," Gyva said softly, knowing the truth of it, the bitter weight of it. "And you have made vows until death. What more do you ask?"

Bright Flower looked back at her with hurt-filled eyes, and departed to the station she had been assigned, next to the forest by the playing field. If worse came to worst, the braves, falling back, were to lead Jackson's men onto the open field, and the women, concealed in the trees, were to open fire on them.

Sadly Gyva watched Bright Flower walk away. Then she saw the messenger race to Torch's wigwam, and a moment later Torch rushed out and leaped into the saddle upon the back of the white stallion.

"We go to the river!" he cried to the braves who would fight with him. "Now hasten. We must succeed on the river, for Jackson approaches from the north faster than we had thought."

Then he rode from the village, and Gyva watched him go. But for some secret reason of the heart, she did not think for a moment of battle and death, but was transported in memory back into the past, saw him again as he had been in the young days when she had been growing into her womanhood: how his body had moved as he strode across the dusty ground in the village, how he had looked at her for the first time, in the manner that a man looks at a woman, and how he had said, his voice filled with new meaning, wordless promise, *"Ixchay,* Dey-Lor-Gyva. Are you well?"

"Ixchay!" she had responded, a little flustered, a little surprised, but delighted beyond description. But before she was able to say anything more, he had gone away.

Now he was going away again.

No, he is not, she decided. And, mounting a horse, she galloped into the forest after Torch and his war party.

There were three parts to the battle, which lasted from mid-afternoon until dusk. Torch and Gyva participated together in the first, which took place on the river to the west of the village. The jackals had been surprised by the Chickasaw waiting in ambush, but fought fiercely with superior numbers, fought with firearms against arrows and knives, and would readily have prevailed had not Torch and his braves and Gyva arrived to offer support to the beleaguered Indians.

Simultaneously, on the river to the east of the village, the second part of the battle was taking place. In this engagement the jackals triumphed, leaving braves dead and dying in the river and upon its banks, and sending red, bloodied water down the current, like curtains of war paint thrown across the river, like scarlet streaks of dye in the blue sky.

Jackson heard the sounds of these two struggles

and nerved his men for an immediate attack. "The Indians are occupied now," he said, "just as I planned. Let's hit the village."

He counted, of course, on the village being defended, but he had underestimated the number and ferocity of its defenders. He erred, too, in thinking that the river battles would not be over as quickly as they were. But it was Jackson who not only participated in but served as focal point for the third and main part of the battle. Before he and his contingent reached the village, their senses were numbed by the screaming and shooting that rose from the river engagements; Firebrand was one jump ahead of the white men, and Jackson knew it. Opposed by a foe even cannier than he had suspected, the general exhorted his charging men: "Fight hard and fast. If our men on the river lose, Firebrand and his braves will be back here, and on our necks!"

Not one of them needed a repetition of this advice.

The Tennesseeans charged out of the forest and across the meadow. Before them crouched the wigwams of the Chickasaw, the dwellings of their home village, which had never before received a militia assault. Jackson led the charge, brandishing a sword, riding hell-for-leather toward the village, his white mane flowing. Beside him, behind him, the Tennesseeans pounded on, brandishing rifles and pistols and knives. They had already begun firing. Yet, captured as they were by the momentum of the charge, they could not fight back all the terror that rose from a strange and savage cry that the Indian defenders were making:

Chula Harjo! Chula Harjo! Chula Harjo!

Over and over came that cry, like a chant, an incantation, and the chilling sound of it pierced the soul.

Too late it struck Jackson as odd that so many of the braves seemed out in the open, that they had not taken more pains to conceal themselves. And too late he knew why this was so. At the edge of the meadow, just where it reached the village, holes had been dug and covered with grass, vines and ropes had been strung taut between stakes in the ground. The horses reached this place, plunging at full gallop, and their legs were snapped like matchsticks. The terrible cries of the horses, rolling in agony on the ground, matched in extremity and horror the cries of the Tennesseeans.

As soon as the horses and riders began to fall, the Chickasaw braves dashed forward with knives and tomahawks, leaving their women behind barriers to cover the attack with bows and arrows. A wicked, slashing, ferocious battle commenced, just as Torch and his party galloped forward, elated by their success down at the river.

Chula Harjo! Chula Harjo! Chula Harjo!

Jackson, grappling with a sinewy brave, saw Torch coming, and then, disbelieving, saw beside the chieftain a woman of incredible beauty, racing toward him like a mountain cat on the attack, her face full of rage and radiance. He knew immediately who it was. *I should have killed her when I had the chance,* he thought sadly, as he sent his Bowie knife between the ribs of the brave with whom he was struggling. He had time to half turn to see the eyes of Gyva and Torch upon him.

Well, it had come. The time to settle everything once and for all.

Then Fes Farson leaped forward, or blundered forward, into Jackson's line of sight. Gyva, riding toward the general, decided in an instant, and slashed at Fes with her knife. At the same moment Firebrand dived from his horse, sailed over Farson, and landed on General Jackson. The two men crashed down into the bloody dust.

Gyva and Torch had ridden at the head of their party, from the scarred banks of the river where the battle had taken place, and now they were approaching the village. "Jackson's already attacking," she heard Torch say, and she spurred her horse to keep up with him. They flashed past the place of the willows, clattered up over the smooth white stones, and then galloped up the meadow, across the playing field toward the village.

Jackson's men were already fighting in the village, and the melee spilled over into forest, onto field. The original plan—to lure the jackals onto the playing field so that they would become prey to archers in the woods—was not working, as so many things planned for battle do not succeed. Delia felt the surging power of the horse between her thighs, felt the wind in her face. Oddly, in spite of the fact that she was riding toward what might be death, she felt free. Torch was riding at her side, Chula Harjo waited in the village; she had the feeling of completion, of all things coming to pass. It was as if destiny had planned these things for her, aeons ago.

Chula was on a big gray, and Gyva knew that Torch would go for him. Then she saw the man at Chula's side, and the blood of hate boiled hot. From the belt at her waist she pulled the knife—she held Red Stick and reins in her other hand—and at that moment decided to remove the life from Fes Farson, if she could. The entire village, the forest, the very sky— all were pandemonium. A wall of shouting sound rose above, and the battle ebbed and flowed. She saw Torch leap from his horse onto Jackson, and then she saw Farson's hand coming up at her, with a gun in it. The black, empty barrel of the gun reminded her of the Choctaw riding toward her in the raid upon the village long ago; and, as she had then, Gyva reacted, twisting sideways in her saddle. A puff of smoke appeared at the muzzle of Farson's gun—the report of the weapon was drowned out by the howls of battle—and Gyva felt something whistle past her head. She regretted having lost her own pistol during the river battle.

Farson's face seemed to hang there against the sky, his mouth opening in astonishment that he should have missed hitting her at such close range, and already his eyes starting to show fear as she brought her knife around toward his throat. Her horse collided with Farson's mount, which reared, and Gyva's knife slashed empty air. Farson fell from his horse into the dirt.

A long, lean man with white hair wrestled a brave in the nearby dust, and Gyva saw the flash of serpent bracelet. But she had no time to think of that. She leaped onto Fes Farson as he struggled to his feet; she smelled the sweat of fear on him, the essence of him, a slippery veneer of grease and ooze, like his smile, which came now as a grimace of effort and desperation.

"Die!" she gritted, and sent the knife upward toward his pumping heart. The knife touched bone, but he fell backward, rolling in the dust. The horses were rearing. Farson was trying to bring up his pistol for another shot. Torch had his Red Stick lifted to club Jacksa. Gyva dived forward, too eagerly, too quickly. With a movement that was more luck than anything else, Farson sidestepped, Gyva tripped and fell; and then the four of them—Gyva, Farson, Jackson, Torch—seemed caught in a terrible frieze, all movement suspended, all time stopped. Torch's arm was raised to strike a blow; and Jackson, pinned beneath the chief, was lifting one arm to ward it off, bringing up the other, which held a knife. Farson's gun was up, ready, his mouth half-open in a guttural cry of panic and decision. Gyva was on the ground, half-turned, braced upon one arm, trying to rise. She saw, as if all movement were frozen, the trampling hooves of frenzied horses, the dust rising in the murky air, the green leaves of the forest flashing beyond.

Then time began again. Fes Farson's arm swung to the side, and he squeezed the trigger. Torch jerked once, and a thin spume of blood burst from the back

of his head. Jackson's eyes widened in sudden astonishment, and he drove his knife upward between Torch's
ribs. Gyva screamed and leaped toward Jackson, felt
his forearm deflect the thrust of her knife, heard
Torch roar in pain, twitching in the dust. Then
Jackson was beneath her, and her knife was flashing
down. She knew where his heart was, and her knife
sought it; and even with the tears in her eyes there
would be no missing, no missing this time.

Her entire body was struck a blow then, and she
was knocked off Chula, rolling once more into the
dirt, and this time Fes Farson had the upper hand.
Diving toward her, he had knocked Gyva from the
general's body, prevented Gyva from striking her
blow, and in so doing had saved Jackson's life. Later
Fes would not remember having done this; but he
did remember, with considerable pleasure, sticking
the black barrel of his gun in Gyva's panting mouth,
and squeezing the trigger tighter, tighter—

"Hold it!" Jackson ordered.

Fes did not pull the trigger. In her mouth Gyva
felt the barrel hot and hard. Torch was moaning on
the ground next to her, and everywhere the battle
raged. She saw Fes Farson's obscene, vengeful sneer,
the twisted grin of an evil conqueror, and she saw
Andrew Jackson tall and gaunt against the sky.

"Let me," Fes pleaded. "Let me blow the bitch's
brains out."

"No," said Jackson. "I might need her."

Perhaps Jackson would not have needed Gyva—
old Teva spoke English, too—but out of some involved
combination of motive and impulse, he stayed Fes's
trigger finger. Their leader's struggle with the Indian
had brought a dozen men toward Jackson, and these
now fought in a circle around him, keeping away
those Chickasaw who might try for the scalp of the
old and fierce one.

"We got their chief right here," Jackson shouted.

"He's near dead, I think. If we can just show him to the rest of these red bastards, it might drop their morale a little."

Suggestion became command, and in a few rough moments Torch's bleeding body was hoisted aloft on the arms of several horsemen. Blood spilled down on Gyva, still pinned beneath Fes Farson; and beyond his leering face she saw the blank, unconscious face of her beloved. The soldiers lifted him like the carcass of an animal dead and doomed, and immediately a howl of sadness, rage, and woe rose from the fighting Chickasaw. They did not cease to fight—not then, not at that moment—but Gyva, lying in the dirt, gauged the sound and knew that the battle was ended, knowing, too, that an age had ended for her people, that the blue, smoky mountains would be home no more.

"Pretty sight, eh?" grunted Farson, glancing up at Torch, then back down at Gyva. "That your Indian lover, eh?"

She glared at him and did not answer.

He slapped her hard across the face. "I astya a question."

She did not answer.

He slapped her again. Her ears rang. Her eyes were filled. Her face was on fire.

"That your Indian lover?"

She spat at him, struggling to free her arms, which were pinned to the earth beneath his knees.

"Why you . . ." she heard him grunt, "I'll . . ." and she waited for the next blow.

But it did not come. Jackson was giving a series of quick orders. "Okay, boys," he was yelling, "we got 'em on the run. Fes, get the woman over there to that big wigwam. You boys get the chief over there, too. In a couple of minutes I'm goin' to try and organize a push from here to the meadow."

The meadow! Gyva thought, with one last hope that the women in the trees would be able to turn the tide with their arrows. But this hope was dashed as Jackson went on. "That river party coming from the east took a whole lot of women prisoners. Got 'em pinned down by the river now. All right, let's get the job done. One last big push and we got 'er licked."

Chula was right. (Ah, but was Chula ever wrong?) By dusk the battle was over, and an age was done. The jackals heaped Indian dead in the center of the village, laid their own dead out in a row along the wall of the forest, covering each with a saddle blanket or a poncho until burial plans were decided. Those braves who had survived were tied hand and foot, their ankles and wrists bound together behind their backs, and made to lie facedown on the playing field, where the spring earth grew cold, where the new grass dampened with dew. Now and again a jackal guard would walk over to give some helpless brave an indolent kick. "That's fer Howie Regis," the jackal would say, and you could hear the thud of the kick and the Indian's grunt of pain. "Howie was a friend of mine. He died today." And then another kick. The Chickasaw were symbolized by that bound brave; the Chickasaw were defeated, vanquished, whipped and helpless. Just before nightfall, the women who had been keeping watch over the infants and small children began to drift in from the woods across the river, and the holocaust was complete.

Jackson, as soon as the battle was decided, had set up headquarters in the big council wigwam, and from there made the decisions as to the disposal of the dead, the treatment of the survivors, and the provisioning of the village. Squaws would be allowed to prepare the meals, and thus would not be bound, although, of course, they were restricted to the village. Children would be kept together, under guard, in the wigwams, because a redskin of even four or five years could be dangerous.

Gyva's face showed disdain when she heard Jackson give the order to keep children under guard. She and Teva were in the wigwam with victorious Chula

Harjo, translating for him, and passing his orders along to the defeated Indians. Neither had wanted such a task, but Jackson minced no words. "Now, I don't speak Chickasaw, an' you do. The Chickasaw don't speak English, 'ceptin' you two. The battle's over and I don't want no more people to get hurt, but that's what's goin' to happen if the Chickasaw can't understand what it is I want them to do. My men are goin' to be none too gentle if their orders ain't carried out real quick."

And so Gyva had served as translator, but the order regarding the children infuriated her.

"I said somethin' wrong, Miz Randolph?" Jackson inquired.

Gyva met his eyes. "It is not my place to speak," she said.

"That's absolutely right," he agreed. "You tied up your lot with the redskins, an' you got whipped. It's *not* your place to speak." Then his eyes softened, and in them she saw herself not as an Indian enemy but as a woman. "But what do you want to say?" he asked gently.

"The children need not be confined," she said. "It is unnecessary." Beside her the old seeress nodded vigorously.

"Miz Randolph, Miz Randolph," Jackson said. "You got to understand. It's for their own safety. Let's say they're runnin' around the village, an' run into some frontiersman who's been tryin' all day to keep from gettin' killed. Now, Miz Randolph, bad as battle is, it's not the time atrocities take place. Atrocities take place after the battle is *over*. That's what I'm trying to prevent."

Gyva understood. In old times, after a Chickasaw victory, the captives of other tribes would be brought back into the village, to be killed slowly, lingeringly. Gyva passed along the order to keep the children under guard, and explained it to her people. They understood. The entire population could be massacred in minutes, with the braves hogtied in the meadow and only women and children walking about. They understood.

Gyva also cooperated because she *had* to be in the council wigwam, because there Torch lay on a pallet, dying. Farson's bullet had gouged the lower back of his head, dangerously near the spinal column; and in spite of Teva's ointments and bandages, the knife wound in his chest was still bleeding. He was unconscious and breathing in short, ragged gasps; and when Gyva bent down to touch his face, she felt with her fingertips the hot flush of his fever. The witch-woman examined Torch for a long time, then looked at Gyva and shook her head.

Jackson, who had just sent Fes Farson out of the wigwam with instructions for tethering the horses, saw Teva's gesture and came over. Kneeling down, he, too, looked at Torch.

"So this is the one they call Firebrand?" he asked, not without sympathy.

"A lie!" Gyva retorted. "It was always a lie." She explained how Rupert Harris had originally, unjustifiably, pinned the name on Torch-of-the-Sun.

"So that's his real name, eh? Sounds like the name of a fine man."

"He is, and—"

"What's yours?"

"What?"

"I don't suppose you're Miz Randolph up here in the mountains, now, are you?"

"I am Dey-Lor-Gyva. It means Beloved-of-Earth."

Jackson nodded. "Now what was it you called yourself down in the flatlands?"

"Delia. My name was Delia."

"This Torch here—he your husband?"

Teva snorted.

"No, he is our chief."

"I know that. But you was sure fightin' next to him like he was more than—"

The sound of an angry confrontation began outside the wigwam, and a woman's voice pleading, in
Chickasaw, to be permitted entrance. Bright Flower.
"I must see my husband!" she was saying, over and
over, but the soldiers did not understand.

"What the hell is that?" asked Jackson, getting up.

Gyva felt impotent, and hurt. And surprised. She
had forgotten all about Flower. She had every right
to be here, and yet to Gyva she seemed an intruder.

"It is the woman of our chief," the seeress told
Jackson.

The general stuck his head out the entrance and
barked a few curt orders. Bright Flower came inside,
proud, but afraid. She looked at neither the witch-
woman nor Gyva, not even at Harjo, but went straight
to Torch and knelt down beside him. She listened to
his breathing, examined his wounds, felt his hot skin,
and kissed his face. She did not weep. She, too, was a
Chickasaw.

"And who shall lead us now?" Bright Flower asked
no one in particular, as she stood up.

"It is an improper question," said the old woman.
"We cannot name a new chieftain until the present
leader is dead."

The comment served to brace Gyva, who had for
the past moments, watching Flower with Torch, let
her mind give way to sorrow and feelings of helpless-
ness. Now was the time, now was precisely the time,
that such feelings must not be entertained.

"What is to happen to us?" she demanded of Jackson in English.

"Let's eat," he said. "We got a lot of talking to do."

Bright Flower tried to spoon broth into Torch's
mouth, failed, and then kept his lips moist with a
wet cloth. She had little interest in political matters.
Her husband was dying.

Gyva longed to be next to Torch, but she knew it

was unseemly. She sat beside the witch-woman, eating chunks of horsemeat, mopping gravy with bread and eating it, too, waiting for Jackson to tell them what the fate of the Chickasaw was to be. He was in no hurry to do so, but whether from reluctance or anticipation Gyva could not tell.

"What does that mark on your face mean?" Jackson asked Teva. Sitting there comfortably around the wigwam fire, he might have been chief himself, or a wise elder. Gyva watched him, listened to him, judged the manner in which he acted, and ate, and spoke. She had vowed to kill him, and had not. She had tried to kill him, and had failed. She bore a great share of the responsibility for her people's misfortune at his hands. How might she redeem her failure? Could she ever do so? Her life was so inextricably linked with that of Jackson, and because it was, she hated him and yet she did not hate him.

The seeress was explaining the significance of her birthmark.

"Interesting," Jackson said. "Interesting. So you already know what is going to happen?"

"There is a great river," Teva grunted.

"And?" prodded Jackson, as if he doubted her powers.

"And we cross it," said Teva.

"What does that mean?"

"It means you jackals are going to possess our homeland," accused the old woman heatedly. "It means we will be sent somewhere else."

For an instant Jackson looked away. Then he was hard again, and so were his words.

"The law is the law," he said. "You're goin' to have to go."

"Not our law!" cried Gyva.

"Your law don't count no more."

"Why not?"

"Because you lost," Jackson said, with dread finality.

"This here is the United States of America, in case you didn't know, an' Indians that go makin' war against peaceful settlers got to take the consequences."

"But there are treaties," Teva began.

"That's true, that's true. I checked all this out before I brought the militia down here. If you Indians run amuck, like you did over to Harrisville, you don't have your treaty rights anymore. You got to go. It's in the treaty, too. The law is the law."

"But the *Choctaw* were responsible for Harrisville!" Gyva explained, her voice quivering. "It was Red Dagger and his people. They disguised themselves, and—"

Jackson was shaking his head. "No use," he said, "no use."

On his pallet Torch groaned, long and painfully.

"His time is coming!" exclaimed Bright Flower, shrinking back a little. "Teva?"

"Why is it no use?" Gyva demanded, torn between a desire to rush to Torch and a need to do something to save her people's homeland.

"Because to Washington, D.C., to white settlers here in Tennessee, to my men out there, and, frankly, to me, I don't care what tribe or nation done it, I just know *Indians* done it. That's the entire point of the Indian removals program. You got to go."

Torch moaned once more.

"Teva!" cried Bright Flower, down on the pallet next to her husband now, as if clinging to him might hold life imprisoned inside his body.

"Don't you understand? You *lost!*" Jackson was explaining to Gyva.

"But—"

"If you don't go peaceful, you'll all be killed," Jackson said, the tension of truth in his voice. "You haven't any choice, don't you understand?"

"Where will we go? How?"

"I'll check on that. I'm sure there's a place for you

Chickasaw somewhere—like over the river, like she said."

Teva had scurried over to Torch and was studying him closely, gauging the nearness of death. Now Jackson and Gyva knelt beside her. Bright Flower still embraced him, more desperately than before. The young chief stirred and seemed to make a sound. Gyva felt her heart would burst, would break, seeing him there before her, unable even to touch him. Life was a trick, a snare, a series of deceptions. Behind every promise of joy lurked a savage truth. After the death of Jason and Andrew she had vowed that nothing similar would ever again happen to those whom she loved. Her heart had been pure, her vow holy. And now Torch lay dying and her people were about to be visited with an exodus to unknown regions. She had come back after so long to know Torch's love once more; and as soon as it had been given, it had been snatched away.

"I . . . see . . . it . . ." Torch moaned, his words faint and far away.

"He speaks!" cried Bright Flower joyously, bending her ear to his lips.

Gyva allowed herself an instant of hope. Perhaps Torch would not die. Perhaps he would return to consciousness, recover.

The chief's right hand moved, moved again, as if sweeping something aside, as if digging.

"Here . . . here it is . . . I . . ."

Then he shuddered and spoke no more, some spell broken, some chord gone. Yet he breathed.

"He is in delirium," snorted old Teva. "I believe he has returned in his mind to the place of his vision." She shrugged. "I hope he finds it this time, and remembers the words on the stick. We all have need of them."

"What are you talking about?" Jackson demanded in his rough yet not uncourteous manner.

"The secret of life," Gyva told him, telling him the vision of the golden stick.

Chula stood for a long time looking sadly down upon the suffering brave; but whether he believed that life held a secret great enough to fill visions, or was merely touched by the fact that Torch thought so, none of them could say.

"Good hunting, Chief," Jackson said softly. "Good hunting."

CHAPTER IX

Gyva arose at dawn that morning, sensing that something had happened within her soul during the course of the night. She did not at first know what it was, only that she felt a strange, unexpected peace within. Last night, around the fire in Teva's wigwam, not even the heavily pungent smoke of the drugged pipe had been able to diminish her rage. For orders had come from Washington, D.C., and Jackson had told her: "Inform your people to prepare for the march. Tomorrow is the date of your eviction."

Although this news had been expected, Gyva's anger was almost uncontrollable. "Fire in the spleen will avail you nothing," old Teva had tried to advise her. "Empty your soul. When acceptance is the only recourse, accepting is the only hope as well."

"Hah!" Gyva had raged. In the end, she had gone back to her own wigwam, consumed by a hatred of the jackals that was so strong it seemed the whole earth would burst into flames if she but spoke the word. But now, in the morning, she felt peace, and after some puzzled moments she began to understand why. When one has lost everything, there is nothing left to lose. It is like the muttering stillness after a great battle. It is like the eerie quiet after a terrible storm.

Then she went outside, into a golden dawn that was as incongruous as this odd new quiet in her heart. The white soldiers on guard at the council wigwam, in which Jacksa Chula slept, followed her with their eyes, and one called out, "Well, if it isn't my trailmate." Fes Farson. He seemed ebullient this morning. Why? What did he mean? She ignored him and walked to a much smaller wigwam, into which the dying Torch had been moved.

Bright Flower looked up as Gyva entered, and her eyes were those of a cornered animal who has determined to fight to the death.

"He lives?" breathed Gyva, barely able to rest her eyes upon the fevered form of her life's great love.

Swallow nodded.

Gyva's heart was torn. Torch would not be allowed to remain here. All the Chickasaw must leave. A special sling had been fashioned for the chief, that he might ride between two horses on a stretcher of saplings and leather and pelts. But she was certain that the trail would kill him. Would it not have been better, and kinder, for him to have died here in the Chickasaw homeland, to be buried in the river bank beside Four Bears, beside all the other chiefs, whose reigns stretched back and back and further back into time immemorial? Would that not have been better?

No matter now. He would be taken with them. If Ababinili intended that Torch's death be on the trail to the west, then so be it. Ababinili had his reasons. Sad, but still with quiet heart, Gyva left Torch in the care of his wife and walked toward the council wigwam.

"An' how's yer boyfriend this mornin'?" Fes Farson drawled.

She did not answer. "I must see the general," she said.

He reached out and grabbed her arm. "You know," he said tersely, "I'm gettin' a little tired of you. Seems like that big chief Firebrand did, too. I see he's got him another woman. Fact is, I think I like her even better'n you."

Gyva shook him off, gave him a look of such cold disdain that it penetrated even his dull-witted arrogance.

Jackson was drinking coffee and gathering maps and papers into a leather case when Gyva entered the wigwam. She saw what was in his eyes, and did not like it.

"I do not need your pity, nor do my people. Even more, is not pity misplaced in a man who would do what you do to us this day?"

He said nothing, but with a gesture he bade her sit, and offered a steaming mug of coffee. This she accepted. He sat down beside her. "Things are all set. Are your people prepared?"

They were, and she told him so. For many days the Chickasaw had rested their horses, gathered food, folded tents and blankets, prepared backpacks and packs to be carried by beasts. All that remained for the people was to assemble this morning in the center of the village, organize the order of march, and ride away. It will be a simple thing, she reflected, if we just do it, just do it without thinking.

"What I got to tell you," Jackson said, after she had sipped a good measure of the coffee, "is your route of march."

She glanced at him in surprise. "Are we not allowed to choose even that?"

He shook his head. "According to my orders, you've got to be escorted to the western border of Tennessee. I'm sending Farson and some of the other militiamen with you."

Gyva could not believe it. Fes Farson would *still* be part of her life? She was just about to protest, but suddenly another thought came to her. If Farson had been assigned to guard her, that was the way it was meant to be. The morning's peace did not desert her. Farson would be with her for a reason, even if she did not yet see the reason clearly.

"The men respect Fes," Jackson was saying, "especially as how he accounted well for himself in the battle, and he's given me every assurance none of your people will be bothered on the trail."

"My trailmate," Farson had said. Now Gyva understood. All right, so be it.

"When you reach the border of west Tennessee," Jackson was saying, "you'll run into the Mississippi River. Turn south there."

"South? I thought we were going—"

"West? Yes. You follow the Mississippi south until you come to another river that flows into it. That's the Arkansas. Turn west there, where the rivers meet, and follow the Arkansas home."

"How far?"

"Far as Oklahoma."

Gyva was startled. In her tongue *okla* meant "red" and *houma* meant "man."

"This is an Indian land?" she asked.

"It will be," he said. "It's where you're goin', at any rate."

"What is it like? Is it like here, with mountains and rivers and green forests into the horizon?"

He did not meet her eyes. "I don't think so," he offered, "but there's plenty of room. No one will bother you there, and you won't have all these wars and such."

Her look was cold and regal. "Ah, but the white men will follow us there, too," she said. "They will always follow, and there will be war again. But next time we shall not be driven away."

He held up his hand. "No more," he said. "The only thing I can tell you is that I will not battle against your people again. That is a promise."

"It comes too late."

"Most things come too late. Now, go and tell your people to get ready."

She rose. "But we have no chieftain," she said. "Not one in proper health to give that command."

"Then *you* give the orders," he said.

Teva agreed. "Do it," she told Gyva, when the younger woman sought her advice. "The people respect you now, and who else will rise from our de-

moralization to lead? As long as Torch lives, there
can be no other chief."

And so for the last time the Chickasaw people
gathered in the center of the village. Skins had been
stripped from the wooden frames of the wigwams,
and all that was left of an ancient settlement was a
jumble of stakes and bent branches, as if strange fire
had swooped down in the night, to wither and consume.

Farson and his men were mounted and armed,
ready to go. The Indians formed up into a long file,
Torch on his stretcher, oblivious to this leavetaking,
some on horseback, many more on foot. Gyva ascer-
tained that all was in readiness, and strode to the
head of the column. Here waited Torch's white horse,
with Teva holding the reins. On its back was the
saddle captured long ago at Roaring Gorge, with the
golden letters *A. J.* affixed to it.

Jackson left the council wigwam and approached.

"Take off this saddle," Gyva ordered one of the
braves.

Jackson heard the instructions and countermanded
her order.

"It is yours," he said. "A battle prize once taken
fairly by a strong man."

"I want nothing of yours," she said, with neither
heat nor defiance. It was a simple statement. "Your
contributions to the life of my nation have already
been more than sufficient."

He smiled, but it was a painful smile.

The saddle was removed, and Gyva mounted bareback, pulling old Teva up behind her. She gazed at
Jackson, who stood in the dust looking up at her,
squinting into the sun.

"Farewell," he said. "There are few words for
tragedy."

"No," Gyva said, cutting him off, lifting her voice
so that all could hear. The morning mood was still
with her, and the march lay long and difficult ahead.

She would not have her people further assaulted by talk of tragedy and loss.

"No," she said again, letting her hand gesture toward the rich forests, the silver river, pointing at last to the Twin Mountains, purple against the morning sky. At her belt she wore the leather pouch, and she touched it now, feeling inside it the smooth white stones with which Torch had once summoned her for loving. "Let us speak of what has been good and holy. The many moons and sunny days we have lived here will long be remembered by us. The Great Spirit has smiled upon us and made us glad. But we have agreed to go."

She paused, her eyes still hard on those of Chula Harjo. She saw the ferocity in him, the strength. And—yes—the suffering. He, too, had suffered in life, like herself, like her people. Ignorance had harmed him, just as it had complicated her own life at times. But the hard struggle for wisdom was etched in the lines on his face; the price of courage was marked by the scar at his temple, which Four Bears had dealt. In the end, he knew as little of his destiny as she knew of her own.

"We go to a country we know little of," she said, her voice softer now, speaking to him. "Our home will be beyond a great river on the way to the setting sun. We will build our wigwams there in another land. In peace we bid you good-bye. If you come to see us, we will welcome you."

In silence the exodus began. The Chickasaw began to move, and Andrew Jackson watched them as they passed toward the forest, and then down along the river, westward toward home. Finally the village was empty and silent, a relic beneath heaven; and Chula Harjo, feeling quite old but not at all fierce, stood alone and listened and listened, but could not quite understand, could not quite decipher, the secret words of wisdom that were hidden in the haunting wind-voices of the high country.

CHAPTER X

"Why don't you leave us now?" Gyva demanded of Fes Farson. "We are going. We shall not turn back. Your company is useless."

Three days had elapsed since the departure from the village, three hard days of struggle on the trail. Torch still clung to life, and Gyva continued to ride at the head of the column. No one had accosted them, even though they were now in Choctaw territory. At times Gyva imagined Choctaw laughing behind trees, behind hedges, rolling on the ground in delight at the Chickasaw plight. Red Dagger's perfidy still burned in her brain.

"Well, I'd hardly say we're useless to ya," Fes allowed. "Wouldn't want the slavers to get you, would ya now?"

"Slavers?"

"Hell, I know you Injuns don't make the best kinda slaves. Got to be whipped too much an' it ruins your health. But even so, a good driver what knows the ropes could get a couple years work outa most of you." He paused, snickered, and stuck a wad of tobacco far back inside his cheek. "But I *did* promise Old Hickory to see you safe as far as the Tennessee border. Lot of slavers in Memphis, too," he added, winking.

Gyva knew Fes by now, knew the bizarre ambitions and impulses that shaped his strategems. He would make certain the Chickasaw reached the Mississippi, left Tennessee. He was too smart to defy Andrew Jackson. But the letter of his promise required only that he accompany the Indians until they left Tennessee. Whatever happened afterward was something else again. Did Fes plan to maneuver them into a captivity that was too horrible to contemplate, and take a profit in the bargain? Gyva wondered.

"Could be," he was saying, "that somebody what knows the ropes might steer you safe around Memphis."

Gyva had watched Jason bargain often enough, trading horses and cattle. She had studied Rupert Harris's ways when he pursued his acquisitive instincts for land.

"What do you want?" she asked bluntly. "Me?"

If so, she thought, I will be the last woman he ever tries to possess.

"Maybe you," Farson replied. "Or maybe one o' them others." He jerked his head, indicating the group of women not far away.

She kept her face expressionless. "You have orders to take us to the Tennessee border, and that is all. If you so much as touch a hair on a Chickasaw woman's head, you will pay for it."

Heavy anger gathered behind his eyes, smoldering like a bad fire. "I'll take what I want," he muttered. "And don't forget, you're in Choctaw country. What if me an' my men was to just of kind of . . . sleep extra heavy one night, and not pay no attention to them Choctaws? We got the guns. You people don't even have a bow an' arry betwixt the whole damn lot of you. Main Choctaw village ain't no more than two miles upwind, too. Consider them apples, lady."

With that, he got up and stomped off. Gyva noticed, though, that he lingered in Bright Flower's sleeping area, just watching and grinning. But Gyva had other things on her mind. Teva was unwell and needed much care. She was growing older every day, it seemed, and the trek westward took more and more of her energy. Gyva went to her wigwam and saw the witch-woman as she lay upon her blankets, worn out and weak voiced. Only her eyes were alive. The hand-print on her skin was pale and dry, as if no omen-blood would pulse again beneath it.

"How is your health?" Gyva asked.

The seeress grinned ruefully, toothlessly. "All there is of my health is yours to observe. But do not think upon it, not yet. There is one thing in life I wish to see before I quit of it, and that is the look of the sun setting in the lands beyond the great river. I have heard that its appearance is quite different from sun-set in the mountains. I shall live until we get beyond the Mississippi. It is all settled. I have spoken with Death. He has agreed to let me wait that long."

"Oh, Teva!" Gyva exclaimed. "What is to become of us? Without you—"

"Without me you will be without me, and that is all. Why make a great thing of it?"

"But your wisdom, your power to see what will be . . ."

"Hah!" I remember a day, and not so many years ago either, in our home village when Four Bears was still chief." Teva's eyes clouded with memory and with the effort to remember; her voice was a pale rasp. "And in those days all seemed right with the world. Few came to me then for counsel. They did not need to. All was well." Then she laughed, a cackle. "It is only in the bad times that they come to me, and need me, and think that my words are important. But let me tell you something, little daughter—" and now her eyes flared and burned, and scorched the far fields of Gyva's soul—"let me tell you, as I have always told you, that my power is as nothing. It is mist, the stuff of hope alone. You yourself have more power now, and insight, too, perhaps, than I have had since . . ."

Her voice trailed off.

"Since?" Gyva prodded, wanting to know.

"Since I was young!" the old crone snapped. "Like

you. That is where you get your strength. Just see that you take me to the lands beyond the river. For now, let me sleep."

"There is one other thing," said Gyva.

"Yes."

"We are in Choctaw territory."

"So?"

"We are but scant miles from the Choctaw village."

"And?"

"Red Dagger," Gyva said simply.

The two women, young and old, looked at one another. They knew how the canny old chief had conspired to sully the Chickasaw name, to destroy the Chickasaw nation. Red Dagger's success had been quick and savage. What glee he must be enjoying, even tonight, around his campfire. No matter that the jackals would destroy the Choctaw, too, in due course. No matter about that. Red Dagger would be laughing tonight, joking about the trail of bitter tears upon which the Chickasaw were being driven by white outlaws and adventurers.

And beyond Dagger's dishonor in his treatment of Torch, Gyva had other reasons to hold him in contempt. It was he and his men who had killed Jason, sent her on the run so that, in the end, her son Andrew had perished as well. Certain things in life, by their very natures, emanate such evil that revenge is demanded, lest the evil grow greater. There are times when forbearance is a crime, when simple acceptance of fate is the highest of sins.

Old Teva's mouth hardened, and even her dessicated jaw became firm. "Red Dagger," she spat. "Get him!"

Gyva rose to leave. It was dark, and the night was passing. She would have to hurry.

Gyva's blankets were cold and the fire was waning when she made a display of going to bed for the night. Farson's armed men were spaced in regular intervals

along the edges of the Indian encampment, half of
them on guard, half of them asleep. Gyva knew the
white men were tired, too. The trail was no easier for
them than for the Chickasaw, and if Farson had not
promised them a share of the money he intended to
make in his putative bargain with the Memphis slave-
traders, some of them would already have quit the
march, militia responsibilities notwithstanding. Gyva
knew the white men—their sudden, bloody enthusi-
asms, their quick discouragement, their easy disillusion. They had not lived in these mountains for
thousands of years. They did not know in their souls
the peaceful immanence of time, the failure of patience. They did not know how to wait.

But she did. She watched as first one sentry and
then another grew bored standing watch and betook
themselves to sit beneath trees. Soon they were nodding, and not much later they dozed. She slipped from
her blankets and crawled across the damp grass. In
moments she was in the bushes, and then in the forest
itself. North, Farson had said. The Choctaw village.
The night had but a fragile bend of moon, but starshine lit the woods, and she made good progress. After
not too long a time, she could smell the village:
leather, campfires, horses. The Choctaw had a smell
to them, too, of course, but Gyva did not wish to
think of it.

The village lay before her, as she peered from
behind the shield of underbrush at the edge of the
forest. She knew what to look for: a wigwam before
which stood the totem of the chief. And there it was.
Did Red Dagger sleep with a wife? Did he have a
wife? Or did he spend his waning nights delighting
in the eager charms of obeisant young women who
would do anything he asked, and more?

Gyva was here to kill one person, and one person
only. Like Bright Flower and the others, she had a
knife good enough for the cutting of meat, the slashing of hide; and such a knife was also sufficiently

strong to slip through the flesh of a man. But such a quick thrust was too charitable. She remembered little Andrew, bleeding from the fall upon the rocky ledge, coughing and shivering against the coldness of water and wind, and she unable to warm him. She recalled laying down his tiny body next to the others, quickness gone from it forever, and his vibrancy fled as if it had never been. She remembered casting the beads of her necklace upon the graves of son and husband. No, a knife was too easy.

The sentinels paced and peered from the borders of the village, pausing, looking. They were nervous. Jackals were in the territory, and even jackals guarding vanquished Chickasaw might find it in their unpredictable minds to make a raid.

Gyva moved along and beneath and around the underbrush feeling her way, coming nearer and nearer to the wigwam of Red Dagger, and studying the plants and leaves. Finally she touched what she was looking for: the thick, supple vines of a climbing flower. Deftly she cut a long length of vine and wrapped it carefully around her wrist, then continued to move along the floor of the forest. Red Dagger's wigwam loomed against the night sky, not far from her. She would have to cross open ground, beneath starlight. The sentinels paced. She waited.

The two sentinels met at the juncture of their rounds, spoke a few quiet words to one another, and separated, going in opposite directions. Gyva did not waste a moment. Half crouching, she shot soundlessly from the covering foliage and dashed to the shadow of Red Dagger's wigwam. By the time she had settled to her knees, the little knife was doing its work, slashing a flap in the skins that covered the shelter. And by the time the sentinels turned to retrace the steps of their appointed rounds, Gyva was inside the wigwam, the flap pulled shut, and she was breathing—barely breathing—in the inner darkness.

And by his breathing did she first have awareness

of the presence of the perfidious chieftain. Heavy and rasping, it came deep and regular. That he should have life, and little Andrew none! That this piece of Choctaw scum should dream with full belly while Jason lay cold in the earth, while Torch-of-the-Sun fought for life, a captive on the trail of tears! Soon, by fading light from the embers of Red Dagger's fire, and by starlight from the smokehole in the roof of the wigwam, Gyva made out the bundled outline of the chief's sleeping form. He was alone. The Great Spirit was with her.

Carefully she crept closer, examining the chief. He might, in daylight, be a bold, sagacious, duplicitous leader, but asleep he was an old man, and he slept like one. His mouth was half-open, and a sheen of drool coated his chin. Now and then, involuntarily, he puckered his lips, and they flapped together with an obscene kissing sound. He lay on his side, half curled into himself, his bearskin blanket bunched at his midriff and pulled tight beneath his chin. An aging baby, slipping day by day into the great darkness. Well, he was not going to slip anymore. He was going to plummet.

And he slept in his moccasins, too, this bloody old coot! With deft fingers Gyva unlaced the long rawhide thongs by which the footwear was bound, tied the two lengths together, fashioned a loop on either end, and slipped the loops first around his ankles and then—carefully, carefully—around his wrists. Red Dagger stirred as she eased his arms around, but he did not awaken. Then she unraveled the vine from her wrist, fashioned a noose on one end, and curled it over his head. The free end she fastened to his wrists, which were bound behind him by the rawhide. The vine was taut. By pressing downward on his arms, it would grow even tauter, pulling the noose tightly around his throat, cutting off his breath.

Abruptly she rolled him onto his stomach and put pressure on his bound arms.

Red Dagger awoke with a jolt of pain and surprise, tried to cry out, felt his breath and his voice cut off by the vine around his neck. He thrashed about wildly for a moment, then realized that his struggles were only making his plight worse, and stopped fighting. He sought his assailant with his eyes, showed surprise when he found a woman looking back at him.

"Do not make a sound and I will release the pressure somewhat," she said. "I must tell you certain things."

Red Dagger jerked his head, a gesture of agreement if not of submission.

Gradually, so that she might reapply the pressure if the chief attempted to cry for help, Gyva allowed the noose to loosen.

Red Dagger could call for no one, not yet. He spent his time gasping for air. "Who . . . are you? What—?"

"I am Dey-Lor-Gyva. Chickasaw. I was Delia Randolph. You killed my husband. Because of your raid on Harrisville, my husband and child died. Because of you, my people have been cast out of our homeland."

Red Dagger could not help but smirk. All these things she had recounted—because of *him* they had come to pass. Mighty deeds!

An instant later he was sorry to have betrayed such glee. Gyva pushed down on his wrists, the vine tightened, and he gulped and gulped for air that was not there. When he had first seen that it was a woman who accosted him, he had relaxed. What could a woman do? He could deal with her. He was very confident of that. So he smirked, and—

She jerked the noose tight and let him suffer. He felt explosions of brilliant light going off inside his skull before she slackened the noose again. He was not afraid, not Red Dagger, but he was not so confident anymore, not at all.

"Why are you here?" he croaked.

"Revenge."

He choked for air, thinking, Revenge is a thing for warriors.

He twisted his head to one side and looked into her eyes. They did not move from his own. They blazed. She smiled and a shudder passed through his body. He was looking into the eyes of a warrior as implacable as any he had ever beheld. And he knew that he was about to die. But his heart would not permit him to believe it.

"For your husband, for your child, I am sorry," he said, bargaining for time. "We did destroy Harrisville. It was a glorious thing, and had to be done."

"It is more than that," Gyva replied.

What else? Red Dagger wondered. Oh, yes—Torch-of-the-Sun!

"As you know," he choked, "your chieftain did not join us in the battle—"

He suddenly felt the vine tighten around his neck, and her voice came hard in his ear as he choked for air, one word after another, like slaps: *"You did not wait for his message and you disguised yourselves as Chickasaw!"*

This time she kept the pressure on until he knew he was going to die. Then she released her grip, and let him swim up, up, back into the ocean of air that was sweeter than anything else on earth. It was a long time until he felt even half-alive. She was still there, a terrible presence. And, warrior though he was, had been, Red Dagger despaired. Still, he would not plead or babble. He would apologize, if that would do any good, and even if he meant not a word of it. But he would not grovel or whine or beg.

"I come," she told him, "to avenge my chieftain and my people. Torch-of-the-Sun has more honor in his fingertip, in his glance, in his heartbeat, than do you in your whole body and entire life. He would avenge himself, were he able."

"It was—the thing was—we had to destroy Chula Harjo," gabbled Red Dagger, seeking to call up the image of the great jackal and thus win Gyva over to his point of view.

"Chula has more honor in a moment than do you in your lifetime circling the sun."

That stung him, and he tried to cry out, but the noose was tight again.

"Farewell, Red Dagger," she was saying. "In mere moments, you shall know what lies in wait for those Indians who manipulate and betray their own kind, who sully the bright blood of our race."

She twisted his head to the side, and Red Dagger saw those coal-dark eyes burning down on him, through him, as again he fell down and down and down to where there was no air, where there was nothing. His lungs were bursting, like the blown bladders of pigs that were used in sport, and his heart was pounding in his chest, in his head, and his blood was roaring. Just one breath, he thought desperately, just one breath! But then her words hovered in his mind—*know what lies in wait*—and the thought struck him as terribly important. He had always believed that a warrior who does his duty, holds his post with honor, would join He-Who-Dwells-in-the-Clear-Sky. He had always believed that he, as a chieftain, would meet the dark horseman Death and ride with him out beyond the fiery field of heaven, forever to romp in joy and glory, hunting in the fields that lay beyond the North Star. But now, suddenly, he doubted, he wondered. In the thrashing throes of death, he had to admit his blatant perfidy in betraying a promise to another chieftain, in lying to the Chickasaw, in duping them. He had to admit that what he had done was heinous, not only according to the code of honor, but even more so according to the canons of simple honesty.

What transpired when a renegade chieftain crossed the great divide? What hunting was provided for a warrior who had, with malicious intent, practiced deceit upon an ally, and thus destroyed his own blood brothers?

Gyva's eyes were upon him when Red Dagger moved toward such terrible knowledge. She kept the noose tight and never flinched or wavered, simply pressed her weight upon him when his last violent struggles caused his body to jerk and writhe upon the earth.

Ah, the earth, he thought. So easy to come to, and so hard to leave . . . .

It was then that Red Dagger perceived the horseman Death come for him, riding over black vistas, dark mountains, veiled in a cape as blue as infinity, darker than the skies beyond Orion. Red Dagger's heart thundered when he saw the horseman, for he knew now that he had done great evil in these last days of his life, evil for which there was no longer time to make amends. Then Death was before him, and from beneath the eternal cape of night a skeletal hand reached for him. Trembling, Red Dagger touched Death with his soul. Heaven gave him one flashing instant to know he would have no reward. And the spirit of Red Dagger was extinguished forever from heaven and from earth.

CHAPTER XI

Fes Farson had posted his sentries for the night and given them their instructions. Then, nursing his lust along with a jug of whiskey, he sat against his rolled-up blankets and his saddle and considered how to get between the legs of that fetching little Bright Flower with a minimum of fuss. The more he thought about the swell of her breasts, the curve of her haunch, the more he had to have her.

All he had to do now was figure out how to do it. The chief couldn't put up no fuss, nosiree, but Fes couldn't just walk over there and put his John Thomas to the girl, because all them Indians was sleepin' on the ground. Very least they would wake up. He could have the sentries tie up the men, true, but that would get 'em all het up, all that extry work, et cetera—and, what the hell, Fes Farson was not a man who had to have an army guard him while he got hisself a piece of tail, even red tail. Naw, there had to be a better way. Bright Flower, get ready, he thought.

He took another big slug of the drink and thought it over real hard. The Chickasaw had few good braves left, after the way Fes an' Jackson had whupped 'em, but they were all savages, even or especially the women, an' Fes was not about to get himself in a bind where a bunch of them squaws might see fit to retaliate onto his personal parts, a danger he might face should he be caught with his pants down, so to speak. The woods was the only place to do what he

had in mind. So having decided on *where*, he had to
go on to *how*, which was harder. Can't go over and
drag her out, because that would set 'em all hoppin'
and yelpin'. There must be a way, he thought.

He got to his feet and made his way between the
sleeping bundles of the redskins. Slept almost jes'
like they was human, too, they surely did. Pretty soon
he got over to where Flower and the chief was sleepin'.
The chief was still breathin'. He saw the squaw's eyes
in the fire-lit darkness. Awake. An' that would probably be one of them little knives pokin' out from
beneath her blanket.

"Nev'mind me," he grunted, hardly able to restrain
himself from jumping her right here. "Nev'mind me,
I jes' come to bring ya a message. That old woman
wants ya."

She looked a little surprised, but he could tell she
believed him.

"Yeah, the one with the ugly mark on her face.
She said tell you to meet her over there by that big
rock, next to the clearing. I think it's got something
to do with that Gyva woman," he added, congratulat-
ing himself on a beautiful improvisation. Talk about
competition, he could for sure an' hell see there was
some between Delia and this Flower, what with the
same boyfriend and all. Hell, you could take any
woman an' bet your bottom dollar she would still be
jealous about some man. Well, that was natural,
wasn't it? That was the way good ol' God made the
world. Bein' jealous about a man was perfectly under-
standable, 'specially if that man happened to be ol'
Fes.

After giving the squaw his message, Fes wandered
away, pretending to check that everything was quiet.
But once he got out of sight of the campfires, he went
hell-for-leather over to that big rock, trying to smother
his expectant chortle as he saw Bright Flower, back
there among the Indians, rise up an' think it over an'
wait around and think it over some more.

Finally she headed toward the big rock.

Fes was ready and waiting.

He knew she had that little dinky knife, of course. All he had to do was watch out for that, an' he would be perfectly all right. Just get the thing, toss it away, an' hey, but wouldn't he have hisself a time. Two times, possibly three. It all depended.

As Flower crept around the shadow of the rock, light-footed and quick, Fes shot out and grabbed her, putting his knife to her throat. "Talk an' I'll kill you," he grunted. "Otherwise, you'll have plenty of fun."

She didn't move, and didn't cry out.

With the tip of his knife he slit her buckskin dress from collar to hem, leaving a thin red line where the tip of the knife touched skin. Blood began to seep out slowly and pearled like beads at the places where the knife had been.

Flower moaned softly. To be defiled by a lust-filled brave was bad enough, but to be raped by a white man was worse than anything. Worse than death. It did not matter that a maiden might struggle against him to the end of all effort. Such resistance could neither reduce nor erase the taint left in her body and soul by the jackal. Indeed, to be taken against one's will by a white man was like having coupled with a dog, a goat, a stinking wild boar. In ancient times, according to the stories, the women thus assaulted were lucky to be banished from the tribe. Those who were unlucky received a far crueler sentence: to be tied down in the center of the village and set upon by actual dogs. A maiden true to herself was expected to end her own life rather than submit to a white man's rape.

"Not a sound," Fes warned again. He checked her all over. She was bare-ass naked, and what a piece she was. But no knife. Wasn't in her mouth, he knew that, and the only two other places where it might possibly have been it wasn't. He checked both. He was no damn fool. Never trust a redskin. There was no end to the tricks they had.

So now she stood there all ready for his purposes, as lush a female as he had ever had, 'cept—to his credit, he chuckled—he had a knife of his own in the hand that was wrapped around her neck. He switched the knife to his other hand and touched the cold tip of the knife to her nipples, which rose and swelled with fear.

"That's it," he said. "That's what I like to see."

She didn't make a sound now, so he knew she was ready. She just stood there on her bare feet, those thick braids of black hair hanging down on either side of her face. God, for a moment he wished she was a lovely white girl and he something other than what he was. But Fes Farson had long ago stopped thinking about what might have been. Now he was thinking only of the slave-trading money in Memphis, and going back to "Farsonville" to get rich on pore old dead Rupert's coal—and how it would feel to shoot every liquid ounce of his whole being into the ripe body of this redskin.

She didn't resist—couldn't, probably, because of the knife. But wasn't she acting kind of funny? She *should* resist. That was the way it was supposed to be. That would make it better.

But she didn't.

What the hell. He slipped a leg behind her and flipped her down on the ground behind the rock. Keeping the knife at her throat, he spread her legs with a hard hand, rolled in between, and found with his fingers what he was looking for. Poised above her, Fes balanced himself with one hand in the dirt beside her shoulder and kept the knife in his other hand, in case she was to get any smart ideas. He had the point of the knife aimed just between those two fine breasts of hers. Still balancing on his arm, he targeted his body, straightened, and shoved himself into her. The sudden, excruciating pleasure shot through his

body, and even had he cared, he could not have understood the sense of unspeakable violation that Bright
Flower was suffering.

What he could understand, though, even as he
pumped away at her, was that she was trying to get
the damn knife! She grabbed his knife hand and
seemed to be trying to wrestle the weapon away from
him. "Whoa there!" he grunted, making ready to
give her a little slap on the side of the head, when
suddenly he realized she was not trying to pull the
knife away from him. She was trying to pull it into
her body—and she did. Choosing the only way she
could think of to save her sense of spiritual honor,
Bright Flower pulled Fes's hand down, and the knife
with it. The blade slipped into her heart, and blood
leaped from her body even as Fes Farson's seed shot
into her. But she was dying, and in her eyes Fes
Farson saw a final gleam of triumph. She died, and
Fes withdrew from her and leaped to his feet in
stunned confusion. God, now why did she have to go
and do *that*? He might have a heap of trouble with
them redskins now, for Christ sake. Jesus! He looked
down at her perfect, naked, dead body. Bright Flower's
eyes were still on him, boring into him, as if she saw
his fate. He shivered and yanked up his trousers, trying to decide what to do with her. Couldn't leave her
here, that was for sure, an' digging a grave would
make no end of noise, wake everybody . . . .

Hey, they were all asleep, he reasoned, getting
shrewd and canny again. If he could just sneak her
back . . .

So, not looking at Bright Flower's eyes, he hoisted
her up on his shoulder and, before carrying her back
to her sleeping place, peered cautiously all around.

But not cautiously enough. He did not see Teva
observing him from behind the bushes at the edge
of the woods.

CHAPTER XII

Gyva returned to the encampment not long before dawn. She had not slept at all, but she felt as if she would never have need of sleep again. A great thing had been in need of settling, and she had done it, for Torch and for the tribe. She had shrunk from the killing of the raiding Choctaw long ago. She had killed Harris because only by his death was her freedom to be won. But the killing of Red Dagger was like a final responsibility, without which the tribe's old life could not be left behind.

"Is it done?" muttered Teva.

"Yes."

"Now there is another."

The witch-woman explained. She had seen Gyva leave the encampment. She had watched Fes Farson cross to Flower and depart. And she had seen Flower go to the place of the rock.

Such a fate Gyva would not have wished upon anyone, and she silently praised Flower's hard courage in the face of unspeakable violation.

"And Torch?" she managed.

"He sleeps."

"Farson has seen enough circlings of the sun," she said.

"I agree," Teva nodded.

"Where is Flower's body?"

"Farson carried it back, and laid it down next to Torch. All were asleep. It will seem like a self-killing, accomplished by Flower out of despair."

Gyva bit her lip. Even in crisis—though it must have affected him—Fes Farson seemed to have a reservoir of desperate and icy calm. She and Teva would have to match and exceed the level of his self-containment if they meant to destroy him.

And they did mean to do so.

Morning came, and once again the Indians formed their long column, which wound its slow way through their ancient, well-beloved country, on into a land whose face they did not know. But before setting out, the dead had to be tended. Each day, each night, an old woman or a young child or a brave wounded in the battle with Jackson would succumb to the rigors of the march. They were buried along the trail, and each morning a prayer was made over their graves.

This morning the bodies of Bright Flower and Bright Badger were laid to rest. Teva said the prayer:

O Great and mighty Spirit,
Thou who hast from thy well of in-
scrutable wisdom caused thy children to
be cast out of their heartland,
accept unto thy care today
the spirits of those whose bodies
have already been accepted by thy earth.
Take unto thyself Bright Flower
and take Bright Badger, too,
that they should know the love of the infinite,
and that their deaths shall have meaning.

Gyva did not weep. Her heart held too much fury for mere tears. She was waiting. She and the seeress had prepared Flower's body for burial, and had given other members of the tribe to understand that the maiden had succumbed to sudden fever, compounded by malaise. If the real cause of death became known, the people would rise up, even in this bleak hour of extreme travail. And if they rose up, the jackals would crush them utterly, kill them to the last living soul. Flower would be avenged in due course, but not now. She watched the blanket-wrapped body as it was lowered into the red earth, and thought, I knew you, Flower, better than you believed. Because we were both women, and knew love. I knew you because of Torch. So go in peace, and know that I love you, too, in the end.

She felt simple sadness when Bright Badger was lowered to his final resting place. The poor boy seemed to have been born under the mark of the black star, his life a luckless series of mishaps and accidents and disasters of greater or lesser magnitude. After Jason had helped him escape from Gale Foley's place in Harrisville, he had returned to the tribe to enjoy, for a short time, a measure of respect and admiration hitherto beyond his experience. But he was essentially a good-humored, shallow, loutish lad, and the manner in which he boasted of his captivity and escape, the manner in which he basked in well-meant but routine praise, soon turned his fellows against him. He became something of a laughing-stock, until there were those who all too gleefully recalled that it was Bright Badger's own slow-footed stupidity that had caused him to be captured by Harris in the first place. Bright Badger ceased to boast then, and he went on to live as quietly as he could, tending cattle—rather carelessly—and caring for the horses in a manner not much better. Indeed, a horse had laid him low. Setting up the encampment on the previous evening, a tired, skittish mare had kicked him in the head. It was not meant for Bright Badger to lay eyes upon the strange, distant land of Oklahoma.

And for how many another Chickasaw, thought Gyva, watching the earth being tossed down now upon the bodies, would such a view be forbidden?

She glanced around discreetly. Most of the jackals were completing their breakfast at a campfire not far

away. Fes Farson was with them, but he was not
sharing in their mean chatter. No, he stood watching
the burial scene and looking over the Chickasaw. He
is probably calculating what Bright Badger might
have brought on a slaver's auction block, Gyva reflected. Or how many pieces of gold Flower would
have fetched from the owner of one of those houses
where the jackal men purchased with hard coin what
they could not win with loving tongue and gentle
heart. Bright Badger and Flower might be lucky to
have died before the unfolding of unknown horrors
lying in wait.

Then she saw Farson's eyes on her. There was
puzzlement in them. He was wondering about Bright
Flower. Did he know that Teva had seen him with
the maiden? He did not seem to.

She looked away, not abruptly, just let her gaze
pass casually from him. He must not know. He must
wonder. He must guess. He must begin to worry. But
could Fes Farson worry? Did he have it in him to
agonize over a thing, until he began to come unraveled, to make mistakes? That was the question.

Before the march began that day, Gyva went to
Torch and helped lift him onto the stretcher on
which he traveled. He was conscious, but he seemed
to have difficulty recognizing her. The wound on his
skull had covered itself, but Gyva had no way of
knowing how much damage had been wreaked inside
his head. The wound in his breast was infected, and
daily changes of dressing revealed pockets of festering
pus.

"Where . . . are we . . . bound?" he asked dully.

She touched his forehead gently. Hot and dry. A
bad sign.

"Oklahoma," she said. She motioned for a dipper,
then slowly gave cool water to her chieftain and
beloved.

"Is it far?" he asked, when he had ceased drinking.

She did not wish to tell him how far it was, lest

he give up his fight to live. "Only beyond the river," she said soothingly. "Just sleep, and in a time we shall be there."

"The river," he sighed, trying to smile, "and the bend where sand is gold . . ."

For the first time, Gyva allowed herself to hope for his recovery. He was not delirious now, and neither was he hallucinating. He remembered his sacred vision. As he spoke, his eyes seemed to clear a little, his gaze sharpened, and she saw herself reflected in his eyes.

"*Ixchay*, Dey-Lor-Gyva . . ."

But that was all, just then.

"Come on, let's move out!" Fes Farson was shouting. "Be mid-mornin' before you lazy-ass redskins get your breechcloths organized, fer Christ sake."

Once on the trail, Gyva guided her horse away from the jackals and whispered to Teva, who rode behind her. "What about Farson?"

"I have considered it. Today, ask of each woman and maiden the gift of one glass bead or ornament."

"What?"

"A present for Mr. Farson," Teva explained obscurely. "Before we reach Memphis, we must make a present to him for the fine care he has bestowed upon us."

Gyva did not understand Teva's plan, if indeed she had one. But nevertheless she went from woman to woman, explaining nothing, telling them only that the seeress had need of fragile ornaments. Shrugging, they complied. Perhaps Teva had one last trick that might save the Chickasaw, in which case the offering of a bead or trinket was more than worthwhile.

Days passed, and they came down out of the hills and onto the sweltering flatlands that led to the Mississippi valley.

"I reckon we'll reach Memphis in a coupla days," Fes allowed late one afternoon. He had brought his horse alongside Gyva's. "Once we get to Memphis, my responsibility to y'all is over. Unless, of course, I decide to sell you all to some nice plantation owner."

"No," Gyva said. "We shall cross the river and seek our destiny."

"Wait!" old Teva interrupted. "Mr. Farson, do you truly harbor in your heart plans to turn us over to slave traders?"

He cackled. "That's fer me to know an' you to find out, as the man says."

"Perhaps if I might make an offer of wealth in excess of any you might receive from a slaver?"

What was Teva thinking about? wondered Gyva. Was she thinking that the pitiful collection of beads and jewelry taken from the women of the tribe would assuage Farson's greed? The seeress must be growing senile. History did not so readily reverse itself. The trinkets that the white man had once used to rob the red man of his land would not now buy back from the white man the very lives of the Indians themselves.

"So you got some hidden gold, eh?" Farson was gloating. "Tell the truth, I always expected as much. How much you got?"

"Come tonight to our fire," Teva told him. "And we shall count how much it is."

"It better be plenty," grunted Farson, sawing the reins and turning his horse back toward the center of the column.

When they stopped that night to make camp, Gyva walked the long line, asking after the health of her people, gauging how much damage had been done by the day's march. Several women had collapsed. Three children were sick with exhaustion. One brave —young Grey Bough—was dead, his body thrown over the back of a horse for burial in the morning. A bad day, but there had been worse. The Chickasaw regarded her with dark, patient, suffering eyes. "The river lies before us now," she told them, with as much hopefulness as she could summon. "After we cross the river we shall be free."

"Tomorrow?" they asked.

"Maybe tomorrow. We must circle Memphis, and pass down the bluffs. Then we are free."

She saw in their eyes that they wanted to believe her, and such desire would help them through at least another night. She walked back to Teva, and found the old woman painstakingly at work over a fire. A small kettle bubbled with a succulent stew, which immediately made Gyva aware of her hunger. She took her tin bowl from the saddlebag.

"No," Teva commanded. "It is for our guest. Only rabbit, I am afraid, but the most tender parts thereof, and also tubers and wild onion for taste."

Truly the stew gave off a most enticing aroma. But if the seeress thought a mere meal would warm Farson's heart, her old mind was softer than Gyva had imagined.

"And what do you hope to gain by this?"

"Whatever there is to be gained," said the old woman, stirring the stew.

It was no use to argue with Teva. Her heart was in the right place, whatever might have happened to her mind. Gyva sat down, rested, and chewed a chunk of bread that had grown hard and dry in her saddlebag. Perhaps Farson would not gorge himself on all of the stew. There might be some remaining.

Fes swaggered toward them, sat down peremptorily, and sniffed the air. He had his whiskey jug with him, but he did not offer it. No redskin lips ought to touch that upon which a mighty white man places his thirsty kiss.

"So? What're ya waitin' fer? I'm hungry."

Teva got up slowly, her old joints protesting, and went to the kettle, spooning sweet, steaming rabbit stew from the kettle to a heated bowl. She stuck the spoon in the bowl, hobbled back to Farson, handed it to him, and sat down. He poked the pieces of tender rabbit, and his eyes lit up. "Hey!" he said, "this ain't half bad!" He took a big mouthful. "Ain't half bad at all," he repeated, chewing happily with his mouth open. "Now, if you don't mind talkin' business while I eat, how much money have you got?"

"Money?" asked Teva, as if confounded.

Gyva almost sighed in exasperation. The witch-woman herself had invited Farson here tonight in order to discuss money, and now she had forgotten all about it.

"That's right," said Fes, gulping another enormous mouthful of rabbit stew. So tender was it that he didn't even bother to chew. Didn't have to. "You said you was goin' to make me an offer an' buy me off. 'Cause of the slavers. Why, you stupid old bat! Don't you even remember?" He gave Gyva a disgusted glance, circled his finger round and round next to his temple as if to say, See? Daft as a loon she is, and took another mighty mouthful of the stew. Gyva watched him eating. Her poor stomach was rumbling, her mouth wet with a hunger stirred by the aroma of the food. Farson finished his bowl and shoved it forward. "More," he said.

Teva made as if to rise, but Gyva beat her to it. She would give Farson some more, and while doing so she would have some stew herself.

"Come on now, where's the gold?" Farson demanded.

Gyva was halfway to the kettle, which simmered happily over the fire. Teva seemed to be trying to make some cautionary gesture, as if to tell Gyva something dangerous lay in wait for her, something to be avoided. And Fes Farson was demanding money.

Then he became totally silent, completely still, for the shred of a terrible instant. In that instant he clutched at his gut, eyes wide with horror and a dawning awareness of what had happened.

"*Nooooo!*" he cried, "Oh, no!" He leaped up as if

to run, realizing at the same time that running would do no good. It was too late to run.

Gyva stood, stunned and horrified, midway between Farson and the fire. Old Teva just sat there on the ground, smiling now, with a look of tremendous triumph on her face. The blood beneath her pale mark even pulsed and surged a time or two. And Farson held his belly, eyes wide as ever, mouth open, as from his mouth the blood began to come. Some strange, inexplicable pain seemed to hold and possess him. Screaming, he ripped off his clothes, rolling upon the earth now. Indians, summoned by the commotion, gathered around, and the jackal guards raced over to regard Festus. He flopped naked and bloody upon the earth, the blood coming from his nose and mouth, and then from his genitals, too, and from every orifice upon his body. It seemed as if blood would emanate also from the very pores of his flesh, but this he was spared. He did not die quickly, but neither did it take too long for him to succumb, and he flopped and gasped one last time beneath the horrified gaze of his men, beneath the obsidian, implacable eyes of the Chickasaw.

When at last Farson was still, old Teva got up and addressed the jackals. "It could not be helped," she told them. "It was a curse."

The guards looked at her, then at Farson. It had certainly been a curse, all right. Two of them began to vomit and raced for the trees. The rest backed away, to gather at some distance, talking fast and low.

"You killed him, Teva, did you not?" the Indians asked.

"No," she grinned, toothless and indomitable. "We all killed him."

"It was the stew, of course," Gyva guessed.

Old Teva grinned some more. "No, no. How could it have been the stew? The stew was splendid. Do you question my skill with kettle and condiments?"

She gave a high, cackling laugh. "It might, however, have been the beads I ground into fine powder, and which I used to flavor the stew. I will not say it was not that."

During the night the jackals disappeared into the forest, and in the morning all of them were gone.

CHAPTER XIII

Torch struggled to raise himself, bracing his body upon an elbow. He squinted toward the west. He could not see land, only brilliant sunlight, and water equally brilliant, which seemed to stretch on forever.

"How can a river, one river, be so wide?" he asked.

"But we have reached it, and that is the issue," said Gyva, smiling at him. She knew in her heart that the river, reached with such difficulty, marked the beginning of a new life for her people and for herself. A new life and a better one.

After their fortuitous abandonment by the Tennessee militia, the spirits of the Chickasaw had begun to recover. They were dispossessed, true, but they were no longer under the guard of their conquerors. They were on their own. Torch was slowly beginning to recover, but he was by no means strong enough to take an active part in deliberations. Gyva herself had called the Indians to council. Not only braves this time—few of them were not in some way wounded or incapacitated—but women, too, and young people who had accredited themselves well upon the trail.

"There is the white man's city called Memphis somewhere ahead of us," she had told them. "And flowing by the city is the river which we seek, and which we must cross. Then we go south, as Jacksa Chula has spoken, until we reach the place where the Mississippi and the Arkansas meet, and then we go west, toward home."

There were a few protests, and even cries of "No!
No! Perhaps Chula has lied!"

Gyva refuted these doubts with the strength of her
own belief. "Chula was many things, but he was not
a liar," she snapped. "We had best decide right now
to let old battles die, for they will but weigh upon
our hearts. Our first problem is reaching the river.
We cannot venture near the city. So we must each
of us call upon all that we have learned in the lost
hills of home, and travel by guile and stealth and
cunning."

So the Chickasaw traveled by night, and on the
morning of the third day they reached the blazing,
sun-struck river.

Torch leaned upon his elbow, still borne in his
stretcher between the two horses, and regarded the
colossal expanse of the Father of Waters.

His eyes darkened, struggling with a memory. "I
have seen this before . . . ."

He seemed stronger now, though by no means fit
to leave the litter. Far away to the south, Gyva could
see, were a great white house and numerous outbuildings of a plantation. Even now, gangs of black
people were being herded together outside some of
the sheds, to be driven to work out in the cotton fields.

"We must cross at once," Gyva told him. "We have
no boats, no rafts. What say you, my chief? How
shall we do it?"

Torch turned his head and saw the plantation. It
meant the presence of hostile white men. Discovery
now would mean doom, as would delay.

"We shall cross together," he said, falling back
upon the stretcher. "Place the children and the
wounded upon our horses. Everyone else must swim.
Some of us may be lost, but the river of summer
moves slowly, and perhaps we shall be fortunate.
Where is Bright Flower?"

He looked around, seeking his young wife. No one

spoke for a time. Gyva did not know what to say. Torch's health seemed slightly better, and he was lucid again. The news of Bright Flower's death—to say nothing of her manner of death—would surely wound him grievously in spirit. Then, too, there was the knowledge of all that had transpired between Torch and Gyva. No, she should not be the one to answer his question.

Old Teva knew this. She tottered over to the stretcher and gazed at the chieftain. "Bright Flower is gone," she said simply. "I will tell you of it some-day, but not now. Just let me say, so that your mind will be at rest, that your wife died with courage and honor, with more of both than most of us will ever possess."

The young chieftain's eyes darkened and he sagged back down on his stretcher. He lay there for a moment, flat and motionless; then he spoke. His voice was weak, but the words were given with an air of command. "Let us go west toward home," he said. "Cross me as I am, between these horses. Only let someone swim beside, lest some accident occur."

"Dey-Lor-Gyva shall do it," said old Teva. "She has taken you—she has taken *us*—all this way."

Torch looked up at Gyva. He did not speak. But his eyes overflowed with gratitude. And admiration.

And so did Gyva and her people move on, across the river and into the trees. They forded the Mississippi that morning, the Chickasaw did, holding their children and the reins of horses in their hands, holding hope of safe haven in their hearts. Gyva, swimming, struggling against the suddenly swift midstream current, remembered—almost as if the memory were a prayer—the stories of her rescue by Four Bears at Roaring Gorge. With Jackson lying wounded and presumably dying in the trampled grass near the thundering falls, Four Bears had given his braves the order to mount up and ride. "Now we go west toward home," he had told them. West toward home, thought Gyva. Swimming, she matched the words to her stroke. West toward home.

The horses panicked slightly in midstream, where the current was strongest; but Gyva, who had been swimming beside them, crawled upon the back of one and seized the reins, patting the horse's neck and crooning. It calmed, and so did the other horse. Between them, on his stretcher, Torch was soaking wet.

"How is the crossing?" he asked, not thinking at all of his own safety.

From the horse's back Gyva looked up the river and down. Spread out on the water, the tribe was struggling, swimming, fighting for the shore. But they were past mid-river now, and they would be safe.

Only then did Gyva allow herself a smile. "We have done it!" she told him softly, with pride and triumph, in spite of everything.

"No," he said, looking up at her. "I believe that when the future legends are told around the fires, it will be said that you were the one who led us to do it."

"I did only what I had to do," she answered, guiding the horses up the western bank of the great river that Ababinili had created.

"Just as a chieftain," said Torch.

Gyva halted the beasts and turned to assure herself that the Chickasaw were safely across. They were, and the warm sun beat down, drying them, soothing them. She looked back at Torch.

"A chieftain?" she said, smiling. "You must know that our people cannot have two leaders at the same time. Also, I have a desire for a different position in life."

"And what is that?" he asked, smiling, too.

"To be the one closest to our leader," she said, "in every way there is."

Their eyes were fixed upon each other; they touched eyes and gave each other all that they were and would be. One life had ended, but a greater one had just begun.

"That is a serious aspiration," he said, reaching out and taking her hand. "But I do not think we need hold further council upon the matter. Beloved-of-Earth and of me, I grant you your desire."

EPILOGUE

One beautiful evening, as the setting sun melded red dusk and the dry red plains of Oklahoma, the old woman decided that it was too hot to sleep inside the wigwam. "Come," she said to her husband, "let us go out, as when we were young, and sleep again beneath the stars. We have not done so in . . . how many circlings of the sun?"

He smiled at her, half amused, half touched by tender memory, and together they took up their blankets and found a spot not far from the village. It was a quiet village, and a peaceful one; and the prairie that lay about it, once so alien and inhospitable, was full and fragrant with blossoming crops. Fat cattle grazed, tended by children, and a pale ghost of the moon that would shine tonight rode the eastern horizon. They spread the blankets on the grass, sank down, and embraced with long affection. The woman was smiling mischievously when the embrace ended, and the man wondered why.

"I found something today," she said.

"What is it?"

"Oh, it will mean nothing to you, I think. You will have forgotten." But still she was smiling.

"I have forgotten nothing," he countered, slightly vexed. "As you well know."

From beneath her buckskin skirt the woman withdrew a pouch of leather, the leather itself dry and cracked with age, but still delicately beaded. And from the pouch she withdrew small white polished stones.

"Just as I feared," she teased. "You do not remember."

He kissed her for an answer. "Fifty years," he said. "More."

They touched eyes and did not speak, thinking of time. Andrew Jackson lay cold in his grave in distant Tennessee. He had captured his dream, and presided tumultuously over his nation, but with a sad heart. His beloved Rachel had passed on before the power came to him.

So many people had died since those times—including old Teva, whose last prophecy had told of black gold lying in wait beneath the dry grass and red dust of Oklahoma. Everyone thought she had become addled in her last days, that she was thinking of the coal in the mountains of Tennessee. Yet not everyone discounted prophecy. Four Bears had been right, for example. One with a name strange to the Chickasaw had appeared to save them, and she had been Dey-Lor-Gyva, returned to the tribe as Delia, the name bestowed upon her by Jason Randolph, her white husband. Indeed, to live fully, one could not safely ignore the veracity of prophecy, the power of dreams.

Once, too, long years ago, a young chieftain called Torch-of-the-Sun had awakened at dawn, while the Chickasaw were encamped at the juncture of the Mississippi and Arkansas rivers. They had been on their way to Oklahoma then, and he had turned and gently shaken the beautiful young woman asleep beside him.

"I have seen them," he whispered, his face alight with joy and discovery.

"What?" she asked, struggling out of sleep. "What have you seen?"

"The words. The words of the vision."

He told it. He had found his way back into the dream, the vision of his manhood ritual. He had found his way back within sleep to the river of a second sleep, and to the sand in the bend of the river where the golden stick lay buried. This time he had been wise; this time he had not forgotten.

"What is the secret?" she had asked, barely breathing.

"I am a little surprised, though," he faltered. "It is not at all complicated or portentous."

"Tell me, so that I may judge."

" 'The future is filled with hope only if the past is free of regret.' " he said, speaking very slowly, reading the words from the image of the stick he had captured with his mind, " 'and the sunset is as beautiful as the dawn.' "

That is it? she had wondered at the time, lying beside him on that long-ago morning. That is the secret of life?

But now, so many years later, lying beside him still, she knew that his vision had been true. The secret of life was very simple, but difficult to understand, for it required the patience and wisdom that only time could bring.

The sun had dropped below the horizon now, and it was growing dark. Cattle lowed in the distance. Crickets called, and frogs, croaking in the wet sand by the well. Another day gone, time passing, and all the deeds of long ago took shape in memory. Dey-Lor-Gyva accepted the memories. She was at peace with herself and had no regrets. All prophecies would come to pass; all tales would eventually be told. Even those things that could not be accomplished on earth, those things for which there was no time, did not really matter. Because, in the end, all that was left undone upon the earth would be completed beyond a river even greater than the Mississippi, beyond a final sunset. Dey-Lor-Gyva, who, as her grandfather had prayed, was both beloved *of* earth and beloved *on* it, gazed up at the star-riven sky, and for a moment she was no longer upon the red plains of Oklahoma,

but already where she would be one day, with Four
Bears and Jason, with Andrew and Teva and all the
others, far out among the flowering fields of light,
beyond the North Star, where dawn blazed forever,
and would never die.

Torch-of-the-Sun died in 1876, while riding along
the Chikaskia River in northern Oklahoma. He was
alone at the time, and had apparently stopped and
dismounted to allow his horse to drink. His body
was discovered by one of his seven sons—he and Gyva
also had four daughters—who had been sent after
him when he did not return for the evening meal.
His visage was composed and showed neither suffering
nor alarm. A warrior, he was buried along the Chikaskia, near the sound of flowing water. A bracelet in
the form of a serpent circled his arm in death, and
his widow tossed into the grave what appeared to be
a very old leather purse.

Years afterward oil was discovered in Oklahoma,
and a great deal of this black gold was found beneath
Indian lands. Dey-Lor-Gyva and her children became
quite wealthy, and over the decades exerted much
influence on behalf of their people. Today the grandchildren and great-grandchildren and great-great-
grandchildren of Firebrand's woman live in all parts
of the country. Her blood lives on in their veins, and
her adventures live on in their tales. Gyva herself
died while on a visit to Tulsa in 1893 and, according
to her wish, was buried in the mountains south of
Knoxville, Tennessee. Upon her gravestone is a design
to puzzle the tourists and quiet passersby:

The continuation of
the exciting six-book series that
began with *The Exiles*

The SETTLERS

WILLIAM STUART LONG

Volume II of *The Australians*

Set against the turbulent epic of a nation's birth is
the unforgettable chronicle of fiery Jenny
Taggart—a woman whose life would be torn by
betrayal, flayed by tragedy, enflamed by love and
sustained by inconquerable determination.

A Dell Book $2.95   (15923-7)

Dell BESTSELLERS